Pride and Prejudice in Space

PRIDE AND PREJUDICE IN SPACE

ALEXIS LAMPLEY

UNION SQUARE & CO.
NEW YORK

UNION SQUARE & CO. and the distinctive Union Square & Co. logo
are trademarks of Sterling Publishing Co., Inc.

Union Square & Co., LLC, is a subsidiary of Sterling Publishing Co., Inc.

ISBN 978-1-4549-5411-8
ISBN: 978-1-4549-5413-2 (paperback)
ISBN: 978-4549-5412-5 (e-book)

For information about custom editions, special sales, and premium purchases, please contact specialsales@unionsquareandco.com.

Printed in China

2 4 6 8 10 9 7 5 3 1

unionsquareandco.com

Cover and interior design by Erik Jacobsen
Cover and interior illustrations by Alexis Lampley

To Josh. None of this would have happened
without you, in so many ways.

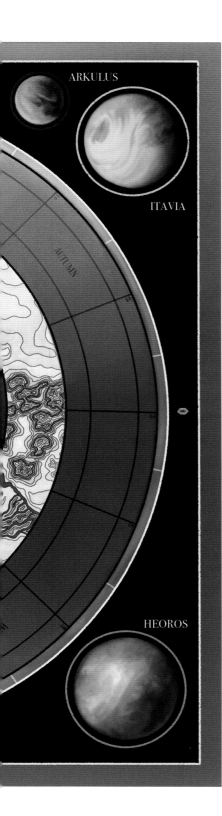

ARKULUS

ITAVIA

AUTUMN

HEOROS

AS DAYS AND TIMES vary per moon, a standard for inter-lunar commerce within the Londinium system is essential. Londinium has several time zones, but the universal lunar standard (denoted in abbreviation form "LS") is the only one used outside of the planet itself. Some moons have adopted the lunar standard completely. Most use a dual time system, to better function within the natural rhythms of their days. This is especially true for a populace that doesn't often, if ever, participate in inter-lunar travel. Dual time systems are most commonly observed on the outer moons, which have larger orbits and suffer the most dissonance from adhering to the lunar standard. While this system has its drawbacks, it is a necessary tool for the complexities of the Londinium System. Nowhere else in the solar system are so many moons equally habitable. While some of this was engineered by the initial inhabitants, the fact remains that Londinium and its moons are a one-of-a-kind phenomenon.

HEOROS
HEOROSIAN SATELLITE SYSTEM

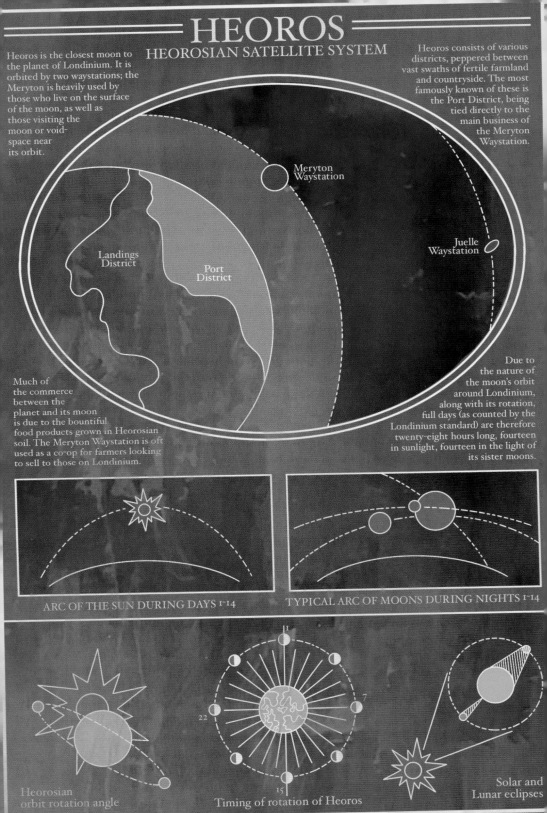

Heoros is the closest moon to the planet of Londinium. It is orbited by two waystations; the Meryton is heavily used by those who live on the surface of the moon, as well as those visiting the moon or void-space near its orbit.

Heoros consists of various districts, peppered between vast swaths of fertile farmland and countryside. The most famously known of these is the Port District, being tied directly to the main business of the Meryton Waystation.

Meryton
Waystation

Juelle
Waystation

Landings
District

Port
District

Much of the commerce between the planet and its moon is due to the bountiful food products grown in Heorosian soil. The Meryton Waystation is oft used as a co-op for farmers looking to sell to those on Londinium.

Due to the nature of the moon's orbit around Londinium, along with its rotation, full days (as counted by the Londinium standard) are therefore twenty-eight hours long, fourteen in sunlight, fourteen in the light of its sister moons.

ARC OF THE SUN DURING DAYS 1-14

TYPICAL ARC OF MOONS DURING NIGHTS 1-14

Heorosian
orbit rotation angle

Timing of rotation of Heoros

Solar and
Lunar eclipses

CHAPTER
01

Flyleaf Starship, Inter-Lunar Travel Route 19-A, Londinium System

It is a truth universally acknowledged, that a single, space-faring man in possession of a good fortune must be in want of a wife.

Whatever the intentions of such a man may actually be upon entering the atmosphere, this truth is so fixed in the minds of the land-bound families that he is considered a guaranteed match for one of their daughters.

The Bennets, being one such family, were returning from holiday on Nagalea, the sixth moon of Londinium, when news of this very kind reached them.

"Have you heard?" exclaimed Mrs. Bennet as they boarded the Flyleaf Starship. "Netherfield Landing is finally claimed."

Mr. Bennet replied that he hadn't.

"Well, it is," she continued. "I've had a waive from Mrs. Long, and she told me all about it."

Mr. Bennet beckoned his daughters to keep up rather than answer.

"Are you not interested in who leased it?" Mrs. Bennet's impatient voice echoed off the metal walls of the Flyleaf's vestibule, eliciting an offended look from a stately woman at the threshold of her compartment door.

"*You* are interested, therefore, I am, too," said her husband.

This was invitation enough. "Well, Mrs. Long says that Netherfield Landing has been claimed by a young man of large fortune—from Kaels, if you can believe it. Such a distance, I must say. He descended on Monday in a Chase-N4 to inspect the land, and was so pleased with it that he ordered his brand-new starcruiser be named the Netherfield in its honor. The ship will be docked on the grounds by the end of next week."

Mr. and Mrs. Bennet reached the compartment first and the door slid open. This was just enough distraction for Mrs. Bennet to stop talking. Seizing the moment, her daughters chimed in.

"How large a fortune?" Kitty started, as Jane asked, "What's his name?"

"Bingley," Mrs. Bennet answered.

Lydia twirled through the door, bumping into Elizabeth and then Mary in the process. "Single?"

"I wouldn't bother telling you about a *married* man." Mrs. Bennet followed the stragglers through the door and elaborated. "A single man with a fortune of something like four or five thousand aurum a year. Such great news for you girls."

"His fortune can't affect them," Mr. Bennet said.

"It will if he marries one of them."

Elizabeth laughed at her mother's words as she and her sisters swept through the common area of the suite.

Her father coolly prompted, "That's his reason for settling on Heoros?"

"Nonsense." Her mother waved his words away. "But it's very likely that he *may* fall in love with one of them, so you must visit him as soon as we return home."

"I see no occasion for that." Mr. Bennet pulled his comcard from the pocket of his dusk blue travel jacket, checking the time against projected launch, muttering "fifteen," before returning his attention to the conversation. "You and the girls may go," he said, heading toward the stateroom. "Or you can send them by themselves— which would be preferable, since you're as lovely as any of them. Mr. Bingley might otherwise take a liking to you instead."

Mrs. Bennet, following him in, said, "My dear, you flatter me. I certainly *was* beautiful in my youth, but I don't pretend to be anything extraordinary now."

The youngest two girls trailed their mother like ducklings, giddy and giggling, with Mary shaking her head in vague disapproval behind them. Elizabeth and Jane, lightly entertained by it all, followed after. Their mother gestured toward them. "When a woman has five grown daughters, she ought to stop caring about her own beauty."

Their father stood by the bed, examining the luggage in the storage closet, ensuring it was secured properly. "Ah, I see. And in such cases, what little could be left of beauty, after all that effort spent on others?" He caught Elizabeth's eye as she crowded with her sisters in the doorway, and winked at her.

"You tease," her mother retorted, "but my dear, you really must go and see Mr. Bingley the moment we re-enter the atmosphere."

"Ought I not wait till we make landfall?"

Their mother huffed and dismissed him. "You know perfectly well what I mean. You must go the very day we return."

"That's more effort than I'd like to exert after a long journey." Apparently satisfied with the room, he shooed the girls out to the kitchen, his wife trailing him like a plume of exhaust. "Go check your rooms and luggage, girls," he ordered them, not unkindly.

They obliged, the youngest ones lingering so as not to miss anything. Elizabeth knew they'd still be able to hear their mother, even through the relatively thick walls. She and Jane headed toward the room they'd be sharing with Mary at the back of the sitting area.

"Think of your daughters," their mother said. "This is such an opportunity for one of them. Sir William and Lady Lucas are determined to go—for the very same reason—and you know they don't visit anyone new. Oh, you must go. It'll be impossible for *us* to visit him if you don't."

"I'm sure Mr. Bingley won't object to the informality of seeing you without me. I'll send a note along with you to assure him that he's allowed to marry whichever of the girls he chooses, though I must put in a good word for my little Lizzie."

Elizabeth smiled and shook her head, catching Lydia sticking her tongue out at her before disappearing through the doorway.

"You'll do no such thing," she heard her mother saying. "Lizzie isn't a bit better than the others. She's not half so beautiful as Jane, nor half so good-humored as Lydia, but you constantly give *her* the preference."

Mary, pulling a book from the luggage secured in the compartment below her in-wall bunk, gave Jane and Elizabeth a long-suffering look, and whispered, "What are Kitty and I? Cousins?"

"None of them are half so like me," their father replied.

"Yes, so very witty!" Lydia chimed in loudly.

As the girls filtered back to the common area, their father went on. "Elizabeth does certainly have her share of my wit. But you are all still silly little girls in my eyes."

Their mother *tsk*ed. "How can you talk about your children that way?" She sat in the chair beside him, fiddling with the catch that would release the seatbelts for launch. "You take delight in vexing me. You have no compassion for my poor nerves."

"You're mistaken, my dear. I have the utmost respect for your nerves. They've been my companion for twenty years at least."

"You don't know how I suffer," she declared, raising her voice to be heard as the intercom clicked on to alert passengers of impending takeoff procedures.

Elizabeth found a seat between Jane and Kitty on the couch.

"I hope you'll survive it, and live to see many young men of great means alight on our little moon," her father replied.

"It won't matter if there are twenty who breach our atmosphere, since you refuse to visit them."

"Depend upon it, my dear, that when there are twenty, I will visit them all."

Mr. Bennet was such an odd mixture of intelligence, sarcasm, indifference, and fickleness that Elizabeth doubted her mother would ever fully understand his character. They were so different, and her thoughts so bent on her children and social life, that most of his wit went over her head. But it was entertaining to him, nonetheless, and with Elizabeth—and sometimes one or two of her sisters—sharing in his little jokes, he made the most of it.

OBSERVATIONS BY MARY BENNET
PERSONAL JOURNAL / COMCARD ID: HC-3095.D3.MB
TIMESTAMP: 2.9-18:01:33.LS / LOCATION: VOIDSPACE

THOUGHTS UPON LEAVING NAGALEA

This cruise has truly been a once-in-a-lifetime excursion. I know that our moon system is easy enough to traverse, and yet we don't often travel further from home than to the planet itself. There are six other moons in the system full of people and natural wonders, yet we've hardly left our own. Heoros is wonderful. I don't mean to disparage it. But I think I understand Lizzie's love of flight more now. There is so much to explore.

We started our trip by visiting Aunt and Uncle Gardiner in St. James City, which I wouldn't count toward us exploring the system, since we've visited Londinium so many times before. It was a lovely visit, though, and a proper easing into the larger journey. This was also a necessary stop, of course, because we boarded the Flyleaf Starship from upper St. James (Cloudtop, colloquially).

We left Londinium and began the tour by heading to Itavia. Though the moon is further out from Londinium than Apollia, with its current position in orbit, it was easier to get to. Apollia's red hue is nearly as familiar in the Heorosian sky as the teal and emerald Londinium, so I didn't mind skipping it.

Itavia was a jewel. Bustling cities and large swaths of land. I enjoyed our time there. If you asked any of my sisters, we'd all choose wildly different parts of our stay as our favorite, but mine was of course the bookstores. One thing you can count on wherever you travel, it seems, is finding a building full of books and readers to inhabit it.

Since this trip was mostly a cruise through the void itself, Itavia was one of only two landings we made. This doesn't count stops on waystations for refueling, but there's no abundance of activities to be had on most of those. They aren't much like the Meryton Waystation. It's unique, I think, in that it's almost its own little moon to Heoros. Unique due to its proximity to Londinium as well as its access to our Port and Landings districts. One side of Heoros is filled with feats of engineering and machines; the largest lunar port within the inner rings of orbit. The other is idyllic estates and fertile farm lands, dotted with homes and the occasional landing zone for those who wish to have a home that can travel the stars as well as becoming one with the landscape around it. I imagine there's nothing quite like having a front porch that could look out on acres of golden fields one day and the velvet black of space the next.

But I digress.

From Itavia, we cruised through the void for a time, watching the moons dance with one another along their orbits. Unfortunately, we weren't able to stop on Dyberion, though it boasts the most beautiful and unique natural sites. I don't think my father would have enjoyed that sort of exploring as much, so it was no loss to him. But Lizzie, ever curious about the worlds, and Kitty, who has always been a lover of all things in nature, certainly had their share of disappointment. Their feelings were outmatched only by Lydia's, knowing that she would be but one moon away from Arkulus, which is home to the Alesadran Academy of Arts, a place I know she dreams of seeing one day.

Instead, we made it only as far as Nagalea. (Kaels was on the other side of Londinium, so there was no chance to stop there.) Though Nagalea is one moon shy of the farthest orbit, it was still something special to see the planet from such a distance. I can only begin to imagine what Londinium must look like to those living on our neighboring planet. It must be but a speck to those on Wenhal. Not that many of us will ever know. We've kept mostly to ourselves because of the asteroid field. Travel between us is very hazardous. Jane says it's probably for the best, as there is so much to wonder at in our own little system. If we look beyond it, we may forget to appreciate what we have here. I believe it is human nature to wonder at what lies beyond our grasp, but I agree with her, overall.

Speaking of travel, ours is nearly at an end. Now that we have left Nagalea, it's a straight shot for home. The only stop will be refueling at the Balico Waystation, which is by far the largest satellite in the inner rings. While the Meryton is a hub of business for the more common populace, the Balico is home to the ship builders' staging port for the wealthiest buyers. All the big ships are finished there. We ought to keep a sharp eye on Lizzie while we're docked, or it's possible she'll slip away to get a closer look at the ships and never come back. One sleepless night in service of keeping our dear sister from absconding on a StarHawk, and then we'll be on our way again in the morning.

CHAPTER 02

Flyleaf Starship, Inter-Lunar Travel Route 19-A, Londinium System

Mr. Bennet's knowledge that the recent ship acquisition by Mr. Bingley would put the man on the Balico Waystation at the same time as the Flyleaf meant that he was among the earliest of Mr. Bingley's new Heoros connections. He'd always intended to visit Mr. Bingley, but decided it would be a good bit of fun not to mention anything until after he'd made his initial introduction during refueling.

That evening, observing his second daughter as she added notes to some ship schematics, he said, "I believe Mr. Bingley would like the look of that, Lizzie."

"We don't know *what* Mr. Bingley likes," said his wife resentfully as she sat nibbling on the remnants of their dinner, "since we won't get to meet him."

"Oh, Mama, you know that isn't true," said Elizabeth. "We'll meet him at the next ball on the Meryton. Mrs. Long promised to introduce us to him."

His wife set her fork down to emphasize her words. "She will *not*. She has two nieces of her own to parade in front of him. She's a selfish, hypocritical woman, and I have no opinion of her."

"Nor I," said Mr. Bennet, leaning in to peer closer at Elizabeth's notes. She seemed to be labeling a Star Chaser from memory. He was impressed. "It's best you don't depend on her."

Mrs. Bennet didn't respond, but instead began scolding one of their daughters. "Do quiet that beeping on your comcard, Kitty. Stars around us!—Have a little compassion for my nerves."

"Kitty has no discretion," he sighed, "to be getting messages at a time like this."

"I don't have a say when the comcard makes noise," Kitty replied indignantly, looking up from the screen. She turned to Lizzie. "It was Maria Lucas asking to borrow a dress. When's the next ball?"

"Two weeks."

"Stars!—It is," cried his wife, "and Mrs. Long doesn't return to Heoros until after we have, so it'll be impossible for her to make introductions, since she won't know him herself."

Mr. Bennet rounded the little chaise where Jane and Lydia sat playing a game, the pieces projected in the air between them. He dipped his hand harmlessly into the projection and pretended to knock the pieces off the board. Lydia rolled her eyes in response. He winked at her, then neared the window, feigning interest in the view as he said, "Then, my dear, you'll have the advantage over your friend by introducing Mr. Bingley to *her*."

"Impossible," she retorted. "Don't tease me. I won't be acquainted with him either."

He nodded solemnly and turned his back to the window. "You're right. Two weeks' acquaintance is not much. How can we really know a man in such a short time?"

A couple of the girls narrowed their eyes at him, suspicious. His wife tittered. "Nonsense."

He inclined his head. "What do you mean, my dear? Do you consider the forms of introduction, as well as the importance of their propriety, nonsense? I must disagree with you there." He turned to his middle child. "What do you have to say on the subject, Mary? You're a young lady of deep reflection, read a great many books, and share many thoughts attained from them."

Mary appeared to have been caught with her mind half-occupied by the book in her hands, and had no answer.

"While Mary is ruminating," he continued, seating himself in a nearby chair, "let us return to Mr. Bingley."

"I'm sick of Mr. Bingley," muttered his wife.

"That's unfortunate news. Why didn't you tell me that before? If I'd known you felt that way this morning, I wouldn't have gone out of my way to make my introductions on the Balico." He sighed. "But since I've already paid the visit, we can't escape his acquaintance now."

He smiled slyly as the compartment erupted with exclamations from his family. They were as astonished as he'd hoped; his wife, as usual, surpassing the rest. When the last sounds of their exhilaration and surprise had stopped ringing off the walls, Mrs. Bennet began to insist that she'd suspected such a move all along.

"Oh, you are too good to us, my dear! I knew I'd persuade you. You certainly love your girls too much to ignore such a potential match. Well, I'm pleased. Very pleased, indeed. And what a joke you played on us, to have met him on Balico without saying a word to us about it!"

His jest at an end, Mr. Bennet stood. "Now, Kitty, your comcard can ring without consequence till our journey's end," he said, and he strode toward the stateroom, suddenly fatigued by the raptures of his wife.

"What an excellent father you have, girls," Mrs. Bennet said. "I don't know how you will ever repay him for his kindness; nor me, for that matter. At our age it's taxing to be making new acquaintances every day; but for your sakes, we'd do anything." As the stateroom door hissed open, she said, "Lydia, my love, as you're the youngest, I can't guarantee Mr. Bingley will dance with you at the next ball."

The door slipped shut behind him, but Mr. Bennet could still hear Lydia's stout reply. "Oh, I'm not worried about that. There'll be plenty of dance partners for me. I may be the youngest, but I shine the brightest."

LONDINIUM SAT[SYS

Communications Log—System Storage 30 Days [Planetary]

[LotteLu] 5.9-19:32:44.LS

Can't wait to see you and hear all about your vacation when you get back!

[LizzieLovesSpace] 5.9-19:43:58.LS

So much to tell you. Did you hear about the new neighbor at
Netherfield Landing?

[LotteLu] 5.9-19:57:23.LS

No! What have you heard?

[LizzieLovesSpace] 5.9-20:10:03.LS

An apparently quite rich and very single man leased it. Mr. Bingley. My father
met with him at our Balico stop. In typical fashion, he thinks he's incredibly
funny by keeping us in the void about the man.

[LotteLu] 5.9-20:25:34.LS

No doubt riling your mother for sport.

[LizzieLovesSpace] 5.9-20:40:48.LS

Indeed. She's talked of little else since. Jane isn't pushy enough to make a
dent in his armor, and Mary's too engrossed in her current book to care for
gossip. Kitty and I have tried more subtle and nefarious means of extracting
even the barest description, but no such luck. Lydia ambushed him in the
corridor and nearly gave him a heart attack, but he wouldn't budge.

[LizzieLovesSpace] 5.9-20:42:16.LS

We just got an alert that we're about to lose personal com links for a while.
Probably a moon interfering. I'll let you know if we manage to crack him.

COM INTERRUPTION . . . REESTABLISHING CONNECTION . . .
COM FAILED-LUNAR INTERFERENCE . . . APPROXIMATING DELAY
LENGTH . . . RETRYING IN [10] HOURS . . . COM LINK REPAIRED . . .
REESTABLISHING CONNECTION . . .

[LotteLu] 6.9-07:08:53.LS

Any luck breaking your father?

[LizzieLovesSpace] 6.9-18:29:17.LS

Mary, believe it or not, managed to get him to admit that Mr. Bingley is Jane's age. But that's all we have to show for an entire day's effort.

[LotteLu] 6.9-18:32:44.LS

I'd say it was better than no intelligence on him at all, except that he actually arrived in port this morning.

[LizzieLovesSpace] 6.9-18:46:13.LS

I should've guessed! He's got a personal ship, after all. He doesn't have to stay on the Flyleaf's pace.

[LotteLu] 6.9-18:57:08.LS

Personal ships really do make travel so much more convenient.

[LizzieLovesSpace] 6.9-19:09:12.LS

Truly. It'll be so nice to sleep in my own bed again. And to see if Mr. Bingley is worth all this fuss.

[LotteLu] 6.9-19:20:53.LS

My father just went to see him. Says he's a handsome man, and very likable.

[LizzieLovesSpace] 6.9-19:31:35.LS

Rich. Handsome. Single. Likable. All that's left to tempt the entire district is his willingness to dance.

[LotteLu] 6.9-19:42:29.LS

Then it appears we can expect a brawl for the pleasure of having his first dance. He's committed to attending the Meryton ball next week.

[LizzieLovesSpace] 6.9-19:59:45.LS

This couldn't have come at a better time. Kitty and Lydia are beginning to snip at each other for lack of entertainment, and Mama has all but given up hope of hearing news, so she complains about it every quarter hour. I shall win the day with this information!

[LotteLu] 6.9-20:13:47.LS

Glad I could be of service! But I'm off! My own younger siblings are diverting my attentions.

[LizzieLovesSpace] 6.9-20:26:03.LS

I'll see you the day we touch ground!

. . . END COM . . .

CHAPTER
03

Heoros, First Moon of Londinium

Jane pulled her arm into the sleeve of her dress as her mother's excited, impatient voice traveled up the stairwell. "Hurry, girls! The shuttle departs in less than an hour!"

As squeals of delight emanated from the younger girls' bedrooms, Jane turned her attention to the closet door, a grin already on her lips in anticipation of Lizzie's inevitable retort.

"It's a private shuttle," her sister said from within its depths. She emerged wearing a floor-length, pale-yellow gown, one hand busy behind her back, the other holding her shoes. "It won't leave without us."

Jane chuckled softly. "Still, we need not be late. The Lucases will be waiting, after all." She beckoned Lizzie over. "Let me help."

"You mean Mr. Bingley will be kept waiting," Lizzie said as Jane looped the buttons into place.

"If the ball is not incentive enough to avoid being late, then consider this: the sooner you get into the ship, the sooner you can hover over the pilot's shoulder and ask him more questions." Her sister had always been fascinated with the inner workings of ships, and determined to know them all should she ever have the chance to fly one of them. It'd be a special man indeed who could excite her mind the same way space flight did.

Lizzie laughed. "On any other occasion, I'd consider that a winning option. But I'm as eager to satisfy my curiosity about Mr. Bingley as anyone."

"If only we'd gotten a better look at him when he came to visit the other day." Jane secured the last button and adjusted the flares on the back of Elizabeth's dress so the line of buttons followed the length of her spine. "It's a shame he couldn't accept Mama's invitation to dinner."

Jane turned to the mirror on the opposite wall, looking herself over one last time. She had dressed in a light blue gown to match the color of her eyes. Though fairer than most of her sisters, Jane's hair was just a shade lighter than Kitty's. Lydia, who had a talent for fashion, had completed the look with a complicated hairpiece that wove through her upswept curls and draped like a metallic lace curtain down the side of her face. It dripped with delicate chains of blue gemstones along her collarbone and down her back. Lydia had said, "No point in my attempting to snag him, so I'll do my best to make sure one of you will," as she'd pinned it in place. Lydia really was a sweet girl, in her own way.

"It might be for the best," Lizzie said. "What with all the women he's supposedly bringing tonight."

Just then, Mary, who'd been crossing the hall, stepped into the room. She wore, as usual, a simpler, darker gown; this one just a step off black and into green, with sheer, shimmering sleeves. Her hair was in a clean, simple updo. She'd clearly not given in to Lydia's attempts to accessorize every sister. It'd be a feat, indeed, if Lydia had managed that. Mary's dark eyes shone with a kind of wary excitement. "Maria Lucas says she heard it isn't twelve like everyone thought. He's only bringing five sisters and a cousin."

"In that case, dear sisters," Lizzie said, "he's practically ours already."

Jane huffed a laugh, plucked her comcard from her bedside table, and tucked it in the concealed pocket in her gown. "Come on, Mary, let's help Lizzie finish getting ready."

As Jane spoke, she flicked a switch on the wall panel to reveal a case behind the mirror. She carefully extracted a short, cape-like shoulder-piece made of an intricate metallic lace that sparkled when it caught the light. The piece arced slightly to sit around Lizzie's neck and shoulders, the lace dangling down the bare stretch of her back between her shoulder blades. Mary deftly looped Lizzie's hair into a Laerian Knot, a loosely braided chignon which walked the line of artful indifference and glamorous elegance that so suited her sister's personality.

"Time to leave!" their mother shouted. The sisters got to their feet, checked themselves in the mirror once more, and—following behind the brightly colored blurs that were Lydia and Kitty—made their way downstairs and out the door.

Having recently come off a vacation where most of their days lacked the telltale shift of the sun, it felt jarring to be back on Heoros, experiencing a predictable rhythm again.

Their transport sat gleaming on its launchpad, the metal sides painted with multicolored light from the triple-moon sunset. It was a sleek Tailwynd series passenger shuttle, the shape of which, Jane had to admit, always reminded her of the jewelbirds native to Heoros.

Mrs. Bennet was practically bouncing on her heels with impatience. "The Lucases are already inside," she said, ushering them up the steps.

The Lucases' eldest daughter, Charlotte, gave Jane a small wave as she and Lizzie situated themselves closest to the pilot; Lizzie, as always, sitting nearest to the command center. Kitty and Lydia found seats in the back row, settling in with Charlotte's younger sister Maria, three vivid splashes of color, giggling to themselves and comparing comcard screens. The mothers, with just as much excitement—and slightly less giggling—sat beside the younger girls, leaving Mary and Jane to take their seats near the front. Poor Sir William Lucas, devoid of a companion, sat alone beside the empty seat reserved for Mr. Bennet.

"Your father not joining us this evening?" he asked.

"He cited a good book and a house to himself as reason enough to stay behind," Jane answered.

Sir William laughed heartily. "Can't say I blame him."

The Lucases were the Bennets' closest neighbors and friends, and lived just a short walk from Longbourn. Sir William and Lady Lucas were both friendly and kind, with easy temperaments that were the perfect counterparts to those of Mr. and Mrs. Bennet. It was luck that such friendships were shared with their children. Maria was an eager and willing participant in any of Lydia's schemes, and Charlotte, who was a dear friend to Jane, was near enough another sister to Lizzie.

As the engines engaged, Jane let her mind wander to what awaited them at the ball. She was glad, when the shuttle's engine noise dropped away, to hear Sir William talking with her mother and his wife about Mr. Bingley and his guests.

". . . said he's only bringing his two sisters and a couple other gentlemen."

"One of the men is the older sister's husband, from what we've heard," added Lady Lucas.

"And the other?" her mother asked.

"A friend. I don't know much more about him."

"Oh, it won't be long into the evening before we've learned the details, I'm sure," her mother said firmly.

Jane quietly agreed. If anyone could be certain to find out every piece of gossip as soon as possible, it was Mrs. Bennet.

The ride was smooth and uneventful, the scene through the viewport shifting from the molten gold sunset clouds of Heoros to the cool dark of space as the shuttle adjusted course. In the center of the square of black, like a rounded cluster of metallic crystals, Meryton Waystation loomed ahead.

In short order, the party docked, disembarked, and quickly bypassed the general public levels—with a scan of their comcards—entering directly into the Grand Ballroom, located at the apex of the waystation's central sphere.

The group spilled into the ballroom with gasps of delight. The entire ceiling was made of glass, allowing the gold and green light of the moon to cast a soft glow over the dance floor, mixing with the warm yellow strands of lights that crisscrossed above them—held aloft by string or drone, Jane couldn't tell.

"I think perhaps the organizers heard of Mr. Bingley's intention to attend," Lizzie said, just loud enough for Jane and Charlotte to hear.

"They've certainly gone beyond their usual efforts," Charlotte agreed.

Musicians were playing at the far edge of the ballroom, and many pairs were already dancing. Small tables dotted the outer edges of the room, and a banquet was set along the wall nearest their entry. The younger girls bypassed the drinks proffered by the wait staff, in favor of joining a group of their friends from town. Jane and the others gratefully accepted drinks and the rest of their party slowly split up as they wove through the ballroom, talking and laughing, stopping occasionally to procure another drink or a bit of food.

"There are some very fine dresses here this evening," Jane noted, as a girl Mary's age swept past them in a vibrant, intricately woven, faceted emerald gown.

"Everyone's outdone themselves," Charlotte agreed.

Lizzie flashed a knowing smile. "We have an eligible man to impress."

As if her words had called him from the ether, Mr. Bingley entered the ballroom, his sisters and friends flanking him.

Their presence swept a stillness out over the room, like stardust in the wake of a comet. Even the music stalled.

Mr. Bingley—for it must be him, so similar in appearance to the women in his company—was fair and handsome in a fitted navy suit, the high collar of his jacket turned low and opened to reveal the white cravat beneath. White armor-like metal pieces adorned his arms, one hip, and legs. The newest fashion from Londinium. The men behind and beside him were similarly dressed—the tall, darker one in black and silver, the stockier one in blue and gold.

The women wore dresses with a shine captured in thousands of threads of silver and gold, far beyond anything the women of Heoros and Meryton had adorned themselves in. Their ornate shoulder-pieces seemed far too impractical for movement, and seemed to indicate that they wouldn't be dancing among the crowd.

Lydia startled Jane, having drifted behind her and the others with Kitty, as she whispered excitedly, "Astral lace! Oh, it may as well be made of starlight. I bet it's as delicate as a spider's web. I'd love to touch it."

"You will absolutely not," their mother scolded quietly, also sneaking up on them.

Jane couldn't deny a slight flutter in her stomach when she looked at Mr. Bingley. Though he didn't smile as the Netherfield party moved through the ballroom, she couldn't shake the feeling that he was very kind.

"So, what have you discovered about them?" Kitty asked her mother.

Mrs. Bennet's eyes gleamed. "Mr. Bingley is the slighter one there in front," she told them. "The matching man and woman in the blue and gold are most likely Mr. and Mrs. Hurst, who are of no use to us."

"Mama," Jane chastised.

"Well, I'm not wrong."

"And who is Tall, Dark, and Handsome there behind him?" Lydia prompted.

Lizzie stifled a chuckle.

"Mr. Darcy," Mrs. Bennet answered. "He runs a large estate on Dyberion. Makes something like ten thousand aurum a year."

"He *is* very handsome," Kitty noted.

Lydia nodded sagely, squeezing Jane's and Elizabeth's hands. "You should be trying to attract *him*. Don't let my hard work go to waste." Then she was off again, dragging Kitty and Mary with her toward the refreshment tables while everyone else was distracted.

As the ballroom slowly returned to dance and conversation, Sir William Lucas ushered the Bennets over to meet the Netherfield party, having been in conversation with them for several minutes prior.

"Mr. Bingley, let me introduce my wife and daughter," Sir William said, Lady Lucas and Charlotte bowing slightly in turn. "And here we have Mrs. Bennet and her daughters."

"These are my two eldest," her mother said, "Jane and Elizabeth. I have three others. They're off with the younger crowd."

Mr. Bingley smiled warmly at Jane. "Very nice to finally meet you all." Were his eyes lingering on her?

He went on to introduce his own party. Mr. Darcy barely nodded and didn't smile. Miss Bingley inclined her head as far as her adornments would allow, which wasn't much. Mr. and Mrs. Hurst were less stiff in their acknowledgment, but seemed more interested in their surroundings than the group in front of them.

"Miss Lucas," Mr. Bingley said. "I'd be honored to start the evening off with a dance, if you'd oblige?"

Charlotte's cheeks colored, turning a similar shade to her dress. "Happily," she said, taking his outstretched hand.

The two groups parted slightly to let them through, and as they passed, Bingley's eyes caught Jane's for just a moment, sending a thrill up her spine. And then he was gone.

Mrs. Bennet followed Lady Lucas and her husband as they bowed out of the group to watch Charlotte dance and, no doubt, discuss their thoughts on Mr. Bingley away from his friends.

Jane was immediately thankful for Elizabeth, who wasn't one to let a conversation slip into awkwardness. Her sister turned to Miss Bingley and Mr. Darcy, the only two of their group still affecting an interest in socializing; the Hursts now talking quietly among themselves, their eyes on the glass dome above them.

"Have you been down to Heoros yet, or is Meryton your first stop?" Lizzie asked.

"We arrived this morning," Miss Bingley answered.

Jane offered her a smile. "It must've been nice to reacquaint yourself with soil after such a journey."

"Indeed. Though we came only from Londinium."

"St. James City?" Lizzie asked.

Nods from them both.

"This ball must pale in comparison to the ones you've been able to attend in Cloudtop," Jane noted.

Miss Bingley looked around her, taking in the scene. "They are quite grand, yes."

"Do you often dance on such evenings?" Lizzie asked. "Your shoulder-piece seems to prohibit much movement."

"It does," Miss Bingley replied.

Elizabeth turned to Mr. Darcy. "And do you enjoy dancing?"

"Not particularly, no," he said stiffly.

Elizabeth gave the appearance of commiseration, but Jane knew by the quirk of her brow that she was holding back a great deal of opinion.

Sensing that her sister was likely to grow politely antagonistic, Jane took advantage of the end of the song. "Oh!—Lizzie, I believe Lydia's coming this way. Let's go meet her."

Elizabeth narrowed her eyes at Jane a moment, then assented.

"Lovely to meet you," Jane said, before taking her sister's arm and dragging her away.

They moved nearer to the dance, the sound of the crowd allowing their words some semblance of camouflage.

"Mr. Darcy seems determined not to enjoy his evening, doesn't he?" Lizzie said. "Did he come to the ball simply to look superior and stare down his nose at everyone?"

"Lizzie, he wasn't that bad. He's probably shy."

"I'd call him forbidding and disagreeable over shy."

Before Jane could reply, Mr. Bingley was beside them. "Miss Bennet, would you please honor me with a dance?"

Jane could feel the heat rise in her cheeks. "It'd be a pleasure," she said, as he took both her hands in his and pulled her gently into the line of dancers.

As Jane was swept into the dance, she saw Charlotte step into the space beside Lizzie, and then she had no more attention to spare for her sister.

Jane's and Lizzie's gowns for the Meryton Ball.

The vintage style definitely served Jane well. I knew it would! She caught Mr. Bingley's eye (and half the guests here, as usual).

I think Lizzie would've gone with a more modern style. It suits her better. She does love to be contrary though.

She looked as docile as Jane, but we all know she isn't.

~ Jane

Jewelry details

Lizzie ♡

Probably why Mr. Darcy passed her over. His loss.

CHAPTER 04

Meryton Waystation, Heoros Orbit, First Moon of Londinium

Elizabeth was glad to see Jane enjoying herself so much. Mr. Bingley could hardly keep his eyes off her, and Jane was having no more success avoiding looking at him. He was lively and unreserved in a way that felt promising for her older sister. Compared to his guests, Mr. Bingley was disarmingly charming and downright eager to be acquainted with everyone. At one point Elizabeth heard him mention that the ball closed far too early, and should he have one at his estate, time would be of no consequence.

This elicited varying looks of alarm and annoyance from his companions, especially Mr. Darcy. Unlike Mr. Bingley, his friend had spent the better part of the evening brooding by the windows, and barely speaking to anyone outside his own party. His character was quickly decided. The general consensus was that Mr. Darcy was the proudest, most disagreeable man within the inner rings of the system.

Elizabeth was not the only one to notice Mr. Darcy's disinterest. Mr. Bingley soon came darting out of the dance and over to him.

"Darcy, come dance," he said, his voice traveling along the walls to where Elizabeth sat, in that unique way that circular rooms offer. "I insist. You look ridiculous pouting in a corner over here."

"There are no corners. It's a dome."

Bingley laughed and shook his head. "You really ought to dance."

"I'd rather not dance with people I don't know well. And who here would be worth knowing well? No, dancing with any of the women here would be a punishment."

"You couldn't bribe me with a moon to be so particular," said Mr. Bingley. "Honestly. I've never met so many pleasant girls as I have this evening. There are several who are uncommonly pretty."

"*You've* been dancing with the only pretty girl in the room," said Mr. Darcy, his eyes on Jane.

"Oh, she's more beautiful than a seven-moon sunrise," he exclaimed.

Elizabeth couldn't help grinning at his description.

"But her sister Elizabeth is also very pretty, and enjoyable company."

Her heart skipped as he said this, and Mr. Darcy turned toward her. "Which one?" He caught her eye and quickly withdrew his gaze. "She's tolerable, but not pretty enough to tempt *me*. I'm in no mood to elevate the status of any of these women, let alone one already slighted by other men."

Elizabeth huffed. She hadn't been slighted. She'd chosen to sit out a few dances.

"You'd better return to your partner and enjoy her smiles," Mr. Darcy continued. "You're wasting your time with me."

Mr. Bingley dismissed his friend's words with another laugh and rejoined the dance. Mr. Darcy dislodged himself from his sulking place and strode stiffly past her.

She sat in stunned silence for a moment, then stood to find Charlotte and relay what she'd heard. It was too ridiculous a situation to not laugh at it with someone, even if it was at the expense of her pride.

She found Charlotte amid a small party, and told them all the story.

"Lose him in the stars," Lydia said. "He's obviously got no taste."

"Consider it good fortune," Mary offered. "If he'd shown as much interest in you as Bingley's showing Jane, you'd be forced to dance with him in silence."

"Or stand beside him glowering out the windows," Kitty added.

The group had a good laugh, then Mary changed the subject.

"I actually overheard something quite nice." Her cheeks colored a little as she continued. "Mrs. Bates told Miss Bingley that I was the most accomplished girl in the district."

Lydia gave her sister an obnoxious squeeze of a hug. "That's because you work so very hard at it, Mary, dear."

Two boys came over then, and enticed Lydia and Kitty back onto the dance floor, leaving the other three to their approaching mothers.

"Stars alight!—what an evening, girls," Mrs. Bennet exclaimed happily. "Jane has certainly caught the attentions of quite a few."

"No doubt due to the glow from Mr. Bingley's particular regard," Lady Lucas noted.

"The word 'beautiful' was uttered," Mary said.

Mrs. Bennet's eyes bulged with excitement.

The rest of the evening passed pleasantly. Each member of the Longbourn party left feeling satisfied, even if, in Elizabeth's case, it was more for her sister's success than for herself.

The party entered Longbourn house in good spirits, finding that Mr. Bennet was still awake. With a book, he could disregard time—a trait he shared with Elizabeth and Mary—and it was clear that despite his decision not to go, he was very curious about the evening's events.

"We waved at you from the Meryton, Papa," Lydia teased as she flounced through the doorway of the sitting room, kissing him on the cheek and dropping into the empty chair next to him. "Did you see us sparkling in the sky?"

"Oh, my dear," sighed Mrs. Bennet, breezing right past him. "We've had a most delightful evening. I wish you'd been there. I know you avoid large gatherings when you can, but you missed out on a most excellent ball. Jane was so admired by everyone, of course, and Mr. Bingley thought her quite beautiful. He danced with her twice!"

"Who could blame him?" Elizabeth added, giving Jane a wink as she gingerly slipped her shoes off her aching feet.

"She seemed the only one in the room to him for a time," Mrs. Bennet continued, pacing the room excitedly. "When he asked Charlotte Lucas to dance first, I was very displeased. How could *she* be the one to catch his eye?"

"Mama," Elizabeth and Jane admonished from the doorway.

Mrs. Bennet ignored them and carried on. "But it was clear he thought very little of her. Especially with Jane just *existing* beside her."

"He danced with a few others," Mary noted.

"Oh, yes. Miss King. And then Maria Lucas. Then again with Jane. And once with Lizzie, and—"

"If he had any regard for *me*," cried Mr. Bennet, snapping his book shut, "he'd have sprained his ankle in the first dance." He added in a mutter, "Land's sake. Must he dance so much?"

"He was a delight," their mother said, talking over his muttering as if she hadn't heard. "Incredibly handsome. Such a gentleman.

And his sisters. Beyond elegant. I dare say, the astral lace upon Mrs. Hurst's gown—"

"Must have cost a fortune!" Lydia added breathlessly. "The remnants of the fabric alone would pay for my entire wardrobe."

"Yes, yes," their father said, not at all interested in this line of conversation. "Everyone was beautiful and rich. What else?"

This led Mrs. Bennet to the topic of Elizabeth. With bitterness, and not without exaggeration, she relayed the shocking rudeness of Mr. Darcy.

"I can assure you, Papa," Elizabeth interjected, as she and Jane stood to leave the sitting room, "it was no great loss on my part."

She and Jane made their way quickly upstairs to their room and shut the door, muffling any continued conversation from the sitting room.

Elizabeth eyed her sister stealthily as she dropped her shoes beside her bed, waiting. Finally alone with the person she trusted most, Jane admitted to Elizabeth just how taken she was by Mr. Bingley.

"He's exactly what a man should be," she said, slowly working her fingers into her hair and removing her adornments. "He's sensible, good-humored, kind; and I've never seen anyone so genuinely content with their circumstances."

"He's also handsome," replied Elizabeth, scooping their sleepwear from a drawer, "which doesn't hurt."

Jane laughed. "Indeed. I was so flattered to be given so much of his attention. I didn't expect such a compliment." She gave Elizabeth a little twirl gesture.

Elizabeth backed up to her, letting her undo the buttons. "I expected it for you. But that's the greatest difference between us. Compliments always take *you* by surprise, and *me* never." She turned around, cupping her sister's face in her hands for a moment. "Why would he not ask you to dance over and over again? It was clear to anyone there that you're prettier by far than every other woman in the room—or the whole of the waystation, for that matter." She removed her cape and placed it back in its case. "Well, he does seem to be a good one. I give you permission to like him. You've liked far stupider men in the past."

"Lizzie!"

"You constantly give men—people in general, really—too much credit. You never see a fault in anyone. All the universe is good and agreeable in your eyes."

Jane began the complicated task of slipping her arms out of her sleeves. "I wouldn't want to judge unfairly or too soon; but I always say what I think."

"I know you do," Elizabeth said, wiggling her way out of her own dress. "And that's exactly what makes you such a wonder. With *your* good sense, to be so honestly unaware of other people's nonsense. Faking sincerity is nothing new—we see it in every city on every moon in the system. But to be so candid without being pretentious—to accept the good in everyone and say nothing of the bad—that is a trait of yours alone." The dress slipped off and pooled at her feet. She stepped out and flicked the edge with her foot, catching the fabric in her hand. "To that end, what are your thoughts on Mr. Bingley's sisters? Their manners are . . . unequal to his."

Jane's reply was muffled for a moment as she dragged her sleep shirt over her head. "They're pleasant enough company once you spend a little time talking with them." She draped the gown across the dresser top where the staff could remove it without waking them in the morning, then pulled back her bedcovers and climbed in. "Miss Bingley lives with her brother for the time being, helping maintain order aboard the Netherfield. I believe she'll make a fine addition to the district while they remain docked at Netherfield Landing."

Elizabeth was not convinced, but she readied her bed in silence as her sister spoke. She was tempted to point out that Mr. Bingley's sisters didn't appear interested in making friends with the people of the Landings District. They were all smiles and good humor when it suited them, but they were also proud and conceited. Especially Caroline Bingley. Their family was well respected in the northern hemisphere of Kaels; something impressed more deeply upon their memories than that their brother's fortune—and their own—had been acquired by trade. Their father had built the manufacturing techniques used in the coms devices, which had allowed them to move up in the world. Wealthy and well educated, they were clearly accustomed to spending their time with the system's elites. In Elizabeth's opinion, it made them entitled to think well of themselves and meanly of others.

OBSERVATIONS OF PRIDE AND VANITY

The Meryton ball provided us with new acquaintances. The most anticipated, Mr. Bingley, brought a friend—the inspiration for my thoughts tonight. Mr. Darcy was deemed very proud, and I can't say I disagree. But pride is a common failing. Everything that I've read has convinced me so—that human nature is prone to it, regardless of the planet or ship or satellite they call home. Are there any of us who don't feel some level of pride in at least one aspect or quality of our lives, warranted or not? It's unsurprising that this great man would succumb to it as well.

I think it's worth noting, though, that vanity and pride are different things, and the words are too often used synonymously. A person may be proud without being vain. Pride relates more to our opinion of ourselves, whereas vanity is what we'd have others think of us.

I believe the majority of opinions about him that were made at the ball were formed with vanity in mind. Mr. Darcy is certainly as proud as they say. But perhaps that isn't so offensive as it seems. He has wealth and attractiveness and truly everything in his favor. It's no wonder he would think highly of himself. He could almost be forgiven for it. I dare say he has a right to be proud.

It's entirely possible that he (like me) simply does not enjoy social functions in the same way as most, and comes off the worse for it. But we'll likely never know. And so he'll be known hereafter as proud, when what they really mean is vain.

CHAPTER
05

The Netherfield Private Transport, Heoros, First Moon of Londinium

As the Netherfield's private shuttle returned their small party to Heoros, Darcy settled more comfortably into his seat, glad to finally be away from the crowds.

"What an interesting evening," said Louisa, curled next to her dozing husband.

Caroline, lounging along the private shuttle's chaise, said, "That's a word we could use, yes."

"I've never met nicer people or prettier girls in my life," Bingley offered, his legs sprawled into the aisle, as casual and carefree as ever.

"They were a collection of commonly friendly people and ordinary girls," Darcy countered, breathing in the scent of the brand-new upholstery as he leaned his head back on his seat and closed his eyes, his hands fiddling idly with his comcard.

Caroline chuckled but said nothing else.

"Oh, come now," Bingley said. "Everyone was kind and very attentive. It lacked the usual stiffness and formality of these things."

"They're meant to be formal, darling," his older sister added.

He ignored Louisa. "By the end of it I felt as if I knew everyone there."

Darcy lifted his head and looked at his friend, unable to resist a bit of ribbing. "I rather think the balance of attention was one-sided."

"Indeed," said Caroline. "You wouldn't have cared to know anyone, save Miss Jane Bennet."

Bingley's eyes brightened, his expression exaggerated by the glow of the shuttle's surface as they re-entered the moon's atmosphere. "Even a galaxy couldn't outshine her beauty."

Darcy's mouth quirked in an indulgent grin, although he hid it quickly. "She's very pretty. But she smiles too much." It was too soon for Bingley to be comparing her to the universe, especially when he'd seen so little of it or the people in it.

Bingley had inherited assets which amounted to nearly a hundred thousand aurum from his father, who'd intended to purchase land, but didn't live to do it. Bingley now had access to a good ship that could transition from land to space, and the freedom to travel Londinium's entire satellite system. It seemed unlikely he'd settle down anytime soon, and it was important that he made wise decisions.

It was the way of their friendship, which was a strong and lasting one, in spite of their differences in character. Bingley, endearing and easygoing, was the sunlight to Darcy's dark. Reserved and particular as he was, Darcy always conducted himself with proper manners, but lacked Bingley's inviting openness. Bingley was well liked wherever they went, and Darcy was content to let him take on the brunt of the socializing. But Bingley trusted and relied upon

Darcy, holding his judgment in the highest regard. Darcy knew and understood this for the honor and responsibility that it was.

"But she's very sweet," Louisa said, apparently noting the slightly crestfallen look on her brother's face.

"Yes, I wouldn't mind getting to know her better," said Caroline.

"See now," Darcy said, "approval! Feel free to compare her to the sun itself . . . in your head."

LONDINIUM SAT[SYS

Communications Log—System Storage 30 Days [Planetary]

[HurstLady] 25.9-19:39:15.LS

I like Jane better with every visit, but her mother is intolerable.

[Caroline_Bingley] 25.9-19:40:20.LS

How such a woman raised such a daughter, I'll never know.

[HurstLady] 25.9-19:42:56.LS

She and Eliza do seem to have broken the mold. Perhaps it's their father's influence.

[Caroline_Bingley] 25.9-19:43:10.LS

If that's the case, he seems to have given up after the first two.

[HurstLady] 25.9-19:45:53.LS

Lucky for us, Charles admires Jane, who is not at all like her younger counterparts.

[Caroline_Bingley] 25.9-19:47:02.LS

Oh, can you imagine? . . . How much longer is this dinner?

[HurstLady] 25.9-19:48:45.LS

If our past visits are any indication, the game tables will be setting up any moment.

[Caroline_Bingley] 25.9-19:50:34.LS

Good. Make sure your husband picks whatever game the mother is playing. He's too competitive to care how annoying she is.

[HurstLady] 25.9-19:53:10.LS

If we end up playing Circumstance or Press, it won't matter where she's sitting. We'll hear every thought in her head.

[Caroline_Bingley] 25.9-19:55:58.LS

Let's press for Twist, then. Or Pillars—we can play one another and talk freely.

[HurstLady] 25.9-19:57:22.LS

I'd love to win a rare carak off one of them, though. Finer than any we've seen in the St. James circles. It's rather unfair. They need only to stumble upon one in the garden after jewelbird season.

[Caroline_Bingley] 25.9-20:02:57.LS

One point in favor of this miserable little moon, I suppose.

[Caroline_Bingley] 25.9-20:04:28.LS

Charles gave me a look. He's on to us.

. . . END COM . . .

CHAPTER
06

Lucas Lodge, Heoros,
First Moon of Londinium

The Lucases' annual party for the residents of the Landings District was a perfect place for Elizabeth to discuss her thoughts with Charlotte over the many visits between the Netherfield and Bennet households.

"He appears to be more than partial to her," Charlotte said, as she and Elizabeth sat sipping a dry, fruity Gleam, watching Jane and Bingley talking quietly nearby. Jane was dressed in shimmering silver, and Bingley—in blue and silver—looked as if he'd matched her on purpose.

"Based on the number of coms she sends to him each night—out of view of our mother's prying eyes, of course—I'd say she's feeling the same."

"They might both be well on their way to love," Charlotte gathered.

"It seems so. Thankfully," Elizabeth noted quietly, "Jane is so composed and even-tempered, she's not likely to be found out by the gossips until she's ready for everyone to know."

Charlotte twirled the stem of her glass idly in her fingers, matching the lyrical tempo of the musicians. "In general, not involving the public in your romantic life is ideal."

"Certainly."

"But sometimes it can be a disadvantage, being too guarded. If Jane conceals her affections from Mr. Bingley as well as she conceals them from everyone else, she might lose her chance with him. We can all *begin* freely. A slight preference is natural. But there are very few of us who are brave enough to be really in love without encouragement. She ought to show *more* affection than she feels. It's clear to anyone watching that Bingley likes her. But he may never act upon the feeling if she doesn't offer him the same."

"She does. In her own way. If *I* can see it clear as sky, then he'd be the stupidest man in the system not to notice."

Jane and Bingley had their heads tilted toward one another—Jane smiled warmly as he spoke, their desserts long forgotten in front of them. How could Charlotte not see what was between them?

"Remember, Lizzie, that he doesn't know Jane the way you do. He's known her for a few weeks, and you've known her your entire life."

Elizabeth gestured toward them. "She may not have outright told him she likes him, but she's not hiding it either. He'll figure it out soon if he hasn't already."

"Maybe. If he has enough interactions with her. They meet quite often, but it's never long; and always in the company of so many others. Even considering their conversations on coms, I can't see it being enough. She needs to make every moment count when she has his attention. Once she's secured him, there'll be plenty of time for her to fall in love."

Peals of laughter broke through the sounds of many conversations, pulling Elizabeth's attention to Kitty and Lydia, winding their way through the people and tables. Lydia blew a kiss to Jane and Bingley as she passed them.

Elizabeth shook her head, catching Mr. Darcy's gaze as their eyes both shifted from her sisters to each other, before looking away quickly. "It's a good plan, if being well married were all that mattered to Jane. But Jane isn't favoring him because she wants someone rich. She can't even be certain at this point how much she cares for him. She's only known him a few weeks—dancing on the Meryton, a few dinners in company together—and their conversations, though nightly, are not overburdened with depth. She doesn't know him yet."

Elizabeth could still feel Darcy's gaze on her. It made her restless. She turned toward the other side of the long room. Charlotte had done well with the decor. The floral arrangements were a divine concoction of colors in the otherwise muted room. The lighting gave it all a warm, inviting atmosphere.

Charlotte let out a little sigh. "Well, I wish her luck with all my heart. If she were married to him tomorrow, I believe she'd have just as much chance of happiness with him as if she took a lunar year to get to know him first. Being well acquainted or similar in personality when one marries is no real advantage toward happiness. We all still grow after marriage, and that growth is not guaranteed to be the same direction or speed, so issues will show themselves either way. It's better to know as little as possible about all the annoyances of the person you marry beforehand."

"Oh, Charlotte," Elizabeth laughed, "what an argument. I'd like to see you follow your own advice."

Charlotte just shrugged and tipped her drink back.

"It's objectively bad advice," Elizabeth insisted.

"I don't know the full context of what you're saying," Mary offered, sidling up to them, "but I think maybe Charlotte has a point."

"How so?"

"What is growth if not change? Haven't you ever read a book you loved as a child and found it held no appeal to you as an adult? Or the opposite? Marriage, I imagine, is like a book. You have to experience it to truly know the story and your feelings about it."

Sir William Lucas appeared before them with Void Commander Forster at his side.

"Talking of books, are we?" Sir William asked jovially.

"A fine topic," Void Commander Forster offered. "But I must say I prefer ships to stories."

"I love them equally," Elizabeth said, "though one is easier to access than the other. What are you flying these days, Commander?"

"Not much of anything, to tell you the truth," he said. "We've got a new regiment of Star Force reserves in the inner rings."

"I heard," she said. "The Meryton is meant to station them, is that right?"

He pursed his lips and sighed. "It is, yes. For the whole winter. It's a lot more simulation and a lot less time in the black. But once the training has been completed, I do hope to have a shot at flying the new SheerWing."

"I've read the controls on those are quite something," she began, but her thoughts trailed as Mr. Darcy, to her surprise, entered the little circle they'd formed.

Aware of her sudden slip in conversation, Elizabeth prompted the Void Commander. "How does their training compare to real flight?"

"It's not dissimilar. Just a slightly different view out the peripheral windows."

"I imagine it takes some getting used to, considering the hours they must be putting in," Charlotte noted.

The VC nodded gravely. "We work them hard, but it's worth the training."

"Could you not give them a reprieve," Elizabeth suggested playfully, "so that they might, say, host a ball on the Meryton?"

"Ha! No good could come of it, I assure you," the VC replied.

Elizabeth shrugged. "Some good, surely. They'd be loose-lipped enough after a few drinks to give me a rundown of their training. And you never know when one might need to know how to fly a ship."

Sir William laughed heartily at this. "By that you mean you, of course."

"Of course," she agreed, catching Darcy's intent look out of the corner of her eye.

"I can picture it now," chuckled VC Forster, "a fleet of well-bred ladies, bearing down on a target in those glittering gowns and jeweled contraptions you all wear."

"What a sight that would be," Elizabeth said, imagining the scene with some satisfaction.

An officer pulled VC Forster's attention from the group, and the conversation shifted as the other men were drawn into some dealing or other that was of no concern to Elizabeth or Charlotte.

Taking advantage of the momentary distraction, she pulled her friend close and whispered, "What is Mr. Darcy up to? Why listen in on our conversation with VC Forster?"

"That's a question only he can answer."

"If he continues, I'm going to call him out. If I don't allow myself a slight rudeness here, I might grow too afraid to speak to him at all."

She didn't have long to wait before he turned to them again, though not, it seemed, with the intention of speaking.

"Oh, Lizzie, don't you dare," Charlotte whispered urgently.

Raising a brow in defiance, Elizabeth whispered back, "I do believe I will."

ANNUAL DINNER PARTY PLAN
COLLABORATIVE LIST / CREATOR ID: HC-7988.PI.LL [MOM]
TIMESTAMP: 10.9-9:34:10.LS / LOCATION: HEOROS

THE ANNUAL LUCAS LODGE DINNER PARTY IS 20 DAYS AWAY!
ADD IN CHECKLIST ITEMS AS NEEDED.

MENU SMART EDITS ADDED BY [MOM] 10.9-10:02:33.LS
Soup—Spicy Heorosian Jewelbird Bisque

Main Course—Lagroton, prepared three ways: Stuffed w/lemon, ricotta & oregano • Herb encrusted medallions • Rosemary & garlic w/balsamic glazed carrots over smashed vinegared potatoes

Salad—Mixed local greens w/Arkuluan Vinaigrette

Second Course—Grouse & truffle mushroom pie, cheese assortment feat. Laerian jelly

Dessert—Stardust iced cream, Apollian fruit tarts, tea & coffee

LIBATIONS SMART EDITS ADDED BY [DAD] 20.9-15:45:57.LS
Adults—Gleam (Violet, Sparkling, White) • Whiskey • Port District • Brewery's Full Tap List

All—Tea, Coffee, Imbued Waters, Bubbled Juices

ENTERTAINMENT SMART EDITS ADDED BY [DAD] 13.9-11:02:55.LS
Music—Landings District Quartet

Game Tables—Rise: 2 tables • Twist: 2 tables • Galaxies: 1 table • Circumstance: 1 table • Press: 1 table

DECORATIONS SMART EDITS ADDED BY [CHARLOTTE] 11.9-7:58:12.LS
Florals—Nagalean Starflowers, Coral Peonies, Blue Tweedia, Solar Protea, Silver Sage Fern, Comet Tails, Londinium Roses (Kitty Bennet suggested adding Nebula Blooms if we can get them)

Lighting—Holo-Candelabras for dessert tables, Lodge Lighting System set to "Dinner Party" mode, low floral arrangements w/actual candelabras (use digi-flame candles) for dining table centerpieces *don't forget to set up drones for dance floor chandelier!

NOTABLE GUEST ACCOMMODATIONS
SMART EDITS ADDED BY [MOM] 11.9-13:23:17.LS [DAD] 11.9-14:01:08.LS
[CHARLOTTE] 24.9-19:28:34.LS

Seating
—Seat Maria, Kitty, and Lydia together!
—Seat the above closest to children's table
—Seat Netherfield Party gentlemen near myself and Mr. Bennet
—Seat Jane beside Mr. Bingley, but keep Mrs. Bennet at least 5 seats apart

VOICE NOTE ADDED BY [CHARLOTTE] 30.9-20:18:27.LS

Next time let's maybe find a way to keep Mr. Darcy and Lizzie from interacting.

CHAPTER 07

Lucas Lodge, Heoros, First Moon of Londinium

Having at first hardly acknowledged Miss Elizabeth Bennet's existence, Darcy was startled to discover that she was becoming a real object of interest to him. No sooner had he made it clear to his friends that she wasn't attractive, than he began to notice the mirth that sparkled like the stars in her dark eyes, rendering her rather beautiful. This would have been embarrassing enough, but to his dismay, his criticisms regarding the rest of her appearance crumbled steadily faster with each opportunity he had to study her. She had a pleasing figure, and though her manners weren't perhaps ideal for high society, he couldn't deny her intelligence and easy playfulness.

As he turned back from the conversation with Sir William Lucas, Void Commander Forster, and the Lieutenant, Darcy found himself being watched by Miss Bennet and Miss Lucas.

"Do you think, Mr. Darcy," Miss Elizabeth prompted, "that I was too enthusiastic with Void Commander Forster in teasing him about the officers taking time away to host a ball?"

She certainly didn't hesitate to speak her mind.

"It's a subject that always animates ladies, I think."

She narrowed her eyes. "Such an overgeneralized opinion of us, surely."

Darcy furrowed his brow.

"It's *her* turn now to be teased," Miss Lucas cut in. "I'm going to open the piano, Eliza, and you know what comes next."

"You're a very strange sort of friend," Miss Bennet replied. "Always wanting me to play and sing in front of everyone. If I had any desire to pursue a performer's life, you'd be invaluable. As it is, I'd rather not embarrass myself in front of people in the habit of hearing the very best performers on many a world."

But her friend insisted, and Miss Bennet relented. With a grave glance in his direction, she said, "If it must be so, it must." Miss Lucas led her off to the piano.

It was a fine piece of craftsmanship, the piano. With a glance, one could see that it was an antique, and a strong accompaniment to Miss Bennet's simple and unaffected playing. But it was clear after the second song that she was eager to relinquish the spotlight to her sister. Miss Mary Bennet, despite being known as the quiet one, was a much more determined performer. Unfortunately, she lacked the charm necessary to carry her rigid, though otherwise decent, performance.

Miss Elizabeth's youngest sisters eventually did the party a favor by convincing Miss Mary to play more spirited tunes, but their youthful energy soon overwhelmed as they and two or three officers began dancing at the other end of the room.

Engrossed in his own thoughts, Darcy didn't realize that Sir William Lucas was beside him again until he spoke.

"Such an amusing way to spend an evening, is it not, Mr. Darcy? There's nothing like dancing to raise one's spirits. It's without doubt one of the better parts of polished society."

"It's also quite popular among the less polished societies of the system," he replied, shaking off his lingering thoughts to focus on the conversation at hand. "Anyone can dance."

Sir William smiled. "Skill is another matter. Your friend dances well," he added, seeing Bingley join the group with Miss Jane Bennet. "I have no doubt you are adept in the art as well."

To this Darcy had no answer. Instead, he watched Miss Bennet smile serenely at his friend as the two of them circled one another in the dance. Bingley matched her smile with a boyish grin.

Miss Elizabeth was returning, her eyes focused on something past them. Sir William shot out a hand and stopped her. "My dear, why are you not dancing?" He reached for her hand and turned to Darcy. "You must allow me to recommend Miss Elizabeth as a most worthy dance partner. You couldn't refuse with such beauty standing before you, I'm sure."

Darcy opened his mouth to agree, but was momentarily unable to speak.

Miss Elizabeth pulled her hand back. "Thank you, sir, but I don't intend to dance. I hadn't come by this way to beg for a partner."

Darcy found it quite irresistible to request a dance anyway, but it was of no use. She was determined.

"Mr. Darcy is just being polite," she said.

"Certainly, but could you blame him for obliging?" Sir William replied, teasingly. "After all, who could object to such a partner?"

Miss Elizabeth arched a brow as she locked eyes with Darcy. "*You* may find me *tolerable*, Sir William, but let us not make assumptions for others." With this, she gave a small nod and excused herself, already walking away when realization struck him.

She'd overheard him on the Meryton.

Her small rebuke did nothing to lessen his growing regard for her. In fact, he was rather impressed. She'd slipped it in so casually, but it must have nettled at her for weeks. Her composure was admirable. A quick strike and then she was gone. She hadn't even waited to see the shot land. She'd simply turned her back and known it would.

"I can guess what you're thinking." Caroline materialized beside him, shattering his reverie.

"I doubt it."

"You're imagining the insufferable passage of time that life on a moon such as this, with such society, would afford you. I agree entirely. These people. So vapid. So self-important and yet so insignificant. What I'd give for your thoughts on them."

Darcy barely glanced at her. "My mind was more pleasantly engaged. I was considering what a pleasure it would be to find myself lost in the eyes of a pretty woman."

Caroline sharpened her attention on him at once. "A pretty woman, you say! Well, do tell. Who could've inspired such a change in you?"

Darcy clenched his teeth a moment, then replied resolutely, "Miss Elizabeth Bennet."

"Miss Elizabeth Bennet?" Caroline blinked rapidly. "I'm astonished. Stars! How long has she been in your favor—and when might I wish you congratulations?"

Darcy sighed. "This is exactly what I expected you to ask, Caroline. Such a rapid imagination, jumping from admiration to marriage in the flash of a booster."

"Oh, no," she laughed. "If you're serious I'll consider this matter absolutely settled. You'll have the most charming mother-in-law. She'll always be at Pemberley and have ever so much to say."

As she carried on entertaining herself with more grand suppositions and wild fancies, he listened to her with perfect indifference, his eyes trained on Miss Elizabeth.

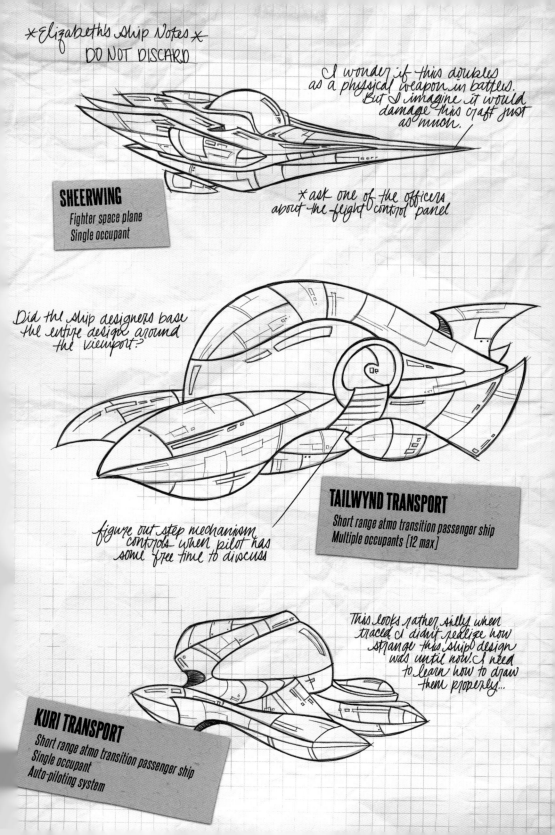

Elizabeth's Ship Notes
DO NOT DISCARD

I wonder if this doubles
as a physical weapon in battles.
But I imagine it would
damage this craft just
as much.

SHEERWING
Fighter space plane
Single occupant

* ask one of the officers
about the flight control panel

Did the ship designers base
the entire design around
the viewport?

TAILWYND TRANSPORT
Short range atmo transition passenger ship
Multiple occupants [12 max]

figure out step mechanism
controls when pilot has
some free time to discuss

This looks rather silly when
traced I didn't realize how
strange this ship design
was until now. I need
to learn how to draw
them properly...

KURI TRANSPORT
Short range atmo transition passenger ship
Single occupant
Auto-piloting system

CHAPTER
08

Longbourn House, Heoros, First Moon of Londinium

One thing Mrs. Bennet was grateful for, now that her children were all old enough, was their ability to visit her sister without her. It was only an hour's ride on the family's Tailwynd Transport ship from the Longbourn Estate to the Meryton Waystation; a very convenient distance for her girls, who often traveled three or four times a week to visit their aunt and the shops on the main level. Kitty and Lydia were particularly frequent travelers, being younger and with fewer demands on their time. The house always felt much quieter without them in it, and Mrs. Bennet was able to give her nerves a break.

The two youngest, who'd risen early in sync with the continually lengthening daylight, were currently chittering like squirrels at their eldest sister. The sun's rays gleamed through the sitting room's window and brightened their already bright, excited faces. The promised regiment of Star Force reserves had recently arrived to the Meryton Waystation, where they would remain the whole winter. With each trip, Kitty and Lydia had learned more of the officers' names and connections, and, thanks to their aunt, they'd eventually been able to meet a few of them.

Mr. Bingley and his large fortune, in their eyes, was worthless in comparison to the flight suits of an ensign.

"From what I'm hearing," Mr. Bennet's deep voice broke through, "you must be two of the silliest girls in the district."

A soft laugh escaped Elizabeth, who'd been hunched over some kind of guide or map at the little drawing table in the corner.

"I've suspected it for quite a while, but now I'm convinced."

Kitty pouted at her father, but said nothing. Lydia, as ever, was perfectly indifferent. She simply continued, loudly admiring Flight Lieutenant Carter and expounding on her hopes of seeing him again soon.

Mrs. Bennet set down her teacup, throwing a stern look at Elizabeth before turning her frown to her husband. "It shocks me, my dear," she said, "that you're so ready to think your own children silly. If I wished to think negatively of anyone's children, it'd certainly not be my own."

"If my children are silly, I hope always to be aware of it."

She huffed and caressed Kitty's hair protectively. "Yes. Well. It just so happens that all of our children are very clever."

Mary looked up from her book and smiled proudly.

Mr. Bennet leaned back in his chair. "On this point, I'm sorry to say, we don't agree. I'd hoped we'd always be of one mind on such things, but I must differ from you here and continue to think our two youngest daughters uncommonly foolish."

Kitty slumped a bit, but then, seeing her little sister's unflinching confidence, straightened again.

"You can't expect these girls to have our good sense at their age," Mrs. Bennet explained. "I remember admiring a man in a flight suit myself at their age. If a smart young Wing Commander, with five or six thousand a year, should admire one of my girls, I wouldn't say no to him. Void Commander Forster looked very handsome the other night at Sir William's, all dressed in his uniform, you must admit."

"Oh! Mama, that reminds me," Lydia cut in, a pout on her lips. "Aunt Phillips says that VC Forster and Flight Lieutenant Carter aren't on Heoros this week. They're engaged in flight training— formations and maneuvers and such. So tedious."

Mrs. Bennet was about to commiserate when an alert sounded from Jane's comcard, lying open on the table. Mrs. Bennet's gaze went straight to the screen, reading it instantly. A waive from the Netherfield, flagged for immediate reply.

Jane's face reddened. "I must've forgotten to turn down the volume." She quickly snatched the comcard from the table and opened the message.

Mrs. Bennet's heart fluttered in excitement for her. "What does it say? Is it from Mr. Bingley? It must be. Oh, just read it aloud, my love! The suspense is too much!"

"It's from Miss Bingley," Jane finally said. She held the screen so Mrs. Bennet could read it.

To: JANE BENNET, LONGBOURN ESTATE, LANDINGS DISTRICT, HEOROS

From: CAROLINE BINGLEY, STARCROSS STARLINER, HEOROS ORBIT

Subject: LUNCH

My dear friend,

The Starcross is in orbit today. I'm sure you're familiar with it. If you're not so compassionate as to dine with

Louisa and me aboard the ship, we'll be in danger of hating each other for the rest of our lives, as a whole day of conversation between two women can never end without a quarrel. Come as soon as you can. My brother and the gentlemen are occupied with a test run of the Netherfield.

Yours ever,
Caroline Bingley

That wasn't at all what Mrs. Bennet had hoped. "A test run. That's very unlucky."

Jane handed Elizabeth the comcard absently. "Can I have the Tailwynd?" she asked.

Mrs. Bennet sat for a moment with this request and considered. Was there a way to turn this to Jane's advantage? She perked up, remembering their old automated-pilot transport. It was overdue for maintenance. "No, my dear," she said, "you'd better go on the Kuri. It needs an update. Take it and the docking bot will flag and lock it. Then you'll have to stay on the Netherfield for the night."

"That'd be a good scheme," said Elizabeth, "if you were sure they wouldn't offer to send her home."

"I'd really prefer going in the Tailwynd," Jane insisted.

"I'm sorry," Mrs. Bennet said, though she wasn't. "It's needed for the groundskeeper's supply run. Isn't that so, my dear?"

Mr. Bennet inclined his head. "It is needed quite often."

"But if it's available today," said Elizabeth, persistent, "then we can avoid this ridiculous plan."

Mr. Bennet then acknowledged what Mrs. Bennet knew already. The transport had launched half an hour earlier in search of supplies to combat a particularly devastating invasion of jewel-birds in the eastern gardens. It wasn't due back until the following evening. Jane was therefore obliged to go in the Kuri, and her mother escorted her to the door with many cheerful predictions of a bad day.

HEOROSIAN
Jewelbird

Fig.

The Jewelbird is native only to Heoros. It is a species that has become a staple of many dishes unique to the moon, most notably, Jewelbird Bisque. The sheds of the Jewelbirds are found across the countryside with great frequency, but they are coveted throughout the system by those who play Circumstance, used as play pieces called caraks. The Jewelbird gets its name from the metallic iridescent coloring of its feather shells, and for being commonly mistaken as a bird during its short flights in and out of the flora of the land.

Jewelbird feather shells do begin their lifecycles as thin, soft, and flexible feather-like material. As the feather ages and lengthens, it begins to harden until it becomes an iridescent shell, metallic in appearance, with a similar solidity to that of a beetle's carapace.

Caraks are often shaped and engraved in various embellishments, which can sometimes add value, but some rare finds value better left untouched.

Fig.

CHAPTER
09

Longbourn House, Heoros, First Moon of Londinium

Elizabeth was disheartened that her mother's plan had succeeded.

Jane hadn't been gone long before a small obscure mechanism malfunctioned during her flight. Everyone was concerned except for Mrs. Bennet, who was delighted.

Jane was certainly not coming back in the Kuri, and the inhabitants of the Netherfield took her in just as her mother had expected.

"What a lucky idea I had," Mrs. Bennet announced several times over the course of the evening, as if the malfunction were to her credit alone. Elizabeth had been glad to escape her mother when it was reasonably believable that she was ready for bed. But morning had come, and with it, news that only strengthened her mother's excitement and Elizabeth's worry.

Breakfast had barely been served when a waive came for Elizabeth from the Netherfield.

To: ELIZABETH BENNET, LONGBOURN ESTATE, LANDINGS DISTRICT, HEOROS

From: JANE BENNET, NETHERFIELD STARCRUISER, HEOROS ORBIT

Subject: UNWELL

Lizzie,

I find myself very unwell this morning, which is likely due to my getting exposed to a chemical from the malfunction yesterday. My friends won't hear of my returning till I'm better, and will continue on with the test run while I'm aboard. They insist also on calling a physician—but don't panic. Aside from fits of vertigo, a small cough, and a head-ache, there isn't much the matter with me.

Yours,
Jane

"Congratulations, my dear," said her father, once Elizabeth had finished reading aloud. "If your daughter becomes gravely ill or dies, it'll be a comfort to know that it was all in pursuit of Mr. Bingley."

Her mother shook her half-eaten muffin at him. "Oh, I'm not afraid of her dying. People don't die of a little exposure. She'll be taken good care of. As long as she stays there, it'll all work out."

Elizabeth, feeling really anxious, was determined to see Jane, though the Tailwynd Transport was still unavailable and the Kuri was undergoing repairs. She had only one alternative. "I'm taking the earliest public shuttle to Meryton. I'll hire a short-range shuttle to catch the Netherfield in orbit with the Starcross."

"Don't be so silly," cried her mother. "When you arrive, you won't be fit to be seen."

"I'll be fit to see Jane, which is all I want."

"You could wait, and I could procure another transport," her father suggested.

"No, I don't mind. Really. It's just a few extra stops. I'll be back by dinner."

"Your intentions are admirable," observed Mary, "but your impulses should always be guided by reason. In my opinion, you're exerting far more effort than is required."

"She's our sister and she's unwell," Elizabeth said. "Every effort is required."

Lydia yawned theatrically. "Don't be so . . . you . . . Mary." She turned to Elizabeth. "Kitty and I will go with you to Meryton." Neither girl had any qualms with using public transport if it allowed them access to the officers aboard the waystation.

Elizabeth accepted, grateful for her offer, even if it was only a way for Lydia to get something she wanted. "Let's get our things and go. Five minutes."

"If we hurry," said Lydia as they stood, "we might be able to catch Flight Lieutenant Carter before he leaves."

In short order, they were upstairs, dressed, and then out the door, walking briskly, the crisp winter air nettling their lungs and shocking away any last vestiges of sleepiness.

The public shuttle station stood on the line between the Port and Landings Districts, green fields at its front giving way to shimmering tech and steel at its back.

Elizabeth wasted no time securing them passage on the next available transport, which was already boarding. She spent the entire flight with her thoughts locked on Jane, her younger sisters' discussion nothing but a buzzing in her ears. Jane wouldn't want them to worry. The fact that she'd said as much as she did made Elizabeth fear it was far worse than she'd let on, and worry occupied all her thoughts.

"Lizzie, are you coming?" Kitty's voice broke through. She was startled to realize they'd already docked on the Meryton.

They reached a bank of elevator doors and Elizabeth saw her sisters safely onto the main level express, Lydia proudly proclaiming her intention of visiting one of the officers' wives as the doors shut. With her attention now on her task alone, Elizabeth scanned the elevators to find which would take her to the Office of Transport at the dock hub. She ducked into the elevator's open door as quickly as she'd found it, and with a short whoosh and a drop of her stomach, she sank to the right level.

When she stepped out, she was in a low-ceilinged lobby with doors and corridors lining the walls on all sides. There was an information desk at its center, staffed by a clerk in a rather pristine, dark violet work uniform. They had a pleasant, helpful expression that morphed into concern as Elizabeth explained her situation.

"So, I need to intercept the Netherfield before it's out of range," she concluded.

The clerk tapped away at the large screen embedded in the counter. "Unfortunately, there are few transports of the kind at the station, and they're all currently engaged. The earliest I can get you on any of these would be this evening."

Elizabeth deflated. But only for a moment. She was determined to find a way. "What else is there available? Something possibly . . . unconventional?"

The clerk's dark brows furrowed over darker eyes. But with a bite of their bottom lip, they tapped at the screen once again. Elizabeth, arms crossed to tamp down the flutter of unease in her chest, tapped her fingers lightly on her arms as she waited, looking down the various corridors to avoid simply staring at the clerk.

"I . . . may have a solution," they offered. "But it might not be something a finely dressed lady such as yourself would be interested in." The clerk gave her clothes a once-over as they said this.

She waved the words off. "Land it on me."

A wary sigh. "We have some small—but sturdy—maintenance vessels available. They're used mostly for runs to and from various ships within and around the dock space." A hesitation. "You'd have to pilot the craft. It's only big enough for a single crew member."

"Okay," Elizabeth said, biting the inside of her cheek as she considered. That was certainly unexpected. But she was smart and while her sisters had simply enjoyed the rides on the family transport, she'd stayed near the controls, learning how they operated. Over the years she'd become as proficient as the pilots themselves, earning her short-flight license the previous year. This was at the upper limits of what she was allowed, but technically within her abilities. "I can do that." The thought of piloting for this length of travel alone thrilled rather than terrified her.

The clerk seemed to notice this, and with more confidence, added, "It does have an automated navigation system, so as long as you can keep on course, you'll be fine. I'll need a few things from you to get you flight ready. I'll have someone take you through a quick tutorial of the operating system."

After the necessary exchange of information, a squat woman in a more faded and rugged version of the clerk's uniform appeared at the desk. Her eyebrows lifted at the sight of Elizabeth, who didn't miss the dubious look the woman cast the clerk before smiling warmly and extending a hand in the direction of a side hallway.

"This way," she said, her voice surprisingly gentle and matronly.

Elizabeth followed her onto a dock suspended in the center of a hangar, listening to her explain the mechanics of the ship all the while. By the time they'd reached the ship itself—an old Void

Crawler—Elizabeth was confident she'd have no trouble reaching the Netherfield before it was out of range.

She settled into the cockpit, noticing—but unaffected by—the mess of mechanical tools and various spillage of oils around the seat. It was a familiar enough setup to the Kuri, with a similar control layout and almost identical automation system. This gave Elizabeth further encouragement, and she completed the flight checks in the cramped cockpit with excitement.

With one last steeling breath, she gripped the levers tight, engaged the craft, and pulled away from the dock. To Elizabeth's right, giant bay doors opened wide, revealing not the black of space but the gray-green of the moon. She eased the levers into position and accelerated, her eyes pricking with moisture as she slipped out into the void. The hairs on her arms stood on end and she shivered with delight.

"Well, fit me for a flight suit," Elizabeth said to herself with a giddy laugh, "I could stay out here all day."

A beep from the navigation panel pulled her focus back. The automation had locked onto the Netherfield's position, with flight specs listed beside the blinking red light.

She activated the thrusters.

With a jolt that shunted her off course—pulling her around and sideways, Heoros suddenly at her back—the ship shot ahead. She yelped and pulled on the thrusters, but quickly shifted the steering until her vessel's dot was aligned once more on both navigation screens. One showed her the distance from the moon that she'd need to maintain so as not to be drawn into its atmosphere. The other showed the direction she'd need to travel. A soft chime sounded as she locked into place on the lines.

She took a moment to breathe deeply. With a laugh and a squeeze on the handles, she engaged the thrusters again. This time she was ready for the feeling, and tensed her arms to keep the ship on track. With that, the Void Crawler barreled forward.

In equal parts impatience and awe, she watched Heoros rotate on her left. It was much faster than when she watched it from the Meryton's windows, given the speed she was traveling now.

As her arms and legs cramped from the exertion of flight, she found herself within view of the Netherfield.

It was one thing to see pictures of land-hybrid ships in space, but it was another entirely to see one so familiar in its grounded state simply floating in the void. But, oh, was it glorious. What had once been a warm, almost stone-like ship on land, had become part creature, with cord tendrils extending outward like grasping vines while large, powerful thrusters protruded from once-hidden compartments in the sides. It glowed slightly green with the refracted light of Heoros against its surface.

A com light flashed on the large flat screen at the center of the control panel, catching her eye.

She tapped the screen. A crackling sounded in the cockpit, followed by a somewhat bored male voice. "Your vessel has locked its navigation onto the Netherfield StarCruiser. If this was your intention, please state your purpose."

Elizabeth cleared her throat. "My name is Elizabeth Bennet. I've leased—"

"Bennet? Miss Jane's sister?" Interrupted a different, female voice.

"Yes. I . . . I'm not exactly sure what to do next in order to dock," she admitted. "This is my first time solo-piloting, well, anything."

"Very impressive," the woman replied with a warm chuckle. "Not to worry. We'll send a code and your system will sync to ours. Follow the steps to engage docking protocol and then sit back and wait."

Elizabeth sighed, feeling a weight lift off her chest. The flight had been smooth enough, but while she felt confident in her understanding of the controls, she wasn't so self-assured about docking.

As the ship guided her in close, Elizabeth stole the chance to look around unhindered. The docking bay, it turned out, was on the bottom of the Netherfield. She craned her neck as her little vessel went underneath it, admiring the intricacy of the underside, which she'd never have seen on land.

With worn body and dirty clothes, but glowing with pride and wonder, she connected to the ship and disembarked.

She was then shown up a set of stairs to the main level by an older attendant, and led into the small dining parlor, where her appearance created a great deal of surprise.

"My stars!—Miss Bennet," Miss Bingley exclaimed. "How did you arrive here?"

"I flew," Elizabeth explained simply, unable to hide the leftover giddiness in her voice.

Mrs. Hurst's eyes widened like exploding suns, but she said nothing. Mr. Darcy, his cup frozen halfway to his lips, was equally quiet. Mr. Hurst seemed too intent on his breakfast to have even noticed her entrance.

Bingley laughed in delighted surprise. "*You* flew? Fantastic, Miss Bennet," he exclaimed. "I didn't realize you were so inclined. Was it marvelous?"

She nodded, a smile quirking at her lips. "It was." Then she refocused. "I'm sorry. I came to see my sister. How is she?"

Bingley drooped a little at this and gave her a small shake of the head. "She slept poorly, from what I understand," he said. "She's been feverish and hasn't been able to leave her room."

Elizabeth frowned.

"Which is down the hall," Darcy elaborated, giving Bingley a look that prompted him to stand.

"Come," Bingley said, moving to her side. "I'll take you to her."

He proffered his arm and she looped hers through. "Lead the way."

ANDSTAR™

STARCRUISERS

float this by Darcy
for possible Netherfield

will need a
similar model

Always at HOME WHEREVER you go

exactly w...
I'm looking for

LANDSTAR

CHAPTER 10

Netherfield StarCruiser, Heoros Orbit, First Moon of Londinium

Caroline beckoned over the servant from the doorway the moment her brother and Miss Elizabeth had left the room. "Surely, she didn't mean she flew *herself* all this way, did she?"

The man nodded fervently. "She did. Took a Void Crawler from the Meryton."

Darcy gave a little *hmph* of admiration that nettled Caroline instantly. "This situation does not warrant such a journey alone. We have everything well in hand."

"It's borderline bad manners," her sister added, bolstering Caroline's confidence in her opinion. "A fine pilot she may be, but she looked almost wild."

Caroline nodded. "She did, Louisa. I could hardly keep a straight face. Why should *she* be flitting about the vastness of space because her sister was exposed to some chemical or other? Her hair was a mess."

"And did you see her clothes? Awash in dirt and oil, I'm absolutely certain."

Her brother-in-law cocked his head in his wife's direction. "Seems expected, Lu," he said. "The Void Crawlers are used as maintenance vessels on the Meryton."

Caroline shuddered at the thought. "I'm not sorry to say it, sister, but I wouldn't dirty myself with a mechanic's cockpit to come to your aid half a day faster than I could in a private shuttle."

"Perhaps she likes her sister better than you like yours," Darcy suggested.

She flashed a playful glare in his direction. "You do love to tease me. But you can't deny that you wouldn't wish to see *your* sister become such a spectacle on your behalf."

"Certainly not."

"To pilot herself so far—in a *maintenance* vessel—alone?" For a moment Caroline's indignation over the entire idea left her bereft of words. But only for a moment. "It seems to show an abominable sort of conceited independence. Such a small-moon indifference to decorum."

"It shows an affection for her sister that is very pleasing," said her brother, who'd slipped back into the room as she spoke.

"Oh, Charles," she sighed. "You're too easily pleased by every-thing." She turned to Darcy, half-whispering to avoid her brother's opinion. "I'm sure this adventure has affected your regard for her fine eyes."

Darcy shrugged, taking a sip of his tea. "Not at all. They were brightened by the experience."

Caroline clenched her jaw. Before she could think of something to say to this, her sister spoke again.

"I do ever so enjoy Miss Jane Bennet. She's really a very sweet girl, and I wish her every happiness. But with such a father and mother, and such low connections, I'm afraid she'll never settle well."

Here again was a chance to highlight Jane's—and by extension, Elizabeth's—shortcomings in front of both her brother and Darcy. "You're so right," Caroline commiserated. "I think I've heard that their uncle is an attorney on the Meryton."

"Yes, and they have another who lives somewhere near Lowland."

"Lowland?" Caroline couldn't stifle her laugh, and Louisa joined in merrily.

"If they had enough uncles to populate *all* of Lowland," Bingley interjected, "it wouldn't make them one speck less lovely."

"But it must substantially lessen their chance of marrying men of any consideration in the worlds," replied Darcy.

Caroline felt a small thrill of success pass through her.

GRATEFUL

So much has happened today I hardly know where to begin. Elizabeth flew all this way to see me. She's such a good and thoughtful sister. I couldn't have asked for a better one. Not that my other sisters aren't also wonderful. But I was touched to see her today. I must admit, I downplayed my symptoms in my initial waive, and was (rightfully, as it turned out) worried for myself. But I didn't want to inconvenience any of my family. Thankfully, Lizzie saw through me. I'm sorry that I was unable to be of much company to her since she arrived. And oh, how she arrived. I can hardly believe it and yet I'm not at all surprised. She's too worried over me to have given me many details, but I know it must've been thrilling for her to finally fly a ship. Even a little old maintenance vessel.

My thoughts are so jumbled with this fever. I hope what I'm typing makes sense. I'm glad Lizzie was here when they sent over the on-board physician from the Starcross to check on me. I wouldn't have wished to burden any of the Bingleys with all that came of it. The physician said I was faring worse than expected, and to be plain, I knew I was. He advised that we hurry to a doctor currently on Apollia who can treat me better for my specific ailment. At this point my vertigo had gotten quite unbearable and my "lungs were in some distress," as he put it. On top of it all I had a terribly sharp headache. I still do.

My wonderful sister has been by my side through it all. Caroline and Louisa have been such caring and affectionate hosts, especially once Mr. Bingley and the other gentlemen were occupied in the control room, setting up to shift course

■ ■ ■

to Apollia. Thankfully, they were planning to slingshot around the moon on their test run, so it won't be wholly out of the way to land there instead.

I'll admit, I indulged some selfishness this afternoon, but I hope I'll be forgiven. Before the boosters fired, Lizzie said she was planning to return to the waystation. Caroline offered her the Netherfield's moon-hopper, assuring her it could tow back the Void Crawler. But I couldn't abide the idea of not having her here with me. I know Lizzie wasn't eager to return either. I'm so grateful to the Bingleys for converting their offer of transport to an invitation to stay with them here for the remainder of the trip. I know it was a bit of a pain linking with the Starcross to acquire a small supply of clothes for us both, but I'll be sure to pay back their kindness somehow.

One small thing I'm happy about today: when Lizzie returned from dinner this evening, she said Mr. Bingley had asked about me quite a lot. She said he seemed rather worried for me. I've noticed—well, I thought maybe I was just hoping it to be true, rather than seeing it— that he's been extra attentive toward me. His attentions have eased my feeling so much the intruder I know I am. It's some extra comfort against this horrible ceaseless headache.

CHAPTER 11

Netherfield StarCruiser, Inter-Lunar Travel Route 33-C, Londinium System

Darcy felt a small shock of surprise. Wondering over the time during a dull hand of cards, an errant thought of Miss Elizabeth had entered his mind, and there she was, standing in the doorway of the dining parlor.

"Miss Elizabeth!" Bingley exclaimed. "Join us. We're playing Rise."

She eyed the table, smiled, and with a tilt of her head, said, "Thank you, but I can't stay long. I'll need to check on Jane again soon."

Bingley nodded gravely. "Of course. How is she?"

"Sleeping, finally. For however long the fever will let her."

He didn't know what possessed him to say it, but Darcy said, "A game might distract you in the interim."

"I can do the same with a book," she replied, not unkindly, and walked toward the bookshelf.

"I can call for others to be brought in, if you don't see any in this room that interest you," Bingley said. "I wish my collection were larger for your benefit and my credit. Honestly, my attention generally diverts elsewhere. I own few books, but have more than I'll personally ever read."

"Is that not a sign of a good library?" Miss Elizabeth replied. "To run out of something new to read would be far more unfortunate than having too many unread books."

Bingley grinned, satisfied. Her response was clever, Darcy thought. She hadn't coddled his friend's insecurity, but leaned into the aspect of Bingley's collection he could be proud of.

Caroline cleared her throat. "I'm astonished that my father left such a small collection of books," she said. "Especially when compared to your absolutely delightful library at Pemberley, Darcy."

"It ought to be good," Darcy replied, watching Elizabeth's slender fingers play over the spines of the books. "It's been the work of many generations."

"You've also added so much to it yourself," Bingley said. "You're always buying books."

"I can't condone the neglect of a family library."

"Neglect," Caroline scoffed. "I'm sure you neglect nothing that adds to the majesty of such a noble home. Charles, when you build *your* estate, I wish it could be half as delightful as Pemberley."

"That is a great wish," Bingley replied.

Louisa, ever eager to add her thoughts to her sister's, said, "I really would advise you to settle on Dyberion, and take Pemberley for a kind of model. There's no finer moon in the system."

Her husband nodded sagely beside her.

Bingley laughed. "I'd buy Pemberley itself if Darcy would sell it."

"We're talking of possibilities, Charles," Caroline said, setting her cards down and sliding them away from her.

"I'd think it more possible to get Pemberley by purchase than by imitation," Bingley said, nudging Darcy in the arm and flashing him a grin.

Darcy absently traded in two cards as Elizabeth drifted over to the table, her chosen book clutched in her hand. At his angle, he couldn't read the title she'd selected. She stood between Bingley and Louisa, observing the game.

It seemed every time he caught himself watching Miss Elizabeth for too long, it was because Caroline was speaking to him.

"Has Georgiana grown much since I last saw her? I'm sure she must be nearly as tall as I am these days."

"I think so. She is now about Miss Elizabeth's height," he said, flicking his gaze to her for a moment. "Or even taller."

Caroline sighed dramatically. "How I long to see her again. She's so very delightful. Such beauty and manners. And so very accomplished for her age."

Darcy couldn't help a small smile at the thought of his little sister. He looked forward to seeing her again, too. It had been too long.

"It's amazing to me," said Bingley, "how all these ladies have the patience to be so very accomplished. They all paint moonscapes, play music, sing, dance . . . the list goes on. I feel as if I've never heard of a young lady spoken of for the first time without being informed that she's very accomplished."

"Your list is of common accomplishments," Darcy said. "But the word is applied too liberally. I couldn't tell you more than half a dozen women in my whole range of acquaintances that are really accomplished."

Miss Elizabeth frowned. "Then you must encompass quite a lot in your idea of an accomplished woman."

"Absolutely," he answered, finding it hard to pull away from her thoughtful gaze.

"Oh, yes," Caroline faithfully assisted. "One must surpass the common idea of the word to be considered really accomplished. A woman must have a thorough knowledge of astronomy, singing, visual arts, dancing, math, sciences, and the modern languages to deserve the word; and besides all this, she must possess a certain something in the way she carries herself, the tone of her voice, her manners and expressions, or the word will be but half-deserved."

Miss Elizabeth straightened as Caroline spoke, her chin lifting almost defiantly. Darcy glanced at the saddle-brown book in her hand as he said, "All of this, yes. But she must also add something more substantial. The improvement of her mind by extensive reading."

To his surprise, she said, "I can't imagine, then, that you know *only* six accomplished women. With a list like that, I wonder at your knowing *any*."

"Are you so severe upon your own sex?"

She shrugged. "We're not a monolith. But *I* have never seen such a woman. Nor saw such capacity, taste, application, and elegance, as you describe, united."

He had to bite back a smile at the indignant cries of Bingley's sisters, who no doubt felt the injustice of her implication that they, whom she *had* met, didn't live up to this standard.

"*You* may not know any," Louisa said, "but we've traveled extensively and have had far more opportunities to meet accomplished women in our circles."

"Are we going to play this game or not?" Mr. Hurst suddenly complained. "I'm sure to win this hand, and you're all ruining the moment for me."

"Yes, do play," Elizabeth said. "I've distracted us all long enough. I should get back to my sister." She raised the book. The title, embossed in gold, read *Objects in Space* and featured a swirling gold pattern circling outward from a small ship. "Thank you for this," she said to Bingley, then took her leave.

"Elizabeth Bennet," said Caroline, mere moments after the door closed behind her, "is one of those women who wish to recommend themselves to the other sex by undervaluing their own. I'm sure this succeeds with many men. But it's a very mean way of getting attention."

"Undoubtedly," Darcy replied, knowing full well that Caroline was aiming her comments at him. "There is a meanness in *all* methods to which ladies stoop for attention. Whatever bears affinity to cunning is despicable."

To his satisfaction, this seemed to put her on her back foot, and she said no more.

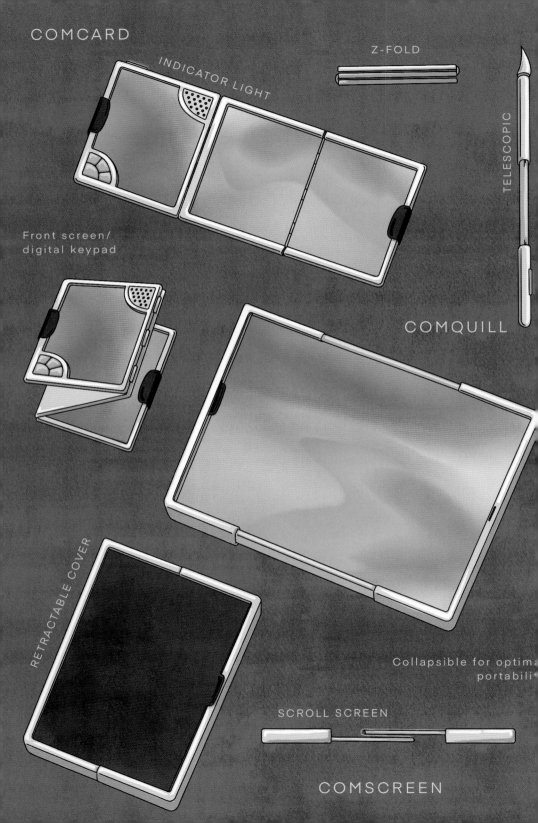

COMCARD

INDICATOR LIGHT

Z-FOLD

TELESCOPIC

Front screen/
digital keypad

COMQUILL

RETRACTABLE COVER

Collapsible for optima
portabili

SCROLL SCREEN

COMSCREEN

CHAPTER 12

Netherfield StarCruiser, Apollia, Second Moon of Londinium

Elizabeth was thankful that Apollia's orbit was so near Heoros that it took them only a day to travel the distance. As the Netherfield descended into Apollia's atmosphere the following afternoon, Elizabeth took Mr. Bingley aside to request a holo-waive with her family when they landed. Bingley enthusiastically obliged.

As the doctor recorded Jane's vitals and asked questions, Lizzie set up the comscreen and began the holo-waive.

Mrs. Bennet's image materialized, projected from the comscreen. Kitty and Lydia appeared beside her a moment later.

"Oh, my dear Jane, how are you feeling today?" her mother asked.

Jane sat up straighter on her pillows. "Sleep seems to have helped."

Mrs. Bennet nodded. "Yes, you look better than Lizzie would've had me believe."

"I didn't exaggerate, Mama," Elizabeth said. "She's improved this morning, but she was fighting a fever until well after midnight."

Mrs. Bennet scrutinized her daughters. Then she turned her attention to the specialist. "What do you have to say on the matter?"

The doctor was a tall, dark woman with a crown of even darker hair. She smiled patiently at Mrs. Bennet. "She's improving, but will need medication and a treatment to fully clear her lungs of the chemicals."

"Hi, Jane," Kitty said, unable to keep quiet any longer. "I miss you."

Jane waved weakly. "I miss you, too," she said. "In fact," she turned her attention to their mother, "I was wondering if we could perhaps be sent home directly from Apollia. There's no need to burden our hosts with whatever additional care will be necessary."

Her mother's features closed off and Elizabeth knew the answer before she'd spoken. "Absolutely not." There was a gleam in her eye reminiscent of the one she'd had when she'd concocted the Kuri plan in the first place.

"If I may," the doctor said. "I would actually agree with your mother. I don't think it at all advisable to try and move you onto a different transport right now. The accommodations would be crowded, and the ease of staying on the treatment schedule would be lessened significantly. I think it's best that you stay on the Netherfield until you're fully recovered."

"If you think that would be best."

The specialist tilted her head. "I do. And now—"

Before she could elaborate, there was a knock at the doorway and Mr. Bingley poked his head around the corner. "Everything well?"

Mrs. Bennet was the first to speak. "Oh, if only that were the case, sir. Unfortunately, my dear Jane is still not well. We've been told not to think of moving her from the Netherfield until she's recovered."

"Removed!" cried Bingley. "I wouldn't dream of it."

Jane, face flushed from what Elizabeth wagered wasn't fever, said, "We must trespass a little longer on your kindness, Mr. Bingley."

"Speaking of trespass," said the doctor, "it's time for me to prepare the necessary equipment for Miss Bennet here, and we'll need the room, if you wouldn't mind."

"Yes, yes, of course," Bingley said. "Here. Let me move this discussion to the parlor." He collected the comscreen and coaxed Elizabeth to follow him with a jerk of his head.

They entered the parlor where Mr. Darcy, Miss Bingley, and Mrs. Hurst sat at the table, engaged in individual pursuits.

Mr. Bingley set the comscreen on the far end, shifting the projection to give the impression her family were seated at the table with the rest. She chose a seat nearest them, dreading, suddenly, her family being on display in this way. Especially these three. If it came to it, she could lunge for the end-com button.

"As I was saying, Mrs. Bennet," Bingley went on, "we're happy to continue looking after your daughter. My sisters, I'm sure, won't hear of her leaving until she's healthy."

"You can be sure, ma'am," said Miss Bingley, with cold civility, "that your daughter will receive every possible attention while she remains with us."

Mrs. Bennet fluttered in her thankfulness. "If it weren't for such good friends, I don't know what would become of her. She suffers so much—though with the greatest patience, which is always her way. She has the sweetest temperament I've ever known. My other girls know they fall well short of her."

Kitty and Lydia shifted in their seats at this last bit, and Elizabeth closed her eyes briefly in embarrassment.

"This room has quite the view at the moment, Mr. Bingley," her mother went on, to Elizabeth's great relief at having changed the subject. "The red is such a contrast to the greens of Netherfield Landing. I hope you won't quit the land in a hurry, though you have such a capable vessel for travel."

"Whatever I do is done in a hurry," he replied. "If I should resolve to leave, I'd probably be off in five minutes. But, for now, I consider Netherfield Landing as much my home as this ship."

"That is exactly what I supposed of you," Elizabeth said.

"You've come to know me so well, have you?" he laughed, turning toward her.

"Oh, yes. I understand you perfectly."

"I wish I could take this as a compliment, but to be so easily seen through feels rather pitiful."

"You're an easy read," she said, "but a deep, intricate character is no more important than one such as yours."

"Lizzie," her mother admonished.

Bingley wasn't offended. "I didn't know you studied characters. It must be an entertaining pastime."

"Oh, yes. And interesting characters are my favorite."

"A sliver of a moon could supply only so many subjects for such a study," Darcy said. "In a district such as yours, even with a port and waystation, you have little by way of variation."

She met his gaze. "But people themselves alter so much that there's something new to be observed in them forever."

"I can't see how traversing the various moons and cities of Londinium has any great advantage over the whole of Heoros," said Mrs. Bennet, causing a knot to form in Elizabeth's chest as she spoke, "except the shops and public places. I'd argue that small, lunar society is rather more pleasant, is it not, Mr. Bingley?"

"When I'm off-world," he said lightly, "I never wish to touch land. When I'm on land, I can't fathom the stars. They each have their advantages and I'm just as happy in either."

"That's because you have the right disposition," her mother said. "But that gentleman," she narrowed her eyes at Mr. Darcy, "seemed to think small lunar districts were nothing at all."

Elizabeth's heart was in her throat. "Mama, you're mistaken. It was clear that Mr. Darcy meant there just wasn't as much variety in the people we encounter in our circle, which you must admit is true."

"Certainly, my dear. But we meet many people outside of our own moon. The waystation makes our society wider than most."

A wild panic overtook Elizabeth. Mr. Darcy had turned his face toward the window, Apollia's red sands shimmering like fire beyond the panels. Miss Bingley and Mrs. Hurst matched smirks as their eyes met each other.

Elizabeth, desperate to turn her mother's thoughts, asked, "Have you seen Charlotte since we left?"

"Yes, she came over yesterday with her father," her mother said, and Elizabeth allowed herself a breath. "He's such a lovely man, Sir William. So fashionable, so easygoing. He always has something to say to everyone he meets." Her gaze locked onto Mr. Darcy again, and dread billowed into Elizabeth. "*That* is my idea of good breeding. And people who think themselves so very important and never open their mouths quite mistake the idea."

"Did Charlotte stay for dinner?" Elizabeth rushed the words, her voice rising in pitch in her failed attempt to cut her mother off.

"She went home," Lydia said, "to help make the pies, I think." Elizabeth could hardly believe her sister had remained quiet for so long. But it seemed she and Kitty were spending as much time whispering to one another as her mother was talking. This didn't reassure her.

"It's unfortunate they don't keep servants for such work," Mrs. Bennet elaborated. "*My* daughters are raised differently. But everyone must do what they deem best for themselves. And the Lucases are very good girls. It's a pity they aren't beautiful."

Elizabeth bit her cheek and wished for a comet to slam into them to end this conversation.

"Charlotte seems very pleasant," Mr. Bingley offered.

"Yes, of course. But you can't deny that she's plain. Her mother has often admitted as much and envied me Jane's beauty. I don't like to boast of my children, but Jane, well . . . one doesn't often see anyone as beautiful. Everyone says so. When she was eighteen, there was a young man who fell so much in love with her during a vacation on Londinium that we were sure he would make her an offer before we left. It didn't amount to one, in the end. They were very young. But he did write her some lovely poetry."

"And so ended his affection," said Elizabeth, seizing the first natural opportunity to steer the conversation away. "Poetry is very effective in driving away love."

"I thought—" Mr. Darcy's voice was a surprise—"that poetry was considered the food of love."

She turned to him, grateful to hear someone other than her mother talking. "Everything nourishes what's strong already. But if it's only a slight sort of inclination, I'm convinced one good sonnet will suffocate it instantly."

"Mr. Bingley?" Lydia asked, with all the self-assurance and bravado of a pretty, pampered fifteen-year-old who felt herself equal to addressing just about anyone, regardless of their status. "Kitty and I were wondering whether you were serious that night on the Meryton about your promise to hold a ball on the Netherfield? It'd be ever so shameful to break a promise."

Bingley laughed in surprise, good-natured as ever. "I'm perfectly ready to keep my promise, I assure you. When your sister is recovered, you shall name the day of the ball. But you wouldn't wish to be dancing while she's ill."

"Oh, yes. We should be sure Flight Lieutenant Carter is on the Meryton again first. We'd better wait."

Elizabeth couldn't wish any harder for that comet.

Thankfully, the call was at an end, and, when her family had said their goodbyes and disconnected, she stood instantly. Barely able to look any of them in the eye, she made her excuses, and returned to the quiet safety of her sister's stateroom. Only when the door was securely closed behind her did Elizabeth allow herself to breathe properly again.

LONDINIUM SAT[SYS

Communications Log—System Storage 30 Days [Planetary]

[Gigi-D] 13.10-15:12:11.LS

I loved your latest waive. It was very useful in warding off the boredom during lessons. You have my permission to write them even longer, with more details. By permission, I mean, I'm demanding it. Tell me more about the woman who flew herself to the Netherfield, please! I can't believe you wrote a single line and thought that would be enough.

[FW.Darcy] 13.10-15:15:34.LS

You are supposed to be learning during lessons.

[GiGi-D] 13.10-15:17:56.LS

. . . I meant . . . between . . . lessons . . .

[FW.Darcy] 13.10-15:19:48.LS

Georgiana, I mean for you to read those when you aren't actively engaged with learning. It's important.

[GiGi-D] 13.10-15:21:34.LS

Yes, yes, FATHER. I promise I'll save your future waives for after lessons. Now tell me about her.

[FW.Darcy] 13.10-15:23:56.LS

Her name is Elizabeth Bennet. She's interesting.

[GiGi-D] 13.10-15:24:13.LS

Interesting?

[FW.Darcy] 13.10-15:25:55.LS

Yes.

[GiGi-D] 13.10-15:26:54.LS

How? Why are you avoiding elaborating?

[FW.Darcy] 13.10-15:28:45.LS

I'm not. I just hadn't really put any of my thoughts about her into words yet.

[GiGi-D] 13.10-15:30:12.LS

Now is a perfect time to try.

[FW.Darcy] 13.10-15:37:24.LS

She confuses me, but in a good way. I found myself studying her last night. When I realized she'd noticed, I tried conversing with her. She met me with silence. When I tried again, she said she "delighted in subverting a scheme of premeditated contempt" and dared me to despise her. I should've been affronted, but there's this mix of sweetness and archness in her manner that makes it difficult to be.

[Gigi-D] 13.10-15:40:34.LS

I like her already. She sounds more than "interesting."

[FW.Darcy] 13.10-15:45:47.LS

To put it plainly, I don't think I've ever been so bewitched by any woman as I am by her. If she weren't so beneath me, socially, I might be in some danger with her.

[GiGi-D] 13.10-15:50:08.LS

What if . . . and I know that I'm not as experienced in the ways of the worlds as you, but, what if . . . none of that actually mattered?

[FW.Darcy] 13.10-15:52:10.LS

It does though, Gi. It does.

. . . NEW COM INCOMING . . .

[Ba_Da_Bing_ley] 13.10-15:52:23.LS

We should delay the takeoff until tomorrow afternoon.

[FW.Darcy] 13.10-15:53:32.LS

What are you scheming?

[Ba_Da_Bing_ley] 13.10-15:54:05.LS

You haven't been to the Celestial Caverns, have you?

[FW.Darcy] 13.10-15:55:56.LS

Once or twice.

[Ba_Da_Bing_ley] 13.10-15:58:34.LS

Apollia is experiencing an Alignment tomorrow morning. I've seen the Caverns, too, but it's apparently an otherworldly experience during an Alignment. And don't tell me it's going to be crowded. I'm working on something that'll suit us.

[FW.Darcy] 13.10-16:00:04.LS

Come upstairs so we can talk about it. I'm in the observatory.

[Ba_Da_Bing_ley] 13.10-16:01:47.LS

I like this idea, Darcy. You better not talk me out of it.

. . . END COM . . .

CHAPTER
13

Netherfield StarCruiser, Apollia, Second Moon of Londinium

The afternoon passed peacefully for Jane, who, thanks to the ministrations of the doctor earlier, was feeling improved. The medicines and breathing treatments had taken enough of the edge off her headaches and constant dizziness that when Lizzie talked of joining the others in the drawing room before dinner, Jane accompanied her.

"Are you absolutely sure?" Lizzie asked. "You still seem weak."

Jane straightened her spine. "I won't get any stronger wasting away in this bed."

They entered the drawing room to exclamations of surprise and delight from the Bingley sisters.

"So nice to have you join us," Caroline said, helpfully guiding Jane and Lizzie over to the plush mustard-colored chair nearest the ornate fireplace—a digital fire crackling merrily, heat pouring gently from the vents tucked in the edges—the two of them fussing over Jane once they got her seated.

Jane smiled and shook her head. "This is all too much. Thank you. I'm fine here." She swallowed a slight sense of nausea as dizziness passed over her with the shift in position.

"Will you be joining us for dinner?" Louisa asked.

She caught her sister's worried gaze before answering truthfully. "I don't think so. I'm improving, but I have a feeling it won't last if I push myself too hard."

Caroline nodded. She and Louisa moved to the bookshelf on the wall beside the fireplace. "Best to enjoy the peace of reading a book and eating a meal in bed while it lasts. You have quite a house full when you get back home, don't you?"

Jane chuckled weakly. "Indeed." She turned to Lizzie, expecting her to share in her mirth, but her sister didn't seem amused.

Before she could examine what was off about Lizzie, she heard Mr. Darcy's voice in the hall. It was followed quickly by Mr. Bingley's.

"I really think someone ought to, since we're here. I mean, the views are hard to—oh." He stepped into the room and his attention fell squarely on Jane.

She felt a buzzing in her ears as his blue eyes brightened and a smile broke across his face. "What a pleasant surprise."

Her heartbeat somehow constricted her throat and she could only smile back at him.

Mr. Hurst and Mr. Darcy followed him in, expressing their delight in seeing her improved.

"Fancy a game of cards?" Mr. Hurst asked her with a wink.

"It's much too early for that," his wife reprimanded him, smacking him playfully on the leg with the little book in her hand.

And then there was Mr. Bingley, crouched beside her chair, his hands in front of the fireplace, testing its warmth. "How are you feeling? Does this temperature need adjustment? I don't want you to suffer for having tried to join us, though I'm so glad that you did."

"I'm well," Jane said. "But please don't trouble yourself over the temperature," she added. "I don't plan to stay long."

His smile faltered and she felt her own slip in response.

"That's to be expected, of course," he said, quickly. "It's best if you take it slow. We wouldn't want you to be stuck here even longer."

Her heart dropped.

His eyes widened. "Oh. No! I don't—I mean—We do want you here longer. Be sick as long as you like. No. I don't want you to be sick any longer than you must. But I'm happy to have you stay . . ." he trailed.

Jane laughed, relief bleeding into her. "I see what you meant," she said. Offering him an escape from his momentary embarrassment, she asked, "Did I hear Mr. Darcy mention something about the Celestial Caverns?"

"Yes." Mr. Bingley stood, grabbed the matching armchair at the other side of the fireplace, and dragged it next to hers so close the arms touched. "I suggested that we delay our takeoff until tomorrow afternoon so we could make the most of the unexpected stop. We happened to land near the site, and it seems a shame not to explore it a bit before we leave."

She sighed wistfully. "Oh, it's a beautiful place."

"You've seen it?"

"Only images." She eyed Lizzie, who, like the others, had found a spot in the room to get comfortable, and was now at the corner of the chaise across from her. "Lizzie found them in a book a few years back."

"Do you have any interest in seeing it in person?" His cheeks reddened. "It's a bit of walking, but we'd have the place mostly to ourselves and could go at our own pace."

For a moment she didn't know what to say. It was such a kind offer, one that felt like an effort beyond that of a gracious host, but she didn't want to assume too much simply because she felt a certain regard for him. "As much as I'd love to say yes, I don't think the doctor would approve."

He furrowed his brow, all seriousness. "Of course."

"But don't let my staying behind hold you back from seeing it," she said. "I can entertain myself."

"No!" He quickly insisted. "No, you wouldn't be holding me back at all. You're my guest and under my watch. It'd be my honor to keep you company while our companions explore the Caverns." He sat a little taller as he said this, his chin lifted ever so slightly, the warm glow from the fireplace settling like motes on the little bristles of hair on his jawline. She had the most compelling urge to run her fingers along it.

She was snapped from her thoughts as Mr. Hurst groaned. "You sneak," he accused his wife, who appeared to have won their first game of Galaxies.

Louisa laughed heartily. "Not sneaky. Just fantastic at deduction, my dear."

The two of them went straight into another game, oblivious to anyone else in the room. Jane turned her attention to her sister, thinking perhaps she was also watching the couple. But Lizzie's attention was on Mr. Darcy and Caroline, her face alight with silent amusement.

Mr. Darcy was writing something with a comquill, and Caroline, seated near him, was watching his progress. She wasn't, however, doing so as quietly as Lizzie—and now Jane. Caroline was repeatedly dragging his attention from the screen to comment on what he was doing.

"You write unusually fast."

He didn't look up. "You're mistaken. I write rather slowly."

"How many waives you must send—and not just for pleasure, but business, too. You must type *some* of these?"

"Of course."

"But for your sister, something more personal."

He nodded and kept attempting to write.

"Please tell Georgiana I look forward to seeing her again."

The moment his comquill stilled, and his eyes closed with the effort of patience, Jane struggled to stifle the laugh. What a pair those two were. It was clear to Jane that Caroline had an affinity for Mr. Darcy, but it was less clear to her what affections, if any, he had toward Caroline. His regard seemed only readable when applied to Mr. Bingley. A fierce friend he was, without a doubt. But his heart was a guarded thing. And though she had, here and there, glimpsed what she thought was an inclination toward Lizzie, it never lasted long enough for her to be sure.

"Oh! And tell her how excited I am to—"

"Would you mind if I defer your raptures until my next letter? At the moment I have insufficient charge to do them justice."

"Oh, yes, that's fine. I'll see her this winter. But do you always write her such charming long waives?"

"They're usually long, but whether or not they're charming isn't for me to say."

"He uses far too many words with four syllables," Mr. Bingley offered. "Don't you, Darcy?"

"My style of writing differs from yours."

"Oh, Charles writes in the most careless way imaginable," his sister cried. "He leaves out half his words and if not for the automated key corrections, I'm convinced half the page would be illegible."

"My ideas flow so rapidly that I don't have the time to express them."

"Your humility guards you against admonishment," Lizzie finally jumped in.

"Nothing is more deceitful," said Darcy, "than the appearance of humility. It's often only carelessness of opinion, and sometimes an indirect boast."

Mr. Bingley leaned forward slightly in his chair. As he did so, his hand brushed Jane's on the armrest, and her breath hitched. "And which of the two do you call *my* little recent piece of modesty?"

"The indirect boast," Mr. Darcy said simply. "You're actually proud of your defects in writing because you consider them as the product of rapidity of thought. The power of doing anything quickly is always prized highly by those who do so, though it's often without any attention to detail. But what's there to praise in quickness that would doubtless leave parts or plans out of order?"

Mr. Darcy was certainly a valuable friend to have around as she tried to get to know Mr. Bingley, that much was certain. He seemed almost an older brother to him. Older siblings did often see more than their younger ones could about themselves. For instance, Lizzie's current body language told Jane that while Lizzie was not aware of it herself, she was intrigued by Mr. Darcy's mind.

"I swear," cried Mr. Bingley, "I believe what I said about myself is true."

"I don't doubt you believe it," Darcy replied. "But you're more dependent on chance than any man I know. If you stepped onto your Dobbin and a friend suggested you stay till next week, you'd stay— and with another word, might not leave for a month."

"You've only proved, Mr. Darcy," said Lizzie, "that your friend doesn't do himself justice."

"I'm glad to have you convert Darcy's words into compliments for me, Miss Elizabeth," Bingley said. "He'd no doubt think better of me if I were to flatly refuse and fly off at once."

Lizzie, ever the quick wit and easy conversationalist, wasted no time in finding some new way to bait Mr. Darcy, for it was clear to Jane that this was her intent. Whether her sister was conscious of this was less certain. "Would Mr. Darcy then consider the rashness of your original intentions to be evened out by your refusal to change course?"

"Here, I think Darcy must speak for himself," Bingley said, easing back in his chair.

A little thrill went through Jane as Bingley's hand once again brushed hers in his movement. She didn't dare look at him, though she anxiously wondered if he'd been intentional.

"I've never actually admitted to any of these opinions you two have made for me. But let's say your representation is accurate. Remember, Miss Bennet, that the friend who wants him to delay his plans hasn't given him any reason to do so beyond desiring it."

"To readily agree to the persuasion of a friend has no merit for you?"

"To readily agree without conviction isn't a compliment to the understanding of either."

It seemed for a moment as though the two of them had forgotten that anyone else was in the room, despite their distance from one another. Lizzie had tucked her legs under her on the couch and leaned over the armrest, too engrossed in the moment to remember that she was a guest and not at home. "It appears to me that you allow nothing for the influence of friendship and affection. In general, would you really think poorly of someone for complying with a friend's small request without being argued into it?"

It gave Jane some unease to see this volley between them. Though it felt playful, because Lizzie so often regarded her arguments as such, there was no way to know if Mr. Darcy felt the same. Was he insulted? He didn't seem to be. But he was difficult to read.

"Should we, before we go any further, figure out precisely the degree of importance for the particular request, as well as the degree of intimacy between the friends?" he asked her.

"By all means," cried Bingley, "let's hear all the particulars. Don't leave out a thing. Especially their comparative height and size. That will hold more weight in this debate than you might know, Miss Elizabeth. I can promise you that if Darcy wasn't such a tall man in comparison to myself, I wouldn't pay him nearly the respect I give him now. I swear, I don't know a more intimidating person than Darcy, in the right circumstances."

She missed Mr. Darcy's initial response to this, for again Bingley's hand brushed hers. And this time, dizzy with the mingled rush of hope and lingering effects of exposure, she risked turning to look at him. He looked directly at her and didn't break her gaze for several seconds. She sucked in a breath—it was much louder than she'd intended—to steady herself. Thankfully, it drew no one's notice, as Darcy spoke at the same moment.

"I see what you're up to," Darcy said. "As ever, you dislike debate, and want to be done with this."

"Perhaps I do," Bingley replied. "Debates are too much like arguments. If you two would mind holding off on yours until I've left the room?"

Here, Jane took her chance while her strength and steadiness remained. "I think I'd better return to my room and lie down. Lizzie, if you'd—"

Bingley was on his feet. "Allow me to escort you." When he took Jane's hand in his and helped her to stand, she was glad for the excuse of her illness, because her legs nearly gave out underneath her with the shock and delight of his touch.

"Oh, please, no, I can take her," Lizzie said, standing as well.

He waved her off. "Sit. You're our guest. Enjoy yourself. Darcy," he shot him a teasing, rueful look, "you ought to finish your letter."

CELESTIAL CAVERNS

APOLLIA

CELESTIAL CAVERNS

APOLLIA

DAILY SCHEDULES FROM RAEFALL

LET TRAMS . . . 6:00, 7:30, 8:00, 9:30, 10:00, 11:30,
2:00, 13:30, 14:00, 15:30, 16:00, 17:30, 18:00, 19:30, 20:00

UTLET TRAMS . . . 6:30, 7:00, 8:30, 9:00, 10:30, 11:00,
2:30, 13:00, 14:30, 15:00, 16:30, 17:00, 18:30, 19:00, 20:30,
21:00, 21:30, 22:00

CHAPTER 14

Celestial Caverns Park, Apollia, Second Moon of Londinium

The party was off to explore the Celestial Caverns first thing in the morning. Darcy had secured five exclusive early passes into the park which would allow them to witness the Alignment of his home moon in the Cathedral Cavern. Miss Jane stayed behind. And Bingley, who had talked him into this excursion in the first place, chose to keep her company. Darcy couldn't help but wonder with amusement at the thought. Had this been Bingley's plan all along?

The first leg of the journey into the caverns was a subterranean train ride that would lead them safely through the beautiful—albeit less hospitable sections—of the park and into the areas zoned for walking. Their private compartment was a glass-walled tube with lush carpet and comfortable couches lining the sides, so they could see all that was ahead of them in the tunnels.

The advantage of such an early entrance to the park was that there'd be almost no other attendees. The disadvantage, of course, was that they were traveling in a comfortable compartment in semi-darkness, having risen much earlier than usual. The result was that Mr. Hurst dozed on his wife's shoulder as she gazed in a half-awake stupor out the windows, neither of them able to truly enjoy the views they were meant to be admiring.

Caroline, like Darcy, had a guidebook in her hands. He was barely paying attention to the pages he was looking at, his mind on Miss Elizabeth, who sat with her back half-turned to him, her face inches from the glass, her dark eyes full of wonder at the veins of vibrant rock glowing in the tunnel walls around them. For some reason, Caroline kept asking him what page he was on, or some-thing about the image or notation on a given section, forcing him to refocus on the guidebook to answer her before checking it against her own.

It was barely morning and he'd already had his fill of Caroline Bingley. She wasn't even reading from the same guidebook, hers being the volume focused on the walking caverns, and his being that of the tunnels they were currently traversing.

Eventually, she gave up and sighed dramatically. "How pleasant this is. I could read through a guidebook ten times larger than this without growing tired of it. One must always be after knowledge. When I have a place of my own, I shall fill it with books of all the places I've been or want to be. It shall be a grand library, grander even than these caverns."

He wondered if she even believed what she was saying.

She yawned and tossed the guidebook onto the seat beside her. Apparently displeased with the lack of response, she changed course. "By the way, is Charles really serious about holding a ball on the

Netherfield? I think he ought to consult the rest of us before he decides on anything. There are certainly those among us who would view a ball as more punishment than pleasure, wouldn't you say, Darcy?"

Darcy shrugged. "They could always retire early and avoid the whole thing." He turned his attention back to the guidebook.

"I'd like the whole affair better if it were approached differently. There's something so insufferably tedious about it all. Surely, it'd be more rational to make conversation the point of the evening, rather than dancing."

Her sister, pulled from her stupor by Caroline's complaints, said, "Much more rational, my dear Caroline, but not near so much like a ball."

Darcy watched Caroline roll her eyes, but she said nothing else. She stood, almost restless, and strode to the door of the compartment, peering through the little window into the pod behind them, then turned back to their pod. She was elegant and graceful in her movements, but that was her way. Always the air of drama.

"Miss Eliza, could I persuade you to stand with me at the window, so we might have a better look at the tunnels?"

Miss Elizabeth agreed immediately, and Darcy abandoned his spot in the guidebook as he closed it, his attention well and truly shifted to her.

"Will you join us as well, Darcy?" Caroline asked.

He shook his head. "There can be only two real motives for your actions, Caroline, and I'd be interfering in both by joining you."

"What could he mean by this?" Caroline asked Miss Elizabeth. "Do you understand him?"

"Not at all," she replied. "But I'm sure he means to judge us, and our surest way to disappoint him will be to ask nothing about it."

Caroline, never one to disappoint Darcy on purpose, couldn't leave it grounded, which, of course, he'd anticipated. "You must tell us," she said.

"I don't object to explaining. You either wish to discuss something secretive, or you're conscious that your figures appear to the greatest advantage standing there crowned in the tunnel's glow. If the first, I'd be completely in your way. If the second, I can admire you much better from here."

"Shocking!" cried Caroline. "You're incorrigible. How shall we punish him for such a speech?"

Miss Elizabeth narrowed her eyes at him, considering, but the corners of her lips twitched with the ghost of a smile. "Tease him. Laugh at him. As well as you know each other, you must surely know how to go about it."

"Oh, no. I don't," Caroline insisted. "Tease calmness of manner and presence of mind? No, no. We won't expose ourselves attempting to laugh without a subject, and Darcy will give us no openings there, I'm certain."

Miss Elizabeth placed a finger absently to her bottom lip. "Mr. Darcy isn't to be laughed at. Hm. That is an uncommon advantage. And what a shame, for I dearly love a laugh."

"Caroline has given me too much credit," he admitted. "The wisest and best of men—or their actions—may be rendered ridiculous by a person whose goal in life is a good joke."

"There are certainly those types of people," Miss Elizabeth replied. "But I hope I'm not one of *them*. I hope I never ridicule what is wise and good. Follies and nonsense, whims and inconsistencies, are certainly diverting, I'll admit. I laugh at them whenever I can. But these, I suppose, are exactly what you're without."

He warmed a little at this. "Perhaps it isn't possible for anyone, but it's been something I work hard to avoid—those weaknesses which often expose one to ridicule."

Her brow arched. The train curved slightly, and the glow of the tunnel shifted from blue-black to yellow-white, lighting her like the cresting of the sun. "Such as vanity and pride," she offered.

"Yes, vanity is a weakness indeed. But pride, where it's warranted, isn't without its merits."

She turned away from him then, though he caught a smile on her face as she did. What could it mean?

"Your examination of our dear Mr. Darcy is over, I take it?" Caroline asked. "What have you concluded?"

"I'm convinced now that Mr. Darcy has no defect. He says as much himself."

"I've made no such claim. I have faults, certainly, but I hope they aren't of understanding. My temper, I wouldn't vouch for. It's," he considered, "too unyielding. I can't forget the follies and vices of others easily, nor their offenses against me. My good opinion, once lost, is lost forever."

"*That* is a failing indeed," said Elizabeth. "Relentless resentment *is* a shade in one's character. But you've chosen your fault well. I really can't *laugh* at it. You're safe from me."

"I believe there's a fault in every disposition, which not even the best education could overcome," he said.

She looked him over archly. "So *your* defect is to hate everybody."

"And yours," he replied with a smile, "is to willfully misunderstand them."

She held his gaze with the ghost of a smile on her own lips.

"Oh, look, the rock is changing again," Caroline said. "I believe we're nearly there."

Miss Elizabeth's attention was diverted back to their surroundings, where indeed the tunnel grew larger and the stone shifted from veins of sparkling white-gold rock to layers of aquamarine and shades of violet. Even the Hursts had emerged from their early-morning stupor to look out and comment upon the view.

Darcy, after a few moments replaying their interaction in his mind, wasn't sorry for the shift. He began to feel the danger of paying Miss Elizabeth too much attention.

When the train finally stopped, they disembarked at the mouth of the Cathedral Cavern, a wide space that would've felt like a colossal underground cave if not for the fact that the ceiling of the cavern was one great open arch, bringing to mind the idea of standing in the orbital cavity of a long-dead giant. Beyond the cavern, the sky grew pink. The sunrise, combined with this particular alignment of moons, would set off a reaction in the crystalline interior that would flood the cavern floor in refracted light.

From their vantage point, the Cathedral Cavern looked like a vast garden of vegetation-like rocks and crystal formations, the pastel colors so myriad it seemed more like the inside of a jewelry box than anything one might call a garden. According to the small brochure tucked in his guidebook, when the light finally shifted into the opening, the colors would become so vibrant they would be nearly unfathomable. And because they'd come early, they'd be in the center of it when the light hit.

He wondered how the colors would reflect in Miss Elizabeth's eyes.

Darcy followed her with his gaze for a moment as the Hursts led her to a sign on a pedestal near the entrance, which further explained the phenomenon they would soon witness, and which offered little cards showing the top-down layout of the mazelike paths.

"I hope," Caroline said, walking close beside him, "that you'll give your mother-in-law a few hints about holding her tongue, and possibly cure the younger girls of running after the officers, if you can manage it."

Darcy cocked his head. "Is there any other advice you'd like to impart for my nonexistent married life?"

"Oh, yes. Do hang the portraits of your new in-laws in the gallery at Pemberley. As for your Elizabeth's picture, you mustn't have it done, for what painter could do justice to those beautiful eyes?"

"It'd definitely not be easy to catch their expression. But their color and shape, and the eyelashes—so remarkably fine—might be copied with a skilled enough hand."

At that moment their party converged once again at the opening to the walking path, the Hursts casually clinging to one another as usual, Miss Elizabeth twirling a card between her delicate fingers.

"I hope you didn't plan to go on without us," said Louisa.

"I'd never dream of it, dear sister," Caroline said, and hooked her arm in her sister's, leaving Miss Elizabeth to walk by herself. The path was not wide enough for five across.

Darcy felt their rudeness, and immediately said, "We can't all walk in a row like this. We'd be much better off splitting up."

But Miss Elizabeth just laughed and said, "No, stay where you are. You look so charming together. Like an old postcard. I'd ruin the picture trying to split you up. I'll explore on my own a while," she lifted the little map, "and meet you in the center for the Alignment."

Without giving them a chance to stop her, she curtsied, turned on her heel, and strolled down one of the narrower paths, her expression open and unguarded as she took in the sights around her with obvious wonder.

LONDINIUM SAT[SYS
Communications Log—System Storage 30 Days [Planetary]

[MyMyMissJane] 14.10-7:45:13.LS

How is it? I'm sorry I won't get to see the Alignment.

[LizzieLovesSpace] 14.10-7:47:01.LS

The most beautiful thing I've seen. I'm sure our host feels differently.

[MyMyMissJane] 14.10-7:50:43.LS

Don't tease. He's been very attentive.

[LizzieLovesSpace] 14.10-7:53:51.LS

How are you feeling? Ready to be home?

[MyMyMissJane] 14.10-7:55:03.LS

Actually quite improved. Are you?

[LizzieLovesSpace] 14.10-7:57:34.LS

I just think we've intruded on them enough.

[MyMyMissJane] 14.10-7:59:47.LS

I do feel bad for having them go to so much trouble. Though I can't say I'm completely broken up about it.

[LizzieLovesSpace] 14.10-8:01:05.LS

Oh, no, how could you be? With such a caring nursemaid at your side!

[MyMyMissJane] 14.10-8:03:25.LS

No, indeed. When are you thinking we should try to return?

[LizzieLovesSpace] 14.10-8:05:01.LS

As soon as we're back in orbit?

[MyMyMissJane] 14.10-8:07:36.LS

That's soon, actually. Mr. Bingley told me during breakfast that their final test will bring us back around Heoros.

■ ■ ■

[LizzieLovesSpace] 14.10-8:09:55.LS

So, tomorrow?

[MyMyMissJane] 14.10-8:11:42.LS

Yes.

[LizzieLovesSpace] 14.10-8:13:20.LS

Perfect. Let's tell Mama.

[MyMyMissJane] . . . ADDED . . . **[MamaB]** . . . TO THE GROUP . . .

[MamaB] 14.10-8:20:24.LS

Engaged yet?

[MyMyMissJane] 14.10-8:22:48.LS

I'm feeling much better. We're hoping to come home when we're back in orbit, maybe tomorrow.

[MamaB] 14.10-8:25:29.LS

That's great, dear. I don't want to see you until I see the ship on Netherfield Landing.

. . . better yet, until you have a proposal.

[LizzieLovesSpace] 14.10-8:27:05.LS

Mother. We've imposed enough.

[MamaB] 14.10-8:30:58.LS

Lizzie, don't be dramatic. We can't possibly come get you that soon.

[LizzieLovesSpace] 14.10-8:32:25.LS

You can't spare the Tailwynd?

[MamaB] 14.10-8:35:11.LS

Absolutely not.

[LizzieLovesSpace] 14.10-8:37:08.LS

We'll figure something out. See you soon.

[MamaB] 14.10-8:40:38.LS

No you won't.

[LizzieLovesSpace] . . . DROPPED . . . **[MamaB]** . . . FROM THE GROUP . . .

[LizzieLovesSpace] 14.10-8:42:00.LS

The Netherfield has a shuttle.

[MyMyMissJane] 14.10-8:43:49.LS

We can ask about it when you get back. Go enjoy your time!

[LizzieLovesSpace] 14.10-8:45:56.LS

Enjoy all that attention.

. . . END COM . . .

CHAPTER
15

Celestial Caverns Park, Apollia,
Second Moon of Londinium

Elizabeth couldn't deny that nature was, as ever, most diverting. The Celestial Caverns were a wonder. She wandered the maze, which wasn't at all difficult to navigate, stopping often to inspect a particularly intriguing formation or investigate the play of light through the crystalline leaves of so many rocky trees. Taken with her exploration, she was nearly late in meeting the rest of her party for the Alignment.

Mr. Darcy was the first to notice her approach. The central clearing was the size of the Meryton's ballroom dance floor. Its curved garden walls reminded her of that experience and she flinched, remembering his words.

Admittedly, something had shifted in him since then. He was more willing to have a conversation, at the very least, and she felt his gaze upon her more. Even there in the center of the Cathedral Cavern, as the third moon drifted into view above them and sunlight refracted, spilling into the cavern and lighting the tips of the crystalline vegetation like so many colorful candles, his eyes were turned toward her.

She glanced down at herself. She'd chosen a simple white dress. In doing so, she'd become a canvas, the spectacle of light bouncing from gemstone to gemstone playing color like a kaleidoscope across the entirety of her.

She couldn't help but laugh and catch the eye of whoever was closest to share in this with. It just so happened to be Darcy. For an instant, his expression mirrored her own, and they shared a brief, unspoken moment of joyful awe.

The Alignment lasted only a minute, and it took everything in her not to twirl in the light like a little girl. She closed her eyes and let the light dance across her eyelids. When it was over, she lingered in the feeling, and soon, the party split again to explore adjacent caverns.

For the rest of the excursion, Mr. Darcy was puzzlingly attentive. While she was never alone with him long before Caroline appeared at their side, he pointed her to the caverns most worth visiting, noting shortcuts or showing her some particular detail to look into whenever they happened upon one another on the paths.

She couldn't account for it, and while she wasn't one to worry, she did wonder if perhaps she was offending him in some new way. There was always a chance that he was doing his best to distract her and keep her out of their party. It would make as much sense as anything else, she supposed.

About the time she decided to be more mindful of his attentions to her, they stopped. Caroline and her sister spent so much of the return ride talking of all they'd seen that no one else got in a word, so at first it wasn't noticeable. But once aboard the Netherfield, he seemed to be almost avoiding the very sight of her.

At lunch, he made no conversation with her, and soon afterward engaged himself in searching the bookshelf before settling in an armchair by the fireplace to read. For a brief time after the dishes had been cleared, they were the only two in that room, and yet he never so much as looked up from his book.

She was sure now that they'd overstayed their welcome, at least in his eyes, and was even more adamant that the plan she and Jane had made would be put into motion.

When the others had once again joined them, Elizabeth decided to broach the subject with a cautious glance toward her sister. "Jane and I were discussing when it might be most convenient for everyone for us to return home. We know you have certain flight tests to conduct that you put off for our sake."

"And we are ever so thankful," Jane added, eyeing Mr. Bingley.

"Rather than the entire ship descending out of orbit, we would like to request use of your shuttle. You can drop us off and continue on your way without another delay."

"Oh, but wouldn't it be safer for you to remain?" Mr. Bingley asked.

"I'm already feeling much improved," Jane answered.

"Thanks to your most gracious ministrations, brother, I'm sure," Caroline added.

He nodded fervently. "It was the least I could do," he said, smiling warmly at her. But then his frown returned. "Though it must be too soon. Would you not be better off staying a couple more days?"

"While I appreciate your concern," Jane said, kindly, but firmly, "I believe returning to my own atmosphere would be more beneficial than avoiding another change in transports at this point."

Mr. Bingley seemed to deflate slightly, but he nodded. "I understand. We'll get everything in place this evening."

Elizabeth glanced at Mr. Darcy, but he was still engrossed in his book.

CELESTIAL CAVERNS

Identifying the rock formations of Apollia's greatest park

Elizabeth at Alignment

Lunar Attractions Guide Issue 72

J. 1|10\30

CHAPTER 16

Longbourn House, Heoros, First Moon of Londinium

When Elizabeth and Jane returned home, their father's relief was palpable. It appeared he had felt their absence acutely. But their mother wasn't at all pleased to see them. She barely welcomed them in, and went straight to scolding them, insisting that Jane's health would relapse.

Elizabeth chose not to engage her mother's attempts to guilt them and focused on the news her younger sisters had to share. Mary told them her favorite parts from the books she'd read. Lydia detailed every bit of gossip she'd heard in their time away, while Kitty added observations throughout—including information gleaned from dinners spent around several officers, hinting that Void Commander Forster was soon to be married.

Mr. Bennet wasn't without news, either. When the younger girls had divested themselves of words, he alerted them to the imminent arrival of a guest. "About a month ago," he told them, "I received a waive. I took a bit of time to consider before replying, as I felt this was to be handled with some delicacy, but I did in fact reply. The waive is from Mr. Collins, who, when I'm dead, may scatter you among the moons as soon as he pleases."

"Stars imploding," Mrs. Bennet hissed, "I can't bear to hear you talk of such things. It's unfair how tangled the affairs of our estate are. To take away the only home our children have ever known. Unthinkable. I would've done something about this long ago, if I were you."

Elizabeth sighed. Between herself, Jane, and their father, they had tried to explain the complicated circumstances surrounding the entail. But Mrs. Bennet seemed incapable, or perhaps stubbornly unwilling, of understanding them. It made little difference whether she understood or not. Their home would be inherited by a distant cousin when their father died. It was out of their hands.

"Nothing can clear Mr. Collins from the guilt of inheriting Longbourn," Mr. Bennet replied. "But if you listen to his waive, you may perhaps be a bit softened by his manner."

"I'm sure that I won't," Mrs. Bennet said. "How dare he write you at all. So hypocritical, to pretend to be a friend. Why could he not continue his father's quarrel with you?"

"Why, indeed," he said, then lifted his comcard to read the message aloud.

To: HEAD OF HOUSEHOLD, LONGBOURN ESTATE, LANDINGS DISTRICT, HEOROS

From: HUNSFORD PARSONAGE, KENT ORBITAL STATION

Subject: OLIVE BRANCH

Dear Sir,

The disagreement subsisting between yourself and my late honored father always gave me uneasiness. Since his unfortunate demise, I've frequently wished to heal the breach; but for some time was kept back by my own doubts, fearing that it might seem disrespectful to his memory for me to be on good terms with you. My mind, however, is now decided on the subject. I've been so fortunate as to be distinguished by the patronage of the honorable Lady Catherine de Bourgh, who preferred me to the rectory of the Kent Orbital Station, where I'll endeavor to ingratiate myself with her at every opportunity, and be ever ready to perform those rites and ceremonies which are instituted by the Temple of the Everlasting Light.

As a man of the Light, I feel it's my duty to promote and establish the blessing of peace in all families within my sphere of influence. On these grounds I flatter myself that my present overtures are highly commendable, and that my part in the entail will not lead you to reject the offered olive branch. I beg leave to apologize for being the means of potential discomfort on the part of your amiable daughters, and assure you of my readiness to make them every possible amends.

If you'd have no objection to receive me into your home, I will have the satisfaction of staying with your family beginning promptly at 7:00 in the evening on Monday, October 18th. I shall likely trespass on your hospitality till the second Saturday following, which I can do without any inconvenience, as Lady Catherine is far from objecting to my occasional absence during times of worship, provided there's someone to perform the duties of the day.

I remain, dear sir, with respectful compliments to your lady and daughters, your well-wisher and friend,
William Collins

"At seven, therefore, we may expect this gentleman," Mr. Bennet said, tapping the screen to close the waive. "He seems to be a most conscientious and polite young man. I'm certain he'll

prove a valuable acquaintance, especially if Lady Catherine should
be so indulgent as to spare him often." He glanced at Elizabeth
with mischief in his eyes. "There's some sense in what he says
about the girls. If he's disposed to make them amends, I won't
discourage him."

"It's difficult to guess," Jane said, "in what way he thinks he
could make any sort of atonement. The wish to do so is certainly to
his credit, I suppose."

Elizabeth frowned. "He thinks very highly of this Lady
Catherine, and seems quite dedicated to the Temple. Though I
think he must be a bit odd. I can't make him out. His writing style
is pompous. And what *can* he mean by apologizing for the entail?
Does he really think we believe he had any say over it?" She bit her
bottom lip for a moment, considering. "Is he . . . a sensible man, do
you think?"

Mr. Bennet chuckled. "Oh, no, my dear, I think not. I have
great hopes of finding him exactly the opposite. There's a mixture of
subservience and self-importance in his waive, which promises well.
I'm impatient to meet him."

They didn't have long to wait before the desired meeting
occurred. Mr. Collins was punctual, and was received with great
politeness by the whole family.

He was a short, stocky man of twenty-five. He had a grave
and stately air about him, and his manners were formal, but he
seemed neither in need of encouragement, nor inclination to
be silent.

As they sat for dinner, he said, "I'd heard much of the beauty of
the Bennet women, but fame has fallen short of the truth. I have no
doubt you all are constantly gaining the attention of the local gentlemen. You'll all be married in no time."

"This is off to a great start," Elizabeth muttered in Jane's ear,
taking stock of her sisters' reactions. Lydia's annoyance was instant.
Kitty gave him a wary look before turning her attention to the cup of

tea in front of her. Only Jane and Mary appeared to accept this statement as a compliment and return any sort of smile.

"You're so kind," her mother told him. "I wish with all my heart
that it'll prove to be true, since they'll be destitute when their father
dies, with things settled as they are."

"Ah, yes. You allude to the entail of this estate," said Mr.
Collins.

"Indeed, I do. It's a terrible situation for my girls. Not that
I can fault *you*, of course. It was settled long before we came to
this point."

"I'm sensitive to the hardship this will cause them, and could
say much on the subject, but I don't want to appear too forward. I
can assure you I come prepared to do them a service. When we're
better acquainted—"

He was interrupted by dinner arriving at the table, and Elizabeth
could barely hide her relief. Whatever service he came to do for
them, she was certain she wanted no part in it. The man was tedious.

Though she had to admit, it was funny to watch her mother's
face as she fought conflicting emotions. Elizabeth ventured a guess
that her mother was proud of all the compliments to her home while
simultaneously horrified by the notion that he might be taking note
of all his future property.

"Please tell me to which of you fine ladies I should impart my
thanks for this excellent meal," said Mr. Collins.

"We're perfectly able to keep a cook," Mrs. Bennet said immediately. "My daughters have nothing to do with the kitchen."

"I apologize most profusely," he replied, dipping his head hum-
bly. "I didn't mean to displease you with my assumptions."

Her mother waved him off. "It's no matter."

But he continued to apologize long after any of them cared
to listen.

Thankfully, her father put a stop to it by prompting, "Tell us of
Lady Catherine. You seem fortunate to have such a patroness."

The subject elevated Mr. Collins to a more than usual solemnity of manner. "I've never in my life witnessed such behavior in a person of rank—such affability and condescension—as I've experienced first-hand from Lady Catherine de Bourgh. She was gracious enough to read through and approve two of my recent sermons. She's also asked me to dine twice now at Rosings Sector, and sent for me just last Saturday evening to complete her party for a game of Penumbra."

Elizabeth was unsure if Mr. Collins had taken a proper breath yet. But he was far from done.

"Lady Catherine is mistaken as proud by many, I know. But *I've* never seen anything to that effect. She's always spoken to me as she would to any other gentleman, and made no objections to my joining the society of the Orbital Station. She's even been gracious enough to advise me to marry soon—provided I choose with discretion, of course—and paid a visit to my humble quarters, where she approved all the alterations I've made and even suggested many herself. I was most taken with her idea for a secondary hatch into the wall garden. Quite ingenious."

"That's all proper and civil, I'm sure," said Mr. Bennet.

Elizabeth deliberately avoided eye contact with her father to keep from laughing.

"I dare say she's a very agreeable woman," her father went on. "It's a pity that great ladies in general aren't more like her. Is it a grand station, the Kent?"

"One of the largest in the system. The gardens of Rosings Park abut my humble sector, and cross nearly half the station's fifteen-mile expanse."

"I think you said she was a widow?" Mr. Bennet said. "Does she have any family?"

"She has one daughter. The heiress of Rosings."

"Ah," her mother cut in, "then she's better off than many girls. And what sort of young lady is she?"

Mr. Collins bobbed his head as he responded to each question, taking dainty bites from his fork between each answer. "She's most charming. Lady Catherine herself says that, in point of true beauty, Miss de Bourgh is far superior to the handsomest of women, because there is that in her features which marks the young lady of distinguished birth."

"Light's end, how are any of us to compete," Elizabeth muttered into her glass, leaning toward Jane beside her so that only her sister heard.

There was a ghost of a smirk on her sister's face, but Jane shook her head ever so slightly to warn her off.

Mr. Collins remained oblivious. "She's unfortunately quite sickly, which has prevented her from making the progress in many accomplishments in which she would have succeeded. But she's perfectly condescending, and often comes by in her little Faeton glider."

"I don't think I've seen her name among the St. James society papers," Kitty mentioned quietly.

"She wouldn't be. Her indifferent state of health prevents her from being on land; and so—as I told Lady Catherine one day— has deprived the worlds of its brightest star. Her ladyship seemed pleased with the idea."

Elizabeth couldn't help herself any longer. This man was so absurd. "You have such a way with words, sir."

This time Jane kicked her in the shin. But it was worth it, and Elizabeth only winked at her before turning her eyes expectantly on Mr. Collins to await his answer.

"I'm happy on every occasion to offer those little delicate compliments which are always acceptable to the ladies. I've often observed to Lady Catherine that her daughter seemed born to be a duchess, and that her rank in society, rather than giving her consequence, was elevated by her existence. These things please her ladyship, and it's a sort of attention which I believe myself particularly bound to pay."

"You judge properly," Mr. Bennet said. "What luck that you possess a talent for delicate flattery. Are these pleasing attentions an impulse of the moment, or the result of previous study?"

Elizabeth eyed Jane fully now, and gave her a look to say, "if only you could reach *his* shins."

Jane narrowed her eyes playfully in response and covered her grin by taking a sip of her wine.

"They arise mainly from what's passing at the time. Though I sometimes amuse myself with suggesting and arranging little elegant compliments that may be adapted to ordinary occasions, when they arise." His gaze lingered overlong on Jane as he said this, and Elizabeth suppressed a shudder.

"Though I always wish to give them as unstudied an air as possible," he added.

Elizabeth caught her father's expression as she turned from Mr. Collins. It was clear that this man was all her father had hoped he'd be. This man was absurd, and for her father that would bring keen enjoyment. As he sat there, the picture of composure, there was a twinkle in his eye that she knew too well. He was immensely pleased.

As dinner came to a close, and the family moved to the drawing room for tea, Mr. Bennet exposed his daughters to more torment by inviting Mr. Collins to read aloud to them. Mr. Collins was more than eager to oblige. Her father handed him a book from their family library. But when Mr. Collins examined it, seeming to recognize it as a work of fiction, he handed it back with apology. "I don't read novels."

"You *what*?" Lydia said incredulously.

"It's not like you do either," Kitty replied, shrugging.

Lydia stuck out her tongue. "I prefer listening to them. It amounts to the same thing. I know the story just as well as anyone else."

"Maybe not the spelling," Mary countered.

Lydia was unaffected. "Certainly the pronunciation."

Mr. Collins cleared his throat. Digging in his bag, which hung from the coat rack near the door, he revealed a book of his own. "I was reading this on the flight here. There's a particularly interesting chapter on the Light in each of us, which I'd be delighted to share."

Lydia gaped openly at him, and before he'd managed, with monotonous solemnity, to read more than three pages, she interrupted him by turning to their mother.

"Did Uncle Phillips tell you he's thinking of letting Void Commander Forster hire his clerk? Aunt Phillips told me so herself."

"Lydia, don't be rude to poor Mr. Collins," Jane admonished.

Clearly offended, Mr. Collins shut his book and set it aside. "I've often observed how little the youth of today are interested in books of a serious stamp, though written for the benefit of us all. It amazes me, I confess, for certainly there can be nothing so advantageous as knowledge. But I'll no longer bore the young lady."

"I'm so sorry, Mr. Collins," Mrs. Bennet said. "That was incredibly unlike her—"

Elizabeth choked in surprise and played it off as a cough.

"—and will never happen again. Please feel free to continue. The rest of us would be delighted to listen. Wouldn't we, girls?" Her mother raised her eyebrows and stared daggers at them.

Mr. Collins lifted a hand. "Truly, it's of little consequence. I should be winding down. Retiring early would be best after a long day of travel. She did me a favor."

"See," Lydia hissed to her mother as Mr. Collins put away his book. "I did literally *everyone* a favor."

THE RIGHT AND DUTY TO MARRY WELL
18.10-10:54:21.LS

I'm on my way to Longbourn and will arrive this evening. What with a stable home and income, my intention to marry has been at the forefront of my mind. In seeking a reconciliation with the Bennet family, it is, naturally, my intention to choose one of the daughters as my wife—if their beauty and amiable natures (so often reported) do indeed appear to be faithfully represented. This is my plan of amends for inheriting their father's estate. An excellent plan, if I allow myself to be so bold. They're eligible and perfectly suitable to a man of the Light such as myself. It's excessively generous, for my part, to even entertain such an offer before setting eyes upon them.

18.10-20:37:57.LS

I'm glad to say that this plan of mine hasn't changed now that I've seen them. Jane is beyond expectations. Absolutely lovely from head to toe. Gentle and well spoken. More than adequate form. The jewel of the bunch. Since I must do this fairly and observe seniority, I will of course have to choose her for my wife. I shall broach this subject with her mother as soon as I'm free to have a moment of conversation with her.

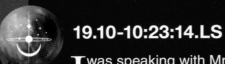

19.10-10:23:14.LS

Iwas speaking with Mrs. Bennet about my rectory this morning, which led naturally to the avowal of my hopes that a mistress might be found for it here in Longbourn. I showered her with praises over her eldest daughter, and in doing so was gently warned that Jane is in fact the object of a Mr. Bingley, who is anticipated to be asking for her hand any day now. While this was quite the grievous blow to my plans, Mrs. Bennet assured me that none of her other daughters were spoken for.

I now admit that while Jane is indeed a jewel, she isn't the only pleasing option of the ladies. Her sister Elizabeth is closest to her in age and beauty. She seems a bit livelier company, but she also has a pleasing form. She will do well as my wife.

CHAPTER 17

Longbourn House, Heoros, First Moon of Londinium

Jane was looking forward to the plans her youngest sister had made before they'd all gone to bed. It would be nice to visit the Meryton. This was the first time she'd felt truly herself since the exposure, and she was brimming with energy.

Every sister but Mary had chosen to come along, which would've been a wonderful way to gain some quality sister time, except that Mr. Collins had decided to join them. Her father had, of course, nudged him into such a choice. Mr. Bennet was a man who found solace and tranquility in his study, but none could be found while Mr. Collins was in the house. She could all but see the weight in his shoulders that morning as her father stood trapped in his own library while Mr. Collins touched all the books and talked about each as he did so.

It was that which led her to sit beside Lizzie on the Tailwynd. They cast each other looks of tested patience as the transport broke through the cloud cover, Mr. Collins filling the cabin with words, leaving barely a breath of silence in which any of them could respond with more than a civil nod.

Jane attempted to listen intently as he turned to her, pointing out the wide viewport.

"You see how the sunlight colors the clouds there?" he asked, continuing before she had even replied. "This is a clear indication of . . ."

Despite herself she tuned him out. She admired his passion for the things he spoke about. She simply couldn't muster the same enthusiasm.

She couldn't quite stifle her sigh of relief as they docked at the Meryton and they no longer had to feign interest in his musings.

Mr. Collins couldn't hope to hold their attention, especially the younger girls, their gazes immediately wandering along the wide thoroughfare of the atrium. He quickly begged off on business in a small temple not far from the entrance, and they parted ways with the intention of meeting again at their aunt's quarters for lunch. The atrium was all grand colors and boisterous crowd noise. People milled about in the central space, which was as broad as a transport ship, with a ceiling far enough above them to feel like open air—not that it could be seen clearly through the lines of colorful lights and fabric that wove across the thoroughfare from the second stories of a few buildings. Nothing but the most eye-catching dresses in a shop window, or a particularly fine artisan's work, could drag them into any semblance of focus.

Jane smiled warmly, enjoying her sisters' laughs and exclamations of excitement. She inhaled the faint metallic scent of the way-station interior infused with the yeasty, floured warmth of baking breads and the sparkling tang from the sweet-crystal shop—losing herself in the feeling of a summer day in a small town's shopping district captured in a bottle.

Their attention was finally snared by a young man they'd never seen before, walking with an officer on the other side of the atrium.

"Stars around us!—what luck! There's Mr. Denny!" Lydia exclaimed. "Who's that with him, I wonder."

"He's very handsome," Kitty said with a giggle.

"Oh, we must meet him," Lydia announced. "Come. We'll pretend to be after something in that shop just there ahead of them. They won't be able to miss us if we time it right."

Lydia and Kitty hurried along, determination in their steps.

The plan succeeded, and Jane couldn't help but see the similarity to her mother in that moment. Lydia deftly coaxed the two men and her sister into one group.

As she and Lizzie approached, Jane heard Mr. Denny introduce the man as Mr. Wickham.

"We returned together yesterday from Londinium," Mr. Denny added.

Mr. Wickham nodded. "I've accepted a commission with the squadron," he said. Jane thought of how he would look dressed in a flight suit, and felt it suited him. She sensed the effect he had upon her sisters immediately—even Lizzie—and it was no wonder why. He had a velvet, pleasant voice, and the kind of features sculptors covet.

She found herself momentarily lost, not hearing what they said, as her mind wandered to Mr. Bingley. She'd grown accustomed to his company during their time on the Netherfield, and she missed his quieter, more fumbling brand of charm.

Her gaze drifted down the thoroughfare. She was only dimly aware of a shift in the crowd as Mr. Bingley and Mr. Darcy emerged on the central avenue.

She gasped, so startled by the object of her thoughts suddenly materializing in front of her eyes. "Lizzie," she said softly, elbowing her sister to get her attention.

But Lizzie had noticed the two men as well.

Bingley caught sight of Jane first. Then Mr. Darcy, at a word from his friend, shifted his focus to their little group, his gaze on Lizzie. They increased their pace and quickly closed the distance.

"Jane, what a surprise," Bingley said, his smile contagious. "I'm so glad to see you at full health."

She felt her cheeks burn. "All thanks to you," she said. Then quickly added, "What brings you to the Meryton? Have you completed the tests on your ship?"

"Yes. All is well. I was actually here to . . ." he trailed off and didn't meet her eyes.

Mr. Darcy stepped in. "We were here to look for a gift for you. Something to wish you a speedy return to full health."

Mr. Bingley's face blazed red. "But it seems you beat us to it. Your health has returned."

"Indeed, it has," she said. "Though that's very kind of you. It should be me who gives you a gift. As a thank-you for your hospitality."

"Your company is gift enough," he said earnestly.

She was now at a loss for words. She glanced toward her sister. But rather than the playfully devious look she expected to see, instead Lizzie's eyes were narrowed in something like suspicion. She followed her gaze to Mr. Darcy and Mr. Wickham. The latter was giving the barest of nods to the former, who did likewise.

Jane had missed something. But Lizzie had caught it. She'd hear all about it when they were finally alone, certainly.

"I'm so sorry," Mr. Bingley said, pulling her attention back to him. "But we have to go. We have a reservation. Send me a waive when you return home?"

She nodded. "Of course. Please, don't let us detain you."

He took her hand in his, squeezing lightly. The gentle brush of his skin on hers sent a comet of electricity through her. It lingered long after he'd disappeared into the crowd.

"Perhaps they have a small replica of our fighters," Mr. Denny was saying.

"Oh, I know they do," Lydia replied airily, pulling Jane's attention to a shop across the thoroughfare. "And you must show me all the little details that match it."

They crossed to the other side, the broad windows behind the buildings giving the illusion of being at a night market on the moon.

The clear doors hissed open as Kitty stepped forward, and the sounds of whirring and buzzing plumed out to meet them.

The shop was a veritable garden of mechanical marvels. Ships and flying creatures hung from the ceiling like creeping vines, every wall filled with cases of figures and parts on display, while the walkspace was nothing but a grid of single-person-width lanes carved between displays on square tables.

As they entered, Jane heard Lizzie ask Mr. Wickham about his new position.

"Yes, the Red Squadron," he told her. "As Flight Lieutenant."

"And what draws you most to the profession?"

He lifted a hand to gently touch the metallic petals of a flower toy as it bloomed with the softest of clicks. He plucked it from the little vase where it stood and handed it to Lizzie with a noble flourish. "The chance to meet such new and . . . intriguing people."

Jane turned her gaze away as she saw her sister's cheeks flush and her mouth draw into a smile. She couldn't help smiling herself. Wishing to give her sister space to enjoy this attention, Jane drifted to the wall of toys behind her, and was delighted to find shelves of miniature creations. Tiny horses and houses, people and transports. Each with its movement on display. It was enchanting. She bent to peer closer at a little set of people walking hand-in-hand around a small hedge maze. The sign below it indicated that this was called "The Lovers" and she cocked her head, imagining that the male figure looked a little like Bingley.

She wasn't sure how long she watched them, but when she heard Lydia's voice call, "Jane!" she stood and turned too quickly, momentarily disoriented.

Lydia was at the front of the shop. "We're famished. Let's head to Aunt Phillips's for lunch."

"Mr. Denny and Mr. Wickham said they'd join us!" Kitty added, clutching the flower Mr. Wickham had handed to Lizzie earlier in one hand, her little wallet in the other. Jane imagined Kitty would add the toy to one of the many plants she tended to at home.

Mr. Denny and Mr. Wickham made pleasant conversation with them as they made their way to the elevators. The quarters where the Phillipses lived overlooked the atrium on the non-window side, and was one of many levels. Theirs was not too high above the shopping district. It was a great place to people-watch, almost in the same way as Jane had watched the mechanical "lovers" walking through their hedge, only with many, live people, and the echoing sounds of hundreds of conversations rising to meet them.

When they reached their destination, their aunt threw open the door and beckoned them all in with a wave and a loud invitation of welcome. As they filed merrily into her house, she spotted Mr. Collins shuffling behind them and ushered him in after them.

"It's so wonderful to have you all here," she said. "Please, come join us. We've made too much lunch, I'm sure."

"I must profess," Mr. Collins began, "I'm terribly sorry for such an intrusion, especially as we've never met and I'm here in your home. I do hope you'll excuse me, as I'm of course acquainted with your nieces. We could certainly have acquired lunch within the atrium and saved you the trouble. However, I do appreciate the most excellent hospitality, and will be more than delighted to partake

PRIDE AND PREJUDICE IN SPACE

in what I can only imagine will be a gratifying meal." He looked around. "What a fine home you have here, Mrs. Phillips."

Her aunt was a woman of simple pleasures, and took an instant liking to him after such compliments. "I do hope you enjoy the game of Circumstance, Mr. Collins," she said. "You'll certainly have a willing partner in it with me."

THE ATRIUM *at the* MERYTON

ATRIUM WALK   1

SHOPS
 2 Parhelia Books
 3 Dreamlands
 4 Halcyon's
 5 Shelf & Square
 6 Rae's Atelier
 7 The Astrolabe

TOYS AND GAMES
 8 Moons of Adventure
 9 Dolls & Delights
 10 Marvels
 11 Beren's Hobby Shop

RELAXATION
 12 Atrium Park
 13 Apartments at the Atrium

RESTAURANTS
 14 Drea's
 15 The Emerald Dragon
 16 Lavore's Cupcakery
 17 Atrium Park Overlook

CHAPTER 18

Meryton Waystation, Heoros Orbit, First Moon of Londinium

Elizabeth was grateful that the entirety of the table was between her and Mr. Collins, so that she hadn't been forced to politely listen to him speak. He had an attentive listener in her aunt, who became the buffer for her younger sisters, freeing them to converse merrily with Mr. Denny and a couple other officers from the Red Squadron. The officers had dropped by to speak with her uncle and were offered a place at the table. They were in general good company, but in Elizabeth's opinion, Mr. Wickham outstripped them in person, countenance, and general manner.

She was so intrigued by the strangeness that had passed between him and Mr. Darcy in the atrium. Upon meeting, one had gone red and the other pale as starlight. The atmosphere also seemed to have dropped in temperature by at least two degrees. Whatever could it mean? It was impossible to imagine, yet equally impossible not to long to know.

She was pleased Wickham had turned out to be such pleasant company. There was, perhaps, a chance to learn what conflict existed in their acquaintance.

At last, the game tables were brought out, and the party broke apart.

"I know little of the game," Mr. Collins told her aunt as they sat with her uncle and the latecomers from Red Squadron at the Twist table. "But I'll be glad to improve myself, for in my situation in life—"

Her aunt had shifted into game mode, and didn't wait for his reasoning. She simply dealt the cards and cut into his sentence with instructions.

Elizabeth, from her seat at the other table, chuckled softly at her aunt's shift in demeanor. Mr. Wickham sat between her and Lydia. For a moment Elizabeth was uneasy, expecting that her sister's nature would divert his attention. But this table agreed to Circumstance, and Lydia was fonder of the game than of flirting, so she merely said, "I hope you're prepared to lose handsomely, Mr. Wickham," and then immediately started making bets and announcing what prizes she thought would be best.

The structure of the game allowed him plenty of time to talk, and Elizabeth was an attentive listener, though what she hoped to hear of she dared not ask him.

"How often does the Netherfield party come to the Meryton?" he asked, inadvertently relieving her curiosity.

"I'm unsure. At least as often as we do, lately," she replied.

He glanced at the cards in his hand. After a moment's silence, he asked, "How long has Mr. Darcy been aboard the starcruiser?"

"About a month," Elizabeth said, and unwilling to let the lead slip away, added, "He has a large property on Dyberion, I believe."

Mr. Wickham nodded, a stray lock of his hair falling in front of his blue eyes. "It's a noble estate. An easy ten thousand aurum per revo. You couldn't have met with someone more capable of imparting this information than myself. I've been closely connected with his family from birth."

Elizabeth couldn't hide her surprise.

"It is surprising, Miss Bennet, to hear such a thing after you saw the cold manner of our greeting. How familiar are you with Mr. Darcy?"

"As much as I ever wish to be," she said honestly. "I find him disagreeable."

"I have no right to give *my* opinion over his agreeableness," said Mr. Wickham, "I've known him too long and too well to be a fair or impartial judge. I believe your opinion of him would, on the whole, astonish. I'd be careful to express it strongly outside of your family's orbit."

"I say nothing that this entire station—nor those in the landed districts—don't say. In all spheres but his own aboard the Netherfield, he's thoroughly disliked. He's too prideful, and none could find a favorable word toward him on all of Heoros."

"I can't pretend to be sorry," said Wickham, as he set out three caraks and discarded. "No man should be esteemed higher than deserved, but it happens often for him. The worlds are blinded by his fortune and importance, or frightened by his imposing manners. They see him only as he chooses to be seen."

Lydia exclaimed as she won the first set of Circumstance, then turned to him. "I did say handsomely," she said, winking, and scooped his caraks into her hand.

Wickham laughed and pulled new cards, then turned to Elizabeth again. "I wonder whether Darcy is likely to be within the Heoros system much longer."

"I don't know, but I didn't hear of plans to leave when I visited the Netherfield," she said, pulling her own cards into her hand.

"I hope your time with the Red Squadron won't be affected by his being among our society."

"Oh, no—it isn't *my* place to be driven away by Darcy. If *he* wishes to avoid seeing *me*, he must go. We aren't on friendly terms, and it's always painful for me to meet him. But I have no reason to avoid him. Though it's difficult to resist announcing to all the system how ill-used I've been by him."

Elizabeth nearly bent the cards in her hand with suspense.

"The late Mr. Darcy was one of the best men that ever lived, and the truest friend I ever had. I can never be in the company of young Mr. Darcy without grieving a thousand tender memories of his father."

Her throat tightened at the sadness that seemed to cloud his eyes.

"Darcy's behavior toward me has been scandalous, but I truly believe I'd forgive him entirely if it meant not disappointing the hopes and disgracing the memory of his father."

Elizabeth was shocked into silence by this admission. Her mouth went a tad dry as it hung open, but she mastered herself enough to close it.

He turned the conversation to more general topics: the way-station, the Port and Landings Districts, the society—highly pleased with all he'd seen and experienced thus far. He spoke with such gentle and intelligible gallantry, and she found herself mesmerized by the way his lips moved.

"It was the prospect of such good society," he admitted, "that was the ultimate factor in my choice to join the Star Force Reserves. I knew it was a respectable occupation, and Denny tempted me further with his account of the quarters and people I'd expect to find on the Meryton. I thrive in company, and wither in solitude. A pilot's life may not have been what I intended, but circumstances have made it so. I should have been in possession of a valuable property on Dyberion by now, had it not been for the interference of the gentleman we spoke of earlier."

"Is that so?" she half-gasped.

He nodded gravely. "The late Mr. Darcy left me a small estate in his will. He loved me as though I was his own child. I can't do justice to his kindness. He meant to provide for me amply, and thought he'd done so, but when all was done, the estate was given elsewhere."

"Great eclipse," cried Elizabeth, "but how could *that* be? How could his will be disregarded? Why couldn't you fight it?"

"The terms were informal enough that I had no chance using the law. A man of honor wouldn't have doubted the intention, but Darcy chose differently—treating it as a conditional recommendation, and insisted I'd forfeited all claim to it by extravagance and imprudence. When the estate became vacant, it was given to someone else. Perhaps I have spoken my opinion of him and to him too frequently in our youth, but I can think of nothing worse. The fact is that we're very different sorts of men, and he hates me for it."

"I'm shocked. He deserves to be publicly disgraced."

"Someday he will be, but not by me," Wickham said confidently. "Until I can forget the father, I can never defy or expose the son."

In her regard, he grew somehow handsomer at these words. "But his dislike couldn't have been motive enough to behave this way?"

"It was more than dislike. It was pure jealousy. Had his father liked me less, Darcy may have tolerated me more. But his father's uncommon attachment to me irritated him since childhood. He didn't have the temper to bear the competition—the preference his father often gave me."

Elizabeth frowned. "I didn't think Mr. Darcy was so bad as this. I've never liked him, but I didn't think him capable of descending to such malicious revenge—such injustice—as this."

They were quiet a moment, neither of them very involved in the game, though no one else appeared to notice. After a pause, she spoke again. "I do remember him boasting one day on the Netherfield of his unmoving resentments and unforgiving temper. He must be absolutely dreadful."

"I won't add my thoughts," Wickham said.

She stared through her cards for a while, her thoughts reeling. "It's so callous. To treat not only a friend, but a favorite of his own father in such a way. Someone like *you*, who's nothing but amiable . . . and was his companion from childhood . . ." she trailed off, shaking her head.

"Indeed. We were born on the same moon; within the same district; the greatest part of our youth was passed together. My father declined an illustrious career to be of use to the late Mr. Darcy. He devoted all his life to the care of the Pemberley property. He was most highly esteemed, and a dear friend to the man, who considered himself grateful to have such a superintendent. Shortly before my father died, Mr. Darcy promised to provide for me, and I'm convinced that he felt that promise to be as much a debt of gratitude to *him*, as it was affection for myself."

"How strange. How horrible. I can't help but wonder at Mr. Darcy's pride. Surely, if from no other motive, his pride would've stopped him from being so dishonest."

"Oh, all his actions may be traced to pride, certainly," Wickham said. "He and pride are the best of friends. But no man is consistent, and I believe there were stronger impulses than pride at play here."

She frowned. "Has such pride ever done him any good?"

"Yes. It often led him to be generous, hospitable, assist tenants, or relieve the poor. Family pride, and dutiful pride—for he is proud of his father's legacy—have done this. It's a powerful motive for him to avoid disgracing the family or losing the influence of the Pemberley Estate. And brotherly pride and affection makes him a kind and careful guardian of his sister. You'll hear him generally considered the best and most attentive of brothers."

She had heard that. "What sort of girl is Miss Darcy?"

He sighed and frowned in consternation. "I wish I could say she was lovely. It pains me to speak ill of her. But she's too much like her brother. Very proud. As a child she was sweet and pleasing, and extremely fond of me. I've devoted hours and hours to her amusement. But we're nothing to one another now. She's handsome, and highly accomplished. She has lived at the family's Londinium home since her father's death. There's a lady who lives with her and oversees her education."

Elizabeth let the conversation stall momentarily, engaging in the game of Circumstance a bit more, trying to clear her head. But she couldn't let the subject drop.

"I'm even more surprised at Mr. Darcy's closeness with Mr. Bingley, now. How can Bingley, in all his good humor, maintain a friendship with such a man? They can't possibly suit each other. Do you know Mr. Bingley?"

He shrugged. "Not at all."

"He's sweet-tempered, charming, and nothing but goodness. He must not truly know Mr. Darcy."

"Maybe not. But Darcy can be pleasant when he chooses to be. He doesn't lack the ability if he thinks someone's worth his time. Among those he considers equals, he's an entirely different man than when he's around those less prosperous. He's ever prideful, but with those he deems worthy, he can be just, sincere, rational, honorable. There's no shortage of generosity for the right fortune and figure."

Elizabeth started to say more, but the occupants of the other table had finished their game and were now out of their seats, gathering to watch the ongoing game of Circumstance.

"I do apologize," her aunt said to Mr. Collins. "I've never seen someone lose every point in such a spectacular manner."

Mr. Collins puffed his chest and replied, solemnly, "Not to worry, madam, I assure you. It's but a trifle. Don't make yourself uneasy over your victory on my behalf. I can stand to lose five aurum. Thanks to Lady Catherine de Bourgh, I'm removed from worrying over such small sums."

Mr. Wickham's attention was diverted. He observed Mr. Collins steadily for a full minute, then turned again to Elizabeth and asked in a low voice, "How familiar is this man with the family of de Bourgh?"

"Lady Catherine has recently gifted him a position at her station temple," she whispered back. "I don't know the situation of the introduction, but he hasn't known her long."

"You know that Lady Catherine de Bourgh and Lady Anne Darcy were close cousins, and that she's considered nothing short of Mr. Darcy's aunt?"

"No! I knew nothing of her connections, nor her existence, until Mr. Collins arrived."

"Her daughter, Miss de Bourgh, is set to inherit a large fortune. It's believed that she and Darcy will unite their two estates."

This information made Elizabeth smirk, as she thought of poor Caroline Bingley and all her vain attempts to garner Mr. Darcy's affections. He was destined for another. "Mr. Collins speaks very highly of both Lady Catherine and her daughter, but from some of the details he's mentioned of her, I suspect his gratitude misleads him, and though she's his patroness, she's an arrogant and conceited woman."

"I haven't seen her for many years, but that's the truth of her," he said. "I never liked her. She was an insolent dictator of her tiny queendom with a reputation for being remarkably sensible and clever. But I believe she gets that reputation more from rank and fortune and an authoritative manner. The pride of being connected to Mr. Darcy is an added factor."

Elizabeth nodded, feeling validated in her assessment of the Lady and content to discard all thoughts of the wretched Mr. Darcy in favor of the pleasure of her present company.

When the game finally ended and the visit concluded, the Bennet sisters and Mr. Collins made their way to the docks to head home for dinner. Elizabeth, for her part, went away with her head full of Mr. Wickham. She could think of nothing else on the flight but of him and of what he'd told her. She was so distracted, she barely followed the pilot in his checks as usual. There wasn't time for her to mention his name as they went, as neither Lydia nor Mr. Collins was ever quiet for more than the space it took to suck in a breath. Lydia talked incessantly of Circumstance, and Mr. Collins seemed compelled to describe her aunt and uncle's home and hospitality in painstaking detail despite their all having just been there. They both had more to say than either could manage before the Tailwynd landed at the Longbourn House.

LONDINIUM SAT[SYS

Communications Log—System Storage 30 Days [Planetary]

[Ba_Da_Bing_ley] 19.10-19:38:20.LS

I know that I asked you to send me a waive when you got home, but I couldn't wait. I just wanted to say that it was such a pleasure to see you earlier, and I'm sorry that I couldn't stay to talk with you longer.

[MyMyMissJane] 19.10-19:40:32.LS

We've just handed, actually. You have incredible timing! It was such a nice surprise to see you, even if the visit was cut short.

[Ba_Da_Bing_ley] 19.10-19:41:25.LS

Now that I know you're back to full health, it seems I have a promise to keep your youngest sister.

[MyMyMissJane] 19.10-19:44:36.LS

Oh! That's right. The ball. She has mentioned it a few times.

[Ba_Da_Bing_ley] 19.10-19:46:22.LS

Please ask her what date she thinks would be best.

[MyMyMissJane] 19.10-19:47:08.LS

I'll be sure to remind her that you'll need time to prepare. Otherwise, she may just tell you to throw it together for tomorrow.

[Ba_Da_Bing_ley] 19.10-19:48:58.LS

While it would be a delight to see you again so soon, I would very much appreciate the prep time.

[MyMyMissJane] . . . LIKES MESSAGE . . .

[MyMyMissJane] 19.10-19:50:20.LS

I'll let you know as soon as I can.

[Ba_Da_Bing_ley] 19.10-19:53:45.LS

Whatever the date may be, let this be my official invitation to you and your family.

[MyMyMissJane] 19.10-19:55:41.LS

On behalf of the entire family, I gratefully accept.

. . . **END COM** . . .

CHAPTER
19

Longbourn House, Heoros, First Moon of Londinium

Jane sat on the edge of her bed, plucking the strands of Lizzie's braids apart as her sister filled her in on all that Mr. Wickham had said. Her fingers worked more steadily than her mind as she took in the words. How was she supposed to believe that Mr. Darcy was so unworthy of Mr. Bingley's friendship? And yet, what reason did she have to question the truthfulness of such a friendly and open man as Mr. Wickham?

As she pulled the last of the braids apart, she remembered her voice. "They've both been deceived somehow," she said. "We don't have the information to put the pieces together. Things must've been misrepresented at some point for one or both of them. It's possible neither of them is to blame."

Lizzie turned and placed her hands on Jane's. "Yes, and please be sure to say something good about anyone else involved in this matter. We can't forget to clear them of wrongdoing before I'm forced to think ill of somebody."

The glint in Lizzie's eye was full of loving mischief. She was teasing Jane, of course. Still, Jane said, "Laugh as much as you wish, but you won't laugh me out of my opinion. At least consider how disgracefully this would color Mr. Darcy if his treatment of Mr. Wickham proves true. It's impossible. No man with common human decency or any value of character would be capable of it. And how would his closest friends not know of it? There's something not right here."

Lizzie's features grew stern. "I can much more easily believe that Mr. Bingley's kind and generous nature might be taken advantage of than that Mr. Wickham might invent such a history of himself as he did this afternoon. He had names, facts, everything—all of it mentioned casually. If it isn't true, let Mr. Darcy contradict it. But there was truth in Wickham's eyes."

"This is so distressing." Jane pulled her hands from her sister's. "I don't know what to think."

Lizzie crossed her arms. "You know exactly what to think."

But Jane was certain on only one point—that Mr. Bingley, if he'd been taken in by Mr. Darcy, would suffer much from his acquaintance if this ordeal became public.

Jane's comcard, lying on the bed beside them, flashed blue, the glow coloring the white covers temporarily.

"Bingley?" Lizzie asked curiously, as Jane scanned the device.

Jane smiled as she read the screen.

[Ba_Da_Bing_ley] 19.10-21:03:18.LS

I hope you won't mind me asking here for your first dance at the ball?

She quickly typed back in the affirmative, then set the com-card down again as her youngest sister called from the bottom of the stairs.

"You *could* thank Jane, of course, for the ball, but really, it was *I* who spurred Mr. Bingley into committing," she said airily.

Lizzie cast a look at Jane, a smirk spreading on her lips. Lydia could be excitable and a little too focused on herself, but she could be endearing and sometimes amusing. Neither would admit it aloud, for fear of inflating her head, but they could acknowledge the sentiment quietly between them, as they did with many other things.

"While I do enjoy the solitude of my mornings," Mary said, footfalls echoing in the stairwell, "I can sacrifice my evenings for an occasion such as this. Society has claims on us all, and recreation and amusement are necessary for everyone."

Lydia appeared first in the hallway, barely glancing into her eldest sisters' room as she looked back at their middle sister. "I love you dearly, Mary, but you don't need to sound so Mr. Collins about it. Just say you're excited—you don't need to explain why."

As the other girls disappeared down the hallway, Kitty followed and said, "Would you rather dance five dances with Mr. Wickham or one dance each with five different officers?"

"Why not both?" Lydia said, their door snapping shut behind them.

Lizzie laughed out loud and Jane found herself chuckling as well, dispelling some of the anxious tension she'd felt over the drama of Mr. Wickham and Mr. Darcy.

Suddenly their mother poked her head around the doorframe, startling them both, her eyes alight with excitement.

"Lizzie, dearest," she said, "Mr. Collins has asked for your first dance at the ball. I believe he's looking forward to the occasion, so I agreed on your behalf." She flashed her palm to stop Lizzie's choked attempt to reply. "He's our guest and he's shown you *special* deference. I expect you to behave accordingly."

Lizzie, her back to Jane as her mother said this, stiffened, pulling her shoulder blades together. With a huff, she replied, "Fine."

Their mother smiled, satisfied, and bid them goodnight.

Lizzie slipped off Jane's bed and stood, took one step to her own bed, and fell dramatically into it. "I was momentarily imagining myself dancing with Mr. Wickham to start the evening," she muttered.

"That's an unfortunate turn of events," Jane commiserated.

Lizzie buried her face in her hands. "Do you think . . ." she began, her voice muffled. Her hands dropped away, her arms flopping to her sides. "It's not possible that Mr. Collins . . . that his choosing me—especially the way our mother just implied—could mean he sees me as some possible marriage opportunity? That's . . . an irrational thought, right?"

Jane shrugged, uncertain.

"He's been increasingly conversational toward me—always complimenting me about things. Not that he doesn't compliment every one of us, but—oh, now that the thought is in my head, I can't help but suspect a pattern."

Jane had never felt luckier to be the object of Bingley's attention. She hated to say it, but her mother seemed well pleased with whatever had transpired during her conversation with Mr. Collins.

The smile she'd had on her face in the doorway matched the one she wore when she was scheming. It didn't bode well for her poor sister.

"You know what," Lizzie said, more forcefully. "It doesn't matter. Even if what I'm now thinking might be true, he might never have the courage to make an offer. Until he does, I'm going to go about my life just as I was before this horrible revelation."

"Excellent plan," Jane said, then sneaked a peek at her comcard again. Her screen, still open to the conversation Bingley had started, showed a new message.

[Ba_Da_Bing_ley] 19.10-21:07:33.LS

Tuesday can't come soon enough.

for the ball: commission that artist
Charles always mentions (N. Valentina)
as a surprise!

CHAPTER
20

Netherfield StarCruiser, Heoros Orbit, First Moon of Londinium

E lizabeth had never considered that Mr. Wickham might not attend the ball until she entered the drawing room of the Netherfield. Not a single man in Star Force dress reds was the one she was eager to see. In the days leading to the ball, he hadn't given her any indication that he'd be missing from their ranks. She'd dressed with more than usual care, going through several gowns before settling on one she felt was right—a gold complementary to the red of his uniform, which laced intricately from her diaphragm to her collar in the front, and dropped low and open in the back, sleeves made entirely of delicate chains and sparkling red jewels. She'd felt like a star, shining bright with anticipation and enthusiasm, as she'd stepped off their transport and into the docking bay of the Netherfield.

As she fruitlessly scanned the crowd for Wickham's face, a dreadful suspicion rose in her at the thought of Mr. Darcy purposefully omitting him from the invitation to the officers. Would he have had that kind of influence over Mr. Bingley?

"What, no Wickham?" Lydia asked without ceremony as Mr. Denny approached them.

He nodded reluctantly. "Wickham had to travel planet-side on business yesterday and hasn't returned." He leaned in closer and, in a conspiratorial whisper to Elizabeth, added, "I doubt that business would've been as pressing if he hadn't wanted to avoid a certain gentleman here."

Elizabeth found Mr. Darcy in the crowd almost at once, and glared at him. He was with Mr. Bingley, and she realized then that the two were purposefully moving toward them. For Jane's and for Bingley's sake, she was able to arrange her features in a more neutral expression as they drew near. But she could barely look in his direction, let alone reply civilly when Mr. Darcy actually spoke.

"Was docking as smooth as last time, Miss Elizabeth?"

For him to appear so pleasant and conversational was too much to bear. Giving him any attention or showing him patience was nothing short of condoning his past behavior. She was resolved against responding in any way that would further a conversation. "Indeed," was all she managed, then excused herself.

Once out of his immediate vicinity, the dark storm of her mood cleared somewhat. Though every prospect of her own was destroyed for the evening, it wouldn't keep her spirits low. She was at a beautiful party, drifting like a mote in the void. How could she not enjoy herself?

She found Charlotte Lucas on the far end of the ballroom and was able to shift her anger at Mr. Darcy into annoyance at Mr. Collins and the dreaded first dance her mother had promised him.

"It might be best to get it over with quickly," Charlotte suggested. "Then you'll be free of vexation for the rest of the evening."

Elizabeth agreed. So, when Mr. Collins came near a moment later, she voluntarily caught his attention and offered to get the dance over with.

The moment they stepped onto the dance floor, she regretted showing him that sliver of positive reinforcement.

"I thank you for so readily agreeing to my request," he said solemnly. "Your mother assured me you were eager to say yes, but I had my doubts. And then you come so soon to find me . . ."

She used every bit of her willpower not to roll her eyes at the thought of her mother exaggerating on her behalf.

The dance called for a turn away from each other, but Mr. Collins pulled her toward him instead, forcing her to awkwardly twirl with him and pulling looks from the surrounding dancers before they fell back into step.

She hoped theirs was the shortest song of the night.

"I'd like very much—" he began, before the dance called for them to move out of range from one another, and suddenly Mr. Bingley crossed her path.

"You sparkle this evening, Miss Bennet," Mr. Bingley offered, as they locked forearms to weave through the dancers.

She smiled warmly and gave him a wink as they broke apart, shifting partners once again before returning to Mr. Collins.

He seemed to have been holding his thought, his eyes now so intent on her face that he flubbed the steps and bumped into the woman next to him. He didn't appear to notice. "—to remain close to you throughout this evening."

She made her face impassive. What she'd give to just walk off the dance floor at this moment. But her mother would cause more of a scene in witnessing it than the walking off would, so she clenched her teeth and gave him nothing.

Thankfully the dance shifted them apart again before he could say more, and her sister appeared beside her.

Jane was glowing. Whatever starlight Elizabeth thought she'd had when she dressed was nothing compared to Jane's radiance. The dress she wore, with its bioluminescent lace, would've overpowered anyone else who attempted to wear it. But on Jane, it seemed a mere afterthought—a beautiful accessory to the true jewel wearing it.

Elizabeth leaned toward her. "Will he be sharing you at all this evening, dear sister, or are you his own personal sun to revolve around?"

"The latter, I hope," Jane said, that wish glittering in her eyes.

They spun away from each other, and there was Mr. Collins again.

"You don't have to hold back your smiles from me, Miss Elizabeth. Your eagerness is endearing."

The smile Jane's mere presence had coaxed onto Elizabeth's face froze and warped as she realized he'd been watching her throughout the entire dance and believed her smile for him.

Could he be so obtuse? She shook her head. Of course he could.

"I feel it's my honor, perhaps even my duty, to reward you—" The dance shifted, but he did not shift with them. Again, he pulled her close to him, mere inches between them, and concluded, "with as much time together tonight as possible."

Her eyes widened. Her thoughts went to static momentarily, before she remembered herself and their surroundings. "The dance, sir," she murmured, eyeing those around them, aware of how this moment might be misconstrued.

To her great relief, he stepped back into the dance, and the song finished without incident.

Before he could say another word, Elizabeth blurted, "Excuse me, Charlotte expects my return." It took everything in her not to run, but to walk with dignity and grace back to her friend.

She was so focused on getting to Charlotte that she nearly slammed into Mr. Darcy as he stepped into her path.

She gasped and stepped back. "My apologies," she said, too stunned at his appearance to be anything but polite.

"Miss Elizabeth, would you do me the honor of a dance at the start of the next set?"

Whether it was the thought of Mr. Collins trailing her, or simply the shock of his sudden appearance, she replied, "Yes."

He bowed slightly and disappeared, leaving her to lock eyes with Charlotte.

"What is happening?" Elizabeth mouthed.

Charlotte shook her head, a slightly bemused smile on her face.

She moved to Charlotte's side, an incredulous laugh escaping her. "Have I gone mad? Have the worlds? Did we slip into an alternate dimension? What is happening tonight?"

Charlotte laughed and patted her shoulder. "It seems you aren't meant for a night of leisure and calm."

"I just endured one of the most awkward dances of my life and now I've agreed to what will absolutely be another."

"Dare I say, you may find Mr. Darcy quite the agreeable dance partner?"

"That'd be inconvenient, since I'm determined to hate him."

They both laughed, and then Charlotte waved down a server and grabbed them each a glass of imported Kaelsian White, its soft, sweet scent bubbling off the surface as the liquid shifted.

"Perhaps this'll give me the fortitude to endure my next dance partner."

Charlotte grinned, but then she grew somber. "Lizzie, I know you're upset by what Wickham told you, but do please be smart about Mr. Darcy. He has so much more influence than Wickham, and it'll do you no favors to be unpleasant. For your family's—your sister's sake—if not your own, don't antagonize him."

Elizabeth groaned, then downed her drink as Mr. Darcy approached, hand outstretched. "I'll try."

The Netherfield StarCruiser Inaugural Ball
—N. Valentina, Special Commission by Caroline Bingley

CHAPTER
21

Netherfield StarCruiser, Heoros Orbit, First Moon of Londinium

Miss Elizabeth's fingers slipped across Darcy's as she took his hand. His skin felt suddenly electrified where it touched hers. The sensation lingered, throwing him into momentary silence as they moved into position for the dance.

In the ensuing quiet, he realized that this was the first time he'd be seen dancing with anyone outside of his own party since they'd arrived on Heoros. He wondered if she felt the weight of it also. The amazement on the neighboring dancers' faces made him uneasy. But it was too late to change course now.

The dance started, and they continued in a comfortable silence, which allowed him to follow the traces of her thoughts as they played across Miss Elizabeth's expressive face. Each time she locked her gaze with his, he felt a momentary jolt of anticipation, but then her face would shift into another emotion and still no words followed. She flitted between something like stubbornness, curiosity, confusion, and then an expression more resolute settled in her lips. Her dark eyes narrowed.

"This dance is a good one," she said, "though rather complicated."

He lifted his chin slightly to match her air of assurance. "The footwork trips many." What else he could say on the matter felt too dull.

She studied him as if looking for meaning. "It's *your* turn to say something now, Mr. Darcy. *I* talked about the dance, now *you* ought to remark upon the size of the room or the number of couples."

He smiled, caught off guard by the lack of usual rote pleasantries, which by now he should have anticipated from her. "Whatever you wish to be said, I'll say. The room is large and well equipped for so many couples."

"That reply will do for now. Perhaps I'll then observe that private balls are far more pleasant than public ones. And now we may be silent."

Her self-assurance was endearing, and pulled on a thread in him that made him rather eager to converse. "Do you talk as a rule, then, while dancing?"

"Sometimes. One must speak a little, you know. It'd feel odd to be entirely silent. And yet for *some*, conversation ought to be arranged in a way that they have to say as little as possible."

Was she teasing him? "Are you consulting your own feelings in this case, or do you imagine you're gratifying mine?"

"Both," replied Elizabeth archly, "for I've always seen a great similarity in our minds. We are both generally unsocial and taciturn, unwilling to speak unless we expect to say something that will amaze the whole room and be handed down the generations with all the pomp of a proverb."

She was teasing him. He was sure of it. And yet, this didn't irritate him. "This doesn't sound like you at all," he said. "How near it may be to me, I can't pretend to say. *You* think it an accurate representation, undoubtedly."

"I must not decide on my own."

Was this an invitation to show her more of himself? It felt that way. But she'd have to work harder to discover his inner self than by baiting him into revealing it.

The music swelled and the dance parted them momentarily, his attention caught on Jane. It was good to see her well. It'd been a surprise to see her and Miss Elizabeth at the waystation so soon after their stay on the Netherfield. When they reconnected, he thought to ask, "Do you and your sisters travel to the Meryton often?"

"We do, yes. To visit my aunt." She paused a moment, then added, "In fact, when you met us there the other day, we'd just been forming a new acquaintance."

He knew immediately she was referring to Wickham. For a moment the rush of blood behind his eyes made it difficult to think clearly. After several steps in the dance, carefully constraining his words, he said, "Mr. Wickham is blessed with such a pleasing personality which ensures him the ease of *making* friends. Whether he's equally capable of *retaining* them is less certain."

"He's been unlucky enough to lose your friendship," she emphasized, "and in a way he's likely to suffer from it all his life."

Darcy didn't immediately respond. How could he, rationally? She was more familiar with Wickham than he'd expected. It unsettled him greatly. He needed a moment to collect himself, lest he said too much.

Sir William Lucas appeared in that moment beside them, cutting through the dance—likely to reach the other side of the room—but stopping to give Darcy a bow. At any other time, he might have been irritated, but it was a welcome distraction.

"It's wonderful to see such lively and skilled dancers like yourselves on the floor this evening," Sir William said jovially. "I hope to see this pleasing connection often in the future," he leaned in conspiratorially, "especially when a certain desirable event will take place."

Darcy followed the old man's gaze to where Bingley and Miss Jane danced together, and was struck by what the general population must interpret between them, and by the depth of Bingley's attachment. But this was a problem for a different day.

He turned his attention back to Miss Elizabeth. They'd lapsed into silence. Spurred by her challenge, he was determined to find something they'd both enjoy talking about. He remembered how much she'd read during her stay, so he smiled boldly and said, "What about books?"

"Books! Oh, no. I'm sure we never read the same—or not with the same feelings."

A disappointing reaction, to be sure, but not one he couldn't counteract. "I'm sorry you think so. But if that is the case, we'll never run out of conversation. We can compare our different opinions."

She shook her head. "I can't talk of books in a ballroom. It's far too distracting."

"The *present* always occupies you in such places, does it?" he asked, letting her see his doubt with a tilt of his head and a lift of one brow.

"Always," she said almost absently, her gaze drawn upward to the dome of windows above them, Heoros looming at its edge. He was struck with the thought of her flight from the Meryton, and, cursing himself for not suggesting flight first, was about to mention it, when her features shifted and she added suddenly, "I remember hearing you once say, Mr. Darcy, that you hardly ever forgave, and that your resentment once created was inflexible. You're very cautious, I'd hope, in the *creation* of that opinion?"

It was an odd shift in the conversation, but wherever she was going with it, he was intrigued enough to follow. "Absolutely," he answered.

"And you never allow yourself to be blinded by prejudice?"

"I hope not."

"It's particularly important for those who never change their opinion to be very sure they've judged true at first."

A burgeoning suspicion took hold in his chest. "May I ask where these questions are leading?"

"I just want to get a clear illustration of your character," she said, some of the seriousness leaving her face. "I'm trying to decipher it."

"Any success?"

She shook her head. "I hear such different accounts of you that I'm exceedingly puzzled."

He remembered then what they'd been discussing before Sir William had come over. What had Wickham told her? How much could he have said in so few days since they'd met? Carefully, he answered, "I'm sure that reports may vary greatly in regard to me. I do wish, Miss Bennet, that you wouldn't decide my character at the present moment, as there's reason to fear that it'd reflect no credit on either of us."

Her face darkened with a grave determination. "But if I don't take your likeness now, I may never have another opportunity."

He could see that Wickham had said enough to put her on guard against him, and there was too little time in the dance now to change her mind. "I'd by no means suspend any pleasure of yours," he replied coldly, unable to keep at bay the anger he felt for Wickham interfering yet again in his life. At least Georgiana was no part of it this time.

Miss Elizabeth said nothing else as the dance came to an end, and they parted in silence. What had started with the promise of knowing her more had come to a bitter and dissatisfying end.

Lizzie wore the gold dress tonight. I told her the chain sleeves would work best with drop-back of the dress. She actually took my advice. She should do that more often. She even caught Mr. Darcy's attention, and he hates her. More proof that the right clothes can change your life. Speaking of life-changing... Jane in that blu dress! It may as well have been made for her. It took everything in me not to run my hands across her back all night. Thankfully, she let me draw little pictures on her while we were on the Tailwynd. To see the lace light up under my fingertips was magical. The bonus: watching the colors change every time Bingley even barely grazed her sleeves or placed his hands on her hips or shoulders in the dances. Stars! it was

Mesmerizing!

My dress is a Lydia Bennet original. ...I don't have access to the kinds of fabrics I want yet, so it was lacking in texture. But in design, I'd say I absolutely rivaled my sisters, and got as many compliments on mine as theirs.

Mary's and Kitty's were fine. But Mary doesn't care about standing out and Kitty picked her favorite...again. Whatever they're comfortable in, but it's no wonder they didn't get as

CHAPTER
22

Netherfield StarCruiser, Heoros Orbit, First Moon of Londinium

Before Elizabeth had a chance to sort out her feelings about how the conversation had ended with Mr. Darcy, Jane met her with a smile and a glow of happiness that suffused the air around her. It appeared that her sister was satisfied with the events of the evening thus far. Elizabeth's resentment toward Darcy, and her disappointment with the absence of Wickham, gave way before the hope of Jane's happiness, and she softened her words significantly before speaking.

"I wanted to know," she said, finding herself mirroring her sister's smile, "what you've learned about Mr. Wickham. But perhaps you've been too pleasantly preoccupied to think of anyone else. In which case, rest assured you've already been pardoned."

Jane laughed. "I haven't forgotten him. But I don't have much to tell. Bingley knows little of the details that caused Mr. Darcy to despise the man. But he vouches for the good and honorable nature of his friend and is fully convinced that Mr. Wickham deserved even less attention from Mr. Darcy than he received. I'm sorry to say it, Lizzie, but Mr. Wickham appears not to be a respectable man and has deserved the loss of Mr. Darcy's good graces."

"Bingley doesn't know Wickham himself?"

"No, he'd never seen him until the other day on the Meryton."

"So, what he knows is based on what Mr. Darcy has told him."

The look of concern marring her sister's blissful countenance wasn't one she wanted to encourage. Elizabeth grabbed Jane's hands in hers. "I have no doubt of Bingley's sincerity. But forgive me if I'm not convinced by his assurances alone. Bingley does right by his friend in defending his honor. But since he's learned what he has from Mr. Darcy himself, I have no choice but to continue thinking of them both as I did before. And you can go back to thinking of neither one of them, and focusing all your attention on Mr. Bingley."

This did the trick. Jane's eyes glittered in delight. "I don't want to assume anything prematurely, but I do really think he feels the same for me as I do for him."

"Anyone could see it, even in the darkness of space," Elizabeth encouraged, gesturing around them at the windows.

"He never leaves us at the end of a dance without securing another, and I feel—oh, it's silly. I'm sure this is wishful, but—well, it feels like even when we aren't dancing or talking together, his attention's on me. Perhaps it's that I'm so aware of *him*, that I notice whenever he's looking in my direction . . ."

"It's absolutely not because of that," Elizabeth assured her. "He watches you every chance he gets." She peered over Jane's shoulder, spotting Bingley in half a second. He wasn't far away, in conversation with a few of the officers, his attention unfixed. The moment he caught Elizabeth watching him, he smiled at her, then begged leave of his company and headed toward them. "He couldn't even stand to be away this long." She winked at Jane as Bingley touched her lightly on the shoulder, the gray lace glowing suddenly teal under his touch.

Not wishing to intrude on this moment, Elizabeth caught sight of Charlotte and locked course for her immediately. She'd had enough on her mind in the past half hour to forget about Mr. Collins, and only as he intercepted her trajectory did the memory of their dance return.

She clenched her teeth in anticipation of what he'd say next.

"Miss Elizabeth," he said. "I have wonderful news. I've just, through sheer happenstance, discovered that there is now, in the room, a near relation of my patroness. I overheard the gentleman himself mentioning to one of his companions the names of his distant cousin, Miss de Bourgh and her mother, Lady Catherine. How wonderful when these sorts of things occur! Who would've thought of my meeting with someone so close to Lady Catherine de Bourgh at this great gathering. I'm most thankful that I discovered this in time to pay my respects to him. I must do it immediately and hope that he'll forgive my not doing so the moment we boarded the ship. My total ignorance of the connection must plead my apology."

"You're not going to introduce yourself to Mr. Darcy."

"I am indeed. And I'll beg his pardon for not having done it sooner. He is, for all intents and purposes, Lady Catherine's nephew. It's within my power to assure him that her ladyship is quite well since last I spoke with her."

"But Mr. Collins, I'm sure if he was at all worried or curious about her, he could ask her himself. He won't thank you for addressing him without an introduction. He'll see it as impertinent. It's unnecessary for you two to speak, but if it were, the onus falls on

Mr. Darcy, the *superior* in status, to begin the acquaintance." How did he not know this?

Mr. Collins listened to her with all the attentiveness of a small child being told not to eat the snack in his hand. He had eyes only for the snack. He gave her a patronizing smile. "Dear Miss Elizabeth, I have the highest opinion in the worlds of your excellent judgment in all matters within the scope of *your* understanding, but permit me to say that there must be a wide difference between the established forms of ceremony among the elite and those of us who commune with the Everlasting Light. I must profess that I consider my position to be equal with the highest rank in the system, provided that proper humility and decorum are maintained. I must follow my own conscience in this matter. Pardon me for neglecting your advice, which on every other subject will be my constant guide. But, in this case, I am better suited to determine what's right than a young lady like yourself."

She stiffened and glared at him, but he didn't notice or care. With a low bow he left her to accost Mr. Darcy, whose reaction to his advances she eagerly watched. It was evident that Mr. Darcy was astonished at being addressed so informally, Mr. Collins having gone so far as to interrupt a conversation already in progress. Elizabeth would've buried her head in her hands in vicarious embarrassment had she been able to look away from the disaster.

Mr. Darcy turned as the man prefaced his speech with a solemn bow. She nearly groaned out loud, but instead, grabbed a drink from Charlotte's outstretched hand as her friend came to stand beside her.

"I'm making out 'apology' and 'Hunsford' and . . . 'Lady Catherine' maybe?" Charlotte said.

They watched in silent, horrified awe as Mr. Collins spoke long past when he should've stopped to breathe.

When at last Mr. Collins allowed Mr. Darcy time to speak, he replied with an air of distant civility, which, she had to begrudgingly admit, was kinder than he needed to be. Mr. Collins, however, wasn't discouraged, and Mr. Darcy's features morphed from polite tolerance to seething annoyance to hardly concealed contempt. He ended the conversation with a slight bow, then turned back to his previous company.

Mr. Collins returned happily to Elizabeth. "That went well."

Elizabeth took a drink to obscure her reaction, the wine more bitter from her distaste of him. Apparently too high on his perceived success to limit his recounting to Elizabeth and Charlotte, Mr. Collins quickly begged off in search of more attentive victims.

Having no other obstacle for the evening, Elizabeth turned her attention on her sister and Mr. Bingley. The visions of pleasant possibilities which emerged from her observations made her nearly as happy as Jane. She imagined her sister settled on the Netherfield, happy in a marriage of true affection, content to be together wherever the ship might take them. Elizabeth could even find it in herself to like his sisters in such a circumstance.

Her mother's thoughts were clearly bent the same way. At dinner, Elizabeth was deeply distressed to discover that her mother was seated next to the one person—Lady Lucas—she'd talk freely, openly, and loudly with, and they spoke of nothing else but her expectation that Jane would soon marry Mr. Bingley. It was a subject which animated her mother greatly—and she seemed incapable of growing tired of listing the many advantages from such a match.

"Oh, he's so very charming, and so rich," her mother said laughingly, "and Netherfield Landing is so close to the Longbourn Estate we could visit every day!"

Elizabeth pressed her lips together as if somehow the action could force her mother to do the same.

"And stars around us!—how lovely it is that her future sisters adore her. It'll make the times she's away from us, traveling from moon to moon, that much easier."

Elizabeth chanced a look in their hosts' direction, and while Bingley was thankfully too preoccupied with Jane, Mr. Darcy, sitting only two spots to her right, appeared to be overhearing it all.

"What a promising situation this'll be for her younger sisters," Mrs. Bennet carried on, wine spilling over the edge of her glass as she gesticulated. "Jane marrying so well will certainly throw them into the way of other rich men, and then I'll be at my leisure, and I'll be able to go into company only when it pleases me, rather than as necessity. As you know, there's no one more likely to find comfort in staying home than I."

She giggled like her youngest daughter and Elizabeth grew desperate enough to whisper-yell across the table. "Mother, please lower your voice. This isn't a conversation for mixed company."

But her mother simply *tsk*ed at her and said, "Nonsense, Lizzie, everyone else is in their own conversations. You're the only one being nosy."

"I'm not. I can't help but hear you and I'm not the only one." She gestured covertly to Mr. Darcy.

"What is Mr. Darcy to me? Should I be concerned with his opinion? No. We don't owe him such civility, saying nothing unless it pleases him to hear it."

"For land's sake, Mama, speak lower. What possible advantage could offending him have? You'll never recommend yourself to his *friend* if you keep this up."

But nothing she said had any influence on her mother, and Elizabeth was left to blush in shame and bear the continued spectacle. She couldn't help but frequently glance toward Mr. Darcy, though each time only confirmed her dread that his attention was fixed on her mother. The expression on his face changed gradually from indignant contempt to a composed and steady gravity.

Eventually, her mother had no more to say, and Lady Lucas, who had grown visibly tired of the repetition of delights she was unlikely to share in, was left to eat in peace.

The respite was long enough for Elizabeth to revive and con-sider enjoying herself again. But it wasn't long lived. When supper was over, a few of the younger attendees discussed a bit of singing, and she had the acute mortification of seeing Mary, of all sisters, orchestrate the means for an impromptu concert.

Elizabeth attempted to stop her, wanting to explain that this wasn't the place for her to show off, but she couldn't get the words out in time. The opportunity to exhibit her talents was too promis-ing, and Mary began her song.

Unable to look away, Elizabeth was forced to endure. Mary wasn't talented enough for such a display. She loved her sister dearly, but her voice was too weak for this large a room, and she took her-self far too seriously.

Elizabeth was on the verge of melting into the floor from the embarrassment. She looked to Jane, but she was talking to Bingley. She looked at his two sisters and recognized a vicious derision in their mannerisms. Mr. Darcy's grave expression remained unchanged. In desperation, she looked to her father. For one shining moment she thought that he understood her plight and recognized her silent entreaty to interfere, lest Mary should sing all night.

Instead of a tactful and discreet removal, however, her father cut into her song before it had finished, saying, "You have delighted us all with your performance long enough. Now let the others have their turns."

Mary, though she pretended not to hear, grew disconcerted. Her face whitened as she noticed the room's attention, no longer able to believe they were admiring her performance. Elizabeth felt sorry for her and sorrier still that their father had gone about ending the embarrassment by certainly creating more.

"If I were so fortunate as to be able to sing," Mr. Collins offered loudly enough to be heard by half the room, "I'd take great pleasure in obliging the company with a song. A man of the Light such as myself has much to do, however. And I don't think it of little importance that I should be attentive to the worlds and people around me, especially to those who are due preferential notice." And with a bow to Mr. Darcy, he concluded his speech.

Elizabeth was a breath away from finding the nearest airlock and throwing herself out of it. Had her family made some sort of agreement to expose themselves to such a degree? Her only consolation was that Bingley and Jane seemed oblivious to the indiscretions. It was soured, however, by the certainty that Bingley's sisters and closest friend had soberly witnessed it all, and now possessed extensive fodder to ridicule her family.

The rest of the evening brought her little amusement and no relief. Mr. Collins became an unwanted satellite, perversely orbiting her. He couldn't convince her to dance with him again, but by continuing to stay near her, kept anyone else away. Her encouragements to have him dance with others were in vain.

The burden of his company was lifted somewhat by Charlotte, who joined them often between dances, and politely engaged in conversation with him. The relief of this was somewhat lessened by Mr. Darcy often standing within an uncomfortably short distance of her, though he never came near enough to her to speak.

At the end of the evening, the Bennets were the last of the company to depart. By some scheme of her mother's, they had to wait for their pilot for a quarter of an hour after the rest of the guests had disembarked. It emphasized just how heartily they were wished away by some of the family. Mrs. Hurst and her sister barely opened their mouths except to complain of fatigue. They ignored every attempt of conversation by her mother, though there was no real silence in the wake of this, for there was always the long speeches of Mr. Collins. Even Lydia was too exhausted to utter more than the occasional, "I could sleep for an entire month!" accompanied by a violent yawn.

Finally, their transport was ready, and they rose from their chairs to leave. Her mother graciously thanked their hosts and encouraged them to come soon to Longbourn. "We'd be delighted to have you over for dinner any time. No need for a formal invitation," she said to Bingley.

"Thank you, madam," Bingley replied. "I'd be equally happy to accept that offer the first chance I get after we return from Londinium. I must attend to a few things there for a short while."

"We're so grateful that you took the time to host this ball before you departed," Elizabeth said. "I hope your night was well worth the effort."

His eyes flicked toward Jane for a moment. "It was indeed."

And with that, they finally parted company, heading down the stairs to the docking bay. Elizabeth only hoped they were well and truly out of earshot when her mother started itemizing the necessary preparations for Jane's upcoming nuptials.

Wish list dress

Something that drapes effortlessly but is actually rich in texture, detail, and, well, I guess it'd probably be more complicated than *effortless* to make, but that's what makes art... *♥ art ♥* ...and me an artist!

Possible textures or details:
Astral lace
Bi-lu silk
Jewelbird pattern (hand-beading)

♥ Bioluminescent Silk, Magenta base*
Item#:BIS36003-1092

Made from bi-lu strands produced on Kent Orbital Station, the silk reacts to touch by glowing brightly in a myriad of colors.

ål. 364\79 _yard)// ...stars! that price...

Make a test dress something cheaper first— not a wasted scrap! → Maybe some kind of hair piece.

CHAPTER 23

Longbourn House, Heoros, First Moon of Londinium

Elizabeth sat at the dining table with Kitty and Lydia, listening to them recount the night's events while absently snacking on pastries the staff had set out.

"There was not a single boy our age of the same caliber as that spread of food, Lydia, and you can't deny it," Kitty said.

Lydia gave a great sigh. "You only say that because you didn't dance with Denny."

Their mother wandered blissfully in. "Talking of the ball, are we?"

"There's not another subject worth discussing so early, Mama," Lydia said airily.

Mrs. Bennet smiled and patted Lydia on the head, taking the seat next to her. "Too true, my dear." She surveyed the table, her attention snagging on the pitcher of water, which she grabbed and poured into an empty cup.

As she took a long drink, Mr. Collins walked in. He was stiff-backed and serious, dressed as carefully as he'd been last evening. He was even wearing shoes. It was off-putting for so early in the day.

He approached their mother and cleared his throat. "I'd like to formally solicit the honor of a private audience with Miss Elizabeth at some point within the morning hours."

Before Elizabeth could do more than pale in surprise, her mother answered, "Oh, yes, certainly. I'm sure Lizzie will be very happy—she can have no objection. Now is as good a time as any. Come, Kitty, Lydia, you're needed upstairs." She stood, hastily snatching a few of the rolls from the table and shooing her youngest daughters out of their seats.

"Wait, no, please," Elizabeth called out. "There's no need to leave." She turned to Mr. Collins. "Excuse me sir," then back to her mother, "but there's nothing he can have to say to me that needs to be said in private. In fact, I was just leaving as well." She stood, with every intention of fleeing the room.

But her mother stopped her with a look. "Nonsense, Lizzie. Stay where you are. I *insist* that you hear him out."

Her entire body was primed to bolt, but reason kept her in place. She needed to face this situation, reject his proposal, and be done with it. She returned to her seat.

When they'd gone, Mr. Collins began to speak.

"My dear Miss Elizabeth, I appreciate your modesty. You would've been less perfect in my eyes had there *not* been this little unwillingness. I am certain that you know what I am about to offer, though your feminine nature may lead you to feign ignorance. My attentions have been too marked to be mistaken. Almost as soon as I entered the house, I singled you out as the companion of my future life. But before I'm swept away by my feelings on the subject, I think it advisable to state my reasons for marrying, and for coming into Heoros with the design of selecting a wife."

The idea of Mr. Collins, with his solemnity and seriousness, being swept away by feelings amused Elizabeth so much that she missed the chance to stop him saying more.

"First, as a man of the Light, it is my duty to set the example of a stable home life for my followers. Second, I'm convinced it will add greatly to my happiness. And third, it is the particular recommendation of that exquisitely noble lady whom I have the honor of calling a patroness. Twice, she has condescended to give me advice on this subject. 'Mr. Collins,' she said, 'you must marry. Choose properly, choose a gentlewoman for *my* sake; and for your *own*, let her be an active, useful sort of person, not reared to think too highly of herself, but able to make a small income go a long way. Find such a woman as soon as you can, bring her to the station, and I'll visit her.' Allow me, by the way, to observe that I'm certain the notice and kindness of Lady Catherine de Bourgh is not among the least of the advantages to this offer of mine. Your wit and vivacity, I think, will be acceptable to her, especially tempered with the silence and respect which her rank will inevitably excite. Now, you may wonder why I chose Longbourn for this marital mission, rather than the Orbital Station, where I can assure you there are many eligible young women. But the fact is, as I am to inherit this estate after the death of your honorable father, I resolved to choose a wife from among his daughters, so that the loss of him could be the only loss in that event. This has been my motive, and I flatter myself it won't lower me in your esteem. And now nothing remains but for me to assure you in the most animated language of the violence of my affection, and to assure you that when we are married—"

It was absolutely necessary to interrupt him now.

"Slow down," she cried. "I've given you no answer. Let me do it without any further delay. I appreciate the compliment you're paying me. I'm very sensible of the honor of your proposal. But I can only decline."

"I'm not new to the idea," Mr. Collins said, dismissive, "that it's common practice among young ladies to reject the first addresses of the man they secretly mean to accept; and that sometimes that refusal is repeated a second or even third time. I am by no means discouraged by your response, and shall hope to lead you to the altar soon enough."

"Galaxy's end," Elizabeth cried, "your hope is extraordinary after my response. I assure you, I'm not one of those women who are so daring as to risk their happiness on the chance of being asked a second time. I'm perfectly serious in my refusal. You couldn't make me happy, and I'm convinced that I'm the last woman in the world who could make you happy. In fact, I'm sure your Lady Catherine would find me ill-suited for the situation in every way."

"I can't imagine that her ladyship would at all disapprove of you," Mr. Collins said very gravely. "You may be certain that when I see her again, I'll speak in the highest terms of your modesty, economy, and other amiable qualifications."

"Mr. Collins, your praise of me will be entirely unnecessary. Allow me to judge for myself and pay me the compliment of believing me. I wish you happiness, and by refusing you, I'm doing all I can to assure it. Your offer has satisfied your feelings with regard to my family. Take possession of Longbourn estate, whenever it falls, without guilt. This matter is settled." And rising as she spoke, she would've left the room had Mr. Collins not continued.

"When I have the honor of speaking to you next on the subject, I'll hope for a more favorable answer. You've said much to encourage me."

"Really, Mr. Collins," Elizabeth sighed, half exasperated and half amused, "you puzzle me. If what I've said appears as encouragement, I don't know how to express my refusal more definitively."

"Allow me to explain, dear Miss Elizabeth. You wish to increase my love by suspense, according to the usual practice of elegant females. Your refusal is thus merely custom, because I'm not unworthy of your acceptance, and what I offer is highly desirable. My situation in life, my connections with the family of de Bourgh, and my relationship to your own family, are circumstances highly in my favor. You should also consider that in spite of your manifold attractions, it's uncertain that another offer of marriage may ever be made to you. I therefore conclude that you aren't serious in your rejection of me."

"I assure you, *sir*, that I would not torment a respectable man. I'd rather be paid the compliment of being believed. I thank you again for the honor of your proposal, but accepting is impossible. My feelings forbid it." Eager to make sure he truly understood, she said, "I'll be blunt. Don't consider me now as an *elegant female*, intending to plague you, but as a rational creature speaking the truth from her heart."

"You're incredibly charming," he said with an air of awkward gallantry. "I'm persuaded that when given express permission from both of your parents, my proposal won't fail to be acceptable."

His perseverance and willful self-deception left Elizabeth speechless. With nothing to say, and frustration boiling over, she turned silently and left the room. If he persisted in considering her refusals to be encouragement, she'd go to her father. Perhaps *his* refusal could be spoken in such a way as to be believed.

As she exited the dining room, she was met with her mother's eager face. Keen, no doubt, to congratulate Mr. Collins and herself on this scheme, she passed Elizabeth with barely a glance. Elizabeth seized the opportunity to get to her father first.

She swung around the doorframe of the library, finding him seated comfortably in his armchair, book open on his lap. He looked up as she entered.

"What can I help you with this morning, my dear?" he asked, his voice like a soothing balm on her agitation.

"I—"

"Headstrong, foolish girl," she heard her mother say from down the hall. "I promise you she will be brought to reason."

"I need you on my side in this," Elizabeth said firmly to her father.

Mr. Bennet's thick eyebrows slanted in confused concern. "What's happening?"

Suddenly her mother was by her side in the doorway. She shooed Elizabeth inside and pulled the doors shut, talking hurriedly. "We're in an uproar. You must make Lizzie marry Mr. Collins. She has sworn herself against him. If you don't make her see reason, and quickly, he'll change his mind and then *he* will refuse *her*."

Mr. Bennet fixed his gaze on her face with calm unconcern. "It's my misfortune that I can't understand you," he said. "What are you talking about?"

"Mr. Collins and Lizzie!" she yelped, growing increasingly agitated. "Lizzie swears she won't have Mr. Collins—"

Elizabeth crossed her arms as her father turned his eyes to her.

"—and Mr. Collins now begins to think that he won't have Lizzie," her mother finished.

He was silent a moment, gaze sliding back to her mother. "And what am I to do about it?"

Her mother stamped her foot. "Tell her you insist upon her marrying him."

He closed his book and stood. "So, Mr. Collins has made you an offer of marriage, and you have refused?"

"I have."

Her father nodded solemnly. "But your mother insists upon you accepting this proposal. Is that correct, my dear?"

"Yes. Or I'll never see her again."

He studied them both in silence. Then he sighed. "An unhappy alternative is before you, Elizabeth. From this day on, you must be a stranger to one of your parents. Your mother will never see you again if you do *not* marry Mr. Collins—"

"Never," Mrs. Bennet emphasized.

"—and I will never see you again if you *do*."

Relief flooded Elizabeth's body and she ran over to throw her arms around him. "Thank you," she said.

"What do you mean?" her mother asked, incredulous. "You can't be thinking clearly."

"My dear," Mr. Bennet replied, as Elizabeth gave him one more squeeze and stepped back. "I have two small favors to request. First, that you'll respect my intelligence enough to understand this circumstance clearly." He took Elizabeth's chin in his hand and kissed the top of her head. "Second, that you'll return me and my library to solitude."

Elizabeth immediately complied, ducking out of the library before her mother could attempt another word.

LONDINIUM SAT[SYS

Communications Log—System Storage 30 Days [Planetary]

[LotteLu] 28.10-11:45:24.LS

Maria just talked to Lydia. Is what she said true? Did Mr. Collins actually propose?

[LizzieLovesSpace] 28.10-11:47:53.LS

Yes. And now my mother is being insufferable because I refused him.

[LotteLu] 28.10-11:50:03.LS

Naturally. I was going to come by. Is it horrible? Should I stay away?

[LizzieLovesSpace] 28.10-11:53:36.LS

My mother has tried threats, she has tried coaxing, she has tried to turn Jane on me. I'm sure she'll try the same on you. The choice is yours.

[LotteLu] 28.10-11:54:53.LS

Perhaps if I'm there she will be on her . . . better . . . behavior?

[LizzieLovesSpace] 28.10-11.56:42.LS

One would hope. If nothing else, you'll be very welcome company for me.

[LizzieLovesSpace] 28.10-12:00:29.LS

. . . AUDIO RECORDING TRANSCRIPT START . . .

. . . and no one is on my side. I'm being used so cruelly. None of you care for my poor nerves. And there she sits, with her comcard, looking as unconcerned as ever, caring no more for any of us than if we were lost in the outer reaches of the system, as long as she gets her own way. But I'll tell you this, Miss Lizzie, if you go on refusing every offer of marriage like this, you will never get a husband at all. I'm sure I don't know who will take care of you when your father is dead. I certainly won't be able to. I'm done with you from this day on. I told you I would never speak to you again, and I'm as good as my word.

[LotteLu] 28.10-12:02:02.LS

I'm on my way.

. . . END COM . . .

CHAPTER
24

Longbourn House, Heoros,
First Moon of Londinium

Coming down the stairs the morning after the event, Elizabeth heard her mother sighing dramatically —no doubt between lamentations of her daughter's disobedience—and then Mr. Collins cleared his throat.

"Let us be silent on this now," he said, his voice marked with displeasure. "Far be it from me to resent your daughter's behavior. The clarity of hindsight has shown me that this outcome is best for all our happiness. I have meant well through this whole affair, but forgive me if I have conducted myself in any way that you find objectionable. My goal has been to secure a companion with due consideration to the advantage of your family."

Elizabeth slowed to be sure she wouldn't come upon just the two of them in the hallway. The normally iridescent screen of her comcard suddenly lit with the blue of an incoming waive. Her heart skipped at the name of the sender, and she read eagerly.

To: ELIZABETH BENNET, LONGBOURN ESTATE, LANDINGS DISTRICT, HEOROS

From: COL. GEORGE WICKHAM, [LOCATION CONFIDENTIAL]

Subject: Re: ABSENCE

Miss Elizabeth,

I'll be honest, that you noted my absence makes the fact that I wasn't there to dance with you worse. I'm quite frustrated by the situation, I assure you. But as the time drew near, I felt that I'd better not meet Mr. Darcy. To be at the same party, in the same room with him for so many hours together wouldn't have been endured well on either side. Considering that this ball was held in orbit, I didn't fancy the idea of being shoved out an airlock and forced to spacewalk back to the Meryton. It would've ruined the evening for many, in any case.

I should be back within a day or two, and would relish the opportunity to make up for my absence at the ball. We could meet on the Meryton, or if you're willing, I could come by your home. I'll reach out again when I'm in orbit.

Col. Wickham

A fair reason, at last. She felt the compliment of his closing paragraph, and looked to his impending arrival at her home as an acceptable way of introducing him to her parents.

With renewed vigor, she made her way to breakfast.

She entered the dining room to the sight of the rest of her family—and Mr. Collins—finding their seats at the table.

"So nice of you to grace us with your presence," her mother sniped.

A familiar voice echoed from the foyer. "Hello, Bennet family," Charlotte called.

"Just in time for breakfast," Lydia responded.

Charlotte popped her head in and caught sight of Elizabeth. She flashed her a commiserating smile and winked, then made her way over to the empty chair between Kitty and Mr. Collins.

Conversation quickly filled the air. As they waited for the food to emerge, Elizabeth kept a small part of her attention on Mr. Collins. She wasn't sure what she'd expected: embarrassment, dejection, avoidance? Instead, he was stiff and resentful, speaking mostly to Charlotte, whose civility in listening to him seemed almost as much a relief to him as to the rest of the party. She'd hoped that this whole affair might shorten his visit, at least. But his plan remained unchanged. He was meant to leave on Saturday, and till Saturday he intended to stay.

Jane shifted beside her, breaking into her thoughts. Elizabeth watched, out of the corner of her eye, the blue light of the unread waive on Jane's comcard flash to white as she read it under the table.

Jane grew still and straight-backed beside her. Elizabeth turned her full attention to her sister now, whose brows had drawn together as she studied the words on her screen. Elizabeth felt an anxiety coursing off her and she grabbed the hand Jane fisted in her lap, squeezing it encouragingly.

"After breakfast," Jane whispered.

Elizabeth nodded, and they said no more about it until they were able to excuse themselves from breakfast and escape to the back gardens.

As they walked to their favorite corner of the estate—a hidden grove near one of the smaller ponds, with a particularly comfortable outdoor seating area—Jane let Elizabeth read the waive.

To: JANE BENNET, LONGBOURN ESTATE, LANDINGS DISTRICT, HEOROS

From: CAROLINE BINGLEY, NETHERFIELD STARCRUISER, LONDINIUM EXPRESS ROUTE 7

Subject: CHANGE OF PLANS

My dear friend,

I can't pretend to regret anything I'm leaving behind in Heoros except for your company. We must lessen the pain of our separation with a very frequent and unreserved correspondence. I depend on you for that.

When we left yesterday, my brother imagined that the business which took him to Londinium might be concluded in only a few days. Knowing Charles, I'm certain that once in the city, he'll be in no hurry to leave it. Many of our acquaintances are already there for the winter. I wish I could hear that you, my dearest friend, had any intention of being part of that crowd, but it's a moonshot, I know. I sincerely hope your winter holiday on Heoros is filled with the bounty of happiness which the season brings.

While we're all eager to see our Londinium friends again, it's nothing compared to Mr. Darcy's impatience to see his sister. To be honest, *I'm* just as eager to meet her again. I really don't think Georgiana Darcy has an equal in beauty, elegance, or accomplishments. Louisa and I entertain the hope of her one day becoming our sister. My brother admires her greatly already and he'll have the frequent opportunity of seeing her regularly and in much more intimate settings. Her relations all wish the connection as much as we do. I know Charles is most capable of capturing any woman's heart. With all these circumstances in their favor, and nothing to prevent it, am I wrong in indulging the hope of an event which will guarantee the happiness of so many?

Yours ever,
Caroline Bingley

Jane perched on the arm of the little chair beside the chaise where Elizabeth read. Elizabeth had barely lowered the comcard before Jane said, "Did you read the part where she says they won't return to Heoros this winter? It's evident that he won't come back any time soon."

"It's only evident that Caroline means for him not to."

Jane sighed. "Is that any better? And isn't he an adult? It must be his own decision." She stood. "Is it not clear enough? It's obvious that Caroline neither expects nor wishes me to be her sister—that she's perfectly convinced of her brother's indifference—and that she means most kindly to put me on my guard. Can there be any other opinion on the matter?"

"Yes, there can, as mine is totally different." Lizzie said. "Will you hear it?"

"Of course," Jane said earnestly, moving to sit at the foot of the chaise.

"Caroline sees that her brother is in love with you, but wants him to marry elsewhere. She's hoping to keep him away from you and persuade you he doesn't care about you."

"Caroline wouldn't do that."

Elizabeth grabbed Jane's forearm and squeezed gently. "You must believe me. No one who has ever seen you two together can doubt Bingley's affection. Caroline certainly can't. She's not an idiot. Had she seen even half as much love in Mr. Darcy for herself, she'd already have her wedding planned. The truth is, we aren't rich or grand enough for them. But, Jane, even if he does admire Miss Darcy, that can't make him in any way less aware of *your* merit. It is not within her power to persuade him to be in love with her friend when he's clearly in love with you."

"I know you've never thought well of Caroline, and that clouds your view of her. She's incapable of willfully deceiving anyone. All I can hope in this case is that she's being deceived herself."

"You've created a happier idea than I can give you. Believe her to be deceived, by all means. You have now done right by her and can fret no longer."

Jane sighed heavily. "But can I be happy, even supposing the best, being with a man whose sisters and friends all wish him to marry elsewhere?"

"You must decide for yourself," Elizabeth said. "And if you find that the misery of not heeding his sisters' wishes weighs heavier than the happiness of being his wife, then by all means forget him."

"How can you talk this way?" Jane asked. "You know I'd be very sad that they didn't approve of me, but I wouldn't hesitate to marry him."

"I didn't think you would. That being the case, I can't consider your situation with much compassion."

Jane looked out at the water. Elizabeth watched a scrum of jewelbirds flitter in and out of the tall grass in the near field.

Softly, Jane said, "But if he doesn't return all winter, my choice won't be required. A thousand things could happen in six months."

Lizzie crinkled her nose and frowned. "This is nothing but a suggestion of Caroline's wishes. I don't for a moment believe that those wishes, no matter how well spoken, could influence a man so smitten with you."

Jane leaned on Elizabeth's shoulder, quiet in a moment of sisterly comfort. "Time will tell, I suppose," she sighed.

I'M SEIZING OPPORTUNITIES

I pride myself on being a practical woman. I'm happy to help Elizabeth in a bind, especially the one she found herself in recently with Mr. Collins. But I admit I haven't been entirely altruistic in this endeavor. The intent of my kindness extends further than she knows. I'm always glad to be useful to my friend, but in this case, my aim was to direct Mr. Collins's attentions toward myself. It felt as though my scheme (that sounds more sinister than I mean it) was working so well that I was sure nothing short of his impending departure could hinder my success.

I did him the injustice of miscalculating the independence of his character, which led him to escape the Longbourn House this morning and find me at home. I spotted him from an upper window as he walked toward the house, so I set out to meet him accidentally in the lane. I didn't expect the love and eloquence that awaited me there.

He confessed that he was anxious to avoid the notice of his hosts, certain if they saw him they'd know what his plan was. He was unwilling to have the attempt known until its success could also be shared. In this, he did me the injustice of underestimating my encouragement.

Everything was settled between us to our satisfaction with relative swiftness. As we made our way into the house, he earnestly entreated me to "name the day that will make me the happiest of men." I have no desire to trifle with his happiness, but as long as I've secured him and the establishment my marriage to him will provide, I'm in no hurry. The engagement is enough for now.

Mr. Collins is neither sensible nor agreeable. I have no doubt that his attachment to me is imaginary. It's better that way. I'll be well settled and taken care of, free to apply myself to my own interests without worry, and pleasantly preserved from want. At twenty-seven, and without much beauty to help me to it, I think I've positioned myself better than most. For my part, I'm satisfied. I'm getting what I want and taking charge of my future in the process.

My parents agree that he's a most eligible match. I'm ready to have more of a hand in my own fate, and this union holds incredible financial promise. Mother lost herself for a moment and started trying to calculate how many years Mr. Bennet has left to live. Father ought to have reminded her that she was talking about his friend, but he was too busy considering when we might be able to be presented in St. James City. Needless to say, they were overjoyed with the news.

The only point of all this that gives me any unease is the surprise this will cause my dear Eliza. I value her friendship beyond that of any other person. She won't understand. Her feelings might even be hurt by how things have gone. I'm resolved in my choice, however.

I've told Mr. Collins, on his return to Longbourn, to drop no hint to any of the Bennets of what has transpired. I want to tell my friend in person first. He promised himself to secrecy, though it will be a challenge for him, considering his fondness for talking.

Thankfully, he's leaving so early in the morning that he needs only to last through dinner.

CHAPTER
25

Longbourn House, Heoros,
First Moon of Londinium

The next morning, Elizabeth sat at the blissfully Collins-free breakfast table before the rest of her family came down, contemplating their guest's unusual reserve during dinner, when her comcard lit with an incoming waive. She glanced at it, seeing a message from Charlotte, who was on her way over.

She stood and waited for her friend at the door.

When Charlotte arrived, there was a guardedness to her features that put Elizabeth on edge.

"I have some news," Charlotte said, stiffly. "Can we speak alone somewhere?"

Elizabeth led her to the drawing room, knowing her family would be less likely to interrupt them there when they came down. They sat together on the couch, though Charlotte sat much more stiffly than Elizabeth.

"Lizzie, I wanted you to be the first to hear, and hear it from me," she said, her formality reminding Elizabeth slightly of Mr. Collins. "As you know, I have spent more time with you all since the . . . incident . . . with Mr. Collins. In truth, it was not entirely on your behalf. You see, Mr. Collins has asked me to marry him. And I've accepted."

The possibility of Mr. Collins fancying himself in love with her friend had occurred to Elizabeth within the past few days, but that Charlotte would encourage him seemed almost as unlikely as Elizabeth encouraging him herself. Her astonishment was so great that she couldn't stop herself from exclaiming, "Engaged to Mr. Collins! Charlotte. Impossible!"

For a moment, her friend looked confused and admonished, but she gained her composure quickly. "Why should you be surprised, Lizzie?" Charlotte asked calmly. "Do you think it so incredible that Mr. Collins would be able to gain any woman's good opinion, because he wasn't so happy to succeed with you?"

Elizabeth bit her cheek to stop from being unkind in her shock and disappointment. This was not a moment to let her emotions outweigh her friendship. She collected herself and, with a strong effort, assured Charlotte that she was happy for her.

"I understand what you're feeling," Charlotte said. "You're surprised. Of course you are. But when you've had time to think it over, I hope you'll understand what I've done. I'm not romantic. You know this. I never was. Considering Mr. Collins's character, connection, and situation in life, I'm convinced that my chance of happiness with him is as fair as any."

Elizabeth quietly answered, "Certainly," and after an awkward pause she asked if Charlotte would like to stay for breakfast.

Her friend declined politely, gave her a swift parting hug, and left Elizabeth to reflect on what she'd heard.

Elizabeth joined her now-awake family at the table, but spent the majority of breakfast in quiet contemplation. It was a long time before she became at all reconciled to the idea of such an unsuitable match. The strangeness of Mr. Collins making two offers of marriage within three days was nothing in comparison to his actually being accepted. She'd always known that Charlotte's opinion on marriage had differed from her own, but she didn't think it was possible that, when the time came, her friend would sacrifice happiness for worldly advantage. Her dear Charlotte, the wife of Mr. Collins—it was such a humiliating picture. The pain of seeing a friend sink in her esteem was heightened by the distressing conviction that it was impossible for that friend to be even tolerably happy with the life she'd chosen.

Before her mother or sisters could comment on her unusual silence—which they seemed poised to do—she heard her father open the door and Sir William Lucas's voice ringing out in greeting.

Footsteps fell and a moment later the two men entered.

"Hello, Bennets," Sir William boomed jovially. "I've come to share the news."

Elizabeth tensed.

"We'll soon take our friendship to new levels as family—distantly," he went on. "Charlotte is engaged. Mr. Collins has proposed, and we're delighted to make such a connection to our dearest friends."

Elizabeth, unsurprised by this news, was able to focus instead on the reactions of her family. Her mother, with more perseverance than politeness, protested that he must be mistaken.

Lydia, ever unguarded in her reactions, and lacking tact, exclaimed, "Brightest stars!—Sir William, how can you tell such a story? Don't you know Mr. Collins wants to marry Lizzie?"

Unfazed by Lydia's impertinence, Sir William replied, "I don't know of any feelings about Lizzie, but I do know that he stood in my reading room and professed his devotion and intentions for Charlotte just yesterday."

Elizabeth, feeling that it was important now to relieve him from this unpleasant situation, said, "Charlotte came by earlier and told me herself."

Her mother and sisters began to interject, but she talked over them. "Sir William, please accept our congratulations. We're very happy for Charlotte."

"Indeed," Jane added quickly. "We wish her all the joy in the universe. I'm sure she'll thrive on the Kent."

"And she'll be in such illustrious company as Lady Catherine," Elizabeth noted.

"If there's anything we know of Mr. Collins, it's that he's a loyal man and . . . a passionate speaker," Jane offered.

Sir William accepted their compliments with thanks, and soon took his leave.

A great exhalation of breath followed the door closing. Her mother inhaled again before finding her voice. "This is all some elaborate joke. Mr. Collins has been taken in, surely. They can never be happy together. It's not too late for Charlotte to break it off." She huffed, then her attention, which hadn't found purchase, suddenly shifted to Elizabeth. "You're the reason this situation with Mr. Collins has become such a mess. Had you just listened to me, we wouldn't be losing our home to that *girl*. I'm constantly taken for granted by you all." She looked at Mr. Bennet. "Except you, dear."

Her father appeared far more tranquil. When his wife had finally settled into a disgruntled silence, he said, "This gratifies me."

"How could it, Papa?" Kitty protested.

"It's nice to discover that Charlotte Lucas—a girl I used to think tolerably sensible—is more foolish than any of you."

"I must confess, I'm surprised by the match," Jane said. "But if it makes our dear friend happy, then that's all that matters. She deserves happiness."

Kitty and Lydia devolved into chattering about their thoughts on wedding attire and their eagerness to spread the news on the Meryton as soon as possible.

Mrs. Bennet suddenly scoffed. Elizabeth looked to see her glaring at her comcard.

Lydia, happy to peer over her mother's shoulder and read her screen, laughed loudly. "Lady Lucas is enjoying this," she said with a giggle. "'We are overjoyed with the news,'" she read in a singsong voice.

"So insensitive," Mrs. Bennet sniped, her lips curled in a sour smile. "She *knows* this means they'll take our home out from under us, and she's rubbing salt in our wounds with her excitement. *I'll* be *overjoyed* never to speak to her again."

VOICE JOURNAL

COM TAG: LIZZIELOVESSPACE—E. BENNET
PERSONAL JOURNAL / COMCARD ID: HC-3095.D2.EB
TIMESTAMP: 4.11-20:39:12.LS / LOCATION: HEOROS

(4.11-20:39:12.LS) TRANSCRIPTION:

I wish there weren't this tension between us now. We've silently agreed not to speak of the engagement to one another. I hate to admit this, but I don't see how we can ever hope to share the confidences we once did. She didn't exactly break my trust, and yet my sense of trust in her is damaged. I'm so disappointed. It feels almost as if I've lost a friend. If I could be persuaded that she had any actual regard for him, I'd only think worse of her intelligence than I do now of her heart. I can't defend her. Great eclipse! I can't, for the sake of one person, change the meaning of principle and integrity—nor attempt to persuade anyone that selfishness is prudence, and disregard of danger is security for happiness. My only solace is that I could never lose Jane in the same way. The foundations of my belief in her could never be shaken. She's exactly the person I know her to be.

(5.11-14:17:52.LS) TRANSCRIPTION:

My unsettled . . . ness—that's not a word—over Charlotte has become secondary to my unease—that's the word— for Jane. I grow more anxious over her situation with Mr. Bingley with each passing day. He's been gone a week now and has said nothing to her of his return. He's barely saying anything to her at all. He told her initially that he had some business to take care of in Londinium, but in so casual a way that there was little doubt of his return. I've insisted that there's no way he knows about the waive Caroline sent, but I can see Jane's resolve crack- ing. Bingley used to send her a waive every night, but now it's a

■ ■ ■

moonshot whether she'll hear anything from him at all. I'd dust it up to him being busy, except that Caroline has already filled Jane's head with the idea that he's moved on.

Curse Caroline Bingley for planting those seeds of doubt.

(7.11-18:39:17.LS) TRANSCRIPTION:

A rumor reached us on the Meryton. People are saying that the groundskeeping crew for Netherfield Landing has been alerted of a winter's-long absence of the ship. Mama snapped at three different people who brought it up—said it was a scandalous falsehood. I'd have liked to do the same, so for once I'm glad she holds her composure together so poorly. Even still, I must admit this isn't a good sign. I'm starting to worry—not that Bingley is indifferent, I've never suspected that—but that his sisters are meddling to keep him away. Unwilling as I am to entertain the idea of them being so callous, and him being so unstable a companion, I can't prevent the thought occurring. The combined efforts of his sisters, who care nothing for Jane's happiness, and the overpowering nature of his friend (compounded by the multitude of amusements to be found on Londinium—especially in Cloudtop) might be too much for the strength of Bingley's attachment. I hope I'm wrong. But we'll see.

CHAPTER
26

Longbourn House, Heoros,
First Moon of Londinium

When Jane finally received a reply from Caroline Bingley, the waive put an end to all her doubt. The very first sentence assured her that the party was all settled on Londinium for the winter, and the waive concluded with her brother's regret at not having had time to say proper goodbyes before he left the moon.

Hope was entirely over; and when Jane could focus on the rest of the waive, she found little, except the warm affections of a friend, that could give her any comfort. Most of the waive was filled with praise of Miss Darcy, whom Caroline had always adored. She wrote at length of her beauty and talents, and boasted of their growing closeness, hinting once again at the hopes she had for her brother, and the success she felt was imminent in that regard. She wrote with great pleasure of her brother staying at Mr. Darcy's house and mentioned something about plans for the restoration of an old table from Dyberion.

The first chance Jane got, she intercepted Elizabeth in her usual rainy day escape to the hangar of the Tailwynd, and shared the waive with her. She wasn't sure what she hoped to hear by doing so.

Lizzie read in silent indignation, her face shifting from concern to resentment. After a moment she said, "I'll say my piece, if you're willing to hear it?"

Jane nodded her acceptance.

Lizzie took a deep breath, held it for a moment, and then began. "I don't believe that Bingley is partial to Miss Darcy. Whatever's going on, his feelings for you couldn't have changed so quickly. I've always liked him, but I must admit that I can't think any longer without anger—even contempt—of his malleable temperament."

Jane bristled at this, but didn't interrupt.

"Had his own happiness been the only sacrifice to the whims of his friends, then he could do with it as he pleases. But your happiness is involved, and he knows that. It isn't as if he can't just send you a waive and explain himself."

Jane had held her tongue on that particular subject, not for any reason other than her fear of speaking it into existence. He *hadn't* reached out to her. But if she held on to hope, perhaps he still would. She watched the rain fall like a curtain out the hangar doors. "If only Mama had better control of herself. She has no idea of the pain she causes me with her constant complaints about him." She took a breath and gathered herself. "But I won't let this drag me down. It can't last long. He'll be forgotten and we'll be as we were before."

Lizzie merely looked up, doubt in her eyes, and said nothing.

Jane felt heat rise in her cheeks and squeezed her comcard tighter in her hands. "You doubt me," she said, more impassioned than she expected herself to be. "You shouldn't. He'll live in my memory as the friendliest man of my acquaintance, but that's all we were. Acquaintances. Count our stars lucky, I've not been hurt *that* badly. A little time is all it'll take and I'll be better than ever."

She knew full well that she was talking herself into this, but it was necessary. "I have this to comfort me: that it was a misjudgment of my own and that it has done no harm to anyone but myself."

"My dearest, sweetest Jane," Lizzie exclaimed, setting aside her notes and crossing the distance between them before pulling her into a much-needed hug. "You're purer than aurum. Your disinterest is commendable. I don't know what to say to you."

Jane huffed a laugh as her sister pulled away. "You're far kinder and more loving than anyone gives you credit for."

"Stall the engines," Lizzie said, shaking her head. "This isn't fair. *You* wish to think everyone respectable, and you're hurt if I speak poorly of anyone. *I* only want to think *you* perfect—though you try not to let me. There are very few people whom I really love, and still fewer of whom I think well. You are one of the good ones. The more I see of the worlds, the more I'm dissatisfied by the inconsistency of the human character. I'm far from blaming any part of Mr. Bingley's conduct to design. But even without scheming to do wrong, or to make others unhappy, there can be error and even misery. Thoughtlessness, lack of attention to other people's feelings, and no resolve . . . if I go on, I'll displease you by saying what I think of people you hold in esteem. Stop me while you can."

Jane deflated. "You still believe his sisters are influencing him?"

"Absolutely. His friend, too."

"I can't believe it. Why would they try to influence him? They can only want happiness for him, and if he *is* attached to me, no other woman could secure it."

"They may wish things for him besides happiness," Lizzie suggested. "Perhaps increasing his wealth and consequence is more important."

Jane gestured weakly at her comcard. "Very clearly, they do wish him to choose Miss Darcy. But this may be from better feelings than what you're supposing. Stars around us . . . don't distress me with that idea. I'm not ashamed of having been mistaken—or at least, it's nothing in comparison to what I'd feel in believing such things of him or his sisters. Let me take it in the best light—in a way I can understand it."

"You could always consider it in the light our father saw it in," Lizzie said, a small smirk creeping onto her lips.

Jane laughed despite herself. He'd found them collecting jewelbird shells in the garden before the rain had come.

"Well, my dear," he'd said, "you've been crossed in love. I congratulate you. A girl likes to be star-crossed now and then." He'd then turned to Lizzie and mock-whispered, "When is it your turn? You can't bear being outdone by Jane for long. Now's the time. There are plenty of officers on the Meryton to disappoint all the young ladies on this moon. Let Wickham be your man. He's a pleasant fellow, and would jilt you creditably."

Lizzie's smirk morphed into the smile she'd given her father then. "Wickham's company has been helpful in staving off some of the sting of Bingley's absence."

Jane nodded. He was certainly good company. But more so for Lizzie than herself.

"And useful, too, in learning more of Mr. Darcy," Lizzie added.

"It's interesting," Jane noted, "now that Mr. Darcy has gone, just how well known the particulars of Mr. Wickham's claims are in our social circles."

"Yes, everyone is so pleased to insist that they've always disliked Mr. Darcy. Several have condemned him as the worst man in all the lunar system."

"That seems egregious. Especially since we never heard Mr. Darcy's side."

"Oh, I heard enough from him at the ball. It feels rather well deserved."

"Perhaps," Jane said, her thoughts trailing. If Mr. Darcy was truly capable of what Mr. Wickham had claimed, then could she entertain the idea that her sister might have a better read on this situation with Bingley than Jane thought? No. She would think better of Mr. Darcy than that, and in turn, could think better of Mr. Bingley.

ANNOUNCEMENTS

Flower Notes

Dear Eliza —

Thank you for agreeing to come visit with Maria and my father in March. The wedding was made truly beautiful by its surroundings. The parks here on the station rival any I've seen on land. I'm sorry you couldn't be there.

Our home is already nicely furnished, thanks no doubt to the gracious Lady Catherine. I feel very much in comfort already. It's such a pleasure to be the one in charge of my home. I have a lovely spot... well, I'll show it to you when you visit.

For now, I must go. We're expected at Rosings. I look forward to hearing from you very soon.

— Charlotte

Nebula Blooms

Star Flower

Solar Protea

Blue Tweedia

Coral Peony

CHAPTER
27

Longbourn House, Heoros,
First Moon of Londinium

Following the wedding of Mr. Collins and her closest friend, Elizabeth was ready for a distraction, and
exceedingly grateful for the arrival of her aunt and uncle
Gardiner for their annual winter visit. Edward Gardiner,
her mother's brother, was a sensible gentleman who was
far better behaved—by nature as well as education—than
either of his sisters. Elizabeth thought ruefully that the
Netherfield ladies would have had difficulty believing that
a man who lived by trade, within view of his own ware-
houses, could have been so well-bred and agreeable. His
wife, Mariane, was a favorite of all the Bennet sisters, being
several years younger than their mother or Aunt Phillips.
There was a particular regard between her and the eldest

two sisters, as the girls had often stayed with her on Londinium over the years.

Aunt Gardiner's first order of business was to distribute presents and describe, to Lydia's great delight, the newest fashions seen around Cloudtop and below. For Kitty, they brought pots with automated watering capabilities. Lydia, inspired by her aunt's descriptions of various new garments, screeched with joy upon receiving several bolts of high-end fabric. Mary was given a recording device that would allow her to layer her voice on top of music. While she was far more reserved that her younger sisters, her manner grew warmer in her quiet happiness. Lizzie was stunned momentarily by the 1,000-piece working model kit of a SheerWing fighter she pulled from the gift box, and was so involved in reading the instructions that she completely missed what Jane had opened. She told herself to remember to ask later. But as the final gifts were given out, they were drawn into Mrs. Bennet's list of grievances featuring the many ways her family had been ill-used since last they were together.

"Two girls on the verge of marriage, and yet here we still are with five at home," Mrs. Bennet complained. "I don't blame Jane. She would've gotten Mr. Bingley if she could. But Lizzie," her mother flashed a glare in her direction. "It's very hard to think that she could be married to Mr. Collins by now, had it not been for her stubbornness. He made her an offer in this very room, and she refused him!"

Elizabeth shrugged, unaffected. Her aunt made eye contact with her and winked, letting her mother continue uninterrupted.

When she and Elizabeth eventually found themselves alone at the table, the SheerWing pieces spread across its surface, her aunt orbited the subject again. "It seems like Jane had a desirable match. I'm sorry it went off course. But these things happen. A young man like Mr. Bingley so easily falls in love with a pretty girl for a few weeks, and when accident separates them, so easily forgets her."

Elizabeth sighed. "She doesn't suffer by accident. Friends interfering to persuade a young man to quit thinking of a girl whom he was violently in love with a few days before does not often happen."

Aunt Mariane picked up one of the little pieces and studied it absently. "*Violently in love* seems to be used so often. It's so doubtful and indefinite, applied as quickly to feelings that arise from half an hour's acquaintance as to real, strong attachment. So, tell me . . . *how* violent was Mr. Bingley's love?"

"Every time they met, it was more decided and remarkable. She drew him in like gravity. At his own ball, he offended two or three young ladies by not asking them to dance. I spoke with him twice that night without getting an answer. He was too busy watching Jane. Could there be more obvious symptoms? Isn't general incivility the very essence of love?"

Her aunt laughed. "Oh, stars, yes." She shook her head. "If that's the kind of love he was feeling, then poor Jane. I'm sorry for her. With her disposition, she might not get over it immediately. It would've been better had it happened to *you*. You'd have laughed yourself out of it sooner." She was thoughtful for a moment, and then, "Do you think she'd be willing to go back with us? A change of world might be useful. A little relief from home, if nothing else."

Elizabeth was very pleased by this idea. "I'm sure she would be."

"I hope her decision won't be influenced by Mr. Bingley's presence there. We live in such different parts of the capital, all our connections are so different, and you know we go out so little that it's quite improbable they'd meet unless he specifically comes to see her."

"And *that* is impossible, since he's now squarely under the gravitational pull of his friend. Mr. Darcy wouldn't suffer him to visit Jane in Lowland. It's unthinkable. Mr. Darcy may have *heard* of such a place as Gracechurch Street, but he'd hardly deign to sully himself in such a place, and Mr. Bingley never goes anywhere without his blessing."

"All the better. I hope they won't meet at all, then. But, does Jane not correspond with his sister still? *She* couldn't help but visit, surely?"

Elizabeth relinquished the pieces of the SheerWing still in her hands. "Caroline will drop their friendship entirely."

In spite of the certainty Elizabeth had affected to make this point, and her thoughts on Bingley being actually withheld from seeing Jane, she felt convinced that the matter wasn't entirely hopeless. It was possible—and sometimes she thought it probable—that his affection might be renewed, and the influence of his friends successfully held at bay, by the more natural influence of Jane's attractions.

Jane accepted their aunt's invitation as readily as Elizabeth anticipated. She even alluded to a hope that, since Caroline mentioned a change of residence during their stay on Londinium, she might occasionally spend a morning with her without danger of seeing him.

The Gardiners stayed a week at Longbourn. Between visits from the Phillipses, the Lucases, and the officers, there wasn't a day without the company of someone. Her mother had planned so many activities for her brother and sister-in-law that they didn't once sit down to a family dinner. When they entertained at home, some of the officers always made up part of the party. Mr. Wickham was sure to be among them.

He was the most welcome distraction for Elizabeth, as their conversations often turned to one of two animating subjects. The first, which she could talk about for hours on end, was his experience with the various ships she had no access to, being primarily used for the Reserves. The second, of course, was Mr. Darcy. In both cases, time seemed to pass faster when they were able to converse. Even the effervescent and lively Lydia could not pull Mr. Wickham's attention from Elizabeth for long.

Her aunt seemed to observe her more closely whenever Wickham was around, but she was usually too engaged in what he was saying to do more than absently note it. Nothing was ever brought up in conversation during their stay, so Elizabeth dusted it up to being mild curiosity on her aunt's part, until she received a waive the day they left.

LONDINIUM SAT[SYS

Communications Log—System Storage 30 Days [Planetary]

[MarianeGardiner] 1.1-10:32:45.LS

I'm sorry to do this over waive, but I feel like I need to say something about Mr. Wickham. You're too sensible to fall in love merely because you're warned against it.

[LizzieLovesSpace] 1.1-10:34:57.LS

The highest of compliments, my dear aunt!

[MarianeGardiner] 1.1-10:37:41.LS

It's nothing but the truth, darling niece. Be on your guard. Don't put yourselves in a position that neither of you can come back from. I have nothing against him. He's very interesting, but circumstances as they are, you would be ill-suited to a life with him. I care about your happiness, and with him it would suffer. For your own sake, don't let your feelings run away from you. You have sense and your family expects you to use it.

[LizzieLovesSpace] 1.1-10:40:12.LS

Depend on it, Aunt Mari. He won't fall in love with me if I can prevent it.

[MarianeGardiner] 1.1-10:42:07.LS

Elizabeth. We are being serious.

[LizzieLovesSpace] 1.1-10:47:29.LS

I know. Mr. Wickham is very enjoyable to be around, but I'm definitely not in love with him. It's best that he doesn't get too attached to me. I can see the imprudence of it. I'd be very sorry to make any of you unhappy. But we see every day that when it comes to lovers, they seldom let fortune—or lack of fortune—hold them back from entering into engagements. How can I promise to be wiser than so many of my fellow creatures if I'm tempted? And how do I even really know if it's wise to resist? I can promise you this: Not to be in a hurry. I won't hurry to believe I'm the sole object of his attentions. When I'm in his company, I won't be wishing. In so many words . . . I'll do my best.

[MarianeGardiner] 1.1-10:53:16.LS

Fair enough. Though perhaps you would do well to discourage him from coming over so often.

[LizzieLovesSpace] 1.1-10:55:28.LS

True. Don't imagine he's usually over this much. You know Mama's incessant need to offer company when you're here.

[MarianeGardiner] 1.1-10:57:08.LS

Oh, yes. Not a dull moment on her watch!

[LizzieLovesSpace] 1.1-11:01:13.LS

But truly, I'll try to do what I think is wisest, when it comes to Mr. Wickham. I appreciate you looking out for me.

[MarianeGardiner] 1.1-11:04:59.LS

Always, my darling.

. . . END COM . . .

CHAPTER
28

Longbourn House, Heoros, First Moon of Londinium

Elizabeth had been getting updates from her sister on Londinium for nearly a month. Despite her wish for Jane to simply seek out Mr. Bingley directly, Jane was determined to trust Caroline. She had at least, while with her aunt on business in Cloudtop early on, gone to visit Caroline, rather than wait for her to come to Lowland.

The waive Elizabeth had received after this visit wasn't promising. Jane was led to believe that Caroline hadn't had any word of Jane being in town, and that Bingley was too busy with Mr. Darcy to visit anyone. There was some mention of trouble with Bingley's comcard, which gave Jane hope that his period of silence would end soon. But nothing Jane relayed of Caroline's information and demeanor gave

Elizabeth any hope. It was clear to her that the only way Mr. Bingley would know that Jane was on Londinium would be by accident.

Every week that followed without word or visit, Elizabeth's certainty of the situation grew, and Jane's faith in Caroline's intentions waned.

To: Elizabeth Bennet, Longbourn Estate, Landings District, Heoros

From: Jane Bennet, St. James City, Lowland District, Londinium

Subject: Don't Gloat

Lizzie,

I trust you will rein in your sense of triumph, but I can now admit that you were right. Caroline deceived me. She was never my friend. But don't think me stubborn to insist that, considering her behavior, my confidence in her was as natural as your suspicion. If the same circumstances happened again, I'm sure I'd be deceived again.

I visited her three weeks ago, and she returned the visit yesterday. She didn't send any word in the meantime. When she showed up, it was so clearly from obligation rather than enjoyment. Her apology for not coming sooner had about as much genuine emotion as a steel wall. When she left, I knew that was the end of our friendship (or whatever it was). I pity her, though. She must know how wrong it was to act the way she did. Even if it was all for her brother. But that's her burden to bear.

I must also admit that I'm doubting Bingley now as well. If he had cared at all about me, he would've reached out or come to visit me by now. He knows of my being planet-side, I'm certain. Caroline let something slip that left little doubt of that. And yet, I can't help feeling, based on how she was talking, that she wanted to persuade herself that her brother preferred Miss Darcy. If I weren't afraid of judging harshly,

I'd almost be tempted to say that there's a strong appearance of duplicity in all this.

But I'll endeavor to banish every painful thought, and think only of what will make me happy. The Gardiners' kindness is invaluable, and I have your loving and protective attentions, as always.

Stars! I made this all about myself. Forgive me. I'm so glad you've heard such pleasant accounts from Charlotte. I know you've been feeling rather unsettled about her decision. But I'm glad you agreed to visit her with her father and sister. I have no doubt you'll enjoy the time there. It'll be good for you both, I think.

With love and stardust,
Jane

P.S. Caroline said something about Bingley never returning to Netherfield Landing again. Of relinquishing his hold on the land . . . but not with any certainty. We'd better not mention that to Mama.

This waive saddened Elizabeth at first, but the consolation was knowing Jane would no longer be fooled—by Caroline at least. Whatever expectations she'd had of Bingley were shattered now. The more she thought of him simply winking out of Jane's life like a distant star, with not a word or effort, the worse she thought of him. She began hoping he *would* marry Mr. Darcy's sister. By Wickham's account, she'd make him seriously regret what he'd thrown away.

Thoughts of Wickham brought to mind her latest conversation with Aunt Mari. Wickham's partiality for Elizabeth had subsided since her aunt's warning. His attention had turned to someone else. Miss King was a young woman whose greatest charm was her sudden acquisition of ten thousand aurum. Elizabeth watched it happen without pain. Her heart was safe. It seemed she had never been much in love. Had she been, she'd detest his very name and wish him lost to the ether. But she couldn't even think badly of Miss King.

The lady was quite young, and while Elizabeth didn't begrudge Wickham his wish for the comfort and lifestyle that kind of fortune could bring, she felt it was a deeply unserious attachment on his part. Even more proof, she thought, that there could be no love tangled in this.

In the end, her youngest sisters had taken his defection more to heart than she had, and she was forced to admit that perhaps her thoughts on love weren't so wholly separated from Charlotte's as she'd originally thought. She'd told her aunt that Kitty and Lydia were too young to be open to the thought that handsome men were just as in want of something to live on as the plain. In saying this, Elizabeth was aware that she was not judging Wickham to the same standard that she had judged Charlotte for similar motives. But she would have plenty of time to break down and examine her prejudices before she met with Charlotte again.

(remind the wife: groundskeeper off-moon third week of Jan through second week of Feb)

>> JANUARY

There's been little to occupy the household this month outside of the news that Mr. Wickham has mishandled the jilting of my dearest Lizzie so extraordinarily that she has not once wandered about the house in despondency. The fool has gone after a girl not yet Mary's age, with a shiny new fortune. Upon reflection, probably best for everyone not to have him around. The house is full enough. The cold of winter has kept the girls inside or in the void. I like to remind them that they ought to stay home, as space is in fact colder than Heorosian winters, whenever the opportunity arises. Their increasingly dramatic eye rolls upon receiving this information are the fuel that keeps me going as a father.

>> FEBRUARY

More of the same. I'm not eager to review our expenses at the end of this winter. Jane has always been responsible about spending, and her aunt and uncle are taking care of most of her needs while she's on Londinium, but I want her to enjoy herself. And Lizzie will be traveling to visit Charlotte next month, so the cost of the trip is coming now. Still, the number of times we've sent the Tailwynd to and from the Meryton will surely deplete our funds before Lizzie has even left, if the younger girls keep this up. Then again, the house has been wonderfully quiet, so perhaps it's worth it. I'm really making a dent in my library.

>> MARCH

Lizzie is on her journey to the Kent. I believe she's been long enough away from her friend that she misses her more now than she judges her. I'm sure the memory of how grating that friend's new husband is has lost its sharp edges. I shall hope for her sake that their first stop, and the chance to visit her older sister while enjoying the sights of Cloudtop, will keep her in good spirits when she does finally face the man again. If not, she can rest easier, at least, knowing that he won't renew his proposals to her. I miss her already.

CHAPTER
29

St. James City, Londinium

Elizabeth, Sir William, and Maria Lucas arrived in Londinium in time to join Jane and the Gardiners in a visit to Cloudtop. They spent the early evening eating and talking in a low-gravity restaurant while the children bounced and floated in the wide-open garden area at its center.

Elizabeth made sure to sit next to Aunt Mari during dinner. She wanted to hear from someone other than her sister about how Jane's time had been on Londinium.

"She's kept her spirits up, mostly. But there have been periods of dejection," her aunt said.

This was disappointing, but not unsurprising.

"I don't expect it will last much longer. From what I can tell, it seems Jane has truly broken off her friendship with the sister."

"Good."

"Now to you, Lizzie. I'm glad to hear you're taking Mr. Wickham's desertion so well."

Elizabeth huffed a laugh. "I believe I may have let my love of ships and flight color my regard for him. He was very useful for all kinds of information," she said, thinking of Mr. Darcy a moment. "And he was easy conversation. I have no doubt, even if Miss King doesn't care for ships, she will enjoy his attentions as much as I did."

"What kind of girl is Miss King? I'd hate to think Wickham is only in it for the aurum."

"Is there a difference, when it comes to marriage?" Elizabeth wondered. "Where does discretion end and avarice begin? This winter you were afraid of the imprudence of our match. Now, as he's showing interest in a girl with ten thousand aurum, you think he's greedy?"

"Tell me what sort of girl she is, and I can tell you what I think."

"She's a good sort, as far as I know. A little young for anything serious, in my opinion. But I don't know what she envisions for her future. To each their own."

"But he didn't pay any attention to her until she gained a fortune?" Her aunt grimaced slightly as Elizabeth nodded. "It feels a bit . . . indelicate . . . to be showing her so much attention so soon after her inheritance."

Elizabeth glanced at her cousins, distracted momentarily as one tossed another in the air, the low gravity costing him no effort, the little girl's hair flowing like flames around her face as she drifted feather-like back down to his arms. Elizabeth shook her mind into focus again. "Some people are in distressing enough situations not to have the luxury of decorum. If she doesn't have an issue with it, I don't see why we should."

"I'd just be sorry to think poorly of a young man who lived so long on Dyberion. You know the fond memories and good connections I have there."

"Well, *I've* got a very poor opinion of men from Dyberion. Their intimate friends from Kaels aren't much better. I'm sick of them all. Thank the stars I'm going somewhere tomorrow where I'll find a man who doesn't have a single agreeable quality—nor manner or sense to recommend him. Stupid men are the only ones worth knowing, after all."

"Careful, Lizzie. That savors strongly of disappointment."

Elizabeth flashed a wry smile, and then the children returned to the table, effectively ending their conversation.

Before the night was out, her aunt and uncle invited her to accompany them on a vacation they were planning for the summer. "We haven't determined how far we'll go," her aunt said, "but, perhaps, to Kaels."

Nothing could've been more agreeable to Elizabeth. She accepted readily and gratefully. Perhaps it was the timing of a happy evening spent among loved ones, but she was almost giddy with the thought of it. "Galaxies around us!—that sounds fun!" she exclaimed. "What are men to moons and planets? What wonders we'll see!"

KOS

KENT ORBITAL STATION

PLACES OF NOTE

1 Hanging Gardens
2 Shopping District
3 Activity Center
4 Restaurant Row
5 Zero Gravity Chaml

COMMAND CENTER

OBSERVATORY

UPPER DECKS

ROSINGS

UPPER RING HALL
HUNSFORD

RING HALL

CREW APARTMENTS
PROCESSING PLANTS
ENGINES

LOWER DOCKS

CHAPTER
30

Kent Orbital Station,
Londinium Orbit, Long Route 7

Elizabeth was in high spirits for the whole of the journey to Kent Orbital Station. When the ship docked on the Kent, her mind turned at once to the Collinses' home, eager to see it in person. Their luggage—Sir Williams's somehow taking up more than either Elizabeth's or Maria's—was loaded onto a small motorized cart that trailed behind them through the corridors like an overeager pet. Every turn held the expectation of a view, but they'd docked in the deep interior, and it was nothing but artificial light and vaguely nature-colored halls until, as they passed the mark of half an hour, they were met, at last, by the wide ascent to Rosings Level.

The scent of soil and vegetation reached them first, before the walls peeled away, revealing a massive oval, cavern-like atrium with a giant expanse of windows to the far left—black with the lightlessness of space. Rather than feeling oppressive, however, it was a beautiful contrast to the acres of vibrant color that comprised Rosings Park.

They'd entered at roughly a story above the actual Rosings Level on an oversized balcony, and looked out across the immense grounds, more than half of which was garden. On the window side of the oval's length, amid the foliage and fields far in the distance, she spotted what could only be Rosings itself, a large estate peeking out from beneath a swath of trees, alone on a hill. On the right, a shorter distance away from where they'd entered, was what appeared to be a small village, its structures kept low to preserve the sense of open sky.

"It looks as if they built an entire ship around a very small planet," Sir William remarked.

Elizabeth quietly agreed.

It was at the meeting point of the village and Rosings Park, nestled against the opposite wall from the balcony, that they spotted the parsonage. "Oh! There's Lotte!" Maria exclaimed, pointing at Charlotte, who waved at them from the doorway.

As they approached, Elizabeth could trick herself into envisioning the home on land, as long as she didn't peer too closely at the wall of the station behind it. The house looked as if it had been plucked from the Heorosian countryside, complete with a fence, small lawn, and gardens.

The Collinses met their party at the gate, behind which a short path led to the house itself.

Whatever lingering uncertainty the two had toward each other before this moment evaporated as Charlotte flung her arms around Elizabeth and squeezed her tightly in welcome. "I'm so glad to see you again, Lizzie," she said, before pulling herself back and embracing her sister and father in turn.

Mr. Collins, it was clear, had yet to be altered by his marriage—his manner the same as it ever was. He greeted Elizabeth with formal civility, asking after all her family, and delaying their entrance into the house only long enough to comment on the walkway, the front garden, and the general appeal of the house. "It's a true sign of her ladyship's grace that we're afforded such a luxurious property upon a ship like this."

"Indeed. We're very grateful," Charlotte said, as she led them toward the door.

"Are you hungry?" Mr. Collins asked. "Thirsty?" He began to describe the options in excessive detail.

Charlotte seemed to have found a rhythm with him. She picked up right where he left off—though it may not have actually been where he was intending to stop. "There's also Gleam, and a local red wine called Rosings Glade. It's rather potent," she added with a grin. "And Maria, we have another local favorite I think you'll enjoy. A sparkling citrus Fiore."

"Hints of spices and florals make it truly one of a kind." Mr. Collins said. "Our systems are built for production of a great deal of specially grown flora for the entire satellite system."

"Certain plants grow beautifully when gravity is less of a factor," Charlotte concluded.

Elizabeth could only look at her friend in wonder. How could she be so cheerful with such a companion? As Mr. Collins waxed eloquent about the parsonage, from the high-speed comfield capability to the elegantly designed custom furniture, Elizabeth searched her friend's reactions. Whenever he said anything that his wife might be ashamed of—which was often—Elizabeth would quickly glance at Charlotte. Once in a while, she'd make out the faintest blush, but in general Charlotte seemed wisely not to hear him.

They spent the next hour on a tour of the gardens of and connected to the parsonage. "Gardening is a very respectable pleasure,"

Charlotte said. "It's certainly something I encourage my husband to spend his time on when he can spare it."

Mr. Collins led them methodically along every path, pointing out every view with a minuteness that left beauty entirely behind. He went so far as to give details about all the homes with—and the publicly tended sections of—gardens in the Hunsford Sector, the village to the ship's stern. But of all the views his particular garden could boast, none compared to the prospect of Rosings, with its bank of windows bordering half the sector. The Rosings Estate was designed to appear as a handsome historical Londinium building, well situated on cleverly engineered rising ground.

When the tour had ended and they eventually found themselves at the dinner table, Mr. Collins said, "Miss Elizabeth, you'll have the honor of seeing Lady Catherine de Bourgh this coming Sunday at Gathering, and I'm sure it goes without saying that you'll be delighted with her. I barely hesitate in saying that she'll include you and Maria in every invitation she honors us with during your stay. Her behavior to my dear Charlotte is charming. We dine at Rosings twice every week and are never allowed to walk home. Her lady-ship's personal Faeton glider is ordered for us regularly. I *should* say, one of her Faetons, as she's designated several specifically for her use."

"Lady Catherine is a most respectable woman," added Charlotte. "And a most attentive neighbor."

"Very true, my dear, that's exactly what I say. She's the sort of woman one can't regard with too much deference."

When the day ended, Elizabeth, in the quiet solitude of her room, reflected on her friend's situation: the degree of content-ment, her way of guiding and composure in bearing her husband. She could acknowledge, looking back on the day, that it was all done quite well. She could also anticipate much of the way her visit would pass: the ease and quietness of their usual company with one another, the vexations of Mr. Collins's inevitable interruptions, and the intriguing possibilities of their visits to Rosings. She was looking forward to the adventure of it all.

The following day, they were invited to visit Rosings for dinner. The temperature and lighting on Rosings Level were set to simulate a mild spring evening, and they had a pleasant half-mile walk across the park, moving ever closer to the windows. Though she appreciated the unique beauty of the park with the backdrop of Londinium floating in the void, she wasn't as in awe as Mr. Collins expected. She was only slightly affected by his detailing of the estate's façade, and his relation of what the station and its peculiar interior additions originally cost the de Bourghs.

The building was rich, polished stone, a vivid contrast to the metal walls of the station. While it was made of natural lunar components, there was still something engineered about it, which only became evident to her as she ran her hand along the wall before they were invited into the entrance hall. The texture of the stone was too perfect, losing some of what made it beautiful in nature.

As Mr. Collins droned on about the proportions of the room and the ornamentation along every facet, Elizabeth spotted the places where the hand-crafted look of old Londinium architecture gave way to the more modern trappings necessary for a life in the void. Automatic doors were inset in the stone doorframes. Lights from the comfield amplifiers hid in vintage sconces. They followed the servants through an antechamber, to the room where Lady Catherine, her daughter, and her governess, Mrs. Jenkinson, sat. Her ladyship stood to receive them, and Charlotte, who'd insisted that introductions should be hers, introduced her guests without any of those apologies or thanks which her husband would've deemed necessary.

In spite of having been to the rich and royal center of St. James City, Sir William was so completely awed by the grandeur surrounding him that he made a very low bow and took his seat without saying a word. Maria, eyes wide, sat on the edge of her chair, taking everything in at once, it seemed. Elizabeth found herself quite

equal to the scene, and could observe the three ladies before her
with composure.

Lady Catherine was a tall, large woman, with strongly marked
features. She might have been considered beautiful, if her manner
were more welcoming and less superior. She wasn't formidable in
her silence, but whatever she said was spoken in so authoritative
a tone as to mark her self-importance. It brought Mr. Wickham to
her mind immediately. From everything that she'd seen so far, she
believed Lady Catherine to be exactly what he'd represented.

Having examined the mother, who reminded her of Mr. Darcy
in manner, she turned her attention on the daughter. There was
nothing in their faces or figures that resembled each other. Miss
de Bourgh was pale and sickly, her features, not unpleasant, but
unmemorable. She would do well for Mr. Darcy, Elizabeth thought,
with pleasure. Miss de Bourgh spoke very little, except in a low
voice to Mrs. Jenkinson, who was dressed unremarkably and who
was entirely engaged in listening to what she said and adjusting the
shade of a nearby lamp to remove the glare from her charge's eyes.

After sitting a few minutes, they were all sent to one of the
windows to admire the view of the sun being eclipsed by the closest
moon. As the flare shield was lowered, Mr. Collins attended them
to point out the splendors of the view, and Lady Catherine kindly
informed them that it was much better worth looking at when multiple moons aligned within their orbits.

The dinner was admittedly incredible. There were as many
servants and plates of food as Mr. Collins had promised. He took
his seat at the opposite end of the table, at her ladyship's request,
and looked as if he felt that life could offer nothing greater. He ate
and praised with delight, and he commended every dish, with Sir
William recovered enough to echo his son-in-law's sentiments. It
was a wonder Lady Catherine could tolerate it. But she seemed perfectly gratified by their excessive admiration, smiling graciously at
them, especially when any dish on the table proved a novelty.

When dinner ended, the party moved to the drawing room, and there was little to do but listen to Lady Catherine talk, which she did without intermission until coffee was served. She delivered her opinion on every subject with such decisiveness that it was clear she wasn't used to having her judgment questioned or challenged. She inquired into more aspects of Charlotte's life than was necessary, and Elizabeth found that there was nothing beneath the great lady's attention, so long as it would allow her to dictate to others. Eventually, she turned her attention on Elizabeth.

"Do you play or sing, Miss Bennet?"

"A little."

"Our instrument is elite. You'll try it someday. Do your sisters play or sing?"

"One of them does." Elizabeth wondered at the intent behind this line of questioning.

"Why didn't you all learn? You ought to have learned. Do you draw?"

It would've been easier to simply ask what they were each interested in, than ask from a list, but Elizabeth wasn't about to tell her that. "A little. My youngest sketches more often."

"This is all very strange. But I suppose you had no opportunity. Your mother should've taken you to Arkulus for the Annual Festival of the Arts."

"My mother wouldn't have minded, but my father hates traveling so far."

"Why could your governess not take you?"

"We never had a governess."

"How is that possible? Five daughters brought up at home without a governess! I've never heard of such a thing. Your mother must've been a thrall to your education."

Elizabeth could hardly contain a smile as she assured her that hadn't been the case.

"Then who looked after you? Taught you? Without a governess you must've been neglected."

"Compared with some families, it might seem we were. But those of us that wished to learn never wanted for the means. Those who chose to be idle certainly might."

"I have no doubt. And that's what a governess will prevent. If I'd known your mother, I would've advised her quite seriously to employ one. Are any of your younger sisters out in society, Miss Bennet?"

Elizabeth was feeling the weight of attention being so long on herself and was beginning to grow anxious. "Yes, ma'am, all."

"All! Stars dimming!—all five at once? Very odd! And you only the second? The younger ones out before the elders are married? Your younger sisters must be very young."

Elizabeth nodded. "My youngest is just fifteen. She's possibly too young to be out among company, but I think it'd be very hard on younger sisters to not have their share of society and amusement simply because their older sisters don't have the means or inclination to marry early. The last-born has as good a right to the pleasures of youth as the first. And to be kept out on *such* a motive! I think it'd hardly promote sisterly affection."

"Upon my word, you give your opinion very decidedly for so young a person," said her ladyship. "What *is* your age?"

"With three younger sisters grown," replied Elizabeth, smiling, "your ladyship can hardly expect me to admit it."

Lady Catherine seemed quite astonished to not receive a direct answer; and Elizabeth suspected she was the first person to have ever dared to trifle with so much dignified impertinence.

"You can't be more than twenty, I'm sure. There's no need to conceal your age."

"I am twenty exactly," she admitted.

Lady Catherine was satisfied.

When the time came for the party to leave, Lady Catherine ordered them a Faeton glider. They gathered around the large, ornate fireplace, its holo-fire crackling realistically in its hearth, listening to Lady Catherine's recommendations for sights to be seen from the windows the next few weeks. A servant appeared to alert them to the Faeton's waiting presence outside, and with many speeches of thankfulness on Mr. Collins's side, and as many bows on Sir William's, they took their leave.

As soon as they'd situated themselves in the open-top glider, Mr. Collins entreated Elizabeth to give her opinion on all that she'd seen at Rosings. For Charlotte's sake, she made her response more favorable than it really was. Her recommendation, as difficult as it was for her to give, wasn't satisfying enough for him, and he was obliged to take her ladyship's praise into his own hands. Elizabeth was happy to let him. It allowed her the opportunity for her mind to wander for the first time in hours.

Lizzie,

Here's a list of places you may want to explore on the Kent during your visit. Please don't feel the need to wait on me to show you around if you'd rather enjoy it on your own time. I'm so grateful to be able to see you each day, but I don't expect to see you all day!

Charlotte

Areas to Visit:

Market Street (Lower Hunsford Sector - B level)
The ceiling is lower in the atrium than the Meryton, but there are colorful and unique decorations all across the ceiling, so it feels fun rather than confining. Worth seeing, even if you aren't shopping.

The Trilogy (a bookshop in Hunsford Sector)
Great selection. They're very aware that we're on this ship and have little other access. Also, the place is three levels and drops down to Lower Hunsford. The shift from quaint village bookshop on A level to hyper-modern ship bookshop on B level is quite an experience on the inside.

Biosilk shop (close to the bookshop in Hunsford A)
Go inside and watch the process of pulling the webs into the spinners if you get a chance. It's mesmerizing.

The Dark Gardens (inner sector of the Ring Hall)
So many amazing flowers! You'll likely want to show Kitty. I thought of her immediately.

The Hanging Gardens (inner sector of Lower Ring Hall) Also worth a visit. The roots from the Dark Gardens are the grasping point for the plants in this sector!

CHAPTER
31

Kent Orbital Station, Londinium Orbit, Long Route 7

Sir William stayed only a week on the Kent, but he seemed to Elizabeth to have been satisfied by his daughter's circumstance, and he left in good spirits. Mr. Collins, who'd devoted his mornings to walking with Sir William along the avenues of Hunsford Sector, now returned to his usual employments. Elizabeth was thankful to find that they didn't see more of him in this shift, for the bulk of his time between breakfast and dinner was now spent in work on the garden, reading, writing sermons, or looking out the window of his own study, which had the best view of the comings and goings from Rosings.

The room Charlotte favored had a single bay window looking out at a small patch of the void beyond the walls of the station. This room more than any other was a reminder that they weren't on land. Elizabeth had been confused by her friend's choice at first, figuring that Charlotte would prefer the dining room for common use; it was a better-sized room, and the window faced the busy thoroughfare, catching much more of the synthetic daylight. But she soon understood that her friend had an excellent reason for what she did. Mr. Collins would undoubtedly have been in his own room far less had she had one equally lively.

Very few days passed in which Mr. Collins didn't walk Rosings Level and the Ring Hall Level, and more often than not, Charlotte felt it necessary to come along. Elizabeth chose to take advantage of these moments of solitude to do her own walking, exploring the list of places that Charlotte had suggested. Maria trailed her a few times, if the destination interested her more than the company of her sister.

Hunsford Sector was Elizabeth's favorite so far. It was a strange and winding village that started at the edge of Rosings Sector, filtered through the wall of the giant dome, and meandered in a vertical back and forth down to the level below where the buildings grew in height and shifted from faux stone to solid metal, stripping themselves of the small lunar town façade. The dichotomy was a delight to experience, and she was always a little sorry to return, even when her legs grew tired from walking.

Occasionally, when she wasn't exploring, and the Collinses were at home, they were honored with a visit from her ladyship, and nothing escaped the woman's observation. She pried into their hobbies, double checked their work—often advising them to do it differently; found fault with the arrangement of furniture, assured them the housemaid was negligent, and if she accepted any refreshment, seemed to do it only for the sake of discovering that Charlotte's taste was questionable.

Elizabeth soon learned the Collinses were not the sole victims of the great lady's attentions. She came forth from her home for the slightest of concerns—whether a tenant was indisposed, discontent, quarreling, or simply too poor—she came to settle their differences, silence their complaints, and scold them into harmony and plenty.

They repeated their evening dinners at Rosings about twice a week. Their other social engagements were few, as the amenities in the upper levels of the Kent were beyond Mr. Collins's means. This was no loss for Elizabeth. She used her days comfortably enough, with many pockets of time spent in pleasant conversation with Charlotte, or meandering through Rosings Park when she was missing the feeling of being on land. Within certain walks of the park, the walls were lost behind the foliage and she could let herself believe she wasn't orbiting the planet in a space station. Her favorite walk, where she went frequently while the Collinses were away, was along the open grove which edged the Rosings Estate side of the park. It had a nice, sheltered path, with vines of royal blue Arkuluan wisteria, which no one seemed to value but herself— though their aroma was intoxicating—and where she felt she was beyond the reach of Lady Catherine's invasive curiosity.

In this quiet way, the first few weeks of her visit soon passed by. A Triple Alignment was approaching—the station's unique orbit allowing for this chance far sooner than would be seen from Londinium—and the week leading to it promised an addition to the family at Rosings. Mr. Darcy was expected among that addition. Though she could think of no acquaintances less preferable to see, his coming would at least give way to a change in the dynamics of their evenings at Rosings Estate.

Mr. Darcy's arrival wasn't a secret long. Mr. Collins had all but made camp by the windows in Rosings Park where he could see the private shuttle bay, so they knew of it within minutes. They had not anticipated, however, that Mr. Darcy would show up on the front step of the parsonage later that day.

"I'd thank *you*, Lizzie, for this gesture of civility," Charlotte said before Mr. Collins opened the door. "Mr. Darcy would never have come so soon to visit just me."

Elizabeth barely had time to deny any right to such a compliment before voices filtered in from the small foyer. Two men stepped inside. She was unfamiliar with the one leading them into the sitting room. He was about thirty, not handsome, but with a most gentlemanlike demeanor. Mr. Darcy looked just as he had on Heoros. He paid his compliments to Charlotte with his usual reserve, and whatever his feelings toward Elizabeth might be, he met her with every appearance of composure. She nodded to him without saying a word.

"Very pleased to meet you all," said the unfamiliar man. "I'm Void Commander Fitzwilliam. I, like Darcy here—whom I'm told you are already familiar with—am Lady Catherine's nearer nephew. My father's Lord Dashell."

"My uncle," Mr. Darcy elaborated.

"Indeed," VC Fitzwilliam said jovially. "Making me your favorite cousin, I'm sure." He didn't wait for Mr. Darcy's response. He turned, taking in the room. "What a lovely room. Just as welcoming as your wonderful garden outside."

"Charming," Mr. Darcy added.

"Thank you both," Charlotte said. "We have the honor of input from your aunt."

VC Fitzwilliam laughed. "I'm certain of that."

Charlotte smiled warmly. "Please, have a seat. Would you like anything to drink? I hope your journey here was pleasant and uneventful."

Mr. Darcy ventured to a chair and sat as his cousin led the conversation.

Charlotte shooed her husband into the kitchen to retrieve sustenance, listening to the VC describe their trip.

"And just in time for the Triple Alignment festivities," Charlotte said, when he'd concluded.

"Indeed! I hear this will be a first for both you and your guests," VC Fitzwilliam said.

Elizabeth didn't hear Charlotte's reply, because Mr. Darcy turned to her then.

She'd drifted unconsciously to an empty chair near the drawing room doorway not far from where he'd seated himself.

"I trust your family is well," he asked.

Surprised, she answered quickly that they were. After a moment's hesitation, she added, "My sister Jane has been on Londinium for the past few months. Did you happen to see her there?" She knew he never had, but she wished to see whether he'd betray any awareness of what passed between her sister and the Bingleys.

She thought he looked a little confused as he answered. "I was never fortunate enough to run into her, no."

This stirred up more questions, but she felt it an inopportune moment to inquire further, so she said nothing more.

He was equally silent, and soon after, the gentlemen took their leave.

ROSINGS LEVEL
Rosings / Hunsford Sectors

ROSINGS
LEVEL

LOWER HUNSFORD LEVEL

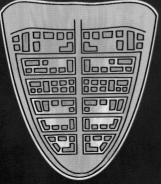

ROSINGS SECTOR

ROSINGS
ESTATE

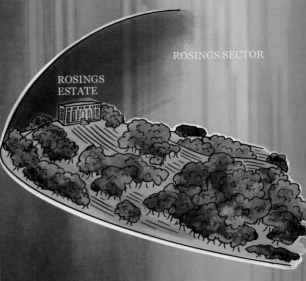

PARSONAGE

HUNSFORD SECTOR
LEVEL A

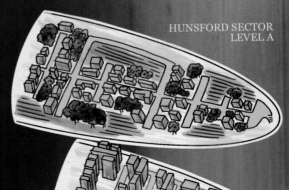

LOWER HUNSFORD SECTOR | LEVEL B

CHAPTER
32

Kent Orbital Station,
Londinium Orbit, Long Route 7

It wasn't until the day of the Triple Alignment, nearly a week since Darcy had arrived on the station, that his aunt invited the Collinses and their guests to a special viewing of the event in the Kent's observatory. His cousin had gone to the parsonage home a couple times during the week to visit, but Fitz had an ease with idle conversation that Darcy simply couldn't match, and he was disinclined to try it, however tempting it might be.

He waited for their guests to arrive with a certain amount of impatience, his gaze drifting to the doorway of the observatory with increased frequency as the interior lights of the station dimmed. He was ready for fresh company. But in some deeper, quieter part of himself, he was also curious to see Miss Elizabeth's reaction to the Alignment. Would her eyes sparkle with the same wonder as they had in the Caverns? This wasn't so immediate a splendor as that had been—no light would paint her skin as the moons fell into line—but it was a vantage point she'd likely never seen of this event.

In an effort to keep his eyes from the door, Darcy turned his attention to the room. His aunt had reserved the observatory for their particular use. The lower level was a long oval room with book-shelves lining the walls, chairs and tables grouped in areas for study as well as conversation. Their party had made themselves at home, and moved pieces around to suit his aunt. Across the room was a large telescope which towered on a raised platform, centered beneath an open circle in the ceiling, so it could be aimed through the dome ceiling of the second level. The bluer side of his home moon shone through the windows beyond the balcony banisters, the swirling gray and red of Nagalea creeping into position behind it.

The sounds of the door opening pulled his attention away from the moons. He turned to see their company filtering in. Mr. Collins, with all his ceremonious pomp, led the way, his wife on his arm. Miss Elizabeth came next, in a simple emerald dress, with the young Miss Lucas wide-eyed behind her. Darcy made eye contact with Elizabeth, and felt a jolt in his chest. The jolt morphed instantly into a light nausea as his aunt, who'd issued the invitation, managed to receive them with equal parts civility and indecorum.

She wasted no time making Darcy the focus of her conversa-tion, allowing him no opportunity to soften the blow of her words.

Through the questions from Lady Catherine and his half-distracted answers, he watched his cousin maneuver to sit beside Elizabeth and Mrs. Collins, and dive quickly into conversation. The three talked animatedly of the Kent and Heoros, of traveling and staying at home, of books, music, and the Alignment festivities they'd enjoyed throughout the week. Darcy's distraction eventually caught his aunt's attention, and she turned it on them.

"What's that you're saying, Fitzwilliam? What are you talking of? I want to hear what it is."

"We're talking about music, ma'am," he said, with more patience for the interruption than Darcy expected. He began to suspect that his cousin was nursing a fondness for Elizabeth.

"Music! Of all subjects, music is my greatest delight. There are few people in the system, I'd wager, who have more true enjoyment of music than myself—or better natural taste. If I'd ever learned, I should've been a prodigy. So would Anne," she gestured vaguely at her daughter in the chair by the hearth, "had her health allowed for it. I'm confident she would've performed beautifully. How is Georgiana doing with the piano, Darcy?"

"She's doing very well. More than proficient at this point. She's lovely to listen to."

"I'm glad to hear she's doing well," said Lady Catherine. "When you speak to her next, remind her from me that she must not neglect her practice."

"I assure you, she doesn't need reminding," he replied.

"Good. I often tell young ladies that no excellence in one's accomplishments can be acquired without constant practice. As I've often told Mrs. Collins, while she has no instrument, she's very welcome to come to Rosings every day and practice on the pianoforte in Mrs. Jenkinson's room. She'd be in nobody's way, you know, in that part of the house."

Darcy lowered his gaze from Elizabeth's face as his aunt's words registered. Fitz, no doubt attempting to ease the blow of her ill-bred comment, suggested to Elizabeth that they adjust the telescope and its view screen so that it would be ready when the moons aligned. She agreed at once, and they moved to the nearest wall to connect the apparatus.

Lady Catherine instructed them on the best angle for the view screen from Anne's seat on the couch, then began talking at Darcy again. He barely paid her any mind. The moment it was clear she wasn't expecting him to answer any questions, he took the opportunity to move nearer to the telescope, positioning himself within the range of quiet conversation with—and a clear view of—Elizabeth.

She took notice of him at once, but said nothing until she had finished adjusting one of the knobs on the massive scope. At that point she turned to him with an arch smile and said, "You intend to unmoor me, Mr. Darcy, by coming over in such a state to monitor my efforts. But I'm stubborn—I never can bear to be subdued by the will of others. My courage always rises at every attempt to intimidate me."

Surely, she didn't believe he'd had any such intention when he walked over. "I've had the pleasure of your acquaintance long enough to know that you find great enjoyment in occasionally professing opinions which are in fact not your own."

Elizabeth laughed heartily at this, the sound like a spark of light in the darkness. She turned to Fitz, who'd circled the telescope and appeared on his right side. "Your cousin will paint quite a picture of me, and convince you not to believe a word I say. How unlucky to meet a person so able to expose my real character, in a part of the system where I'd hoped to pass myself off with some degree of credit." She turned again to Darcy. "How very impolite of you to spotlight all the faults you discovered of me in Heoros. It's provoking me to retaliate, and certain things may come out about you that would shock your relatives to hear."

He smirked. "I'm not afraid of you."

Fitz perked up instantly. "Please, tell me your accusations at once. I'd like to know how he behaves among strangers."

"Prepare yourself for something very dreadful," she said, her tone playfully serious. "The first time I ever saw him was at a ball on the satellite station of Heoros. And at this ball, what do you think he did?" Her eyes sparkled as her gaze flicked between Fitz and Darcy. "He didn't even dance, though there were many willing partners sitting lonely. Mr. Darcy, you can't deny that fact."

"I didn't know anyone beyond my own party."

"True. And nobody can ever be introduced in a ballroom." She eyed him pointedly. "Well, Void Commander, what knob shall I turn next? My fingers await your orders."

Darcy felt the moment slipping from him, but he wasn't ready to let it go. His body leaned forward before his mind decided on a course of action. "Perhaps," he said, his breath catching in a sudden unconscious clench of his throat, "I could've judged better, if I'd sought an introduction. But I'm ill qualified to recommend myself to strangers."

"Shall we ask your cousin the reason for this?" Elizabeth said, still addressing Fitz. "We might ask him why a man of sense and education, who has lived on and traveled to many worlds, is ill quali-fied to recommend himself to strangers?"

"I can answer that question without consulting him," his cousin offered happily. "It's because he won't give himself the trouble."

Darcy felt an urge to be open rather than teasing, and grew sober. "I . . ." he began, "don't have the talent, which some possess, of conversing easily with those I've never met before. I can't catch their tone of conversation, or appear interested in their concerns the way I see others do."

"My fingers don't move over the piano your aunt loves so much in the masterly manner I see so many others do. They don't have the same force or rapidity, and don't produce the same expres-sion," she replied, matching his seriousness. "But I've always supposed it to be my own fault, because I won't take the trouble of practicing. It's not that I don't believe my fingers as capable as any other person who plays better."

A small laugh escaped him. "You're perfectly right. You've employed your time much better. Neither of us perform to strangers."

Her lips opened as if to reply, but she wasn't fast enough for Lady Catherine, who called out, "What are you talking about now?"

Elizabeth immediately put her eye to the scope and reached for another knob.

His aunt approached, and, after watching for a few minutes, said to Darcy, "Miss Bennet would do well to have studied more astronomy. Anne would have had everything in place by now, had her health allowed her to do this herself."

Elizabeth's gaze drifted to him as Lady Catherine said this, though he wasn't sure what she was studying him to discover. Perhaps she expected that he might save her from his aunt's continued remarks, though she bore the many instructions—and comparisons of her and Anne's hypothetical skills—with forbearance and civility.

When the third and final moon nestled itself in line with the others, Darcy was not looking at the sky. He watched the reflection of the Alignment in the depths of Elizabeth's eyes. The expression of joy and wonder on her face transformed their darkness to a star-dappled sky. He would have gladly been lost in them for the rest of the evening. But the moons scattered soon after, and their guests, likewise, parted.

The observatory felt empty after they left.

The Kent Orbital Station is —incredible! I'm surprised by its size, but I'm most impressed by Rosings level. Lady Catherine is graceful and imposing.

Char's front room

Londinium Rising

lunch in the Hanging Gardens

♡ This place is an absolute dream!

Her home is the most beautiful place I've ever seen. I can't believe Char gets to come here so often ♡

I was able to buy a small camera to capture all my favorite things ♡

along the Ring Hall

Hall to the G

As LOVELY

in the Dark Gardens

ap of Rosings

Stars! If I'm even half so lucky!

as all of these gardens are... I wanted most to take the images of Rosings itself but I didn't want to get in trouble. So snuck a couple from the hip before hiding it in my pocket...They came out blurry.

Another snap of Rosings ♡

CHAPTER
33

Kent Orbital Station,
Londinium Orbit, Long Route 7

The morning after the Triple Alignment, Elizabeth chose to remain at the parsonage while Charlotte took Maria to a shop on one of the lower levels. Elizabeth lounged in the window seat of the drawing room, typing out a waive to Jane, occasionally getting lost in the view of Londinium's blue and white northern hemisphere shining in the void. It was strange to see the planet from so many angles, since Londinium and Heoros were tidally locked.

She was startled by a chime at the door, signaling a visitor. There was a small chance it could be Lady Catherine, and with apprehension she tucked her comcard quickly away before moving to the sitting room. She could hear the housekeeper's voice as the door was opened, and to her great surprise, Mr. Darcy, and Mr. Darcy only, entered the room.

He seemed astonished to find her alone. "I'm sorry," he said haltingly, "I was under the impression that all the ladies were here."

"Maria wanted to visit the AstroLab down below," she explained. "After last night, I can hardly blame her." She gestured to the chair by the door. "Please, sit."

He obliged without hesitation and she stifled a smile at his surprising obedience.

"Is all well at Rosings?"

He nodded, but made no attempt to continue the conversation.

They looked about the room. When they made eye contact, it seemed to linger on questions unasked, before he broke the connection and looked out the window.

After a full minute of this, the fear that they might sink into total silence spurred her to say something. She considered where they'd seen each other before, and curious, she said, "You all left Heoros so suddenly in the fall. Mr. Bingley and his sisters were well, I hope, when you left Londinium?"

"They were, yes."

He seemed unlikely to elaborate on that answer. "Is there any truth to the rumor that he isn't planning to return to Netherfield Landing?"

"I've never heard him say that. But he has many friends on many moons, and his friends and engagements are continually increasing."

This line of conversation was at an end. She dared not say too much about his friend. Having nothing else to say, she was now determined to leave the trouble of finding a subject to him.

He took the hint, eventually. "This seems like a comfortable house. Lady Catherine did a great deal to it when Mr. Collins first came to live on the Kent."

"I believe she did. She couldn't have bestowed her kindness on a more grateful subject." She couldn't hide her smirk as she said this. It was unclear whether Mr. Darcy shared the same humor over the man.

"Mr. Collins appears to be fortunate in his choice of a wife."

"He's found one of the very few sensible women who would've accepted him. Charlotte has an excellent understanding." Here she lowered her voice a little, talking more to herself than to him. "Though I can't say her marrying Mr. Collins was the wisest thing she ever did." She cleared her throat as she realized this might've been oversharing. "She seems content, though. In a certain light it's a good match for her."

"It must be nice for her to be settled so close to her family."

"Close? The station can travel, but not on the whim of the Collinses."

"They can easily time their visits. It's little more than half a day's journey when the orbits align. That's very close."

"I'd never consider that inconsistent distance an advantage," Elizabeth said. "And I'd certainly never consider it *close* to her family."

"This is proof of your own attachment to Heoros. Anything beyond the estate of Longbourn, I suppose, would appear far."

As he spoke there was a sort of smile that Elizabeth thought she understood. He likely assumed she was thinking of Jane and the Netherfield, and she blushed as she answered. "I don't mean to say that someone can't be settled too near her family. Near and far are relative and depend on various circumstances. When aurum is no obstacle, neither is travel. But that's not the case *here*. The Collinses live comfortably, but not for the kind of frequent travel that Charlotte would consider *close* to home."

Mr. Darcy shifted to the edge of his chair, leaning toward her. "*You* can't have such a very strong local attachment. You long to experience the moons outside of Heoros, do you not?"

Elizabeth couldn't hide the surprise on her face at his change in focus, and didn't really respond aloud. He reacted to this by drawing away, taking a book from the side table and examining its cover. The book was an in-depth look at the orbital station, with level guides and images of the ship from concept to completion. When he spoke again his voice was colder. "Are you enjoying the Kent?"

Elizabeth was thrown off by his shift in demeanor, especially as she couldn't account for it, based solely on her reaction to his last question. They talked of the Kent for a minute or two, both less candid and more distant in their remarks, and were saved from the stagnating conversation by the entrance of Charlotte and her sister, returned from the lower levels.

Mr. Darcy's presence surprised them. He quickly explained his mistaken belief of their being home as well.

"Did you find anything interesting?" Elizabeth asked Maria.

Maria beamed and quickly set her bag on the low center table to remove its contents. She'd pulled out a small silver tube. "I got a miniature telescope," she said. "The big one was so amazing last night. I wanted to see more. I'm thinking of starting with that red spot we saw the other day on Itavia."

Mr. Darcy stood. "I'd better be going," he said, nodding at them each in turn and then ducking out of the room.

Charlotte's gaze followed him out, then she turned to Elizabeth, her eyes wide. "Well, that was unexpected," she said.

Elizabeth couldn't agree more.

CHARLOTTE COLLINS
PERSONAL JOURNAL / COMCARD ID: KC-677.P2.CC
TIMESTAMP: 21.4-16:45:20.LS
LOCATION: KENT ORBITAL STATION

SOMETHING DIFFERENT ABOUT MR. DARCY . . .

I know Lizzie thinks I'm imagining things, but something is different about Mr. Darcy lately.

He and his cousin have Lady Catherine and her daughter for company, and plenty of options for entertainment on this ship. Whether it's the nearness of our home or the pleasantness of the walk, I can't be certain, but the men have come by nearly every day this past couple weeks. They appear at various times of the morning, sometimes separately, sometimes together . . . every now and then accompanied by their aunt. It's plain as the sun that VC Fitzwilliam comes by because he enjoys our company (especially Lizzie's).

She's mentioned once or twice a certain likeness in his personality to Mr. Wickham (who I know was rather a favorite of hers). I believe the Void Commander would be a beneficial match for her. And he seems to really admire her.

Though I can't discount Mr. Darcy's liking her either. I've suggested it once or twice, but Lizzie always laughs at the idea.

Why, then, would Mr. Darcy come so often to the house? It can't be for the company. He's usually just . . . there. As silent as the void. Hardly animated. When he does speak, it seems to be out of necessity rather than choice. And his cousin's occasional teasing proves that he's generally different (though I've never seen it). I can't help but feel this change is an effect of admiration, the only possible object of that admiration being Lizzie.

I've been determined to figure him out. Whenever we're in his company, or we see him during my husband's sermons, I make sure to watch him. I'm having little success. He certainly looks at her often.

But I can't pin down the expression. It's earnest and stead-fast, but seems to lack the admiration I expect to find there. Sometimes it appears as nothing more than absence of mind.

My husband says I shouldn't press the idea too much with Lizzie, for fear of raising expectations which might only end in disappointment. He's probably right. But I'll say this now: I have no doubt, if Lizzie really believed that Mr. Darcy admired her, all her dislike for him would vanish.

CHAPTER
34

Kent Orbital Station, Londinium Orbit, Long Route 7

Elizabeth often spent her days walking the various trails within Rosings Sector. More than once, she unexpectedly met Mr. Darcy. She felt the perverseness of the mischance that brought him to a trail no one else seemed to bother with. To prevent it happening again, she made sure to inform him that this particular path was a favorite of hers specifically for the solitude it offered. Yet it happened a second time, and then a third. It seemed like willful indifference—or a voluntary penance, as on these occasions it wasn't just a few formal questions followed by an awkward pause and then parting. He seemed to think it necessary to walk with her. He never said much, and she didn't attempt to fill the silence.

One day as she walked, perusing Jane's latest waives and dwelling on some passages that indicated her sister was in poor spirits, instead of being surprised again by Mr. Darcy, she was met by his cousin.

Dropping the comcard into her pocket and forcing a smile, she said, "I haven't see you out this way before."

"I've been making the tour of the park," he replied, "I intend to finish it with a visit to the Collinses. Are you going much farther?"

"I was just about to turn around."

He fell into step beside her toward the parsonage.

"You leave the Kent Saturday?" she asked, running her fingers through the soft, shining white bristles of a hedge full of Kaelian Lightfeather blooms.

"Yes. If Darcy doesn't put it off again. But I'm at his disposal. He arranges the business as he pleases."

"I don't know anyone who seems to enjoy the power of doing what he likes more than Mr. Darcy."

"He likes to have his own way, that's true," VC Fitzwilliam agreed. "But don't we all? It's only that he has better means than most of getting it." He ducked under a low-hanging bough, the large yellow leaves raking his dark hair.

She passed a cluster of Solar Protea in full bloom. The warm, rich scent crept over her and she breathed in deeply. "I imagine your cousin brought you with him mainly for the sake of having someone at his disposal."

This seemed to amuse him. "It's a wonder he hasn't married in order to secure himself such a convenience," he replied.

"Perhaps his sister does the job well enough. She's under his care, so he can order her around as he wishes."

VC Fitzwilliam laughed. "No, that's an advantage he must divide with me. I'm an equal partner in Georgiana's guardianship."

"Are you? How old is she again?"

"Sixteen," he replied.

Too young, then, to be an object of Bingley's affections. She made a mental note to remind Jane of this. To VC Fitzwilliam, she said, "And what sort of guardians do the two of you make? Does she give you much trouble? Young ladies her age are sometimes a little difficult to manage." She thought here of her youngest sister. "If she has the true Darcy spirit, she may like to have her own way."

He was looking at her now with increased earnestness. "Why would you suppose Georgiana would give us any trouble?"

He responded so quickly that she suspected she'd gotten near the truth. "No need to worry. I haven't heard anything about her specifically. I'm sure she's quite well behaved. I just know how that age can be, having siblings currently equal to it. Miss Darcy is a great favorite with some ladies I'm acquainted with—Mrs. Hurst and Miss Bingley. I think you said you know them?"

"I know them a little. Their brother is a pleasant man, and a great friend of Darcy's."

"Stars, yes," Elizabeth said drily. "Mr. Darcy is exceptionally kind to Mr. Bingley and takes an impressive amount of care of him."

"Care of him!" he laughed. "Yes, I really believe he *does* take care of him. From something he told me on our flight here, I suspect Bingley is very much indebted to him. Of course, I could be wrong. I have no right to assume that Bingley was the person he meant."

"What do you mean?"

"It's a circumstance Darcy wouldn't wish to be widely known, since if it reached the woman's family, it'd be unpleasant."

Her stomach flipped and began to sink. "I'll secure the intelligence with double gravity."

He nodded approvingly. "Remember, I don't have much reason to suppose it was Bingley. He was congratulating himself on recently saving a friend from the inconveniences of an ill-considered marriage. He didn't mention names or particulars. I only suspect it to be Bingley as I believe he's the kind of young man to get into a scrap of that sort. He was also with him for the better part of last revo, if I recall correctly."

"Did Mr. Darcy give you his reasons for this interference?"

"I believe there were some strong objections to the lady."

She could feel her breath growing shallow. Had the life support system malfunctioned? "And how did he separate them?"

He shook his head. "That he didn't say. He only told me what I've told you now."

Elizabeth didn't respond. She walked on, her heart swelling with indignation, the flora around them blurring into patches of color as her mind shifted all its power to thoughts of her sister. After a moment, Fitzwilliam asked her why she was so thoughtful.

"I'm thinking about what you've told me," she said, slowing again and frowning at a Comet Tail bush. "Your cousin's conduct makes me uneasy. Why did he need to be the judge?"

"Are you inclined to consider his interference officious?"

"I don't see what right Mr. Darcy had to decide how acceptable his friend's inclination was, or why, on his judgment alone, he could determine how his friend found happiness." She slid the soft taillike petal of a bright yellow flower through her fingers, forcing herself to calm. "But since we know nothing particular, it's not fair to condemn him. We can't suppose there was much affection in this case."

"That does lessen the honor of my cousin's triumph, sadly." He said this jokingly, but it was such an accurate picture of Mr. Darcy that she couldn't trust herself with a reply.

She shifted the conversation to indifferent matters until they reached the parsonage, where she took her leave of him and went quickly to her room. There, she could think, without interruption, of everything she'd heard. The chances of this being about anyone other than Bingley and Jane were minuscule. There couldn't exist, in all the worlds, *two* men over whom Mr. Darcy could have such boundless influence. She'd never doubted that he'd been involved in the measures taken to separate them, but she'd always given Caroline the bulk of the credit. If his own vanity didn't mislead him, then Mr. Darcy was the cause of all that Jane had suffered and continued to suffer. He'd ruined every hope of happiness for the most affectionate, generous heart in the system, and no one could say how lasting an evil he might've inflicted.

Fitzwilliam had said there were strong objections to her sister. Probably the fact that one uncle was a waystation attorney and another was in business in Lowland.

"He couldn't object to Jane," she told herself. Her sister was everything good and lovely, smart and well-read, with more genuine manners than anyone she'd ever met. "There's nothing about my father that could be a problem." He had some quirks. But there was nothing about him that Mr. Darcy could object to. She clenched her teeth, thinking of her mother. Her confidence gave way a little. "No. Mama has her faults. But she can't be such an influence to the relationship." Surely, Darcy would be more worried about Jane's importance in society than her mother's want of sense.

Her pulse pounded forcefully in her temples, a wave of ache coursing like sonar from the back of her head to the crown. Her eyes watered, and she wasn't sure whether it was from the sudden dull pain or the awful circumstance that caused it.

She threw herself down on the bed, and pushed the pads of her thumbs into the corners of her eyes, pressing the bridge of her nose in hopes of easing the growing ache.

A knock sounded on her door soon after.

"Lizzie?" It was Charlotte. "Is everything well?"

"No," she groaned. "My head feels like a supernova."

"Let me get you something for the pain."

The sound of her footsteps drifted away. Quickly, she returned. With a little knock, she entered the room, a glass of water in one hand, a packet of blue powder in the other.

"We were going to Rosings in a bit for tea. I don't suppose you're up for it?"

Elizabeth sat up. The pain only added to her unwillingness to see Mr. Darcy. "I think I'd better rest. I'm sure with sleep and pain-suppressors, this will pass."

Charlotte nodded, handed over her offering, then shooed Elizabeth off the bed to turn down the covers for her. Elizabeth quickly swirled the meds into the water and downed it all.

"Get some rest," Charlotte said, then she left.

Elizabeth sank gratefully into the covers and closed her eyes.

LONDINIUM SAT[SYS

Communications Log—System Storage 30 Days [Planetary]

[MyMyMissJane] 22.4-13.41.39.LS
I was just thinking about how far flung we all are from one another. I miss my sisters.

[Ly.D.uhhh] 22.4-13.45.09.LS
You shouldn't be missing us, you should be adding your beauty to the scene in Cloudtop. Perhaps a fashion designer will stumble upon you and make an entire collection inspired by your eyes!

[MaryB] 22.4-13:46:14.LS
That sounds like your dream, Lydia.
Hi, Jane. Miss you, too. And you, Lizzie.

[KitKitBennet] 22.4-13:47:47.LS
Yes, me also! I hope you're both having the best time, and making some great connections.

[Ly.D.uhhh] 22.4-13:58:19.LS
Lizzie's having the most fun. Hasn't even bothered to reply! I hope she's doing something romantic and exciting.

[LizzieLovesSpace] 22.4-14:02:50.LS
I'm here. I was napping, actually.

[Ly.D.uhhh] 22.4-14:05:09.LS
Well that's boring.

[LizzieLovesSpace] 22.4-14:08:44.LS
Sorry to disappoint you. There's only so much to do on this station, and so far none of it has been romantic.

[KitKitBennet] 22.4-14:10:32.LS
So there's been excitement at least?

■ ■ ■

[LizzieLovesSpace] 22.4-14:13:58.LS
Something like that. Excitement for you, certainly, Kitty. The gardens here are amazing! I've managed to get cuttings of several flowers for you.

[KitKitBennet] 22.4-14:16:22.LS
Really? What ones?

[LizzieLovesSpace] 22.4-14:19:00.LS
I might not have the right names. But I know for sure I've got Stellarite, Kaelian Lightfeather, and Red Gallus. There's also some kind of fern. It shifts hues from the stem to the ends of the branch and leaves. Deep blue to light pink. Do you know what it is? It's very pretty.

[Ly.D.uhhh] 22.4-14:22:41.LS
Shining stars! This just gave me an amazing idea for a dress! Must go draw.

[Ly.D.uhhh] *SILENCED COM*

[MyMyMissJane] 22.4-14:25:30.LS
Can't wait to see what you come up with!

[MaryB] 22.4-14:28:59.LS
There's no chance she saw that before she left.
I'm sorry to say it, but I'm at a really interesting part of the book I'm reading, so I'm going to go now, too. Really looking forward to seeing you both again, but make the most of your time away!

[MyMyMissJane] 22.4-14:32:01.LS
Thank you for stepping away from your reading a minute to say hello!

[MaryB] 22.4-14:35:23.LS
Love you miss you!

■ ■ ■

[MaryB] *SILENCED COM*

[KitKitBennet] 22.4-14:39:11.LS

Thanks, by the way, Lizzie! Jane, I felt the same way this morning . . . it's so strange to be apart like this for so long.

[MyMyMissJane] 22.4-14:42:54.LS

I suppose this is what happens when we grow up. Had any of us already married, we would have been split sooner. Something to be thankful for.

[KitKitBennet] 22.4-14:45:03.LS

I wouldn't have minded, had you ended up with Bingley. You were so well matched.

[MyMyMissJane] 22.4-14:50:14.LS

I thought that as well, Kitty. But sometimes things just don't work out the way we imagined. I'm sure it was all for the best.

[MyMyMissJane] 22.4-14:52:26.LS

Aunt Gardiner needs me. I must go! Kitty, stay sweet! Lizzie, enjoy the rest of your stay on the Kent. I can't wait to hear of all you've done, and more about how you're faring with Mr. Darcy in the mix.

[KitKitBennet] *LIKES MESSAGE*

[LizzieLovesSpace] *LIKES MESSAGE*

. . . END COM . . .

CHAPTER
35

Kent Orbital Station,
Londinium Orbit, Long Route 7

Elizabeth set her comcard on the bed and took stock of her condition. Between the nap and the meds, she seemed to have been revived. She couldn't hear anyone in the parsonage, and felt safe to assume they were still at Rosings. While the conversation with her sisters was a nice and welcome distraction, Jane's final comment reverted Elizabeth's mind instantly to what had distressed her in the first place.

She couldn't stay in this house. Itching for further distraction and not yet ready to be seen by her hosts, she grabbed her comcard, sent a quick note to Charlotte, and escaped the parsonage. The simulated daylight of the station was too much. In need of somewhere darker, she headed to the Hanging Gardens.

As if to exasperate herself to the point of re-inviting another headache, she looked through her comcard as she walked, examining every single message Jane had sent to her since she'd arrived on the Kent.

The waives contained no actual complaint. In fact, there was little within her communication that could pinpoint any current suffering. And yet, in almost every pixel in those lines, there was a want of her usual cheerfulness. Jane's writing, normally imbued with the light of a mind at peace and a heart disposed to kindness, was clearly clouded. With a level of attention she hadn't given it upon her first reading, Elizabeth noted every sentence that conveyed the idea of uneasiness. Mr. Darcy's boast to his cousin had given her a keener sense of her sister's pain.

By the time she had finished reading, she'd reached the Hanging Gardens, and their perpetual verdant gloom. The tall glass walls bordering the gardens were dappled with condensation. As she pulled open the door, she was met with a blast of humidity that stuck to her clothes and skin immediately. She closed her eyes for a moment, taking in the feel of the place, immersing her mind in the soft sounds of foliage under the irrigation system's lulling shush.

She opened her eyes and stepped fully in. Above her, vines and leaves hung like the tentacles of a giant creature, and at her feet were paths of gray stone, bordered by long, velvet-soft, yellow grasses. Walking deeper into the gardens, the feeling of looking up shifted and she could almost believe herself to be walking on a ceiling looking down on a wilderness of unfamiliar vegetation. Were it not for the drops of condensation that fell on her head like a gentle spring drizzle, she might have thought gravity had switched.

She wandered through the flowing natural corridors, grateful for the constant dripping. It kept her from reaching for her comcard to study her sister's words again. But it couldn't keep her mind from finding its way back to Mr. Darcy.

The longer she thought of him, his friend, and her sister, the more agitated she became. The last thing she wanted was to reignite her headache. There was a natural canopy ahead. She moved under it to wipe the water from her face and, hopefully, collect herself.

Then she heard her name and froze.

She turned toward the sound, and to her utter amazement, Mr. Darcy stepped beneath the boughs. Her heart tumbled.

His hair stuck to his forehead and droplets clung to the tips of his eyelashes. If she'd believed it possible, she would've said he looked overcome with emotion.

"I heard you were unwell," he said. "I hope seeing you here means that you're recovered."

"The headache has passed," she said coldly.

He took a slight step toward her, his gaze never leaving her face, something about him almost bristling with an energy she couldn't place. "I've struggled in vain and I can abide it no longer. I knew you were visiting the Kent. You were the only reason I made the trip. I had to see you."

Elizabeth stared, hardly understanding him. This was . . . odd. She barely had the presence of mind to grasp his meaning.

"I've tried to repress my feelings for you, but it's impossible. I'm in agony. You must allow me to tell you how ardently I admire and love you."

Slowly, meaning shifted into place. Then it dropped like a hammer. Her breath hitched as her heart shot into her throat. This was a high compliment, she couldn't deny that, even though she deeply disliked him. But such a confession didn't change her feelings. A tinge of guilt for the pain she'd cause in rejecting him stayed her tongue.

Seeming to take her silence as sufficient encouragement, he continued. "I know better. My family expects better. The inferiority of your birth, your station in life held to the light of my rank and circumstance . . . none of it can diminish this longing in my heart."

Her compassion evaporated in a rush of anger. But she clenched her teeth and held it at bay until he could finish listing all his resentments and objections.

"Your circumstances, your family connections—such a detriment to my social circles—I'll put it all aside to be with you. I can't torment myself any longer. Please do me the honor of accepting my hand."

As he said this, she could see that he had no doubt of a favorable answer. He *spoke* of apprehension and anxiety, but his face showed only self-assurance. The white noise of dripping water around them was replaced by a torrent as her own blood rushed in her ears. But she composed herself, and spoke stiffly to hide the rage. "If I could *feel* gratitude in this moment, I'd thank you. But I can't. I'm sorry to have caused you pain. It was unconsciously done. I hope that it'll be short-lived, as the feelings which you tell me have hindered your regard will help you overcome it."

Mr. Darcy, his eyes still fixed on her face, seemed to catch her words with as much resentment as surprise. His face paled slightly, and the agitation he was feeling was visible in every feature. He was floundering. The pause as she watched his emotions range across his face was dreadful.

Eventually, with forced calmness, he said, "And this is your response? I might ask why, with so little civility, I'm rejected?"

"I might ask why you chose to tell me that you liked me against your will, your reason—even your character? Was this not some excuse for incivility, if I *was* uncivil?"

She stepped toward him, too agitated to stay at arm's length. "I have other reasons. Do you think *anything* would tempt me to accept the man who has been the means of ruining, perhaps forever, my sister's happiness?"

Mr. Darcy's face reddened, but it was only a flash of color, and he gave no indication of interrupting her.

"I have every reason in the cosmos to think ill of you. No motive can excuse the unjust and ungenerous part you played *there*.

You wouldn't dare to deny that you were the main—if not the only—means of dividing them from each other, and involving them both in misery of the acutest kind. Can you deny it?"

His face shifted into a false tranquility. "I don't deny that I did everything in my power to separate my friend from your sister, nor that I rejoice in my success. I've been kinder to *him* than to myself."

Elizabeth ignored this reflection, but its meaning didn't escape her. "It's not just this incident that solidified my dislike. Long before that happened, my opinion of you was decided when Mr. Wickham revealed his misfortunes at your hands. What do you have to say about this? In what imaginary act of friendship can you defend yourself there?"

Mr. Darcy, clearly agitated now, leaned in. "You take an eager interest in that gentleman's *misfortunes*."

"All of them caused by you," she returned. "You've withheld the advantages you know were meant for him, deprived the best years of his life of the independence he deserved. You've done all this. Yet you treat the mention of his misfortune with contempt and ridicule."

Darcy swiped the dripping locks of his hair off his forehead, water splashing her face, but neither of them backed down. "And this is your opinion of me! Thank you for explaining it so fully. My faults, according to you, are great indeed." He paused, casting his gaze down the length of her before returning to meet her eyes. He was so close she could feel the heat of their anger roiling between them. "Perhaps these offenses might've been overlooked, and your bitter accusations suppressed, had your pride not been hurt by my honesty—had I concealed my struggles and flattered you. But I despise falsity of every kind. I'm not ashamed of the feelings I expressed. Could you expect me to rejoice in the inferiority of your connections—to congratulate myself on the hope of relations whose condition in life is so decidedly beneath my own?"

Her rage was white hot, now, and licked like flames behind her eyes. She forced it down enough to speak with composure. She had leaned so close to him she could see the gray flecks in his dark eyes. "You're mistaken, Mr. Darcy, if you think that *how* you declared your love affected me in any other way than sparing me the concern I might've had in rejecting you, had you behaved in a more gentlemanlike manner."

She saw him start at this, but he said nothing, and she continued.

"You couldn't have made the offer in any possible way that would've tempted me to accept it."

Again, his astonishment was obvious. He stepped back with an expression of mingled incredulity and mortification. That didn't stop her.

"From the very beginning," she went on, pressing into the space he'd left between them, "practically from the first moment of my acquaintance with you, your manners established my belief of your arrogance, your conceit, and your selfish disdain of the feelings of others. I hadn't known you a month before I felt that you were the last man in the galaxy whom I could ever be persuaded to marry."

His expression solidified into unreadable stone. "You've said quite enough. I perfectly comprehend your feelings, and can now only be ashamed of what my own have been. Forgive me for having burned through so much of your time."

With these words, he pushed past her, and was lost in an instant to the foliage, leaving her reeling, her legs suddenly too weak to hold her.

To: Jane Bennet, St. James City, Londinium

From: Elizabeth Bennet, Kent Orbital Station, Londinium Orbit, Route 7

Subject: This is all too much

Status: Discarded

Dearest Jane,

I am unmoored. I have no one with whom I can express any of this. Even now, I know that I won't send this to you, though I desperately want to talk to you about it. Perhaps simply getting it out of my head will help me to make sense of it.

Mr. Darcy proposed to me today. Each time I replay the interaction in my mind, I grow more astonished. He proposed, but more than that, he has been in love with me for quite a while. So in love that he wished to marry me in spite of all the objections that had made him prevent Bingley from marrying you.

It's incredible. I'm stunned. And I couldn't be more disappointed to be right about Bingley—the fool—allowing Mr. Darcy to persuade him not to pursue you.

It was gratifying, on some level, to have inspired such a strong affection. But his awful pride—his shameless acknowledgment and unpardonable justification for what he did to you . . . Oh, and the unfeeling way in which he mentioned Wickham. He didn't even try to deny the cruelty he'd inflicted upon his childhood companion. Whatever pity I'd had for him died in that moment. I wish I could just bury myself in the covers of my bed until the station feels like it's no longer spinning. But I'm in no state to encounter Charlotte's keen eyes, so now I'm floundering in the middle of a small rainforest at the center of a giant ship.

I hate that I can't talk to you about any of this, but I can't break your heart further. I just can't do it. Still, to be lost amid these revelations all on my own . . . I am a ship without navigation and no way to signal for home.

CHAPTER 36

Kent Orbital Station, Londinium Orbit, Long Route 7

Elizabeth woke the next morning to the same thoughts and meditations which she'd fallen asleep to a handful of hours before. She couldn't yet recover from the surprise of what had happened. It was impossible to think of anything else, but she resolved, soon after breakfast, to leave the house again and walk off some of this restlessness inside her.

She started toward her favorite walk in Rosings Park, when she remembered that Mr. Darcy sometimes came that way. Instead, she traveled into Hunsford Sector. She'd planned to bring something home for each sister, and had yet to pick Mary a book. What better way to distract the mind than to peruse the shelves of the Trilogy? She hoped it'd work.

The bookshop was a couple lanes off the main avenue, and she turned as she passed the biosilk weaver, the corner window displays alight with various shimmering silks and a few glowing spiders in lavish cages. The morning was a pleasant temperature, halfway through its steady climb to the simulated midday heat, and the streets were busy in a lazy, small-town sort of way. She meandered along the lane, stopping here and there to admire window displays or smell a new and interesting flower sprouting from vines along a fence. All the while, Londinium rose like a pale blue sun against a sky of black in the wall of windows.

The weeks she'd passed aboard the station had made a great difference in the scenery out those windows, each new view of moon or planet or unfamiliar constellation somehow added something different to the coloring or look of the trees. She reached the lane where the Trilogy stood, the windows and the sloping Rosings Park a jeweled background to the buildings at the end of the lane. Through the gaps in two of them, she caught a glimpse of a gentleman walking with purpose down the avenue. Something about his gait set her on edge. It couldn't be Mr. Darcy, and yet, her mind went to him at once.

She hurried to the bookshop door. The building was faced with uneven stone in various browns and grays. A little wooden bench sat beneath the large window, which was so full of books, seeing inside was impossible. She reached for the door handle, when she spotted the sign and realized that the shop was closed for another ten minutes. She cursed under her breath, then sat, impatience creeping in.

She closed her eyes and breathed in the floral scent of the air, listening to the soft noises of people following their daily routines. Finally, she heard a gentle scraping on the shop door. She turned to look, standing as she did. The sign had been flipped to OPEN. As she reached for the handle, she heard Mr. Darcy's voice. He strode down the lane, near enough to see her face clearly. He moved with eagerness, calling her name. She felt herself lurch toward the door, but reluctantly pulled back. He'd only follow her inside, and she'd rather not be trapped indoors for whatever it was that he might say.

Her heart jumped into her throat as he drew even with her.

Holding out a small bundle of paper, which she instinctively took, he said, with a look of haughty composure, "I've been walking the level for some time in the hopes of meeting you. Would you do me the honor of reading this letter?" Then, with a slight bow, retreated, and was soon out of sight.

With no expectation of pleasure, but with the strongest curiosity—a handwritten letter, on actual paper!—Elizabeth sat back down on the bench and opened it. To her ever-increasing surprise, she unfolded the envelope to discover two sheets of thick paper brimming with closely written script. The envelope was likewise full. It was dated just hours prior. She tucked her legs beneath her on the bench and started to read.

Do not be alarmed by this letter, nor apprehensive of it containing any repetition of the sentiments which were yesterday so disgusting to you. I write without any intention of paining you, or humbling myself, by dwelling on wishes which can't be forgotten for either of us soon enough. The effort of this letter could've been spared had my character not required it to be written and read. You must pardon the freedom with which I demand your attention. Your feelings, I know, will bestow it unwillingly, but I demand it of your justice.

Yesterday, you attributed two offenses of very different nature — and by no means of equal magnitude — to my doing. The first, that regardless of the sentiments of either, I'd detached Mr. Bingley from your sister. The other, that in defiance of law, honor, and humanity, I ruined the prosperity and prospects of Mr. Wickham. To have willfully and wantonly thrown off my childhood companion — a young man dependent upon my family, well-loved by my father, and brought up to expect an inheritance — would be a depravity on a level that could not compare to the separation of two people whose affection had grown over a matter of weeks. But I hope to avoid the severest of the blame you bestowed on me yesterday by accounting here of my actions and motives in each circumstance. If, during my explanation, I must relate feelings of mine that are offensive to yours, I can only say that I'm sorry. The necessity must be obeyed, and further apology would be absurd.

I hadn't been on Heoros long before I — and others — saw that Bingley preferred your older sister to any other in the district. But it wasn't until the evening of the dance on the Netherfield that I had any apprehension of his being seriously attached. I've often seen him in love before. At the ball, while I had the honor of dancing with you, I was alerted — first by Sir William Lucas's accidental information — that Bingley's attentions to your sister had given rise to a general expectation of their marriage. He spoke of it as a confirmed event, of which the time alone was left undecided. From that moment I observed my friend's behavior closely. I could see that his partiality for your sister was beyond what I'd ever witnessed in him. I watched your sister as well. She was open and cheerful, as engaging as ever, but without any look of particular regard. I remained convinced throughout the evening that though she received his attention with pleasure, she didn't invite it with any reciprocal sentiment. If you aren't mistaken here, I must've been wrong. You know your sister better than I. If that's the case, if I've been misled by such error to inflict pain on her, your resentment isn't unreasonable. But I want to assert that the general serenity of your sister's manners is enough that even the most acute observer could be convinced—however amiable she may be—that her heart isn't easily touched. I certainly desired to believe she was indifferent. But my investigation and decisions are not usually influenced by my hopes or fears. I didn't believe her indifferent because I wished it. I believed it on impartial conviction and a desire to see with reason. My objections to the match weren't merely those I acknowledged to put aside for passion, in my own case. The want of connection wasn't so great an issue to my friend as it was to me. But there were other causes of aversion that, while still existing for both him and myself in equal measure, I'd convinced myself to look past because they weren't immediately before me. The causes must be stated, though briefly.

The situation of your mother's family, though objectionable, was nothing in comparison to the total lack of propriety so frequently—almost uniformly—shown by herself, your three younger sisters, and even, I'm sorry to say, occasionally your father. It pains me to offend you. But amid your concern and displeasure at this representation of your family, let it give you consolation to consider that not once have you or your older sister been included in any share of your family's criticism. I'll only add that, from what passed that evening, my opinion of all involved was confirmed, and increased every temptation which led me to save my friend from what I believed was an unhappy match. He left Fleoros the next day, as I'm sure you remember, with plans to return quickly.

My part here must be explained. His sisters' uneasiness about the situation was equal to my own, and once we realized this, we all felt there was no time to lose in separating them. On Londinium, I was more than happy to point out the disadvantages of their match. I described them earnestly. But however much my explanations might've lessened or delayed his determination I don't think it would've ultimately prevented a marriage, had I not followed it up with the assurance that your sister was indifferent. He believed that she reciprocated his affections both sincerely and equally. But Bingley is naturally modest and depends more strongly on my judgment than his own. To convince him that he'd deceived himself wasn't difficult. To persuade him not to return to Fleoros, after what I'd expressed, took no time at all. I can't blame myself for having done all this. But there is one part of my conduct in this whole affair that I'm not proud of. I stooped to concealing your sister's presence from him in Londinium. I knew she was in town and so did his sister. But Bingley is still ignorant of it. That they might've met without unfortunate consequences is possible, but his feelings for her didn't appear sufficiently extinguished for him to see her without some danger. Perhaps this was beneath me. It's done, however, and was done with the best intentions. On this subject I have nothing more to say, nor any other apology to offer. If I wounded your sister's feelings, it was unknowingly done. Though the motives which governed me may appear insufficient to you, I've not yet learned to condemn them.

In regard to that other, more weighty accusation, of having injured Mr. Wickham. I can only refute it by explaining the entirety of his connection with my family. Of what he's particularly accused me, I'm ignorant. But I can summon more than one witness of reputable honesty to corroborate the truth of what I relate to you.

Mr. Wickham is the son of a very respectable man, who managed the entire Pemberley Estate. His good conduct in the discharge of my father's trust naturally inclined my father to be of service to him. So, on George Wickham, who was his godson, my father liberally bestowed his kindness— supporting him at school, and afterward at Cambridge. He assisted financially where Wickham's own father would've been unable to. Even as a child, Wickham was very engaging. My father wasn't just fond of him, but had the highest opinion of him, and hoping the temple would be his profession, intended to provide for him in it. As for myself, it has been many, many years since I first began to think of Wickham differently. The vicious propensities—the want of principle, which Wickham was careful to guard from the knowledge of my father—couldn't escape the notice of someone nearly the same age as himself. I had opportunities to see him in unguarded moments, which my father couldn't have. Here again I may pain you— to what degree only you can tell. But whatever sentiments Mr. Wickham has created, a suspicion of their nature won't prevent me from unfolding his true character. It adds even another motive.

My father died about five years ago. His attachment to Wickham was steady to his last breath. In his will, he specifically recommended to me that I promote Wickham's advancement in the best way allowed for his profession —and if he chose the temple, desired that a valuable homestead would become his as soon as it was available. There was also a legacy of one thousand aurum. His own father didn't live much longer. Within half a year of their deaths, Wickham sent a waive to inform me that, having finally resolved against joining the temple, he hoped I wouldn't think it unreasonable for him to expect some more immediate financial assistance. He hoped to attain it rather than the preferment, as that would no longer benefit him. He had some intention, he added, of studying law. He reminded me that the interest of one thousand aurum would be insufficient support for this career path. I wished, rather than believed, that he was sincere. But I was perfectly ready to accept this proposal. I knew that Wickham and the temple were not compatible. The business was soon settled. He resigned all claim to assistance in the temple, should he ever be in a situation to receive it, and accepted in return three thousand aurum. All connection between us seemed dissolved. I thought too ill of him to invite him to Pemberley, or admit his company in mine on Londinium. I believe he lived in Lowland, mainly. But studying law was a pretense. He was free from restraint, and his life was one of idleness and dissipation. For about three years I heard little of him, but when the homestead he was originally meant to have finally became available, he sent a waive requesting it. His circumstances, he assured me—and I had no difficulty believing it—were exceedingly bad. He'd found the law an unprofitable study, and was now absolutely resolved on being ordained, if I would present him with the homestead in question. He believed there'd be little doubt of receiving it, as he was sure I had no one else to provide it to, and couldn't have forgotten my father's intentions. You can hardly blame me for refusing to comply with his request, or for resisting every repetition of it. His resentment was in proportion to the distress of his circumstances—and he was doubtless as violent in his abuse of me to others as he was toward myself. After a time, our communications stopped. How he lived, I don't know. But last summer he again most painfully intruded in my life.

I must now mention a circumstance which I wish to forget and which nothing less than the present obligation would induce me to tell to anyone. Having said this much, I feel no doubt that you'll keep this secret for me. My sister, who is more than ten years my junior, was left to the guardianship of VC Fitzwilliam and myself. About a year ago, she moved from school to be tutored in an establishment formed for her on Londinium. Last summer she went with the lady who presided over it, to Rackport. Wickham went, too, undoubtedly on purpose, as there proved to have been a prior acquaintance between him and Mrs. Younge—who deceived us all about her true character. Through her planning and help, Wickham befriended Georgiana. My sister has an affectionate heart and a strong impression of his kindness to her as a child. He persuaded her to believe herself in love, and to consent to an elopement. She was fifteen. She isn't to blame for believing him. She can be credited, I'm happy to say, for bringing the situation to my attention. I joined them unexpectedly a day or two before the intended elopement, and Georgiana, unable to bear the thought of hurting and offending the brother whom she almost looked up to as a father, admitted everything to me. You may imagine what I felt and how I acted. Regard for my sister's credit and feelings prevented any public exposure, but I sent word to Wickham, who left immediately, and Mrs. Younge was, of course, removed from her charge. Wickham's main object was unquestionably my sister's fortune, which is thirty thousand aurum; yet I can't help supposing that the hope of revenging himself on me was a strong inducement. His revenge would've been complete indeed.

This is a faithful narrative of every event in which we've been concerned together. If you don't reject it as absolutely false, you will, I hope, acquit me of cruelty toward Mr. Wickham. I don't know in what manner or under what falsehood he imposed on you, but his success is perhaps not hard to understand. Ignorant as you were of everything concerning either of us, you'd have no way of detecting the truth, and you're certainly not inclined to be suspicious of him.

You might possibly wonder why all of this was not said yesterday. In truth, I wasn't master enough of my emotions to know what could or ought to be revealed. To verify anything I've told you, I can appeal particularly to the testimony of VC Fitzwilliam, who, from our close relationship, and as executor of my father's will, has been unavoidably acquainted with every particular of these transactions. If your abhorrence of me should make my assertions valueless, you can't have the same qualms in confiding in my cousin. If you should endeavor to consult him, I'll do my best to put this letter in your hands sometime this morning. I'll only add, take care and be well.

Fitzwilliam Darcy

CHAPTER 37

Kent Orbital Station, Londinium Orbit, Long Route 7

Elizabeth couldn't have anticipated the contents of Mr. Darcy's letter, and yet she read voraciously, too eager to allow herself comprehension, and too impatient for the next sentence that she barely made sense of the words before her eyes.

His belief of Jane's indifference was clearly false. His account of the worst objections to the match made her too angry to give him any benefit of the doubt. He expressed no regret for what he'd done. In fact, he was haughty—all pride and insolence.

But as the subject moved to his account of Mr. Wickham, she was able to read with clearer attention. This relation of events, if true, could eclipse all her strongly held opinions of his worth, bearing such an alarming resemblance to Mr. Wickham's own account. She felt so oppressed by her overwhelming feelings.

"This must be false," she exclaimed, as though discrediting it aloud would make it so. "It can't be. This is a horrible lie."

The bookshop door chimed and Elizabeth noted a woman entering, flashing her a slightly alarmed backward glance.

Her heart leapt in surprise. She'd entirely forgotten where she was. She scanned through the remainder of the letter, hardly processing the last two pages, and stuffed it hastily in her pocket. She wouldn't think of it and she'd never look at it again.

Cutting through a community garden and back to the main avenue, she walked briskly toward the back wall of Hunsford Sector, where she could disappear into the bustle of B level while her mind spiraled and refused to touch down on a single thought.

Hardly realizing she was doing it, in half a minute the letter was unfolded again in her hands. She wove slowly through the people on the walking path, the sounds of conversation and the swish and chime of doors opening and closing all falling into an auditory blur as she began reading again, this time on the parts relating to Wickham.

She commanded herself to examine the meaning of every sentence. At first, both Wickham and Mr. Darcy's accounts aligned, each confirming the other's story. But when it came to the will, the difference was great.

In relation to the particulars, it was impossible not to feel that there was a disturbing duplicity on one side or the other. For a moment she could let herself believe her initial convictions. But as she read and reread that section, she was forced to hesitate.

Lowering the letter, she stood for a moment on the declining road to the B level. The slow and clever shift from stone to metal around her glazed into background behind her memories as she deliberated every circumstance and their probability. She intended to be impartial. It was to no avail.

She shook the thoughts clear, started down the road again, and staying near the wall to keep out of the way, read on. But with each line, a new clarity emerged. She'd never heard of Mr. Wickham before his appearance in the Star Force Reserves, which he'd entered thanks to a friend who hadn't known him on Dyberion. In fact there was nothing known of him or his past within all of the Heoros satellite system other than what he told of himself. As to his true character, she'd never felt the need to investigate. His countenance, voice, and manner had immediately established him as trustworthy.

She tried to recall some instance of goodness or trait of integrity that might rescue him from Mr. Darcy's attacks, but she couldn't. She could picture him standing in front of her, all charm and grace, but there was nothing beyond the general adoration of the district, and the regard which his sociability had gained him among their society.

Thinking about that first conversation she'd had with Mr. Wickham at her aunt and uncle's home, she was struck by the impropriety of such a confession to a stranger. How had she not questioned it before? How bold he'd been to put himself forward like that. How inconsistent his professions had been. He had boasted of not fearing to see Mr. Darcy, yet he'd avoided the Netherfield ball the very next week. He had also told no one other than herself about his story until the Netherfield had left the moon permanently. Afterward, it had been discussed everywhere. He'd had no qualms with voiding Mr. Darcy's character then, though he'd assured her that his respect for the father had prevented him from exposing the son.

Everything now appeared so differently where Wickham was concerned. His attentions to Miss King were predatory and desperate. His behavior toward herself could now have no tolerable motive. He'd either been deceived in regard to her fortune, or had been gratifying his vanity by encouraging the preference which she'd so incautiously shown.

Every lingering struggle in his favor grew fainter and fainter. In further justification of Mr. Darcy, she couldn't forget that Mr. Bingley, when questioned by Jane, had long ago asserted his friend's blamelessness in the affair. Proud and repulsive as his manners were, never in the whole course of their acquaintance had she seen anything that betrayed him to be unprincipled or unjust.

She'd reached the main floor of B level, and the noise and colors had increased. This part of Hunsford Sector was bustling, which made it easier to go unnoticed as she found a bench and sat, shame seeping into her every pore. With both Wickham and Darcy she'd been blind, partial, prejudiced . . . "Absurd," she muttered.

She'd prided herself on her discernment; valued herself for her abilities; often thought less of her sister's generous candor, and gratified her vanity in useless mistrust. How humiliating! Had she been in love, she couldn't have been more wretchedly blind. But vanity had been her folly.

From herself to Jane—from Jane to Bingley, her thoughts reminded her that Mr. Darcy's explanation *there* had appeared very insufficient. She read the letter again. The effect was widely different. He declared himself to be totally unsuspicious of Jane's attachment. She couldn't help remembering Charlotte's opinion on the subject, nor that Jane's feelings, though fervent, were little displayed.

She could also painfully recall every point of Mr. Darcy's mortifying, though merited, account of her family. The circumstances he pointed out from the Netherfield ball couldn't have made a stronger impression on his mind than on hers.

The compliment to herself and her sister soothed, but couldn't console her. Jane's heartbreak had indeed come at the hands of her family. How terribly her own and Jane's credit must suffer by such conduct. Gravity seemed to have multiplied, pulling her heart down with incredible force.

She stood, reconciling herself to a change so sudden and important that fatigue overtook her. It had been too long since she left the parsonage. She strode to the B floor door of the Trilogy. Taking the short path up through the bookstore, heart and mind too unsettled even for the welcome distraction of books, she returned to the Parsonage.

When she entered, Charlotte had lunch waiting. Wishing to appear as cheerful as usual, and resolved to repress any reflections that would make her unfit for conversation, Elizabeth sat with her friend for a time.

"Both the Rosings men came to say their goodbyes," Charlotte told her. "Mr. Darcy only stayed a few minutes, but VC Fitzwilliam sat for nearly an hour before he gave up." Her friend eyed her keenly as she added, "he seemed ready to go looking for you, but I convinced him not to."

Elizabeth could barely summon the visage of concern in missing him. "I appreciate it," she said, taking a sip of tea. The Void Commander was of no concern to her now. She could think only of her letter.

LONDINIUM SAT[SYS

Communications Log—System Storage 30 Days [Planetary]

[FW.Darcy] 23.4-18:08:56.LS

I need to tell you something important, and it's very serious.

[GiGi-D] 23.4-18:12:34.LS

Is it super serious, or usual you serious?

[FW.Darcy] 23.4-18:14:49.LS

You aren't going to be happy about it.

[GiGi-D] 23.4-18:15:58.LS

I'm listening.

. . . Reading.

. . . You know what I mean.

[FW.Darcy] 23.4-18:17:47.LS

I told Miss Elizabeth why I came to the Kent.

. . . I also proposed.

[GiGi-D] 23.4-18:18:25.LS

WHY WOULD I NOT BE HAPPY ABOUT THIS?

[FW.Darcy] 23.4-18:19:53.LS

It was a disaster.

[GiGi-D] *DISLIKES MESSAGE*

[GiGi-D] 23.4-18:21:08.LS

I'm sorry.

. . . But what does that have to do with me?

[FW.Darcy] 23.4-18:24:27.LS

She accused me of some things. Not all were true. I had to write her a letter and correct the falsehoods.

[GiGi-D] 23.4-18:26:03.LS

You wouldn't be you if you didn't.

■ ■ ■

[FW.Darcy] 23.4-18:30:30.LS
What I'm going to say will pain you, Gi. I wish that it wouldn't, but all I can offer is this paltry apology. I'm sorry.

[GiGi-D] *DISLIKES MESSAGE*

. . . The accusation was about Wickham. It seems he's been spreading falsehoods about me and the money our father left for him. I needed her to understand his character and the true nature of our history. I had to tell her what transpired with you. She has sisters as well and is as protective of them as I am of you. I knew she'd understand.

And I believe I've judged her correctly in character—if not in feelings for me—that she won't repeat what I've said about your involvement. So please don't worry.

. . . COM IDLE [16] MINUTES . . .

[GiGi-D] 23.4-18:46:07.LS
I trust you. If you still trust her after she rejected you (I will need to know more about this later) then I trust her, too.

[FW.Darcy] 23.4-18:49:53.LS
Thank you for understanding. I just wanted you to be aware. I'm heading back to Londinium in the morning. I believe by then I'll have sorted my thoughts enough to tell you what happened.

[GiGi-D] 23.4-18:52:21.LS
I impatiently await your arrival.
. . . But seriously, take care of yourself until I can ply you with sweet crystals and sister hugs.

. . . END COM . . .

CHAPTER
38

Kent Orbital Station, Londinium Orbit, Long Route 7

Charlotte couldn't pinpoint what had happened in the past few days, but she felt sure she was missing something important. It was clear that Elizabeth was being guarded, so she didn't pry. Still, she watched and wondered.

Even Lady Catherine seemed to have sensed something off about her friend. After another dinner at Rosings, she observed that Lizzie seemed out of spirits. "It's always hard to leave a place you've enjoyed so much, especially when you're with such good company. If you stay another *month*, I'll be able to escort you to Londinium myself. I'm going there in early June, for a week. You can ride in the Arklight. Dawson is a fabulous pilot. And there'll be plenty of room for one of you. In fact, if the entry into the atmosphere will be smooth, I shouldn't object to taking you both." Here she looked at Maria. "Neither of you are very large."

"You're all kindness, ma'am, but I believe we must stick to our original schedule."

Lady Catherine sighed. "Very well." She turned to Charlotte. "Mrs. Collins, you must send a servant with them. I can't bear the idea of two young women traveling public transport by themselves. It's highly improper."

Charlotte nodded along, knowing Elizabeth would correct the woman momentarily, but not daring to interrupt.

"You must find a way to send someone along. When my niece Georgiana went to Rackport last summer, I made a point of her having two escorts. I'm excessively attentive to all those things. Miss Bennet and Miss Lucas must also have proper escort, Mrs. Collins. I'm glad it occurred to me to mention it. It'd be really a discredit to *you* if they were to go alone."

Charlotte smiled serenely and waited for her friend to set her ladyship to rights.

Reliably, Lizzie spoke. "My uncle has acquired a private compartment for us."

"My stars!—your uncle! I'm so glad you have someone who thinks of these things. Good. Good. We're on the outer orbit now. Where will you stop over? Oh, Apollia, of course. It'll be between us this time of year. If you mention my name at Flight Service, you'll be attended to."

Lady Catherine had many other questions to ask regarding their journey. Though she answered a good many herself, she did occasionally expect their input. Charlotte couldn't say for certain, but she thought this might have been the only reason Lizzie didn't drift completely off into her own thoughts.

She remained only half-present for her last few days on the Kent, though she seemed to be making a concerted effort not to appear that way.

When Charlotte stepped into the dining room on the morning of Lizzie and Maria's departure, she found her friend in conversation with her husband.

"Let me assure you, Miss Elizabeth," he said, "that I can from my heart wish you equal happiness in marriage. My dear Charlotte and I have but one mind and one way of thinking. There is, in everything, a most remarkable resemblance of character and ideas between us. We seem to have been designed for each other."

Charlotte was pleased with this description. How much truth there was to it was a matter best left unstudied.

"I'm glad to know that's the case," Elizabeth said, seeing and nodding at Charlotte in greeting. "I firmly believe that she has every comfort she could hope to have and I'm very happy for her."

"The only comfort I'll be missing is your presence, dear Eliza," she said, honestly. Then she alerted her husband to the arrival of the hover cart.

With their trunks fastened, the group made the trek down to the lower docking bays. The goodbyes when they reached the shuttle were shorter than Charlotte wished for them to be, but without her prompting, her husband would talk to them so long they'd miss their departure time.

"Galaxy's end," Maria sighed happily, "it feels like we only arrived a few days ago. And yet, so many things have happened!"

"So many, indeed," Lizzie said, with something in her tone that told Charlotte that whatever had occurred was still very much bothering her friend. She longed to know, but she was forced to be content until Lizzie was ready to divulge.

VOICE JOURNAL

COM TAG: LIZZIELOVESSPACE—E. BENNET
PERSONAL JOURNAL / COMCARD ID: HC-3095.D2.EB
TIMESTAMP: 26.4-II:04:3I.LS
LOCATION: KENT ORBITAL STATION

(26.4-11:04:31.LS) TRANSCRIPTION:

I've memorized whole passages of his letter. Yet with each reading my feelings shift wildly. When I think about the way he addressed me, I feel so . . . indignant. But then I consider how unfair I was to condemn him and reprimand him like a child . . . and then I'm angry with myself. To think of the disappointment on his face when I . . . I feel sorry for him. I can't lie. I do feel some gratitude that he would have any attachment to me. But I don't want to take back my refusal. I don't even feel the slightest inclination to see him again. Perhaps that's more to do with me?

(27.4-7:23:57.LS) TRANSCRIPTION:

I'm beginning to dread the thoughts of my past behavior. It's a constant source of frustration and regret. And my family. Stars! The distress and embarrassment there weighs heavily. There's nothing that can set that situation right. My father's content to laugh at Lydia and Kitty's wild giddiness. Mama's manners are horrendous. Mary is the quietest of us and still finds negative attention. She's less of a concern, though. I can't even count the times Jane and I have attempted to check our other sisters' indiscretions. But as long as our mother indulges them, what improvement is possible? Kitty follows along with everything her baby sister wants—which only further encourages Lydia's wild, careless spirit. Kitty's forever affronted by our advice, and Lydia never hears a thing we say to begin with. They're both—Stars around us! Mama, too—ignorant, idle, and vain. If there's an officer on the Meryton, they'll flirt with him; and as long as they're easily accessible, it'll go on forever. It can't be helped.

(28.4-22:04:39.LS) TRANSCRIPTION:

Just thinking of Jane. Mr. Darcy's explanation restored my good opinion of his friend, but at what cost? It's only heightened my sense of what Jane has lost. His affection was sincere. He's not to blame for the way he conducted himself. Except . . . it pains me to think that Jane was deprived of such a desirable match—in every way that matters—by the folly of her own family and the misplaced trust of a close friend.

(29.4-14:24:12.LS) TRANSCRIPTION:

I know his letter by heart now. I've studied every sentence with twice as much diligence as anything before. How could I have been so naive about Wickham? I'm not sure what I'm more ashamed of: scolding a grown man while simultaneously being so wrong, or blindly trusting a liar because of his looks and demeanor. I'm smarter than that.

I thought I was.

CHAPTER
39

The Juelle Waystation,
Heoros Orbit, First Moon of Londinium

Jane was reunited with her sister the night before the two of them, with Maria Lucas, left Londinium. They traveled to the Juelle, a smaller waystation that circled Heoros in a wider orbit, where they'd find their home transport—and younger sisters—waiting for them.

Upon disembarking, a bag service took their luggage to where her father's transport ship was docked, and they made their way through the halls to the central chamber. The Juelle was a strange and special waystation to visit. The central chamber was a cylinder, the walls and ceiling acting as more floor. Standing in the entrance, they could look above them and see people walking on a mirroring avenue as if suspended from the sky.

They didn't visit here often. Jane always found it equal parts entrancing and unsettling. She looked to what would've been the left wall, but which was also a steep upward hill, and spotted the street where Mary's waive indicated the tearoom would be. The girls would already be there.

"This way," she told her companions, and led them in the right direction.

As they neared, they spotted Kitty and Lydia in a second-floor window of a narrow starflower-white building with rounded corners and a shimmering curtain of an awning over its wide doors.

The three of them went quickly inside and upstairs, finding the two youngest spread among bags and belongings on a bench seat at a table in the corner.

"We've been waiting for you for an hour," Lydia said by way of greeting.

Kitty nodded excitedly. "Yes, we visited the shop square, sat at the window, and watched a handsome security guard at that entrance just there—" she pointed out the window.

"But then he got replaced by some old guy," Lydia cut in. "So we ordered lunch! Hi, by the way, Maria."

Kitty corrected her sister as she gave Maria a hug. "It's just a salad and snack spread." She released her friend and grabbed Jane's and Lizzie's hands. "Isn't this nice? Such a lovely surprise, right?"

"We're treating you," Lydia added. "But you'll need to lend us the money for it. We spent all of ours at the shops."

Jane shook her head and side-eyed Lizzie, who returned her look of amused consternation, neither of them surprised by this request.

"And where's Mary?" Lizzie asked.

"She found a bookshop. She wasn't done looking through it," Lydia answered.

Kitty squeezed Jane's hand. "I told her we would send a short waive when you arrived."

Jane smiled and squeezed back. Kitty had a thoughtfulness that was often cast aside in favor of mirroring Lydia's silliness. It was nice when she saw glimpses of that sweet little kid she used to be, back in the time before Lydia had grown enough to suck her sister into her orbit.

Lydia twirled around the chairs and slid into the bench seat, instantly rummaging through bags. "Look! I got this hat. It's not very pretty," she picked at the straw-lace, "but its quality is decent. I'll take it apart when we get home and make it better."

"It's horrible," Kitty said, dropping Jane's and Lizzie's hands.

"Truly not up to your—or anyone's—standards," Lizzie added.

Lydia was perfectly unconcerned by this. "Oh, there were a few uglier than this. I'll use some of the fabric scraps from Aunt Mari's Turning gift to trim it. Perhaps some structural changes as well. I'll need to sketch some ideas."

Jane laughed lightly. Leave it to Lydia to purchase a terribly ugly hat and see the beauty underneath. "I have no doubt it'll be revived under your care, Lydia."

"Even if it's only tolerable when I finish, it won't much matter. After the Red Squadron leaves Meryton, who will be around to impress? They're leaving in a fortnight."

"They are, indeed," Lizzie said, with more satisfaction than Jane thought to expect from her.

"They're going to be encamped near Sollaria. I *so* want Papa to take us all there for the whole summer! It'd be such a delicious scheme. And it'd hardly cost us anything at all. Mama would like to go, too, I know it."

"Stars in the sky," Lizzie said lowly, so only Jane could hear. "A whole town of officers and pilots, after we've been overset by a single regiment and the monthly balls of the Meryton."

"Our summer'll be miserable without them here!" Lydia lamented, unaware of her sister's derision. "Oh! I've got more news for you. It's about someone we all like." She gestured them all to the table and didn't continue till they'd each taken a seat. "It's about dear Wickham. There's no danger of him marrying Mary King. She's gone off to her uncle's on Itavia. Gone to stay! Count our stars lucky!—Wickham is safe."

"And Mary King is safe," Lizzie added, "from an unwise connection and unstable future."

Jane noted that the way Lizzie said this suggested something more behind her statement.

"She's a fool for going away if she liked him," Lydia countered.

"I hope there was no strong attachment for either of them," Jane said, Bingley crossing her mind.

"I'm sure there's none on *his*. If you ask me, he never cared about her. But who could? She's so very . . . uninteresting."

Jane thought that was unfair, but knew that Lydia was in no state to listen, should she say so aloud. Instead, she shifted the topic to Mary, who'd finally crested the stairs and was headed toward them.

"What'd you find?" Lizzie asked.

Mary lifted a tote bag and smiled. She thumped the bag on the table and sat beside Kitty. Pulling a little green book from its depths, she handed it to her. "*Stunning Plants of the Planetary System*," she said.

Kitty squealed in delight and took the book with reverence.

Mary revealed a magazine next. "Latest *Designer's Guide*, as requested," she said, handing it to Lydia.

"I didn't forget you, Maria," she said, slipping her a tall, thin tome. "*Crafting with Found Images*," she added. "I heard you captured quite a lot on the Kent."

Then, with both hands, she pulled the remainder of the books from her bag. In quick succession, she handed off two of them. "Jane, this is supposed to be a popular one. Some kind of far-flung romance." She handed off a small silver book with white writing. The title read *Starcrossed*. Jane felt a small slip in her composure, her thoughts turning to Bingley again, and the quip her father had made with the same word months ago.

"If this is the wrong one, Lizzie, I can return it," Mary said, pulling Jane back to the present in time to see a dark blue book with a ship schematic on the cover.

"You're so thoughtful, Mary, thank you," Jane said. The others echoed her.

Mary shrugged and re-stacked the remaining three books, returning them to her bag. "It's been too long since we were all together. Felt like celebrating."

With new treasures in hand, the group settled happily into eating and talking and perusing the pages. Soon, Kitty and Lydia insisted that Maria give them minute details of her stay on the Kent, while Mary and Lizzie got lost in comparing the descriptions of the bookshops they'd both visited last.

Jane was happy just listening and basking in the comfort of having her sisters all around her once again.

When they'd been refueled and felt it was time to go—and Jane and Lizzie had paid—they made their way to the docks and piled in. It was quite a puzzle to fit all their luggage and shopping bags and boxes in the spaces between where they were seated, but they managed it.

"We're crammed in so nicely," Lydia noted as they disembarked. "I'm glad I bought the hat, if only because I'll have another hat box!"

"This feels like the nights we spent when we were younger," Kitty said, turning from the window as the Juelle shrank away from them, looking to Jane and Lizzie, "and we'd cram in with your beds pushed together, and talk all night till we fell asleep."

"Oh, what a great idea," Lydia cut in. "We're all comfy and snug. Let's talk the whole way home! Maria has filled us in on her experience, but what about you two? What happened to you both while you were gone?" She leaned past Mary to ask.

Mary, already lost in one of her new books, simply lifted it over Lydia's head and read on.

"Have you seen any pleasant men? Have you been flirting with said men? I was really hoping one of you might have a husband before you came back. Jane, you'll be too grown and set in your ways soon, and then what man will you want? None. Twenty-three is more than old enough to know what you want and you can get yourself a partner so he can do all the things you don't want to. Without one, you'll be forced to do everything yourself. Stars!—that sounds exhausting. I'd be so ashamed of myself not to have a husband by then. What good is my youth and beauty if I can't use it to snag a man to do all those boring things adults must do for me? And anyway, Aunt Phillips, I'm sure, will help you both. She says Lizzie should've accepted Mr. Collins. I don't think there would've been any fun in it, though. No offense to your sister, Maria," she added, almost as an afterthought.

Jane wasn't offended by her sister's statements. Lydia was young and still feeling out her beliefs and opinions. Though Jane hadn't been as . . . strident as Lydia, she'd certainly changed and grown since she was freshly sixteen. Lydia would, too.

"Imagine if I were married before all of you. *I* could be your chaperone to the balls! We had such a good bit of fun the other day at VC Forster's."

As Lydia talked, Jane noticed that Lizzie seemed to have become lost in her thoughts. Jane said nothing, but watched her more closely.

"Mrs. Forster promised to have a little dance in the evening— oh, we're *such* good friends now, Mrs. Forster and I, closer than the twin moons of Wenhal. So she asked the two Harringtons to come, but Mae was sick, so Emilia had to come by herself. Guess what we did? We helped Chamberlayne dress as one of us girls and made him all up—it was so fun! Nobody could even tell he wasn't a young lady except the Forsters, of course, and Kitty and me. We did have to loop Aunt Phillips in, too, as we borrowed one of her dresses. Whatever you're imagining, he looked better. Honestly,

I should've been jealous, if I wasn't completely secure with myself. And anyway, when Denny and Wickham and Pratt and a few of the other men came in, they didn't even know him! We had such a good evening, and we laughed so much—it was the most fun. You shouldn't have missed it!"

Jane noticed a brief frown cross Lizzie's face at the mention of Wickham. They'd parted amicably enough, as far as she knew. But this was the second indicator that something had shifted. What could've changed her opinion of him when she'd been nowhere near him?

She wouldn't get to find out for some time, because the moment they touched down on Heoros, the family was gathering with the Lucases for dinner, and there was very little time to speak to anyone without being in earshot of someone else.

"Oh, my beautiful girl," her mother said, fawning over Jane immediately, "the Londinium air has been so good to you. As radiant as ever, my dear." She cupped Jane's cheeks in her hands.

"Thank you, Mama," she said, as she heard her father tell Lizzie warmly, "I'm glad you're finally home."

Jane didn't begrudge her parents their little favoritisms, as she knew it was simply a quirk of personality and that way of some people to gravitate toward those they feel resemble themselves most. She knew her father loved and missed her with equal measure, but she could admit that she wasn't such good company when discussing the contents of a library as Lizzie, and recognized the appreciation of that in her father. After all, her mother didn't fawn over Lizzie the way she did with Jane. There was a balance there, in its own way.

The dining room was surely at its maximum capacity, with all the Lucases there to greet Maria and hear the news of her travels. Soon, her curiosity was swept away in the midst of several varied conversations across the table.

As Lady Lucas inquired after the welfare and gardens of her eldest daughter, Lydia was launching an inquisition at Jane as to the state of fashion on Londinium. Their mother was then relaying this news to the youngest Lucas girls in a slightly overloud voice, which made it hard for Jane to concentrate on her answers to Lydia. Her father was speaking some with Mary and Lizzie. Mary had her new book out, reading them passages she had found interesting on the flight home.

"Mary," Lydia scolded, upon seeing the book out again. "You really should've joined us." She looked around the table. "There we all were, crowded in the ship, having a grand time, laughing and talking. And she had her nose in that book! Right there with us and missing it all."

Mary gravely replied, "It wasn't my intention to draw a cloud over the joy of your day, dear sister. It was all very interesting, what stories you told, I have no doubt. But I confess that gossip is not a charm for me. I should infinitely prefer a book."

Lydia had barely heard a word. She seldom listened to anyone for more than half a minute, and paid less than half as much attention to Mary as she'd ever done for Jane or Lizzie. The most important thing in Lydia's mind was whatever Lydia wanted to focus on.

When dinner was finished, Lydia did her best to cajole her older sisters into gaining permission to travel to the Meryton. But between Jane and Lizzie, the idea was grounded before launch.

"We don't want it said that the Bennets can't be home half a day before running off in pursuit of the officers," Lizzie reasoned.

But Jane sensed there was some other driving motive for Lizzie's staunch refusal to the idea. She was looking forward to finally being back in their room and having a chance to talk alone.

Before they retired to their rooms, however, Jane and Lizzie caught wind of Lydia's Sollaria scheme being discussed between their parents. It was clear to them both that their father didn't intend to allow it, but he was so vague in his answers that their mother, though disheartened, didn't appear to have given up on eventual success.

Visit SOLLARIA
Mama, look how beautiful
the water is! And the colors!
Can you imagine seeing it
in person? If only we didn't
HAVE to imagine!
Please, please, please let us go!
You let Jane and Lizzie go
places, but never us! It's
downright unfair!

CHAPTER 40

Longbourn House, Heoros, First Moon of Londinium

Elizabeth's impatience to tell Jane what had happened on the Kent was bubbling over. They'd barely gotten into their room, and Jane had only started to say, "Lizzie, is there something on your mind?" before Elizabeth whirled and nodded fervently.

Jane immediately came over to the end of her bed and sat facing her.

Elizabeth took a moment to ground herself, resolving to suppress every detail concerning Jane and preparing for her to be surprised. Then she sat on her own bed, leaned in, and replayed the scene between Mr. Darcy and herself.

Jane's eyes widened like twin moons as Elizabeth spoke. But her astonishment was soon lessened by her sisterly affection. "Of course he'd admire you, Lizzie. How could he not?" She frowned. "I'm sorry he admitted his feelings in such an ungentlemanly way. Being certain of succeeding was his mistake, for sure, but that must only have increased his disappointment."

"Absolutely," Elizabeth replied. "I'm truly sorry for him. But he had other feelings which will probably soon drive away his regard for me." She was silent a moment, concern clouding her mind. "You don't blame me, though, for refusing him?"

"Blame you! Of course not."

"You might after you hear this next part." She then explained the letter and repeated everything in relation to George Wickham. Jane was aghast. Elizabeth knew her sister would've gladly gone through the worlds never knowing such wickedness existed in all the system, let alone within one man. Not even Darcy's vindication, though it undoubtedly helped lessen the blow, could put her fully at ease after this news.

"There must be some error somewhere. Some way to clear one without involving the other . . ."

Elizabeth felt for her sister. "I'm sorry, but you'll never be able to make both of them innocent. There's only so much merit between them to make one good sort of man. And lately, for me, I'm inclined to believe it all belongs to Mr. Darcy. But you can choose as you please."

After more thought, a determined look settled on Jane's face. "I don't know when I've been more shocked," she said. "Wickham being so very bad . . . it's almost beyond belief. And poor Mr. Darcy. Lizzie, just imagine what he suffered. Such a disappointment. And with the knowledge of your poor opinion, too. He had to relate all of that, and confide his sister's experience. It's all so distressing. I'm sure you must be feeling it, too."

"No," Elizabeth said, "my regret is alleviated seeing you so full of it. You'll do him such justice that I'm growing more unconcerned and indifferent every moment. If you lament over him much longer, my heart will be light as a feather."

Jane cracked a smile, though it was small and quickly dispersed. "Poor Wickham," she mused. "He appears so kind and open."

"There was some severe mismanagement in the education of those two," Elizabeth said. "One has all the goodness, and the other all the appearance of it."

Jane shrugged. "I never thought Mr. Darcy so deficient as you used to."

"I thought I was uncommonly clever to dislike him."

Jane sat straighter, a frown creasing her brows. "When you first read that letter, I'm sure you didn't treat all of this as you do now."

A small laugh escaped her. "Stars!—not at all. I was uncomfortable. You could even say unhappy. I had no one to speak to about what I felt—no ever-thoughtful older sister to comfort me and say that I wasn't as weak and vain and nonsensical as I knew I'd been— oh, it was awful."

"How unfortunate that you spoke so strongly of Wickham to Mr. Darcy," Jane mused. "It now seems quite undeserved."

"Oh, yes. But unfortunately, speaking with such bitterness is the natural consequence of all the prejudices I've fostered." She leaned in. "There's one point of this where I want your advice."

Jane nodded, intent.

"I wonder whether I should—or not—make our general society aware of Wickham's character."

Jane thought for a moment. "Is there a reason to expose him? What's your opinion?"

"I don't think so. Mr. Darcy didn't seem to want his letter public. Everything about his sister I was meant to keep to myself as much as possible. If I attempt to reveal his true conduct, who would believe me? The general prejudice toward Mr. Darcy is quite intense. Half the Meryton's populace would implode if they attempted to believe that he isn't a villain. I'm not equal to the task. Wickham will be gone soon, and then it won't matter to anyone what he really is. Eventually everything will come to light, and then we can laugh at their stupidity for not knowing it before. But for now, I think I'll stay quiet about it."

"You're right. To have his errors made public might ruin his future. Perhaps he's sorry, now, for what he did in the past, and anxious to re-establish his character. We shouldn't make him desperate."

The meteor shower of thoughts and emotions pummeling Elizabeth's mind was quieted a good deal by this conversation. She'd gotten rid of two secrets which had weighed on her for a fortnight, and secured a willing listener in Jane—whenever she might wish to talk about either circumstance again. But there was still something lurking behind that she couldn't ease, because she loved her sister too much to disclose it.

The other half of Darcy's letter would remain a secret. She didn't dare to explain Mr. Bingley's true feelings. She felt that nothing less than a perfect understanding between everyone involved could justify ridding herself of the planet-sized weight of this last mystery. And, if that very improbable event should ever take place, she'd only be telling what Bingley himself would tell much more clearly. The freedom to divulge the secret couldn't be hers until it had lost all value.

She went to sleep feeling that there was nothing left to do but to observe the real state of Jane's spirits.

onday—

Is been a week since my sisters returned and that means there's only a
ek left of the regiment's company at the Meryton. We're all so dejected
re. Except for Jane and Lizzie. They have hearts of ice. They can still eat
d drink and sleep and enjoy their days as usual. I can't even enjoy drawing.
'm all misery.

What is to become of us? What am I to do? Lizzie just smiles when I say
is out loud, as if I'm the most entertaining in my agony.

It least Mama shares my grief. She told me something similar happened
hen she was my age. Said she cried for two days after VC Miller's
egiment went away. She thought her heart had been broken forever.
I'm sure mine will break, too.

f only we could go to Sollaria! But Papa is being so disagreeable.
unbathing and swimming would, as Mama said, set me up forever.

ST
Wednesday—EVER!!

   I could die happy! I've just been invited by Mrs. Forster to
come with her to Sollaria! What luck, that she married the VC
of the entire regiment, and that she's taken a liking to me!
(Though who wouldn't?) She's only known me three months,
ut honestly that's enough. It's going to be such
a great time! And I don't even need to convince
Papa to leave the house!

CHAPTER 41

Longbourn House, Heoros, First Moon of Londinium

Mr. Bennet endured Lydia's excitement upon receiving the invitation from Mrs. Forster, but only just. He reached his limit when that elation was then coupled by his wife's, and joined by Kitty's whining at being left out.

Lizzie attempted with little success to temper Lydia while Jane tried in vain to reason with Kitty. Eventually, Lizzie came to find him among his books. She barely crossed the threshold before she began speaking. "I don't know why Mama's so thrilled about this. Letting Lydia go to Sollaria will be the death of her common sense. She's always had one of us to tether her, and she won't have that with Mrs. Forster. I hate to sound so desperate, but I can't help but beg you not to let her go. She's not well behaved in general. She's not going to grow as a person with a connection like Mrs. Forster, nor with a trip like this. She'll be even more imprudent with a friend encouraging her, and there are so many more temptations there than at home."

He listened patiently, then shook his head. "Lydia will continue to be restless and wild until she's made her mistakes in some public place or other. We could never expect her to do it with so little expense or inconvenience to our family as under the present circumstances."

Lizzie frowned. "Can you not see the disadvantages that would befall the rest of us with such public notice of Lydia's most unguarded, unchecked, and imprudent manner? If you knew what has already arisen from it—I'm sure you'd judge this differently."

"Already?" Mr. Bennet repeated. "What, has she frightened away some of your lovers? Oh, Lizzie. Don't be defeated. Men who can't bear a little absurdity are not worth a regret. Come here," he teased, "Let's see this list of pitiful fellows who've been kept away by Lydia's silliness."

Her features scrunched in consternation, reminding him suddenly of when she'd been a child. "It's not about me. I don't have anything to resent. But our respectability in the system *must* be affected by her wild volatility and disdain for restraint." Her face grew solemn. "I'm sorry, but I have to speak plainly. If you, dear father, won't take the trouble to check her, and teach her that her present pursuits are not the business of her life, she'll soon be beyond reach of change. Her character will be fixed, and she will be, at sixteen, the most determined flirt that ever made herself and her family ridiculous. Not even a discerning flirt—just attracted like a moon moth to anything shining with youth and tolerability. She'll remain ignorant and empty-minded, completely squandering her actual talents, and totally unable to ward off the universal contempt that her voracious need for attention will ultimately attract. Kitty, too, will suffer from this. She follows wherever Lydia leads. Vain, ignorant, idle, and absolutely uncontrolled. Is that what you want for them? Can you not see that they'll be despised wherever they're known, and that Jane, Mary, and I will inevitably be included in their disgrace?"

Mr. Bennet could feel the earnest passion in his daughter's words as she spoke. He felt sorry that he'd teased her, so he took her hand in his. "Don't be uneasy, my love. Wherever you and Jane are known you must be respected and valued. You won't appear to any disadvantage for having a couple of—dare I say, three—very silly sisters. We'll have no peace at Longbourn if Lydia doesn't go to Sollaria. Void Commander Forster is a sensible man, and will keep her out of any real mischief. She'll be less important in Sollaria than she feels here. The officers will be too busy with women more worth their time and efforts than an overeager child. Let us hope that her being there may teach Lydia her own insignificance." He shrugged and added, "At any rate, she can't get much worse. Not without us resorting to tethering her to the moon for the rest of her life," he laughed.

Lizzie did not join in.

LONDINIUM SAT[SYS

Communications Log—System Storage 30 Days [Planetary]

[LizzieLovesSpace] 8.5-17:47:08.LS

He's intent on letting her go. I'm forced to be content, but I'm disappointed and sorry that he can't see how foolish this idea is.

[MyMyMissJane] 8.5-17:48:56.LS

You did what you could and told him of your worries. It's not up to us to raise our sister though we often feel the need to help.

[LizzieLovesSpace] 8.5-17:50:33.LS

I know. No continued anxiety on my part will change things. I can only hope, now, that the trip is as wondrous as Lydia imagines and as uneventful as we wish.

[MyMyMissJane] 8.5-17:52:13.LS

Agreed. Lydia has already filled several pages of her sketchbook with drawings of the beaches, officers dotted along the sand like stars.

[LizzieLovesSpace] 8.5-17:54:01.LS

And herself as the object of all their attention, no doubt. She sees the benefits of a town so close to the base and nothing else. Boardwalks crowded with the youthful and carefree, and handsome by the standards of their flight suits alone.

[MyMyMissJane] 8.5-17:57:23.LS

You aren't far off. On one of the pages, she's drawn a lovely little scene of herself seated beneath a tent, flirting with at least six officers at once as pilots show off in flight across the sky above her. It's quite beautiful. She's very talented.

[LizzieLovesSpace] 8.5-18:01:45.LS

Imagine if she spent even half as much energy on her artwork as she does on seeking attention from officers. But there's no encouragement to be had here. No art schools within a reasonable distance. No support from our parents. Mama would rather live vicariously through Lydia than bother encouraging her to do something more with her life.

[MyMyMissJane] 8.5-18:05:33.LS

I know you're upset with the situation, but I do think there's more than just two options. She's only sixteen. Though much of her personality is set, I would dare to say that she still has the possibility of growth and change ahead of her.

[LizzieLovesSpace] 8.5-18:08:19.LS

Not if she does something ill-advised while in Sollaria. Chances are that's much more likely than a sudden spurt of mental growth. Mark my words, Jane, this will not end well.

. . . END COM . . .

CHAPTER
42

Longbourn House, Heoros, First Moon of Londinium

Elizabeth would only need to see Mr. Wickham in person once more before the Reserves left the Meryton. She'd been in company with him a number of times since her return from the Kent, and her agitations had passed. She'd even learned to detect—in the very gentleness of manner that had originally delighted her—an affectation and a sameness that wearied, and sometimes disgusted, her. He tapped a new source of her displeasure recently by hinting at renewing whatever he thought was between them. This, after what she'd learned, served only to provoke her. While she repressed it, she couldn't help feeling the shame of his believing that, regardless of length of time or circumstance surrounding the loss of his attention, she'd be gratified by its renewal.

Their last meeting occurred at Longbourn, where several of the officers had come to dine. Elizabeth was so disinclined to part on good terms that when he made some inquiry as to her time on the Kent, she felt her hackles raise. "It was enlightening," she said. "Void Commander Fitzwilliam and Mr. Darcy both spent quite some time at Rosings. Are you familiar with the VC?"

He looked surprised, displeased, alarmed; but within a moment, a smile returned to his face. "Yes, I used to see him quite often. He's a fine gentleman. How did you like him?"

She returned an equally overcompensating smile. "I liked him very much. You're right, he was indeed a gentleman."

With an air of indifference, he eventually added, "How long did you say he was at Rosings?"

"Nearly a month."

"And you saw him frequently?"

"Yes, almost every day."

"His manners are quite different from his cousin's."

She felt a bit of a fire alight in her eyes. "Yes. Very different. But I think Mr. Darcy improves upon acquaintance."

"Oh?" Mr. Wickham's look of anxious surprise didn't escape her notice. "Might I ask—" He seemed to check himself, his tone lightening. "Is it in address that he improves? Perhaps he's more civil than usual? I dare not hope," he continued in a lower and more serious tone, "that he's improved in essentials."

"No," Elizabeth said. "In essentials I believe he's what he always was." While she spoke, she held her face as passive as she could. Wickham looked as if he barely knew whether to rejoice over her words or to distrust their meaning. He seemed to listen with an apprehensive and anxious attention as she added, "When I said that he improved on acquaintance, I didn't refer to his mind or manners. But that in knowing him better, his disposition was better understood."

Wickham's alarm now broke through, his face paling and a look of agitation overpowering his features. For a few minutes he was silent, until he shook off whatever he was feeling and turned to her again. With a conspiratorial tone, he said, "Knowing my feelings toward Mr. Darcy so well, you can understand why I might be glad to hear of him at least assuming the appearance of what is right. His pride would certainly deter him from further foul conduct. I do fear that this change is merely for the benefit of Lady Catherine. His fear of her judgment has always been a factor, when they're together. A good deal of that I'd attribute to his wish of nurturing the match with Miss de Bourgh, which I'm certain he has very much at heart."

Elizabeth couldn't repress a smile at this, but she didn't respond. It was clear he wished to bring up old grievances, but she was in no mood to indulge him.

(15.5-15:56:12.LS) TRANSCRIPTION:

I've been thinking lately about my parents and marriage in general. If I had only my family to base my opinions of marital happiness on, I don't know that I'd think highly of it. I believe my father was captivated by Mama's youth and beauty, and the appearance of good humor which youth and beauty usually give. But if I'm honest, her weak understanding of the worlds and her closed-mindedness did little to sustain his affection for her.

Whatever he thought marriage with her was going to be was revealed at some point as nothing more than the mirage of expectation. Now he's amused by her quirks and follies in the same way that he's entertained by Mr. Collins. This isn't the sort of happiness one would wish for themselves in marriage.

I'm not excusing my father, of course. His behavior as a husband is lacking. I've long witnessed it with some pain. Mama doesn't even realize that she's more entertainment than partner, and in some ways I'm glad for her ignorance. Despite her constant complaints, she sees herself as happy in her marriage. As a result, she's spared her husband's more obvious derision. He's not a bad person, he just hasn't made the most of the marriage he chose. I respect his intelligence and am grateful for how he's always treated me, so I try not to dwell on these things. But stars dimming, do I struggle with the way that he exposes his wife to our—his children's—contempt as well. It feels like such a terrible breach of . . . conjugal . . . obligation. And decorum.

I suppose this all just leads to my realization of what disadvantages an unsuitable marriage can bring on. I've never been so aware of the evils that come from such ill-judged direction of talents. Had he put them to better use, it might've preserved the respectability of his daughters, even if incapable of effecting growth in his wife.

(22.5-18:22:37.LS) TRANSCRIPTION:

While I celebrated Wickham's leaving, the unfortunate reality is that my impatience for an event to occur doesn't often bring the same satisfaction as I'd expected when it occurs. I suppose now I must decide on some other future event to hang all my hopes for happiness. I'll set my sights on the tour of Kaels with Aunt Mari. If only I could get Jane to come along with us.

(5.6-20:27:56.LS) TRANSCRIPTION:

Three weeks since Lydia left and while she promised to write often—and profusely—her waives have been long expected and very short. She told Mama little more than that she's visited the library. Officers were there, of course. She described various shops she visited and things she's gotten—a new gown or parasol, which she'd describe if only she had the time. She wrote more to Kitty, but Kitty has shared less of the contents of their waives. In the meantime, cheerfulness has pervaded Longbourn again. It certainly helps that many of the families who left for the winter have returned from Londinium. Warm weather engagements are resuming, which always cheers my mother, and there's enough to entertain Kitty that she isn't sad every time we attempt an outing. This is so promising an improvement that I hope by next winter she may not even mention an officer more than once a day. Unless, by some cruel twist of fate, the Defense Office quarters another regiment on the Meryton.

(19.6-21:42:07.LS) TRANSCRIPTION:

Aunt Mari sent a waive this afternoon. The trip has been altered. We're now starting later and ending sooner. The

Gardiners' business has interfered, and they're unable to leave Londinium till the end of the month. This left too small a window for such a distance as our trip required. There's too much travel and too much to see to really enjoy any of it on the new timeframe. The decision has come to voiding Kaels and going no further outward than Dyberion. There's enough to see on that moon to occupy us easily for three weeks. Aunt Mari is especially fond of the moon, having spent many years on it. We'll actually be spending a portion of the trip in her old hometown.

I must admit, I'm excessively disappointed. I had my heart set on seeing the Great Falls and Lakes of Kaels. There could've been enough time for that. But there will be other wonders on Dyberion. The Matlock Caves, the Sandstone Forests, the Aurawood, the Moon's Teeth. One could be content with those. How could they not? I'm sure by the time our trip is over, I'll have forgotten all about the Falls.

(22.6-7:08:35.LS) TRANSCRIPTION:

Galaxy's end!—Pemberley is on Dyberion. Aunt Mari's hometown is within its district. What if—No. Maybe? Surely, I could enter the district and see a few of its wonders without him knowing I'm there.

CHAPTER 43

Pemberley District, Dyberion, Fourth Moon of Londinium

"Off in pursuit of further novelty and amusement," Elizabeth announced, buckling herself into the seat facing her aunt and uncle as the moon-hopper hummed with readying energy. One thing she could rely upon with her traveling companions was that regardless of possible inconveniences, the Gardiners would endure it all with patience and good cheer. They maintained a level of affection and intelligence that could supply a good time whenever they encountered disappointments.

Thankfully, the first portion of their travels on Dyberion was nothing but marvelous. The moon was rich with unique geological formations and uncommon forests. Each of the places they were able to see before coming to her aunt's hometown felt worth the change in plans, and Elizabeth, so enamored by what she'd seen thus far, nearly forgot what lurked near their current destination.

They were traveling to the little town of North Tōmbal, where her aunt once lived, and where some of her friends still remained.

The journey was not overly long. The moon-hopper used the moon's rotation to its advantage in cutting down the travel time. Before Elizabeth knew it, the ship was breaking through the atmosphere, a new beautiful landscape spreading below them in fractured colors and shapes.

Her breath escaped her in a rush as her eyes greedily soaked in the scene. This was one of the reasons she so loved being in ships—seeing different lands from so distant a perspective as to take in all their beauty at once.

"Pemberley's just over that ridge," said her aunt, as the land grew closer in their approach. She pointed out across a verdant cleft in the hilly countryside. "I'd love to see the place again," she added wistfully.

"Why shouldn't we? It's not far off," said her husband.

Aunt Mari gave her shoulder a squeeze. "Wouldn't you like to see a place you've heard so much about? So many of your acquaintances are connected with it. Wickham spent his youth here, you know."

Elizabeth grimaced. She'd grappled with this question since she learned of the change in their plans, and still she didn't know if it was something she wanted. Curiosity burned in her heart, but she didn't feel that she had any right to visit Pemberley. She feigned disinterest as well as she could. "I've seen enough fancy houses in my lifetime. There are only so many variations of decor."

Aunt Mari *tsk*ed. "If it were merely a finely furnished house, I wouldn't care to see it either. But the grounds are incredible. They have some of the finest woods in the system. Truly a trip worth taking."

Elizabeth agreed. She'd seen the travel brochures in the ship's dispensary. She'd wanted to step foot in every one of the places on those maps and leaving Pemberley off would be a shame. It was simply the possibility of running into Mr. Darcy, while viewing his place, which held her back. The idea played like a nightmare in the forefront of her mind, dread boiling up with it. She felt her face grow warm. It was too great a risk. She had to be honest. "I don't want to seem like an intruder."

"Nonsense, Lizzie," said her aunt. "The house takes visitors all the time, being within such famous woods. We're no more intruders than a visitor to a museum."

Elizabeth bit her lower lip in frustrated forbearance. They were unencumbered by the fear of treading where they weren't wanted, since neither of them had refused the owner's proposals. But there was no good argument for avoiding it that she could share. She'd simply have to inquire privately with the staff as to whether he was home when they arrived. If the answer was unfavorable to her, she'd hide in the transport. Maybe even the woods.

When they arrived and settled at the inn, Elizabeth made it a point to direct her worry toward one of the staff. "I hear Pemberley is a very fine place to visit."

"You couldn't be more right," said the plump woman behind the counter. Her eyes sparkled as she spoke. "Summers in those woods are a sight to rival any in the system."

Elizabeth smiled kindly, putting on an air of innocent curiosity. "Who's the owner?"

"That'd be the young Mr. Darcy," she replied kindly, taking a longer look at Elizabeth and adding, "He'd be a few years older than you, I'd say."

"And is he—" she felt the words catch in her throat as a sudden wave of panic seized it—"his family here for the summer?"

The woman held up a finger. "Let me just check and see if . . ." She consulted something on a com board and shook her head.

"Staffing there appears to be in the absence rotation. It seems the family's away."

Elizabeth sighed in relief. "I see," she said, thanking the woman for the information, then found her way back to the suite, where her aunt and uncle were lounging.

"Did you get what you needed?" Aunt Mari asked with a suspiciously knowing smile. "Are we free to travel to Pemberley tomorrow?"

"Am I so predictable?"

Her uncle laughed. "Only to Mari."

"You had a look about you earlier," she shrugged, taking a glittering silver-white sip from her glass.

Elizabeth grinned reluctantly. "I just wanted to be sure." She walked over and planted herself on the chaise facing them, and reached for the empty glass and tall, dark bottle on the ottoman tray. "Now I can indulge in the mystery of what I'll see without worry."

"Exactly as you should," her uncle said as Elizabeth poured herself a drink and raised her glass.

"To Pemberley we go."

Moon's Teeth *Colossal!*

The Moon's Teeth are wondrous natural structures of fossilized trees on a scope found nowhere else in the system. One of the oldest natural wonders, the Moon's Teeth got their name almost immediately upon discovery. While ominous in name, the sight inspires awe rather than dread.

Makes me feel insignificant—even more so than flying into the atmosphere of Dyberion—or any moon, really.

Artist: Mae Smart

Pemberley District

The Pemberley District is home to Pemberley Estate, and the unique grounds which are a meeting point of three separate ecosystems, including the second largest aurawood grove on Dyberion. The district boasts incredible vistas well worth visiting. It also includes the Pemberley home—itself a wonder, being one of the few original architectural structures still on Dyberion.

fine, this is beautiful, I can admit it

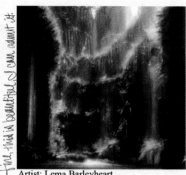

Artist: Lema Barleyheart

Sandstone Forest

The Sandstone Forest is a slight misnomer, as there are no trees in sight. These natural rock formations resemble incredibly large trees, and often give the impression that they are similar in nature to the Moon's Teeth, though with far more branches. Like trees, the Sandstone Forest's structures are equally tempting to climb!! Another family favorite travel location!

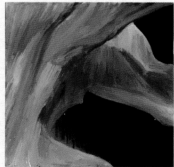

Artist: Petra Barrett

Sky Trees *Saw from a distance — must come back to visit properly. This looks incredible*

The Sky Trees are not for the faint of heart. Travelers be warned, this is a dangerous area for children. It is recommended that no one under the age of ten should venture any closer to the Sky Trees than the demarcation line of white stones. For those who venture to the top, you will be rewarded with breathtaking views of the Northern Dyberion wildlands.

Artist: Leon Ramsey

Aurawood

Go soon— first day in N. Tombal?

The Aurawood derives its name from the slight glow of color the leaves of each individual tree give off against the stark white of the bark. Found in many parts of Dyberion, the largest forest, which holds the name of the Ghost Grove, is located in Tōmbal Valley. The Ghost Grove differs from other aurawood forests in that every tree's leaf coloring is as white as its bark.

Artist: Ari'Valiya Silvain

Cliffs of Weir

100/10 I bet people go missing here constantly. I would have lain in the "grass" until I became part of the land.

The Cliffs of Weir are a lush and verdant cleft in the countryside of Dyberion's southern hemisphere. Covered in densely packed bush, the leaves are so minuscule that many compare the texture to springy moss. It gives the impression of a giant green blanket thrown over the entire landscape. It is a relaxing place to visit, with tourists often falling asleep for hours in the comfort of the flora.

Artist: Emilia Love

Luminous Lakes

The Luminous Lakes, known locally as the Pools of Starlight, are the site of a bioluminescent wonder. Many folktales have been born from this source. There is an inherent sense of magic in walking the edges of the lakes. The term "lake" is given *absolutely* generously here, as the shores are well in sight from any vantage point.

Artist: Liliana Brightwater

Matlock Caves

Beautiful! But my eyes hurt a bit after a while ✷ So vibrant.

The Caves in Matlock district are a vibrant maze of wonder. Perfect for a family tour, these caves are very open and shallow, with easy access in and out at many points throughout the wandering walls. The park spans many acres, so visitors are cautioned to pay attention to the signs at the cave mouths, to be sure the right path is chosen for all who walk through.

Artist: Kimberli Tyler

CHAPTER 44

Pemberley District, Dyberion, Fourth Moon of Londinium

Elizabeth peered out the window of the Cabriol-A, anxious for the first appearance of Pemberley Woods. She wasn't as comfortable about this as she'd intended to be, and there was a flurry in her chest by the time they finally turned in at the entrance.

The grounds were large and quite varied. They entered in one of its lowest points, and rode for some time through a beautiful wood stretching over a wide extent. The tree bark glimmered white as starflower petals, the branches hanging in a rainbow drapery of leaves around them.

Elizabeth's mind was too full for conversation, but she took in everything with admiration and wonder. They gradually ascended for half a mile, and found themselves at the top of a considerable elevation, where the woods tapered off. With the break in the trees, her eye was instantly drawn to Pemberley House, situated on the opposite side of a valley, into which the road wound rather abruptly. It was a large, beautifully constructed stone building, standing well on rising ground, and backed by a ridge of high, tree-dappled hills; in front, a stream swelled across the verdigris lawn of moss-like grasses. Delight overtook her agitations. She'd never seen a place for which nature had done more, or where natural beauty had been so little counteracted by an awkward taste.

Her aunt and uncle exclaimed their praise with the same enthusiasm that she held inside. In that moment, she felt that living at Pemberley might have been something of an inducement after all.

They descended the hill, crossed the bridge, and drove to the door. As they neared the house, all apprehension of meeting its owner returned. She worried that the innkeeper had been mistaken. The urge to look over her shoulder crept up her spine as the Gardiners requested a tour of the place. They were quickly admitted into the hall. As they waited for someone to guide them, she had the freedom to truly wonder at being where she was.

Unlike the stone work at Rosings, Pemberley's was authentic. She could almost feel the years the structure had endured. There was a weight to the air that she couldn't place, other than to say that it felt like the warm hug of a loving, though perhaps somewhat distant, grandfather.

The housekeeper came into the hall. She was a respectable-looking elderly woman, much less fine and more civil than anything Elizabeth had expected.

"Hello, and welcome," said the woman. "I'm Mrs. Reynolds, and I'll be happy to show you around. Follow me."

The first room she led them into was a large dining parlor. It seemed to be made with the outdoors in mind, complementing the colors shining from the large picture windows. Elizabeth strode across the room to enjoy the view better. From here, she could see the hill, crowned with woods, from which they'd descended. Every part of the grounds she could see was meticulously maintained, yet retained the charming wildness of nature. The river, the trees and stone outcroppings scattered on its banks, and the winding of the valley, as far as she could trace it, were beautiful.

As they passed into other rooms, the scene outside shifted, but from every angle it was a living masterpiece. Eventually, she turned her focus more inward, and noted how well suited each space was to its proprietor. She couldn't help but admire his taste. It was neither gaudy nor uselessly fine. It held far less splendor but more real elegance than Rosings. The doors to the rooms were sturdy, beautifully crafted aurawood. She pulled her comcard from her pocket and glanced at the service indicator, which showed a clear connection, but looking around her, there was no sign of comfield transmitters. Everything was elegant and natural.

Though the sheer size of the place gave her a slight feeling of being in a museum, it was one well lived in. "And all of this could've been home," she muttered, as she ran a hand along the sturdy wooden top of a finely crafted sideboard.

By now, had she accepted him, these rooms would've been as familiar as her own. Instead of viewing them as a stranger, she might've been giving this tour herself, welcoming her aunt and uncle as their host.

But, no. She pulled her hand away. That could never be. The Gardiners would've been lost to her. She wouldn't have been permitted to invite them.

This was a lucky recollection. It saved her from something very like regret.

She longed to ask whether Mr. Darcy was really absent, but didn't have the courage to speak it. Thankfully, her uncle had a similar thought.

"Is Mr. Darcy away?" he asked.

Elizabeth froze in anticipation of Mrs. Reynolds's response.

"Yes, but he's expected home tomorrow with a large party of friends."

Elizabeth felt a jolt in her stomach similar to when she had accelerated too quickly on the void crawler so many months before. She could hardly believe her luck. Had they delayed even a day, this visit would've been entirely different.

"My stars! Lizzie, look," her aunt said, waving her over to a series of pictures above a mantelpiece.

She approached, and found herself looking into the painted eyes of a younger Mr. Wickham.

"As charming as always, yes?" Aunt Mari asked, one eyebrow raised.

Mrs. Reynolds noticed who they'd trained their focus on. "That's the son of the late steward. He was brought up right here alongside the Darcy children. He's gone now into the Star Force Reserves." Mrs. Reynolds's smile soured. "I'm afraid he's turned out very wild."

Her aunt looked at her with a smirk, but Elizabeth couldn't return it.

"Now that," Mrs. Reynolds pointed to another of the paintings, "is the young Mr. Darcy. It was commissioned at the same time as the other. About eight years ago."

"Such a handsome face," said her aunt, peering closer at the picture. "Lizzie, does the painting do him justice?"

Mrs. Reynolds's respect for Elizabeth seemed to increase with this discovery. "You know Mr. Darcy?"

Elizabeth's cheeks flushed. "A little."

"He turned out very handsome, don't you think?" Mrs. Reynolds prompted.

Elizabeth glanced at the painting again and felt something in her resolve soften. "Yes. Very handsome."

"In the gallery upstairs you'll see a finer, larger picture of him than this," Mrs. Reynolds offered. "This room here was late

Mr. Darcy's favorite and these small portraits are just as they were when he was alive. He was very fond of them."

This accounted for Mr. Wickham's being among them.

Mrs. Reynolds then directed their attention to a picture of Miss Darcy, painted when she was only eight years old.

"Has Miss Darcy turned out as handsome as her brother?" Her aunt inquired.

"Oh, yes. Beautiful *and* talented. She's a delight. She plays and sings and creates all day long. In the next room is a new instrument that arrived here last week for her. A present from her brother. She's coming here tomorrow with him. It'll be such a surprise for her."

Uncle Edward, ever the easy and pleasant communicator, continued to question Mrs. Reynolds, and it was clear she took great pleasure in talking about the home's inhabitants.

"Is Mr. Darcy often at Pemberley?" he asked.

"Not so much as I'd wish him to be. But I'd say he spends a total of half a revolution here. And Miss Darcy is always landed on Dyberion for the summer months."

Except when she goes to Rackport, Elizabeth thought.

Her aunt offered happily, "If he'd marry, you might see more of him."

A momentary embarrassment fluttered through Elizabeth's chest.

"I agree, but I don't know when *that'll* be. I don't know who's good enough for him."

Elizabeth couldn't help saying, "It's very much to his credit, I'm sure, that you think so."

Mrs. Reynolds placed a hand on her chest. "I say no more than the truth—along with everyone who knows him. I've never known a cross word from him in my life, and I've known him since he was four years old."

This extraordinary praise was quite opposite to Elizabeth's idea of him. She had based her opinions of him firmly on the fact that he wasn't a good-tempered man. This new information awakened her keenest attention and she longed to hear more. Once again, her uncle provided, unknowingly.

"You're lucky to be working under such benevolence."

"I know I am. I doubt I'd meet another on any moon or planet like young Mr. Darcy. He was always the sweetest-tempered, most generous-hearted boy in the system, and the only thing that has changed is that he has grown into a man."

Elizabeth almost stared at Mrs. Reynolds, her mind flooding with a single thought: could this really be the Mr. Darcy she had come to know?

"I remember his father. He was an excellent man," Aunt Mari recollected.

"He was," Mrs. Reynolds agreed. "And his son will be just like him. Just as affable to the less fortunate."

Elizabeth listened, wondered, doubted, and was impatient for more. Mrs. Reynolds could interest her on no other point. She related the subjects of the pictures, the dimensions of the rooms, and prices and makers of the furniture, but Elizabeth dismissed it all.

Uncle Edward leaned in as they ascended the great staircase. "I'm highly amused and very intrigued by this commendation of the Darcys," he whispered to Elizabeth. He winked and caught up with Mrs. Reynolds to prompt her into saying more on the subject.

"He's the best landlord and administrator," she said. "There isn't one of his tenants or employees that wouldn't speak his praise. Some people call him proud, but I've never seen any sign of it. I like to think it's only because he doesn't rattle away like other young men."

"This is such a fine account of him," her aunt whispered. "It's not quite consistent with his behavior to our poor friend."

Elizabeth tensed as thoughts of his letter lifted to the surface. "Perhaps we were deceived."

They reached the spacious lobby of the second floor, and were shown into a very pretty sitting room, recently redone, with a slightly different aesthetic from those below.

"This was just completed as another surprise for Miss Darcy, who took a liking to this room when she was last at Pemberley."

"He's certainly a good brother," Elizabeth said, stepping into the warm light from one of the windows.

"She'll be so delighted when she sees it. That's always the way with Mr. Darcy," Mrs. Reynolds added. "Whatever can add joy in his sister's life, he's sure to do it at the first opportunity. There's nothing he wouldn't do for her."

The picture gallery, and two or three of the principal bedrooms, were all that remained to be shown. In the former were many good paintings, but Elizabeth knew nothing of the art. She gravitated instead to some drawings of Miss Darcy's, in oil crayon, whose subjects seemed more interesting and intelligible.

In the gallery there were many family portraits, but they did little to keep the attention of a stranger. Elizabeth walked in quest of the only face whose features would be known to her. At last, she found it.

The painter had captured Mr. Darcy with a smile she remembered seeing sometimes when he looked at her. She stood several minutes in front of it in earnest contemplation, taking in every detail, and though she was pulled away from it by her aunt—who had spotted a few familiar landscapes she wanted Elizabeth to see— she returned to it again before they left the gallery.

As she studied his face, she felt a warmth wash over her—a gentleness stronger than anything she'd felt toward him at the height of their acquaintance. Mrs. Reynolds's commendation was not trifling. There were so many people whose happiness and well-being depended upon him. He held such power to do good or ill by those in his sphere, and by Mrs. Reynolds's favorable account, he was doing right by them all.

His eyes transfixed her. She couldn't help but think of his regard for her with deeper gratitude than ever. If he was, truly, what Mrs. Reynolds said, then she could feel the warmth of his affection for her more readily. Combined with knowing what he had expressed in his letter, the idea softened the unfortunate way in which he'd expressed that affection.

Head full of new perspectives, she followed the Gardiners and Mrs. Reynolds back downstairs. They were handed over to the groundskeeper, who met them at the hall door. She was grateful for the change of scenery and hopeful that the fresh air might clear her mind a little and allow her not to acknowledge, for a time, the change eclipsing her heart and mind.

LONDINIUM SAT[SYS

Communications Log—System Storage 30 Days [Planetary]

[GiGi-D] 2.7-8:02:50.LS

When you get home, can you ask Reynolds about bringing some treats from Mercers Bakery? I've been thinking about their petal cakes for an entire week!

[FW.Darcy] 2.7-8:04:25.LS

I can take you as soon as you arrive, if you'd like.

[GiGi-D] 2.7-8:05:58.LS

Tempting! But didn't you have some work to do?

[FW.Darcy] 2.7-8:07:43.LS

Yes. I believe I'll be finished before you get in. The whole point of me taking the faster ship was to complete it all today, if possible.

[GiGi-D] 2.7-8:09:17.LS

I know. I appreciate it! But don't work yourself too hard on my account.

[FW.Darcy] 2.7-8:10:33.LS

I can't think of anything that would keep me from my desk today, with the promise of your company in our old rambles tomorrow.

[GiGi-D] 2.7-8:11:57.LS

And this is why I love you so!

. . . END COM . . .

CHAPTER
45

Pemberley District, Dyberion,
Fourth Moon of Londinium

D arcy shut the door of his Dobbin and let out a satisfied sigh. It was a comfort to be home. The choice to return early already felt right. He strode out of the hangar and pressed on up the hill road to the main house, breathing in the fresh, slightly sweet scent of the field of mallow-moss. As he rounded the corner of the house, he noticed Andrew, the groundskeeper, speaking with a group of people on the front lawn. One of the party was a young woman who looked a little like—

He stopped in his tracks.

Elizabeth Bennet.

She was standing no further than twenty feet from him. On the lawn. Of his home.

Her eyes were wide with recognition, no doubt mirroring his own. Her dark hair pooled on her head, loose curls dripping like vines around her rapidly blushing face. She wore a soft blue dress that drifted gently in the summer breeze, the fabric clinging to reveal the curves of her frame on one side, while billowing gently away from her on the other. She was a painting and he couldn't pull his gaze away.

The moment he thought this, the others in her party caught sight of him, and he shook himself free and pushed forward again. He cleared his throat and hoped that when his words escaped, he could address her with—if not perfect composure—at least perfect civility. "Miss Elizabeth. What an unexpected surprise."

She seemed nearly incapable of meeting his eyes. Was it aversion? Embarrassment? Something else? "We were told you weren't home. We didn't mean to intrude."

"I was early. You weren't misinformed."

"Ah," she said, and nothing else.

"Have you been away from Longbourn for some time?"

"A couple of weeks."

"Are you enjoying the visit?"

She turned her head toward the woods. For an escape? In admiration? "Yes, thank you."

"And you've been in Pemberley District how long?"

"We arrived yesterday."

"Ah, I see." This was somehow the most uncomfortable he'd been in his life, including the day he'd sought her out in the Kent. "Your travels have been . . . smooth?"

"And wonderful, yes."

"You left your family in good health, I hope?"

She nodded, concern and something akin to bemusement warring behind her eyes.

The scent of the mallow-moss had become suddenly cloying. The ability to shift thoughts into spoken words had failed him. There was no choice now but to retreat. He looked past her to her companions, doing their best, along with poor Andrew—who seemed to feel Darcy's awkwardness—not to eavesdrop. "I've taken you away from your tour," he said. "Please, go enjoy the grounds. Your guide is the best caretaker on all of Dyberion. I have no doubt he will know all the best views to share with you." He gave Andrew a firm nod, then quickly took his leave and padded up to the house.

As he walked, his mind immediately replayed the interaction. He'd been surprised. She seemed to have been, as well. She hadn't come for him. But she didn't run from him, either. Could there be a possibility that she might not hate him now?

He went quickly to his study and sought her out in the view from his window. It took a moment, but after a few passes across the portion of the grounds he thought they might be, he glimpsed a flash of that blue dress along a walk by the side of the water.

What strange luck that he'd returned early to find her of all people at his home. Had he arrived when he'd planned, he'd have missed her. Even ten minutes later and she would've been beyond his reach. But now . . .

Now was an opportunity. A chance to not let their last meeting be the day he put that letter in her hands.

He paced the room, imagining which path she might take. The walk was lined on one side with the Aurawood, and there were many smaller paths branching off from the main with enticing patterns of trees to explore. But in all likelihood, they'd continue to the higher ground. There, in the spots where the trees thinned to give room for the eye to wander, they'd be met by many charming views of the valley, the opposite hills, the natural stone archways and treelike formations, and the long range of wildly colored woods overspreading many, along with the occasional part of the stream.

It was a ten-mile circuit. They didn't seem dressed for a hike of that length. More than likely, they'd admire the views from the top for a while and return along the path they'd already traversed. The more he calculated, the more certain he became of his next course of action. He could only hope his luck held out a bit longer.

He hurried back outside to intercept her.

Home | Georgiana Darcy, Age 9 | Paint & Pastels

CHAPTER
46

Pemberley District, Dyberion, Fourth Moon of Londinium

It had taken Elizabeth the better part of their walk through the grounds to shake off the feelings of embarrassed vexation and confusion. Thoughts circled like starships coming into port. She blushed again and again over the perverseness of their meeting. And his behavior—so strikingly altered. What could it mean? That he'd even speak to her was amazing, let alone with such civility. She'd never seen him so genuine and relaxed in manners. Never had he spoken with such gentleness as on this unexpected meeting. What a contrast to the last time she'd seen him on the Kent. She didn't know what to think or how to account for it.

She barely noticed the sights along that first part of the walk. Her thoughts were fixed on that one spot of

Pemberley House, wherever it might be, where Mr. Darcy was. She longed to know what he was thinking at that moment, what he thought of her, and whether, in defiance of everything, she was still dear to him. Perhaps he'd been civil only because he felt at ease in his home environment. But there'd been something in his voice that wasn't like ease. Whether it was more from pleasure or pain in seeing her, she couldn't tell, but he certainly hadn't seen her with composure.

When they reached the highest hill, the groundskeeper proudly stated that the entire circuit through the grounds was about ten miles in length. This, her companions felt, was too much to take on. So they decided to descend again into the flowering woods, to the edge of the water, and eventually to one of its narrowest parts.

They crossed a simple bridge that felt somehow as if it'd been made by the flora around it. It was the most unique of the spots they'd yet visited. The valley intersecting two vastly different hills converged here into a tiny glen, allowing room only for the stream and a narrow walk amid the vibrant Aurawood bordering one side and the stone grove trees bordering the other. It felt almost like two paintings torn in half and taped together. Elizabeth longed to explore the winding path, but when they crossed the bridge, and noticed the distance still left from the house, her aunt, whose shoes seemed to be causing her some trouble, admitted that she'd reached her limit and wanted only to get back to the Cabriol-A as quickly as possible.

Elizabeth was obliged to leave the path unexplored, and they made their way toward the house on the opposite side of the river, in the nearest direction. Their progress was slower now, for her aunt's sake, but also due to her uncle. He was very fond of fishing, and was so engaged in watching the occasional appearance of some local fish or other in the water, and talking to the groundskeeper about them, that they advanced very little.

While wandering on in this slow way, Elizabeth was astonished to see Mr. Darcy approaching them again. He was far closer than she would've expected, had she expected him at all. The walk on this side of the stream was much less sheltered than the other side and allowed her to see him before they met.

Though she was as surprised as she'd been earlier, she was at least a little more prepared for conversation this time. It appeared, as he approached, that he was in the same mood as before. She resolved to imitate his calm and politeness.

"These grounds are so delightful," she said by way of greeting. "You must have had many adventures here as a child." She stopped herself from saying more, and blushed, memories intruding. What he told her of his childhood had been in the letter, which she certainly didn't want to bring to mind, and she worried suddenly that praise of Pemberley coming from her might be taken as mischievous rather than genuine.

"Entire worlds made and discovered," he said, before looking past her to her companions. "Would you mind introducing me properly?"

This was unexpected. She could hardly suppress her smile, seeing him now seeking the acquaintance of some of the people his pride had revolted against in his proposal.

"This is my aunt and uncle, Marianne and Edward Gardiner," she said, stealing a sly look at him to see how he bore the news.

That he was *surprised* by the connection was clear, but there was no turning away in disgust. Instead, he fell into conversation with her uncle easily. Elizabeth was consoled, in a small way, that he now knew some of her family weren't embarrassing. She listened intently to all that passed between them and thanked every star in the sky with each sentence her uncle uttered that marked his intelligence, taste, and good manners.

The conversation soon turned to fishing. Mr. Darcy invited her uncle to fish there as often as he chose while they were staying in the district, pointing out the parts of the stream where there was usually the most sport. He even went so far as to offer to supply him with fishing tackle.

Her aunt, walking arm and arm with Elizabeth to ease the burden on her feet, nudged her in the ribs with an elbow and gave her a look of expressive wonder. Elizabeth said nothing, but it pleased her greatly. She felt the compliment of Darcy's attentions. Her astonishment, however, was extreme. She continually wondered why he was so altered. The softening of his manners couldn't have stemmed from her, nor could it be for her sake. Her reproofs at Hunsford Parsonage couldn't have wrought such a change as this. It was impossible that he still loved her.

After walking for some time with the men trailing behind them, the group slowed and descended to the brink of the river to inspect a curious-looking water plant native to Dyberion. When they returned to the path, her aunt confessed that Elizabeth's arm was inadequate support to combat her increasingly aching feet, so she requested that her husband take up the charge. Mr. Darcy took her aunt's place at Elizabeth's side, and they walked on.

After a short silence, Elizabeth found her voice. "Apologies again for intruding. We were assured you weren't home before we left North Tōmbal, and again when we spoke with your housekeeper. Your arrival was quite unexpected."

"It was," he said. "No one knew I was arriving early. I have some business that I wanted to attend to before my guests arrive. They'll join me early tomorrow." Here he paused momentarily, as if gauging her reaction to what he'd say next. "Among them are some who'd claim an acquaintance with you. Mr. Bingley and his sisters."

Elizabeth was careful with her expression, and only nodded in acknowledgment. Her thoughts were instantly rocketed back to the time when Mr. Bingley's name had last been mentioned between them. If she could judge by the shift in his expression, he was also reliving the memory.

"There's one other person in the party," he added tentatively, "who more particularly would wish to meet you. If you'd allow me—or do I ask too much—to introduce my sister to you during your stay at North Tōmbal?"

Elizabeth opened her mouth but was too surprised by such a request to immediately reply. She felt that whatever desire Miss Darcy might have to meet her must be the work of her brother. It was gratifying to know that his resentment hadn't made him think horribly of her. "I . . . would be honored," she finally answered, then, wishing not to make too much of it, added, "You've had a chance to meet mine. Seems a fair trade to meet yours."

"This is very true."

They walked on a bit in silence. Elizabeth wasn't comfortable; that was impossible. But she was flattered and pleased. His wish of introducing his sister to her was a compliment of the highest kind. They soon outstripped the others, and when they'd reached the Cabriol-A, the groundskeeper and the Gardiners were a good distance behind.

"Would you like to go back to the house to rest?" Darcy asked.

"Thank you, but I'm enjoying the atmosphere out here."

He nodded. When he spoke again it was delicately. "Your sisters. They . . . aren't . . . here on Dyberion with you?"

"No" she said, sudden embarrassment keeping her from making eye contact. She shouldn't have brought up her sisters. What had she been thinking?

"Do they have other engagements?"

She laughed nervously. "One of them, yes. My youngest. She was invited to Sollaria with VC Forster and his wife." Not wishing to put the Reserves in his mind, she rushed to add, "If she's not drawing in her sketchbook or—" here she gestured at her dress—"styling outfits for the rest of us, she's socializing."

He looked her over with an appraising eye, and her face flushed with heat. "She styled what you're wearing?"

Elizabeth nodded, mortification strangling her.

"She has a good eye for it."

"Yes, she's very talented," she said quickly, desperate to shift the subject. Speaking of Lydia with him made her uneasy. She wanted to move the conversation to a safer sister, but for once this was not Jane. Instead she lapsed into silence.

They stood quietly together on the turquoise lawn. She wanted to say something, but there seemed to be an embargo on every subject, and she had already flown too close to a few she wanted to avoid. At last she remembered that this visit to Pemberley was just a portion of her vacation. "We saw the Luminous Lakes a few days ago. It's incredible. Have you ever been?"

This seemed to energize him. "Yes. It's one of Georgiana's favorites. If you think it's something now, you should see it in winter."

"I suppose I'll have to come back, then."

"Yes, I'd—" he stopped himself. "I'd recommend it. Have you seen anything else since you arrived?"

"Stars, yes. And it has all been beyond expectation. The Aurawood is massive. I didn't realize a forest could span such a distance."

"Were you able to see it from the air as you landed?" he asked.

"Somewhat, yes. But there was so much to look at."

"There are ways to view them in low atmosphere," he suggested. "If I recall, you're fond of flying."

"I am." Her smiled turned to a bit of a grimace. "What a place to learn. I'd think it'd be a distraction to the actual lessons, though. I'm sure I'd be looking out the window far more than at the controls."

He laughed softly. "I suppose it would be. While I enjoy travel, I would much rather let others do the flying. I do love a good view."

The thought crossed her mind to say that they'd make an excellent team, and she nearly choked at the idea of saying it aloud. What had gotten into her? Thankfully, the rest of their party had finally reunited with them, and she was spared from offering any more inappropriate or embarrassing prompts for conversation.

"Would the three of you like to come in, rest your legs?" Mr. Darcy asked the stragglers. "I'd ply you with refreshments. We have a local tea made from the flowers you may have spotted in a few of the groves."

"We do very much appreciate the offer," her aunt said, "but I think we need to return to the Inn and take a proper rest."

He nodded and smiled slightly. "I understand." With a glance to the groundskeeper, he said, "Go on ahead and have Mrs. Reynolds get you something to drink. Thank you for taking them around."

"A pleasure, Mr. Darcy," the groundskeeper replied, then loped toward the door.

Darcy helped her party into the Cabriol-A, his hand briefly grasping Elizabeth's as he assisted her. The outer layer of her skin felt suddenly electric. So preoccupied by that feeling, she nearly didn't sit in time for the transport to start moving.

While they drove off, Elizabeth watched him walk slowly toward the house, arm strangely stiff by his side.

VOICE JOURNAL

COM TAG: LIZZIELOVESSPACE—E. BENNET
PERSONAL JOURNAL / COMCARD ID: HC-3095.D2.EB
TIMESTAMP: 2.7-20:34:45.LS / LOCATION: DYBERION

(2.7-20:34:45.LS) TRANSCRIPTION:

This morning's events have completely scrapped the rest of the day for me. I can think of nothing else but Mr. Darcy and the change in him. Almost as soon as we left Pemberley, Aunt Mari started praising him. Not at all what I would have expected when I woke this morning. She called him perfectly well-behaved, polite, and unassuming. I can hardly believe it, but I agree. He was so attentive to us all. And suddenly I was being questioned as to why I said he was disagreeable, but how do I explain such a seismic shift when I can't be sure of its reasoning? I gave my excuses as well as I could. I said I liked him better on the Kent than on Heoros, but I was honest with them and explained that I'd never seen him as pleasant as he was today. And then of course Aunt Mari had to remind me that I've only told them one side of the Wickham story. She said that from what she'd seen of Mr. Darcy, she couldn't believe he would behave so cruelly. I had set right what I could on that account, but all I felt comfortable saying was that I learned some things on the Kent and that Mr. Darcy's character wasn't so faulty—nor Wickham's so amicable—as we'd all been led to believe. I told them a few more particulars, without naming my source, to insist that it could be relied on as truthful. This surprised and concerned them, of course, but with so much nostalgia around her and no personal stakes in the matter, Aunt Mari was quickly distracted. Now that we've had a rest and a change of shoes, she's been in quest of old friends. And here I am, in a fog, because there's no room in my heart or mind for new acquaintances. It's all full of Mr. Darcy and his wish for me to meet his sister.

CHAPTER
47

North Tōmbal, Dyberion, Fourth Moon of Londinium

Elizabeth had picked up the menu to peruse brunch options with her aunt and uncle at the restaurant below the inn, when something caught her eye from the window beside her. Mr. Darcy was helping a girl out of a Chase-N4, his eyes trained on Elizabeth. Her mind didn't immediately compute what she saw. When it did, she slid low in her chair to avoid being seen. A moment passed before she sat tall again, realizing that her attempt to hide had come too late. There was no chance he hadn't seen her. She fidgeted in her seat, endeavoring to compose herself as dread and anticipation flooded her body.

The Gardiners looked at her with wide-eyed wonder.

"Mr. Darcy," she explained in a choked whisper. She was amazed at her own discomposure, but there was no doubt in her mind that the girl in the Chase was Darcy's sister. Feeling uncommonly anxious to appear pleasing to the girl, she suddenly suspected that every attempt at it would fail her.

As the thought formed in her head, Darcy appeared. Behind him, his feminine copy.

He scanned the room, found Elizabeth in the crowd, and pressed toward her with purpose and ease.

She had just enough time to convince herself that she wasn't able to escape without him noticing before they were beside the table. Why was she so flustered? She could only account for it by the unexpected timing.

He'd mentioned his friends and sister arriving this morning, but that he would venture to look for her during that time hadn't entered her mind.

"Mr. and Mrs. Gardiner, a pleasure to see you again," he said. "Miss Elizabeth. This is my sister, Georgiana."

The girl inclined her head and gave the quietest of hellos. She appeared at least as embarrassed as Elizabeth. Whatever of pride people saw in her, Elizabeth discovered rather quickly to be incredible shyness. Prying more than a single-syllable answer from her was difficult.

As Darcy spoke with the Gardiners of fishing plans, Elizabeth darted smiles in Miss Georgiana's direction, and took in her appearance.

She was tall, with a naturally larger frame than Elizabeth, but graceful. There was sense and good humor in her face, and her manners were perfectly unassuming and gentle.

Her aunt invited them to sit, and chairs were brought over for them.

Darcy sat beside Elizabeth, and she felt herself tense. He leaned in slightly, causing her heart rate to rocket, before he said softly, "Bingley's looking forward to seeing you, too."

Elizabeth had barely registered the meaning when someone knocked on the window behind her and she jumped. "Great eclipse!" she yelped, too keyed up to handle her surprise gracefully. Bingley waved, jovial as ever, then disappeared from view. A moment later, he was crossing the restaurant to join them.

Elizabeth's anger toward him had long since dissipated, but had she still felt any, it would've crumbled under the unaffected warmth and friendliness he greeted her with. "Is your family well?" he asked, looking around for an empty chair. He spoke with the same good-humored ease as ever.

He spotted a chair and pulled it over to sit between herself and her uncle. She felt a strange combination of familiarity and novelty at being seated between these two men. To her left was the one tied to her in threads of undefined potential that seemed only to be awaiting some realization on her part of who he was and what she was to him. On her right was the one who had seemed a friend from the very beginning, and who she hoped could be a truer one in the future, should circumstances be on her sister's side.

She wondered if Bingley was thinking of her sister now. Was he talking a little less than usual? Was he anxious to ask about Jane specifically?

At a moment when the others were talking, and in a tone of something like real regret, he said, "It's been a very long time since I had the pleasure of seeing a member of the Bennet family." Before she could reply, he added, "It's been over eight months. We haven't met since November 26, when we were all dancing together on the Netherfield."

Elizabeth was pleased to find his memory so exact. "It has been," she said.

"Are *all* your other sisters still at Longbourn?" He accompanied this question with a look that amplified the underlying meaning.

"My youngest is in Sollaria," she answered. "The rest are currently trying to keep the Gardiner children entertained. Though it's probably mostly Jane."

A microcosm of emotions flashed behind his eyes as she spoke, and she couldn't help but smile to herself.

"We wouldn't be nearly as secure in being away from the children so long if it weren't for Jane," her uncle added, having caught wind of their conversation. "The kids may not even know we've been gone. As many times as business has had us relying on the good graces of our nieces, the children see them almost as sisters. They always have such a good time with their favorite cousin. No offense, Lizzie," he added with a wink.

Elizabeth laughed. "I'll be their favorite again when I return with gifts."

Bingley turned to her uncle then, and inquired about his work.

Elizabeth let herself fade out of the conversation, and turned her attention back to Darcy. Being directly next to him made it harder to watch him without being obvious, but engaging in his conversation, even if only to listen, allowed her to pull it off with less awkwardness.

"Yes, Alesadran is the natural choice for anyone hoping for prestige," he said to her aunt, "but if the goal is to stretch your skills beyond what tutors can offer, and not to make a profession of it, I agree, the academies on Londinium are absolutely equal to the task."

"It's a shame that talent alone is not enough for Alesadran," her aunt said, turning her eye toward Elizabeth. "Lizzie, wouldn't you say Lydia would qualify immediately if it were so?"

Darcy looked at her, and she didn't miss the flick of his eyes as he took in the rich yellow of her dress. No doubt, he was remembering their conversation from yesterday.

"Absolutely," Elizabeth replied. "But there are ways to achieve success without formal institutions."

"Such as learning to fly through sheer stubbornness?" her aunt offered playfully.

Darcy seemed amused by this, and Elizabeth felt the sudden need to deflect his attention, lest she read into it. "Yes, or perhaps being proficient on the piano from hard practice, as I hear is true for you, Miss Georgiana."

Georgiana looked startled at the sudden spotlight, but recovered enough to say, "I do love to play. But it wouldn't be possible without my brother's time and effort." She smiled at Darcy with such adoration that Elizabeth could feel it radiating off of her and infecting herself.

"I confess," Darcy said, "that I encourage the playing with some selfishness. It means I'm afforded the pleasure of good music whenever I'd like to hear it."

Aunt Mari laughed heartily at this. "And what of you, Mr. Darcy? Is there anything in particular you would have liked to be, had you not had the estate to inherit?"

He cocked his head in thought. "I don't know that anyone has ever asked me that." He appeared genuinely stumped. As he thought, Elizabeth's mind wandered to Jane again. Like Darcy, Jane was the eldest child. They both had been given a path to walk and had dutifully done so. Jane's success depended upon a marriage, whereas Darcy's was handed down. But in that moment she felt pity for them both, and a sense of gratefulness at being a younger child, who could push against whatever was expected of her in search of her own path. Lydia was of course the extreme of this, but she wondered if it might not be preferable to the strait-laced expectations for Jane or Darcy.

"I believe," Darcy said, pulling her back from her thoughts, "that I would have liked to have done something with writing. Letters and such. I'm fond of handwritten communication, though it's less needed now." His gaze darted to Elizabeth as he said this, and she looked away quickly. But as he spoke, his manner drew her in again.

Watching him build the acquaintance—and courting the good opinion with such openness—of people with whom a connection would've been a disgrace a few months ago, was something. Thinking of his manner during their altercation in the Hanging Gardens, she could hardly restrain her astonishment at the difference in him now. Never in the company of his friends on the Netherfield, nor in the company at Rosings, had he seemed so desirous to please, and so free from self-consciousness as he was now. She could think of nothing he could gain from this particular acquaintance. Surely it would only draw ridicule from the ladies of both the Netherfield and the Kent.

Half an hour passed before Darcy declared that they were expected elsewhere and had to leave. As they stood, Darcy said, "Georgiana and I wish to have the three of you join us for dinner at Pemberley some time before you leave the moon."

Miss Georgiana looked equal parts anxious and eager. "Yes, we would love to be in your company more," she said, her expression betraying her unfamiliarity with giving invitations.

Elizabeth averted her eyes from Darcy's, lest he mistake her surprise as something else.

In her momentary silence, her aunt readily accepted the invitation. "Would two nights from now be acceptable?"

"Absolutely," Georgiana replied, with a quick look of confirmation at her brother.

"I'm so pleased that I'll be seeing you again so soon," Bingley said to Elizabeth. "There's so much more to talk of."

Elizabeth had a suspicion this was his way of wishing for more information about her sister, and she felt a smile creep to the corners of her lips.

Darcy gave a bow, his eyes finding hers last and lingering a moment before the three of them turned and departed.

"That was certainly unexpected," her aunt said.

Elizabeth nodded absently, her mind reeling. "I'm glad you got to meet Bingley," she said, wanting their opinion of him, but eager to be alone, wishing to avoid any hints or inquiries on the Gardiners' part.

"I can see why Jane fell for him," her uncle said.

Elizabeth agreed, then made an excuse about changing into more suitable clothes for the day's activities before escaping the table and their unasked questions.

The day would not be long enough to determine how she felt about Mr. Darcy. She could only hope that it offered enough distractions that she wouldn't need to think of him at all. As she walked to her room, she tried to make sense of her feelings. Hatred had vanished long ago, and her shame at disliking him had grown in its place. She found she was no longer repulsed by the idea of respecting him. That had come with the knowledge that he did in fact have good qualities. With every glowing testimony or example of his benevolence, she could draw him in a more favorable light.

She reached her room and dropped onto the bed, looking out the window where Pemberley sat hidden somewhere in the Aurawood. Respect and esteem he had earned, certainly. But there was something else she couldn't at first place. When it did, she lay quietly with it, unsure what it meant to her.

The feeling was gratitude. She was grateful to him for not only loving her in the first place, but for loving her still well enough to forgive the petulant and bitter way she had refused him. She had flung so many unjust accusations along with it. But rather than avoiding her and considering her an enemy, he had been eager to preserve their acquaintance.

No, it was more than preservation. He'd pushed himself to become acquainted with her aunt and uncle, and had orchestrated a way for her to meet his sister less than a day after he suggested it. It was astonishing.

She drew in a rattling, uneasy breath as she came to a conclusion. Only to love—ardent love—could such a change be attributed.

She sat up to better take stock of her own feelings at this realization. She respected him. She was grateful to him. If she was as honest as possible with herself, she had to admit that she felt a real interest in his welfare. And now she only needed to know how much she wished that welfare to depend upon herself. Could she possess the power, still, to affect his happiness as well as her own? If she should employ that power, could she bring on the renewal of his proposal?

Her heart whispered that she could.

Quite a surprise!
MORE EMBARRASSED THAN I'VE SEEN HER.
She wasn't expecting him
NEITHER WERE WE   Awkwardness,
                           abounds!

B. IS NICE. SAD FOR JANE.
Poor E — seems afraid to
B=READY G=EAGER   disappoint
   D=DETERMINED ⌡TO BE PLEASED
~~do you think maybe~~
⌠   This has been an interesting
EXPLAIN?   couple of days
        ↘ Yesterday... Now this.
Do you think possibly that
            he ... likes her?
LOTS OF EFFORT/ATTENTION
     FOR A MINOR ACQUAINTANCE
So Yes? YES.
The longer I watch, the more certain
I am: One of them knows what
                it is to love.
STILL UNSURE ABOUT E.
Give them time.
Not sure she's noted her own
                feelings yet.

THE LUX
·······································
Special
   åU. 10
Brunch
   åU. 8
Brunch
   åU.
Special
   åU
Tea -
Gle
T

CHAPTER
48

Pemberley District, Dyberion, Fourth Moon of Londinium

As the Cabriol-A drove through the grounds of Pemberley once again, Elizabeth looked for the estate with as much anticipation as her first visit, though this time it was less daunting. Her aunt's plan to return the favor of Georgiana's visit with one of their own had been the clarity her clouded mind needed. It allowed her to be in the space her thoughts kept circling back to, though she knew Darcy wouldn't be there when they arrived. He, her uncle, and a few other gentlemen had gone to fulfill their fishing scheme shortly after breakfast. This would be a time to get to know his sister better, however, and she was looking forward to it.

Upon reaching the house, they were shown through the hall into one of the sitting rooms. The windows were open to the grounds, admitting a pleasant summer breeze, and revealing a splendid view of the high woody hills behind the house. The beautiful Glass Oaks and glittering mineral outcroppings, which were scattered over the mallow-moss lawn, should've appeared dichotomous, but were instead harmonious and breathtaking.

Elizabeth pulled her gaze from the view and settled instead on the women in the room. As they entered, Georgiana stood from her place on the sofa, along with a woman Elizabeth didn't recognize. Caroline Bingley and her sister sat in twin chairs with their backs to the doorway.

Georgiana welcomed them into the room very civilly, though Elizabeth could see how her manner might be interpreted as proud and reserved. It was clear to her that Georgianna was unused to playing host, and was attending to them with some degree of embarrassment—from either shyness or the fear of doing wrong. Elizabeth took pity on her immediately and determined that she'd make the hosting easier for her at every opportunity.

Mrs. Hurst and Miss Bingley turned in their seats and gave little more than a customary welcome. A pause followed. It was awkward, but it was broken by the woman Elizabeth didn't recognize.

She was a genteel, agreeable-looking woman with light hair and even lighter eyes. "I'm Mrs. Annesley. It's so nice to meet you. Georgiana was telling me about her visit with you yesterday in North Tōmbal." Her endeavor to break the silence proved her to be more truly well-bred than either of Bingley's sisters.

"Oh, it was such a nice surprise," Aunt Gardiner said as she and Elizabeth found seats in two of the three still-empty chairs. "We were so grateful for the visit."

"It's a lovely town," Mrs. Annesley noted. "Georgiana and I made sure to stop at the bakery just down the lane from where you had your visit."

"Mercers, yes, it's been around since I was a girl," her aunt said.

Between these two, with Elizabeth's occasional help, the conversation carried on. Georgiana looked as if she wished for courage enough to join in. Sometimes she'd venture a short sentence when there was the least danger of it being heard. Elizabeth made sure to acknowledge her in some way or other. But Elizabeth soon noticed that she was being closely watched by Caroline, and that she couldn't speak a word—especially to Georgiana—without calling her attention.

This observation wouldn't have prevented her from trying to talk to Georgiana, had they not been seated at an inconvenient distance. But she wasn't sorry to be spared the necessity of saying much. Her own thoughts were intruding. She began to anticipate that some of the gentlemen would enter the room. She wished, she feared, that Mr. Darcy might be among them. Whether she wished or feared it most, she could hardly determine.

After sitting for some time without the sound of Caroline's voice, it broke through the barrier of Elizabeth's thoughts in a cold inquiry.

"I trust your family are well, Eliza."

"They are," Elizabeth answered, with equal indifference.

Caroline said nothing more.

Elizabeth wasn't sorry for it.

After many significant looks and smiles aimed from Mrs. Annesley, Georgiana coordinated with the staff and soon they returned with cold meats, an assortment of breads, and a variety of all the finest fruits in season.

There was now, with refreshments, something to employ the whole party. They might not all talk, but they could all eat. The beautiful pyramids of blue grapes, boulades, and sweet mallow-cakes enticed them to surround the table.

As Elizabeth plucked a boulade from the stack, her feelings on Mr. Darcy's potential appearance clarified when he entered the room. In one moment, she believed her wishes to be dominant. In the next, she began to regret that he'd come in.

"I learned that we had visitors," he said, meeting her eyes.

Elizabeth was quick to resolve on being perfectly easy and unembarrassed, a resolution more necessary—though not more easily kept—because she noticed a suspicion from the whole party awakening to them. "We couldn't let such a gesture as yesterday's go unreciprocated," she said.

There was scarcely an eye that didn't watch him. In no face was attentive curiosity so strongly evident as in Caroline's, in spite of her smile.

"It wasn't any trouble," Georgiana offered. "I love the void, but I was ready for steadiness beneath my feet. I was just happy to be home, no matter where my brother took me first." It seemed Darcy's appearance was enough for Georgiana to exert herself more in conversation.

Elizabeth nodded in agreeable understanding. "I think love of the void is made stronger in knowing the solidity of home awaits."

"As you'll recall," Darcy leaned toward his sister, "Miss Elizabeth once piloted herself through the void."

Georgiana's eyes sparkled. "Oh, I haven't forgotten. You still owe me the story, if I recall *correctly.*"

Elizabeth was caught off guard. He'd told his sister about that? She stole a glance at Darcy, and saw him doing the same to her.

She couldn't help giving him a bemused and questioning smile, but, remembering where they were, pulled herself back into the conversation. "It seems your brother thought he was unequal to such a tale," she told Georgiana.

"Best to go to the source," Darcy agreed. "All I could really add is how she looked to us afterward."

Georgiana smiled, easing in their gentle camaraderie. "And how was that?"

"Like she had her own gravity," he said. "She practically floated."

Before Elizabeth could consider what he was saying, Caroline, who was watching them closely, and—driven perhaps from jealousy—took the opportunity to intercede. She sneered, with the barest layer of civility, "Speaking of starflight, Miss Eliza. Do tell. Have the Star Force Reserves left Meryton? There are some particular officers that must be a great loss to *your* family."

In Darcy's presence she seemed keen enough not to mention Wickham's name, but Elizabeth instantly understood the reference. The various recollections connected with him gave her a moment's distress, but exerting herself to repel the ill-natured attack, she answered the question with a tolerably detached tone. "They left a while ago. My family's sufficiently entertained. Especially with our nieces and nephews currently underfoot." While she spoke, she threw an involuntary glance toward Darcy. He was slightly off-color, earnestly looking at her. His sister's face was overcome with confusion. It was fair to assume, she thought, that Wickham was on their minds as well.

"It's good to hear you're getting along tolerably without certain charming connections." Had Caroline known what pain she was causing her beloved friend, she undoubtedly would've refrained from the hint. But her intent was clear. Caroline wanted to raise a subject that might betray the feelings she expected Elizabeth to have, perhaps in hopes of souring Darcy's opinion of her.

Elizabeth stayed calm and collected. She deflected Caroline's attempts with ease and grace, and Darcy's expression soon softened. Caroline, without the satisfaction of whatever reaction she hoped to garner from Elizabeth, dropped the subject, drawing no closer to speaking Wickham's name aloud.

Georgiana seemed to have lost her footing entirely. Though she recovered eventually, it wasn't enough to speak more.

Communications Log—System Storage 30 Days [Planetary]

●●

[LizzieLovesSpace] 4.7-15:46:18.LS

Jane, since you finally saw Caroline Bingley for who she is, I don't feel bad telling you that I was barely civil in response to her snide remarks today during lunch. I didn't miss her.

STATUS: UNDELIVERED

[LizzieLovesSpace] 4.7-16:13:29.LS

Lydia, I have a dinner tomorrow night and I'd love your opinion on which dress to wear. I was thinking about the green one, but I'm not sure if it sets the tone I'm going for. Maybe the blue? It's time for you to shine, little star.

STATUS: UNDELIVERED

[LizzieLovesSpace] 4.7-16:48:25.LS

Are you all just very busy or is there some sort of service issue? I'm having no trouble communicating with Aunt Mari on her comcard.
Moon interference?

STATUS: UNDELIVERED

[LizzieLovesSpace] 4.7-17:01:56.LS

They'll go through eventually, so I'll just keep telling you things.

STATUS: UNDELIVERED

[LizzieLovesSpace] 4.7-17:08:23.LS

Mary, Mr. Darcy's sister just got a new piano. You'd love the acoustics of the room it's in. Much better than what we have at Longbourn. Speaking of Mr. Darcy's sister, Kitty, I think you'd really like her. I don't know whether you'll ever get to meet her, but she reminds me of you a little bit.

STATUS: UNDELIVERED

....

[LizzieLovesSpace] 4.7-17:49:28.LS

I asked about the coms problem. There's an issue with the transmitters around Itavia's orbit line. For now, long-distance coms are out. I look forward to the influx of messages once everything is fixed.

STATUS: UNDELIVERED

. . . END COM . . .

CHAPTER
49

Pemberley District, Dyberion, Fourth Moon of Londinium

Georgiana was sad to see Elizabeth depart from the house so soon after mention of the Star Force Reserves threw everything off balance. It may have been longer, but to her the time seemed to warp while she reoriented. It'd been over a year since the incident, and she was angry at herself for letting such an obscure mention of Wickham affect her so much. She tried to remind herself that it was likely the more recent mention of the man by her own brother—when he told her that he'd confided everything to Elizabeth after his failed proposal—that had Wickham at the forefront of her mind.

The only positive thing that came from her silence at the end of their visit was that she was able to watch

Elizabeth interact with her brother more closely. Elizabeth's composure and deflection had been a welcome balm to both Georgiana's and her brother's nerves, it seemed.

"There are always charming connections to be found," Elizabeth had said, in response to Caroline's veiled mention of Wickham. "Even today, I've had the pleasure of getting to know Mrs. Annesley and Miss Georgiana."

"Perhaps like attracts like," her brother had noted.

Elizabeth laughed softly, "Oh, we both know that isn't true."

He looked at her with more intent and cheerfulness. "There you go professing opinions that aren't your own again."

Georgiana's unease had dissolved with the shock of seeing him so comfortable with someone besides herself or Bingley. Given what he had told her about his terrible attempt at a proposal, she hadn't expected such ease between them. It was a delight to watch.

"There are times, Mr. Darcy, that it's best to misremember the past." Something about this statement seemed to surprise them both as it left Elizabeth's lips.

"And others in which it's not," he said sincerely.

Georgiana had watched them with a growing sense of glee. Their gazes lingered. Elizabeth broke away first, but she recovered faster.

"I will have to be satisfied with you giving me far too much credit in this case, and consider it done on behalf of making me look good in front of your lovely sister." She flashed Georgiana a smile.

"Consider me guilty," he replied.

Georgiana would have paid good aurum in that moment to see them continue their conversation without the prying eyes of the Bingley sisters behind her.

"Then consider me satisfied."

To Georgiana's immense regret, the rest of the fishing group then returned to the house, and the visit came to an end.

While her brother attended their visitors to their vehicle, and Bingley and the other fishermen went their various ways to wash up, Caroline expressed her criticisms of Elizabeth as a person. No subject seemed beneath her to discuss. She seemed unaware—or unbothered—that Georgiana wasn't joining in. Her brother's recommendation would have been enough to ensure Georgiana's favor, had she not had a chance to meet the woman herself.

When her brother returned, Georgiana did nothing to stop Caroline's continued criticisms. She was interested to see his reactions, and curious how far Caroline would go.

"How very ill Miss Eliza looks today," Caroline said in an offhanded manner. "I've never in my life seen anyone so altered. She's so . . . weathered. Louisa and I agreed that we wouldn't have recognized her, had she not been announced when she entered."

He appeared to take it in stride, but Georgiana was able to spot the tiny mannerisms that belied his displeasure. His tone remained cool and unaffected. "I saw no difference other than a slight tan. Which is expected when traveling the countryside in summer."

"For my own part," Caroline continued, "I must confess, I never could see any beauty in her, tanned or otherwise. Her face is too thin. Her complexion has no brilliancy. Her features are not at all handsome . . ."

Georgiana disagreed more with each statement, and shifted uncomfortably in her seat.

". . . Her nose wants character—there's nothing marked in its lines. Her teeth are tolerable, but common."

Suddenly she was a master of the arts?

"And as for her eyes, which have sometimes been called so fine," Caroline put some emphasis here that Georgiana didn't understand. But a quirk of her brother's head indicated that there was some knowledge between them that warranted this emphasis.

"I could never see anything extraordinary in them. They have a sharp, shrewish look. I don't like it at all."

Georgiana masked her growing pity. If she, who had only been around Caroline once in Elizabeth's company, could detect the jealousy, her brother was certainly already aware.

"She has such a manner of self-sufficiency coupled with no fashion—"

No fashion? Elizabeth had been wearing clothes that looked to be designed for her both times they'd met, and from what her aunt had said the day before, it was all thanks to her youngest sister, who was very much keeping up with trends.

"—It's intolerable."

This wasn't the best method of recommending herself over Elizabeth. But angry people weren't always wise.

Her brother was becoming visibly nettled, and remained resolutely silent.

Caroline seemed determined to make him speak. She continued. "I remember when we first knew her on Heoros, how amazed we were to hear that she was a reputed beauty."

Such a strange choice of subject to ingratiate herself.

"Though she seemed to improve for you as the weeks went on. I believe you thought her rather pretty at one time," she chuckled.

"Yes," he replied, and Georgiana knew he'd reached his limit. "But *that* was only when I first saw her. It's been months since I've considered her one of the handsomest women I've known."

He then bowed out of the room, and Caroline was left to all the satisfaction of having forced him to say what gave no one any pain but herself.

For Georgiana's part, she did her very best not to smile at hearing his confession. She hoped that what she saw between her brother and Elizabeth in their short interaction was what she suspected and not just what she wished.

To: Elizabeth Bennet, Pemberley District, Dyberion

From: Jane Bennet, Longbourn Estate, Landings District, Heoros

Subject: Catching Up

Status: Held, Redelivered

Dearest Lizzie,

I believe we're having some connection issues, so I'm trying a waive in the hopes that we can connect. You better be enjoying the beautiful sights of Dyberion. You are, however, missing out on perhaps the most adorable play in existence. The girls orchestrated the entire thing with Kitty's help and the boys were so eager that they played all the parts. My personal favorite was the baby in a dress they made of scarves. He was so sweet toddling around in it.

I'm keeping this short in case this doesn't reach you.

All my love,
Jane

To: Elizabeth Bennet, Pemberley District, Dyberion

From: Jane Bennet, Longbourn Estate, Landings District, Heoros

Subject: [None]

Status: Held, Redelivered

Lizzie,

Something very unexpected and serious has happened. Don't be alarmed. We're all well. But it's Lydia. A waive came through this morning during breakfast, from VC Forster. Lydia has run away. She left her comcard behind and went to Nagalea with one of his officers.

Lizzie, it's Wickham. Kitty seemed to be expecting it. The rest of us weren't. All I can hope is that we're misinformed or that his character has been misunderstood. But my knowledge of his past makes me wary. What could he want with her? She's no Miss Darcy. No inheritance worth extorting. She's sixteen. Does two make a pattern? He's not trying to marry her.

Mama's in shambles. Papa bears it quieter.

The VC suspects that they slipped away last night about twelve. They weren't missed until this morning at eight. We were notified immediately. VC Forster said that he'll be coming here soon. Lydia left a note for his wife, informing her of her intention. She, it seems, plans to marry him. But she's far too young. It'll never happen.

Mama needs me. I've been hiding in our closet just to type this. Sorry if this was poorly communicated. I hardly know what I've written.

Jane

To: ELIZABETH BENNET, NORTH TŌMBAL INN, MARVELS DISTRICT, DYBERION

From: JANE BENNET, LONGBOURN ESTATE, LANDINGS DISTRICT, HEOROS

Subject: APOLOGIES

STATUS: HELD, REDELIVERED

By this time, you've received my rushed waive from yesterday. I hope this is more intelligible, but while I'm not confined for time, I'm so bewildered that I can't guarantee coherency.

The news is bad. I can't hold on to this. There are rumblings of a marriage, but she's too young. It'd be a terrible outcome.

There's reason now to fear that they didn't go to Nagalea. VC Forster arrived yesterday. He left Sollaria the day before, a few hours after he sent his waive. Though Lydia's short note to Mrs. F led them to believe she was going to

Greene Gardens, Denny suggested that Wickham had never intended to go there. VC Forster instantly sounded the alarm and set off from Sollaria hoping to trace their route. He followed them easily to Laudlum, but no further. When they reached the town, they dismissed the Cabriol-A that brought them from Pomes, and got on a Nexus shuttle. All that's known after this is that they were believed to be continuing on the Londinium route.

I don't know what to think. After making every possible inquiry at St. James, VC Forster came all the way to Heoros, renewing his inquiries at the waystation and the inns in the Port District. His efforts yielded no success. No one had seen them pass through. With the kindest concern, he came to Longbourn and confessed his apprehensions to us in an honorable effort to ease our worries. I'm sincerely sorry for him and his wife, but no one can blame them.

Our distress is very great. Papa and Mama believe Mr. Wickham is using her, but for what gain? I'm trying not to think so poorly of him. Many circumstances might be happening that aren't so dire. She's too young to be married on Londinium. If they haven't left the planet, there may still be a chance to get her back from him.

VC Forster doesn't think the best of Wickham. When I expressed hopes that he had no ill intent, there was nothing but doubt on the man's face. He said he feared Wickham wasn't a man to be trusted.

Mama is really ill. She keeps to her room. I wish she'd exert herself a bit, but that seems unlikely. Meanwhile, I've never seen our father so affected. Poor Kitty has the brunt of their anger for keeping the attachment sealed. But it was a matter of confidence. I can't blame her. How could she have expected her baby sister to run off with him when she expresses her adoration for nearly every boy she meets?

I'm so glad that you've been spared some of this distress. But now that the first shock has passed, I must confess, I long for your return. I'm not selfish enough to press for it. That would be so inconvenient. There's nothing you can do that we aren't.

Jane

To: ELIZABETH BENNET, NORTH TŌMBAL INN, MARVELS DISTRICT, DYBERION

From: JANE BENNET, LONGBOURN ESTATE, LANDINGS DISTRICT, HEOROS

Subject: SORRY

STATUS: HELD, REDELIVERED

I'm sending another waive to do what I've told you I wouldn't. But with circumstances as they are, I can't help but earnestly beg you all to come home as soon as possible. I know our aunt and uncle so well that I'm not afraid of requesting it. Though I have still something more to ask of them. Papa's going to Londinium with VC Forster today to try and find Lydia. What he means to do, I don't know. But his excessive distress won't allow him to stay idle, and VC Forster is obliged to be at Sollaria again tomorrow evening. In such urgency as this, our uncle's advice and assistance would be everything. He'll immediately understand what I feel, and I rely on him.

Jane

CHAPTER 50

North Tōmbal Public Library, Dyberion, Fourth Moon of Londinium

Elizabeth pulled a fifth book from the library shelves and stacked it on the others she was holding. It was unlikely she'd finish all of these while they remained in town, but she never shied from a challenge. She turned the corner and stopped short.

"Mr. Darcy?" she exclaimed, then quietly added, "What are the chances I'd run into you here?"

He bowed his head. "Much higher when it's on purpose."

She simply stared at him, too confused to speak.

Correctly interpreting her silence, he elaborated. "I stopped by where you were staying and was directed here. I was hoping to confirm a few things with you about dinner tonight."

"Oh." This was a surprise. But not unwelcome. She glanced at the books in her arms. "Walk with me?" she asked, and tilted her head toward the checkout desk.

He fell into step beside her, and they made their way down the wide stairs.

Feeling bolstered by this unexpected—and unnecessarily civil—extra visit, she said, "I'm just realizing, of all the rooms we were shown the other day at Pemberley, I never saw the library. If I recall, it was the work of many generations."

She watched the smile play at the corner of his lips.

"Your memory is solid—"

As he spoke, she couldn't help but recall what her aunt had said about him a few days ago. There was, indeed, something quite pleasing about his mouth when he talked.

"—and I promise to make up for the error this evening after dinner."

She looked around the warm, inviting space that was the public library, with its beautiful stained-glass dome above the circular foyer. "Is it as grand as all this?"

He looked around, then his eyes trained on hers. "That'll be up to you to decide."

She felt a weight to the words that she was suddenly afraid to examine. They'd reached the crescent-shaped front desk, and she took the opportunity to turn her attention to setting her books on the counter. Reaching into her dress pocket to fish out the library guest pass she'd been given, she moved her comcard out of the way and set it on the books.

A familiar bright light flashed across the screen, and her heart leaped. "Oh! The transmitters must be fixed." She looked closer at the screen, seeing several waives roll in from Jane in quick succession. She frowned. "That's odd." She looked up at Darcy, who watched her with mild, but polite, curiosity. Something about so many waives from Jane caused her unease. "Would you mind giving me a moment? I just need to check . . ." she trailed off, already walking with the comcard toward one of the benches at the back wall.

She was aware of Darcy staying by her stack of books, perhaps to guard it from other library-goers. Her attention, however, had shifted fully to her sister's words, heart sinking with each new waive she opened. She dropped onto the bench as she read, legs losing stability. While reading, time seemed to slow.

Suddenly Darcy was in front of her, and time came screeching back to its proper speed. "Stars rain down!—Miss Elizabeth? What's the matter?" He sounded quite alarmed. She didn't immediately understand why. Then the world blackened at the edges of her vision and her blood seemed to fizz in her veins.

"I—" she was having trouble breathing.

"You're as pale as aurawood," he said, with more feeling than politeness.

"I need to get back. I have to speak with my aunt and uncle." She tried to stand. Her knees trembled under her, and she nearly dropped to the seat again. But then Darcy's hand was on her elbow, and he was helping to steady her.

"You're shaking. Please, Elizabeth, tell me what's wrong. How can I help you?"

She felt sick to her stomach. But she couldn't break down here. She needed to get back to her suite. Taking a deep breath, and doing her best to recover enough to walk and hold the barest of conversation, she said, "I'm well. Well, I'm not sick. Physically. I—I just received some dreadful news. I'm in distress. Sun and stars!" She burst into tears at the thought of it. So much for not breaking down in the library.

Darcy, his face a mask of wretched suspense, could only mutter indistinct encouragements and soothe her with compassionate silence. He disappeared for a moment, only to return with a box of tissues.

She was overcome and frustratingly unable to stop the tears. After a few miserable minutes, she was finally able to regain control and stand. She wiped the tears from her cheeks and looked into his eyes. "I need to return to my suite. I can't explain here."

He nodded immediately. "Are you able to walk?" He seemed genuinely unsure of this answer.

She must have looked a wreck. Straightening a bit to give the appearance, at least, of not falling apart on the inside, she nodded, and led the way to the doors, her books abandoned.

"I just got several waives from Jane," she told him, as they stepped into the bright sunshine. "There was a transmitter issue that was keeping us from communicating. All the coms she'd been sending came through at once."

He stayed close to her as they crossed the road, perhaps afraid her legs would fail her in the midst of oncoming traffic, but he listened intently. In this moment, she hated that he did.

"She told me some terrible news. My youngest sister has left all her friends and run away—has thrown herself into the power of—" she choked from the shame of saying this—"of Mr. Wickham." She could hardly meet his gaze. Did his steps falter, or had she imagined it? "They've gone off together from Sollaria. *You* know him too well to doubt the rest. She has no money, no connections . . . She's completely at his mercy."

Darcy was all astonishment.

She bit back saying more until they had entered the inn and were on the elevator to her suite. Thoughts whirled in her head, eager to spill out.

"When I consider," she finally said, agitated, "that *I* might have prevented this. *I* knew what he was. I should've explained some part of it—something of what I learned, to my own family! If his character had been known, maybe this wouldn't have happened. But now it has and it's all—all too late now."

The elevator door opened and they walked to the suite. "Is there any chance that your sister—that Jane—was misinformed?" he asked.

"No. Their information is coming from VC Forster. What they know is that the two of them left Sollaria together on Sunday night, and were traced almost to St. James City, but not beyond. They've definitely not gone to Nagalea, which was originally believed to be the case."

Darcy's features had hardened, his expression grave.

"My father went to Londinium," she said, opening the door. "Jane is begging for my uncle's help. We'll have to leave as soon as possible. But nothing can be done." She scanned the suite, disappointed but unsurprised to see that the Gardiners were not still here. She sat in the same chair where she'd toasted to their visit to Pemberley just days before, feeling all the cruel irony of the moment. "Exploding suns!—how is such a man to be persuaded? How are they even to be discovered? There isn't the smallest hope."

Darcy found an empty glass and filled it from the purple bottle on the table. He said nothing, but handed her the water with an almost paternal insistence. She took it and downed the whole thing with hardly a breath.

"Galaxy's end! Had I known what I ought—what I dared—to do! But I didn't. I was afraid of doing too much. What a wretched mistake!"

Darcy seemed hardly to hear her. He began pacing the room in earnest meditation, his brow contracted, an air of gloom around him. She instantly understood that with this news, her power was sinking. How could it not under such circumstances? It was proof that her family courted nothing but disgrace and disaster.

She couldn't condemn him, nor be surprised. But the belief of losing his favor for good brought no consolation to her heart and only added to her distress. It was, on the contrary, highlighting the truth of her own wishes. Never had she so honestly felt that she could've loved him, as she did now when all love must be in vain.

She couldn't be worried for herself long. Lydia—and the distress this was causing her whole family—swallowed all her concerns. She buried her face in her hands. Minutes passed as she lost herself to the swirling of questions in her mind. Once again, it was Darcy's voice that pulled her free of the tumult.

Though his manner was compassionate, he spoke like restraint. "I'm afraid I've intruded on your privacy too long. I don't have any excuse other than my real, though ineffective, concern. I wish to the farthest stars that there was anything I could say or do to console you. I hate to mention anything that will cause you more distress, but it must be said. I fear this situation will prevent my sister having the pleasure of your company at Pemberley tonight?"

Her heart dropped even further. "Oh." A thousand curses on Wickham. "Yes, I'm so sorry. Please apologize to her for us. I know I have no right to ask, but . . . conceal the truth from her as long as possible?"

"Of course. You can trust my discretion." He knelt beside her so their eyes were level. "I'm sorry that I'm of no more help to you than this. If you need anything before you leave, you know where I'll be. Give my regrets to your aunt and uncle." With one serious parting look, he stood, and left the suite, taking all the air with him.

Elizabeth was now entirely alone. She couldn't help but feel how improbable it was that they would ever again be to each other whatever it was they were becoming these past few days. Their entire acquaintance was full of contradictions and varieties. She sighed at the perverseness of feeling everything that would have allowed them to become something more at just the right time for that never to happen. How could it, when her family would be tied— perhaps forever, should the worst occur—to Mr. Wickham?

She tried for a moment to believe that what she was beginning to feel for Darcy had been imagined. But the harder she tried, the less honest she felt. Were gratitude and esteem good foundations for affection? Her change of sentiment made it feel likely. If not, then what was there but love at first sight? She'd given that somewhat of a trial in her partiality to Wickham, and it had failed. She found she was more inclined to seek the less interesting mode of attachment. But that knowledge had come too late.

Whatever became of this situation with Lydia, it would affect them all in more ways than they could know. By Jane's second waive, she'd lost any hope of Wickham meaning no mischief toward her sister. But she was astonished that he'd have any interest in her at all. She was boisterous, young, impressionable, and eager for attention. Elizabeth supposed that was sufficient for him, if aurum was not his goal, as it had been—or seemed to have been— for Georgiana. The running away felt somehow like Lydia's idea, though why she would feel the need to do so was unclear. None of them had known of her relationship with him, so she had never been warned off him in a way that might drive her to sneak off. Elizabeth could only conclude that Lydia did really believe she would marry Wickham. Unfortunately, neither her virtue nor her understanding could preserve her from falling prey to him.

Elizabeth was overwhelmingly anxious to be home. She wanted to hear, to see, to be there to share with Jane in carrying the burden of a family so out of sorts. With a father so absent and a mother requiring as much attendance as the four extra children underfoot, Jane was surely suffering. Mary and Kitty might be helping, of course, but Kitty was still a child herself, and Mary had little experience taking charge.

She was immensely relieved when the Gardiners finally returned. In her distress, she'd completely forgotten to alert them. As quickly as she could, she caught them up to speed, reading the three important waives aloud. After their initial exclamations of surprise and horror, they jumped into action.

The following hour was a blur, but it saw their tasks completed. Her uncle had seen to their account at the Inn, her aunt to their excuses and goodbyes to her friends. Elizabeth assured them that their apologies had been made to Pemberley. Nothing else remained but for them to go.

Elizabeth, after all the misery of the morning, found herself, in a shorter space of time than she could've imagined, seated aboard the StarSwift Endurance, and on the journey to Longbourn at last.

LONDINIUM SAT[SYS

Communications Log—System Storage 30 Days [Planetary]

[Ba_Da_Bing_ley] 5.7-11:57:12.LS

Must be going well, I haven't heard from you in quite a while.

[FW.Darcy] 5.7-12:00:41.LS

Plans are grounded for tonight.

[Ba_Da_Bing_ley] 5.7-12:01:55.LS

So going in person to confirm was too much?

[FW.Darcy] 5.7-12:03:12.LS

Not my fault. There was a family emergency. She had to go home.

[Ba_Da_Bing_ley] 5.7-12:04:23.LS

Now I feel like an ass. Is everyone well?

[FW.Darcy] 5.7-12:05:39.LS

Yes. But my plans have changed also. Can you please tell Pierce to ready the Hauler?

[Ba_Da_Bing_ley] 5.7-12:06:53.LS

Of course. I just saw him in the hall. Should I be concerned for you?

[FW.Darcy] 5.7-12:08:12.LS

No. I'll explain when I get back.

[Ba_Da_Bing_ley] 5.7-12:09:58.LS

I'm intrigued

. . . and concerned anyway.

. . . END COM . . .

CHAPTER 51

StarSwift Endurance, Inter-Lunar Travel Route 1280-A, Londinium System

I 've been thinking it over, Lizzie," said her uncle, as the moon diminished from view, "could he really expect her friends and family not to fight for her? And what of his regiment? Did he think he wouldn't be noticed, after such an affront to the Void Commander? The temptation doesn't seem worth the risk."

Elizabeth wanted to believe it, but something in her gut said otherwise.

"It's too great a violation of decency, honor, and interest," her aunt added. "I can't think so very ill of him. Lizzie, can you really believe him capable of it?"

"Maybe not of neglecting his own interest, but in every other neglect I can believe it of him." This wasn't the first time he'd lured a young woman into running away with him. But she couldn't tell them that part, especially since the motives for such a decision appeared so different in Lydia's case. There wasn't a great inheritance coming Lydia's way. "Why else would Lydia have suggested they were heading to Greene Gardens?"

"There's more on Nagalea than Greene Gardens. Perhaps she seized an opportunity to see a part of the system she otherwise wouldn't," Uncle Edward said, rising from his seat and seeking out the food options in their small two-room compartment.

"There's no absolute proof they went to Nagalea," her aunt said.

"But switching shuttles is such a presumption. And no traces of them were found on Barrett Road," Elizabeth observed.

Her uncle returned with three bags of dried assorted fruits, handing one each to his wife and Elizabeth. "Let's suppose they're still on Londinium. St. James would be an ideal location for concealment. It's easy to disappear there, especially in Lowland. And more accessible for the pair of them, with so little aurum to their names."

Elizabeth didn't open the package. She felt too uneasy to eat. "Why run away at all? What good can come from it? This concerns me greatly." She stared at the void beyond the window, her mind projecting imagined scenarios over the inky black. "No, even his own friend was certain this was not love. Wickham would never marry a woman without financial incentive. He can't afford it. Lydia's too young to be married outside Greene Gardens, so if they aren't there, then that isn't his aim." Now Elizabeth stood, too anxious to be still. "Is Lydia's youth and pliability really temptation enough to tarnish his name and disgrace himself in the squadron with such dishonorable behavior? Maybe I'm the wrong person to judge. I don't know what effects such a step might produce. Maybe the men of the Star Force aren't concerned with the implications of what he's done. It doesn't sit right with me, though."

"Do you think Lydia's so lost to everything but her imagined love of him that she can't see the situation she's gotten herself into?" her aunt asked.

"It seems that way," replied Elizabeth, with tears in her eyes. "I shouldn't be shocked that her sense of decency and self-preservation—her awareness—should be so minimal. Yet I am. I don't know what to say. Maybe I'm not being fair to her." She turned to the window. "She's never been taught to think on serious subjects; and for the last several months—no, stars dimming!—more than a revo—she's been occupied with nothing but amusement and vanity. She's been allowed to waste her time in the most frivolous ways, and picks up any opinions that come her way without a moment of reflection. Since the Red Squadron were first quartered on the Meryton, she's had nothing but love, flirtation, and officers in her head. She's primed herself to the idea that love awaits her in the company of officers. And we all know that Wickham has charm enough to captivate nearly anyone."

"But Jane doesn't think so very ill of Wickham as to believe him capable of taking such advantage of her," her aunt reasoned.

"Does Jane ever think ill of anyone?" Elizabeth countered. "Is there anyone she'd believe to be capable of such an attempt until it were proved true? Jane knows, as well as I do, what Wickham really is. We both know that he's been recklessly extravagant in every sense of the word; that he has neither integrity nor honor; that he's as false and deceitful as he is insinuating."

"Do you really know all this?" cried her aunt.

"I do," Elizabeth said, her face warming in the admission. "I told you the other day about his behavior to Mr. Darcy. You heard how he spoke of him, and we know now how much forbearance and liberality he'd actually shown. There are other circumstances I'm not at liberty to—which aren't worthwhile to relate. But his lies about the whole Pemberley family are endless. From what he said of Miss

Georgiana, I was thoroughly prepared to see a proud, reserved, disagreeable girl. He knew his characterization of her was false."

Uncle Edward frowned. "Does Lydia know nothing of this? You and Jane seem so well informed on the matter."

"That's the worst of it." Elizabeth began to pace the width of the window. "Until I was on the Kent, and saw so much of both Mr. Darcy and his cousin, VC Fitzwilliam, I was ignorant of the truth myself. When I returned home, the Regiment was readying to leave Meryton. Knowing that, neither Jane nor I thought it necessary to make our knowledge public. What use could it apparently be to anyone, that the good opinion, which all the district society had of him, should be overthrown? Even when it was settled that Lydia would go with Mrs. Forster, the necessity of opening her eyes to his character never occurred to me. That *she* could be in any danger from the deception never entered my head. That such a consequence as *this* could ensue . . . It was so far from my thoughts."

Her aunt took this in with serious contemplation. "When they all left for Sollaria, you had no reason to believe them fond of each other?"

"Not in the slightest. Had anything of affection been noticeable between them, one of us would have said something. When he arrived, she was ready enough to admire him; but we all were. Every girl on or within an easy flight of the Meryton was out of her senses about him for the first two months. But he never distinguished *her* with any particular attention. After a period of extravagant admiration, her fancy for him gave way, and others—younger ones, who treated her with more distinction—became her favorites."

Little could be added to their fears, hopes, and conjectures on this subject by repeatedly discussing it. No other subject could detach them from it long. They returned to it again and again for the entire journey. From Elizabeth's thoughts it was never absent, fixed there by self-reproach. Her mind did not afford her heart a single moment of ease or forgetfulness for the entirety of the expedited, two-day flight.

LONDINIUM SAT[SYS

Communications Log—System Storage 30 Days [Planetary]

[MaryB] 8.7-16:13:26.LS

I know you've been struggling with all of this, Kit, but I've seen the waives between you and Lydia. This isn't your fault.

[KitKitBennet] 8.7-16:14:49.LS

If I had said something sooner, maybe someone could've stopped it.

[MaryB] 8.7-16:16:25.LS

I believe she would have found another way to get what she wanted. Think of who she is. You know she has never done what was requested or expected of her.

[KitKitBennet] 8.7-16:17:48.LS

Yet she's always rewarded.

[MaryB] 8.7-16:18:04.LS

You aren't wrong, but let us not turn on her. I have a sense that this is not the reward you think it is.

[KitKitBennet] 8.7-16:19:10.LS

I guess we'll see.

[MaryB] 8.7-16:20:19.LS

You are still young. While I'm not a great deal older than you, I think it's fair to say that you see the world differently (much like Lydia, in many ways). It's very likely that while Lydia believes this to be love, she's being manipulated for some other purpose. I know that Jane has hope that it's not the case, but I believe as Lizzie does on this.

[KitKitBennet] 8.7-16:21:59.LS

That's a dreadful thought. I think I'd rather believe as Jane does, for now.

[MaryB] 8.7-16:23:03.LS

I won't begrudge you that. For Lydia's sake, I hope that's the case.

... END COM ...

CHAPTER 52

Longbourn House, Heoros, First Moon of Londinium

J ane opened the door of the study, releasing the little Gardiners like jewelbirds from a cage as the Cabriol-A came into sight in the drive. They flew down the steps of the house to meet it. The joyful surprise that lit their faces radiated throughout their bodies, and whatever stillness she'd managed to coax them into in the hours leading to their parents' arrival was gone.

Lizzie jumped out first, and after giving each of them a hasty kiss, hurried into the vestibule where Jane was waiting in welcome.

They hugged tightly, tears springing from Jane's eyes, then pulled apart with a shared urgency.

"Anything new about the fugitives?" Lizzie asked.

"Not yet. But now that Uncle Edward is here, I hope everything will be well."

"Is Papa still on Londinium?"

"Yes, since last Tuesday."

"Have you heard from him?"

"Only twice. He sent me a few lines on Wednesday to say that they'd arrived safely, and to give me his directions on the house management—which I practically begged him to do. The second came on Friday. He said he wouldn't write again till he heard something of importance to warrant a waive."

"And Mama—how is she? How are you all?"

Jane sighed deeply, but kept as encouraging a smile on her face as she could. "Mama's fine, all things considered. She's greatly shaken. She's upstairs—hasn't left her room. She'll be so glad to see you all. Mary and Kitty, count our stars lucky, are quite well."

Lizzie narrowed her eyes. "But you. How are you? You look pale. You've been through so much!"

Jane was so grateful to now have others to shoulder the load of the past few days that she felt much better than she had. "I'm well. It was challenging, to be sure. I've been mother to six—well, seven, with Mama's needs—and to be perfectly honest, I'm rather exhausted. But otherwise, I'm well." Her sanguine hope of good, which her heart suggested hadn't deserted her, encouraged her to believe that all would still somehow end well, and that every morning might bring some news, from either Lydia or her father.

The children quickly lost interest in the conversations of adults, and wandered back to their activities from earlier in the day. Jane brought Lizzie and the Gardiners to her mother's room.

She received them exactly as expected; with tears and lamentations of regret, cursing the villainous conduct of Wickham, and complaints of her own sufferings.

"Blaming everyone but the person whose ill-judged indulgence allowed Lydia's errors to flourish," Lizzie muttered in Jane's ear.

"If I'd been able to go to Sollaria with all my family as I'd *intended*," said their mother, "this would never have happened. Poor Lydia had nobody to take care of her. The Forsters never should have let her out of their sight. So neglectful. She's not the kind of girl to do such a thing. I knew they were unfit to take charge of her. But I was overruled, as I always am! Poor Lydia. And now my husband has gone away, and he'll be forced to fight Wickham when he finds him, so he'll be killed. Then what will become of us all? The Collinses will turn us out of the house before he's cold in his grave, and if you aren't kind to us, brother, I don't know what we'll do."

They all assured her this wasn't what would happen. Uncle Edward explained his intention to go to Londinium via StarSwift the very next day, and assist Mr. Bennet in every endeavor for recovering Lydia.

"Don't give way to useless alarm," he added. "Though it's right to be prepared for the worst, there's no reason to consider it certain. It hasn't been quite a week since they left Sollaria. In a few more days, we may gain some news of them. Till we know their situation, don't let us give the matter over as lost. As soon as I get to St. James City I'll find your husband, force him back to Gracechurch Street with me, and we'll consult together on what's to be done."

"By the Everlasting Light!" Mama exclaimed. "This is exactly what I most wished for. When you make port, find them out, wherever they may be. Offer her anything to come home. New clothes, new drawing supplies—as long as she comes home. And above all, keep my husband from fighting. Tell him what a dreadful state I'm in— that I have such trembling, such fluttering, all over me—such spasms in my side and pains in my head and flutterings in my heart that I can get no rest by day or night. Oh, my dear brother, you're so kind. I know you'll handle it all."

Uncle Gardiner, though he assured her again of his earnest endeavors in the cause, couldn't avoid recommending moderation, in her hopes as well as her fears. Jane couldn't help but agree.

After talking with her mother in this manner till dinner was on the table, they left her to vent all her feelings to the housekeeper, who'd offered to attend to her in Jane's absences.

As they left the room, her aunt noted quietly, "There's no real reason she should stay sequestered from the family."

Jane grimaced. "I think, for the sake of prudence, we ought to keep Mama's lamentations confined to the housekeeper. We can't be sure she'll hold her tongue around the less . . . fixed . . . of the staff."

Elizabeth agreed. "Yes. By the stars! Let's keep this whole affair contained as long as possible."

When they reached the dining room, Mary and Kitty were already seated at the table, talking intensely to one another. Mary was likely consoling Kitty, who'd been shaken deeply by this ordeal, and had grown more generally fretful.

Jane and Lizzie bookended their younger sisters, Jane beside Kitty, Lizzie by Mary.

"How are you both doing?" Lizzie asked.

"Angry at Lydia for putting herself in this position," Kitty confessed. "Angry at myself for not warning anyone. Angriest at Mr. Wickham."

Jane nodded at that last one.

"This is a difficult situation," Mary said solemnly. "But we must stem the tide of anger and pour into our wounded hearts the balm of sisterly consolation." She grabbed Jane's hand with one of hers, Lizzie's with the other, and squeezed.

Jane smiled fondly at her, then pressed her cheek into Kitty's shoulder in a loving snuggle.

"Why don't we get our minds off this whole thing for a while?" Lizzie suggested. "When we broke atmo, I noticed that the field on the far side of the grounds is at the perfect height for Seven Rings."

Kitty perked up at this, and Jane was inclined to help relieve at least one of her sisters from the oppressive cloud of uncertainty that hung over them all. She stood, deciding for them. "Let's go. Mary, you, too."

Mary cast a longing look at her unopened book on the table, heaved a sigh, and then stood as well. "I'm on your team."

Half an hour later, they had the game pieces in place in the field of golden grass, and their game was underway.

Jane was grateful for Mary's decision to be her partner. It meant that she and Lizzie were, as opponents, standing beside each other on the far border of the playing field.

Lizzie instantly took advantage of this to ask Jane questions which she was just as eager to answer. They both agreed that the entire ordeal was a galaxy-sized disaster.

"But tell me," said Lizzie, tossing her largest ring with precision, "what have I not heard? I need details. Did the VC have any inkling of their plan before they dusted out? He must've seen them together quite a bit."

"He did admit that he'd suspected some partiality, especially on Lydia's side, but nothing that set off any alarms. She's sixteen. Why would he think it anything more than a girlhood infatuation?" Jane lined the rings in order on her non-throwing arm, awaiting her turn. "I feel so badly for him. He was already coming our way to help us when he heard she might not have gone to Nagalea. It made him all the more anxious to reach us quickly."

"Was Denny aware of their intentions? Did the VC mention anything?"

"Yes. But when questioned by *him*, Denny denied knowing anything about their plans, and wouldn't give his real opinion about it."

"Sun and stars!"

"But then Kitty, who found this whole thing rather romantic at first, very triumphantly confessed to knowing more than the rest of us. Apparently, in Lydia's last waive to her, she'd prepared her for such a jump. She'd known of their being in love with each other for many weeks."

Lizzie tossed the last of her rings, but it was clear her mind wasn't on it. "Was this before she went to Sollaria?"

"No, I don't believe so."

"That's something, at least." Lizzie crossed her arms. "What were the VC's thoughts on Wickham?"

"He didn't speak so well of Wickham as he used to. Called him imprudent and extravagant. And, very recently, there are rumblings that Wickham left the Meryton greatly in debt. I hope that's false."

"I have a feeling it isn't."

Jane frowned, and turned her attention to the playing field, trying to channel her frustration into the throws she made with each ring.

"Oh, Jane," Lizzie said. "If only we'd been less secret. Had we told everyone what we knew of him, this wouldn't have happened."

Jane tossed her last ring and turned to face Lizzie, her expression serious. "Don't do that. We just talked Kitty out of the same self-blame spiral. Perhaps it would've been better, I won't deny that. But we acted with the best intentions. We could not have predicted this."

Lizzie growled low in her chest. "You're right. But it feels like it wasn't enough, in retrospect."

"Because it wasn't. But we can't know the future. We did what we could in the present moment, and we'll continue to do so, now."

"You said Lydia wrote a note?"

Jane nodded and pulled it from her pocket and handed it to her. "He brought it with him."

Lizzie read it quickly and then practically growled in frustration. "Galaxy's end! Thoughtless, foolish Lydia!" She handed the page back. "I suppose at least *she* was serious in the idea of marriage. Whatever he might've persuaded her to do after they left, it wasn't any scheme of hers." She shook her head in disgust. "But that makes it all the more unbearable. How did Papa react?"

"I never saw anyone look so shocked. He couldn't speak a word for a full ten minutes. Mama was taken ill immediately, and the whole house was in such confusion."

"Oh, Jane," Lizzie said despondently, "was there a staff member in the whole house who didn't know the whole story before the end of the day?"

"I don't know. I hope there was. But to be guarded at such a time is very difficult. Mama was in hysterics, and though I endeavored to help her as much as I could, I'm afraid I didn't do so much as I might've done. But with the horror of what might possibly happen, I nearly spun out of orbit as well."

"You've given so much of yourself to caring for her and our sisters and the children . . . You need rest. If only I'd been with you! You've had every care and anxiety on yourself alone."

Jane felt the exhaustion as her sister spoke it aloud, but she couldn't see it the same way. "Mary and Kitty have been so kind, and would've helped more, had I let them. I didn't think it was right to put those responsibilities on them. Aunt Phillips flew to Longbourn on Tuesday, after our father left. She was able to stay until Thursday with me and was of great use and comfort to us all."

Kitty gave a little shout of triumph as she landed one of her rings just right. Jane took a moment to celebrate with her before turning back to her conversation with Lizzie. "Lady Lucas has come by as well. She walked over on Wednesday morning to check on us, and offered her services, if they should be of use."

"She'd have been better off staying home," Elizabeth said bitterly. "I'm sure she *meant* well, but with such delicate circumstances as these, one can't see too little of their neighbors. *We* know Lydia's predicament to be distressing, and Wickham to be taking advantage, but not everyone will see them that way. I hope to keep the general public's opinion to a minimum."

Jane couldn't help but agree.

TRIBULATIONS
SUNDAY 17.7-9:01:43.LS

We've been anxiously awaiting a waive from Papa for hours, but our tenth day of sunlight arrived without a single blip from him. We all know he's a negligent correspondent, but at times like this, I'd hoped for some extra effort. I'm forced to conclude that he had nothing worth sending. Even that we'd be glad to know for certain. Uncle Edward has already left.

With his absence comes the steady promise of constant information. He also promised to return our father to us as soon as he could. This was a great consolation to Mama. Aunt Mariane and the children will remain here in the district for a few days longer, which is a great consolation to me. She's been tending to Mama, and is such a comfort to all of us in our hours of excruciating idleness.

MONDAY 18.7-13:03:49.LS

Aunt Phillips has been by a number of times since our uncle left. Her aim is always to cheer and hearten us, though she never comes without reporting some fresh instance of Wickham's extravagance or irregularity.

All of the Meryton now seems to be striving to malign the man who, just three months ago, could do no wrong. I'm thankful that this is not in relation to Lydia's predicament. He was discovered to be in debt to every tradesman in the place, and his intrigues—all labeled as seduction, which unsettles me greatly—have extended into every tradesman's family.

Lizzie doesn't believe more than half of what's been said, but what she does believe makes her assurance of Lydia's endangerment more certain. Even I, who believe less than Lizzie, have become almost hopeless.

TUESDAY 19.7-19:25:22.LS

Aunt M. received a waive from Uncle E. today. He and Papa have been all over the city in search of her. He noted that my father seems entirely disinclined to leave Londinium, and promised to write again very soon. Oh! He also sent a waive to the VC in an effort to find out whether Wickham has any relations or connections who may know what part of town he'd conceal himself in. It feels a stretch, but perhaps there's something to it. We have nothing else to guide us. Now that I think of it, Lizzie could likely tell us about his relations better than anyone else.

WEDNESDAY 20.7-9:56:32.LS

Wickham's parents, both of whom crossed into starlight many years ago, are all the connections he has that Lizzie knows of. It was a dead end after all.

THURSDAY 21.7-20:42:12.LS

Uncle E heard back from the VC. It appears that Wickham has numerous former acquaintances, but hasn't kept much of a friendship with any of them. We have no one who might tell us any news of him. Apparently, it has recently come to light that he has a considerable amount of gambling debts on Londinium. Couple that with the fear of Papa or Uncle E finding them, there's a very powerful motive for secrecy on his part. The VC believes that more than a thousand aurum will be necessary to clear his expenses in Sollaria alone. When Uncle E relayed these particulars, I confess I read them in abject horror.

The only good news is that Papa will be home by Saturday. How melancholy a thing to be happy for. The only one unhappy about this is Mama. She complained of him coming home without Lydia and insists she won't be content until her daughter has been found.

FRIDAY 22.7-11:12:53.LS

Aunt M and the children will return to Londinium tomorrow. She's been studying Lizzie a lot the last few days. It's as if she's waiting for something—some information that Lizzie's withholding. Perhaps I'm reading into nothing, but with all that's been going on, we haven't really focused on talking about anything else.

CHAPTER 53

Longbourn House, Heoros, First Moon of Londinium

Kitty clipped the stem of a flowering Comet Tail and dropped it into the vase on the windowsill. Every day at Longbourn had become a day of anxiety, and tending to her flowers helped her to find a bit of peace.

When her father arrived, he looked as he ever did. He said as little as he'd ever been in the habit of saying. He made no mention of the incident that had taken him away, and it was some time before any of her sisters had courage to speak of it. Being so closely connected to Lydia, and having borne the brunt of a certain level of her parents' anger at the things she'd concealed, Kitty hadn't found the courage even after her sisters did.

It wasn't until the afternoon, when he'd joined them for tea, that Lizzie broached the subject. "I hope you're recovering from your trip. The search had to have been hard on you."

"Say nothing of that," he replied, and Kitty tensed, though he'd said it without anger. "Who should suffer but myself? It has been my own doing, and I ought to feel it."

Kitty felt equally guilty, and wished with all her heart that she could commiserate out loud. But she didn't want to draw his attention on this subject any more than she had to. She hated disappointing him, but hated disappointing herself just as much. And in this case, she had done both, spectacularly.

"Don't be too severe on yourself," Lizzie said.

Kitty hoped the advice was meant for her, too.

"You may warn me against it. Human nature is so prone to fall into it!" he replied, rubbing his left temple. "No, Lizzie, let me once in my life feel how much I've been to blame. I'm not afraid of being overpowered by the impression. It'll pass soon enough."

Kitty nodded.

"Do you think they're on Londinium?" Lizzie asked.

"Yes. Where else can they be so well concealed? The planet is four times bigger than the largest moon."

Silence hung on these words, none of them breaking it for a few minutes.

"Lizzie," her father said. He sounded tired. "I bear you no ill will for being justified in your advice to me last May, which—considering the event—shows some greatness of mind."

Kitty wondered what Lizzie had said. She didn't know her sister had ever argued against the idea of Lydia going. For some reason this comforted her.

Jane came into the room. "Just fetching some tea for Mama."

Papa slapped his hands on his knees and exclaimed, with forced joviality, "This is a parade! It does one good. Gives such an elegance to misfortune. Another day, I'll do the same. I'll sit in my library, in my nightcap and pajamas, and give as much trouble as I can. Or, perhaps, I may defer it until Kitty runs away."

Kitty started, her heart slamming against her chest. "I'm not going to run away, Papa," she cried, her voice more fretful than she would've liked. "If *I* ever go to Sollaria, I'd behave better than Lydia."

"*You* go to Sollaria?" He laughed, and it was as bitter as corona-flower petals. "Land's sake!—I wouldn't trust you so near Sollaria as the Meryton!"

Her heart dropped.

"No, Kitty, I've at last learned to be cautious, and you'll feel the effects of it. No officer is ever to enter into my house again, nor even pass through the district. Social gatherings will be absolutely prohibited unless you're accompanied by one of your sisters. And you're never to leave the house until you can prove you've spent ten minutes of every day in a rational manner."

She looked at him in horror. With each sentence, tears crept closer to the back of her throat. She tried not to let them fall, but when they reached her eyes, they slipped out the corners and slid down her face.

She looked between Lizzie and Jane, a little bewildered, but instead of commiseration, she saw a small grin on the face of the former and pity on the face of the latter. Hadn't they heard him? This was so serious and unfair.

Her father reached out and gently grabbed her chin, sliding a tear away with his thumb. "Now, now," he said. "Don't make yourself unhappy. If you're a good girl for the next ten years, I'll take you to a show on the Meryton at the end of them."

As Jane headed back with Mama's tea, she stopped to put a hand on Kitty's shoulder and lean into her ear. "He doesn't mean it literally, Kit," she whispered, then kissed her cheek and walked out of the room.

Kitty felt marginally better, but she pouted at her father all the same.

To: Mr. Bennet, Longbourn Estate, Landings District, Heoros

From: Edward Gardiner, Lower St. James City, Londinium

Subject: Satisfaction

Dear brother,

At last, I'm able to send you some tidings of my niece. Upon the whole, I hope it will give you satisfaction. Soon after you left me on Saturday, I was fortunate enough to find out in what part of the city they were. The particulars I'll save until we meet. It's enough to know they're discovered. I've seen them both. They aren't married—thank our brightest stars for that—and as we suspected, he had no intention of doing so.

There's a scheme brewing which may be satisfying to all involved. The only requirement on your part is a lump payment of five thousand aurum to the Alesadran Academy of Arts in Dolere on Arkulus, with an annual payment of one hundred aurum per revo. These are conditions which, considering everything, I have no hesitation complying with in your stead.

You'll easily comprehend, from these particulars, that we were able to convince your daughter to separate from him, and that Wickham's character is not so wholly in the dust that he can't see the advantages of walking away and returning to his squadron. But I'll be honest, the Academy may have been the only lure your daughter would bite that's more appealing to her than that man. He had her convinced that he'd be with her for life. We all know this to be false, but it's a delicate matter to disentangle her from him. For his part, the right amount of money is sufficient for him to walk away.

If, as I believe will be the case, you send me full powers to act in your name throughout this whole business, I'll immediately give directions to Hagerston for preparing the paperwork and enrollment process. There'll be no need for you to return to Londinium again. Rest easy at home and depend on my diligence and care.

Send back your answer as fast as you can, and be careful to write explicitly. We've judged it best that our niece will remain in our home under the supervision of the children's governess until it's time for her orientation at the Academy. I hope you'll approve. I'll write again as soon as anything more is determined.

Edward

CHAPTER 54

Longbourn House, Heoros, First Moon of Londinium

Jane handed the comcard back to her father, too stunned to speak.

"Is it possible?" Lizzie said. "Can it be possible that he'll walk away from her?"

"Have you answered the waive?" Jane asked.

"No, but it must be done soon."

"Yes, immediately," Lizzie insisted. "I don't know how they managed this—the Academy! Who would've thought?"

"We've looked into it before," Jane said. "It's very exclusive. *How* were they able to guarantee it?"

"Perhaps the promise of it was enough to get her away?" Lizzie suggested.

"I don't believe anything short of the real thing would do the trick," her father said.

"Then every moment is important in this case. Let's go back inside so you can respond right away." She beckoned them to turn back to the house. "Lydia disappeared with Wickham once. There's no guarantee she won't again. Secure her the spot and we can use it as leverage."

"This is all so much trouble," he grumbled. "But it must be done."

"Do the Academy fees seem . . . off?" Jane wondered.

"Oh, yes. Far too low. I'm ashamed."

Lizzie frowned. "Do you think he's offering the difference?"

Jane nodded. She saw her father do the same.

"And she must go *there*? I know that she was coerced, but what a consequence for running away."

Jane felt certain her sister was biting back the idea of running away herself so she might be admitted to flight school as incentive to return.

"She must," their father said. "You may not see it as such, Lizzie, but I understand it for what it is. A discipline and containment she's never had here."

"She'll be incentivized to grow in a more productive way," Jane considered. "She'll learn discipline and self-sufficiency all while being able to pursue her passion without the distraction of pilots."

"This is all true," her father said. "But there are two things I very much want to know. One is how much money your uncle has laid down to bring this about. The other is how I'm ever to repay him."

"You suspect there was more aurum involved?" Jane asked.

"Wickham's debts were numerous and plentiful. He'll be facing discipline in the Reserves when he returns—*if* they let him return. Only aurum could smooth that over for him. It'd need to be a significant amount. Paying five thousand aurum on deposit, with one hundred aurum per revolution during the course of Lydia's study, is no help to him."

"It hadn't occurred to me," Lizzie said. "It should've. Exploding stars! Uncle Edward is too generous. He's done too much. A small sum wouldn't cover Wickham's debts."

"No," said her father. "Wickham's a fool if he takes a shine less than ten thousand aurum."

"Ten thousand aurum," Jane choked. "Sun and stars! How is half such a sum to be repaid?"

He made no answer, and each of them, deep in thought, continued silently to the house. Their father went on to the library to write his reply, and Jane and Lizzie walked into the parlor.

Seeing they were alone, Lizzie said, with some frustration and awe, "The Alesadran Academy of Arts." She shook her head. "How strange this all is. And for *this* we should be thankful. She runs away, willingly putting herself in an unsafe situation, only to be bribed into attending an incredibly exclusive institution."

"Is there any possibility this was the plan all along?" Jane offered, not really believing her suggestion. "Perhaps his regard for her wasn't false, but also wasn't what we thought it was. This Academy option came out of the ether. Perhaps he had some connection and was trying to get her in . . ." She trailed off, losing what little belief she had in that possibility as she suggested it.

Lizzie just frowned and glared out the window. "That's giving Lydia too much credit. She has her schemes, but nothing so ambitious."

"I can't believe that our uncle gave Wickham anything near ten thousand aurum. He has children of his own, and a business to run. How could he spare even half that sum?"

"If we ever learn what Wickham's debts have been," Lizzie said, "and how much is settled on Lydia's schooling, we'll know exactly what our uncle has done for them, because Wickham doesn't have a fen of his own. The Gardiners' kindness can never be repaid.

Taking her in, affording her their personal protection . . . what a sacrifice to her advantage. If such goodness doesn't make her miserably guilty for her actions now, she'll never deserve to be happy."

"We can be angry at her for her choices," Jane said, hoping to ease her sister's anger. "But we must remember that those choices were made under Wickham's influence. She may very well have been brazen enough to run away without him, but I'm inclined to think you know better than to believe that of her."

They sat in quiet contemplation for a minute or two.

Jane started. "Wenhal's moons! Mama likely doesn't know."

They went to the library and asked their father if he'd mind them giving her the update. He was typing on the comscreen and, without raising his head from the lights of the projected keyboard, coolly replied that they could.

"May we borrow the comcard to read the waive to her?" Jane asked.

"Take it and go," he sighed.

Lizzie took the little irridescent rectangle from his hand with promises of a swift return, and they went upstairs together.

Mary and Kitty were both sitting with their mother on the large bed.

After a slight preparation for good news, Jane read the waive aloud.

At first Mrs. Bennet was uncertain. She was relieved, clearly, that her daughter had been found and seemingly unscathed. But she had never been overly worried about any success of her daughters outside of marriage, and the Academy would likely keep her at arm's length of romance for many years.

It wasn't until Kitty spoke up that their mother's perspective shifted. "You know, Mama, while a marriage would be quite the social win in the short term, having a child in such a prestigious academy—and the opportunities that will allow in time—will more than outweigh even two of us being married. Probably."

Jane's eyes widened, and she looked to see Lizzie with an equally impressed expression.

"She's right," Lizzie said. "The Academy regularly produces the most influential creators, and the graduates are highly sought after from the highest of circles. Imagine: she could become a favorite to those in Cloudtop. What balls and dinners she—and by extension, we—would be invited to then."

A switch flipped in their mother at this, and her joy burst forth.

Jane was happy to see that she wasn't in an irritation as violent from delight as she'd ever been from alarm and vexation. It would be nice to have her mother at full health once again. She was happy and well now, her last week of misery forgotten.

"The light of all suns! My dear, talented Lydia!" She cried. "This is delightful! My good, kind brother. I knew he'd manage everything! How I long to see my sweet baby girl again. But she'll need new clothes! I'll write to Mariane at once. Lizzie, dear, run down to your father and ask him how much he'll give her for a new wardrobe—an Academy wardrobe no less!" She then thought better of it and waved off the suggestion. "Actually, stay. I'll go myself. Ring the bell for Hill, Kitty! I'll put on proper clothes in a minute. Oh, my dear Lydia. How wonderful it'll be when we see her again!"

Jane thought it best to temper her mother's violence of joy with a reminder of the obligations and gratitude owed to her brother. "After all," she added, "we must attribute this happy conclusion to his great measure of kindness. Father believes he's pledged quite a sum to facilitate this."

"Naturally," her mother cried, "it's very right that he should. Who'd do it besides her uncle? If he had no family of his own, he'd allot a great deal of his aurum to me and my children, you know. This is the first time we've ever had anything from him besides a few presents." Now out of bed, she paced around the room with anxious excitement. "Stars! I'm so happy! In a short time I'll have a daughter admitted into an elite academy, and she'll grow to become an influence in all the system's fashion, I'm certain. And at just sixteen. My dear Jane, I'm in such a flutter I'm sure I can't type. I'll dictate and you'll type for me. We'll settle with your father about the aurum afterward, but her things should be ordered immediately."

She then proceeded to dive into the particulars of uniforms and room essentials and would soon have dictated several very plentiful orders had Jane not, with some difficulty, persuaded her to wait until she could consult their father.

"One day's delay will make no difference," Jane offered.

Her mother was too happy to be quite as obstinate as usual. Other schemes populated her thoughts as she put aside the ordering. "I'll fly to the Meryton as soon as I'm dressed, and tell your Aunt Phillips the wonderful news. As I come back, I can call on Lady Lucas and Mrs. Long. Kitty, run down and order the Tailwynd to be readied. Getting out of this room will do me some good. Girls, can I do anything for you while aboard the Meryton? Oh! Here comes Hill. My dear Hill, have you heard the good news? Miss Lydia's joining the Alesadran Academy of Arts! We'll celebrate with a bottle of Gleam tonight!"

Mrs. Hill instantly expressed her joy at this news.

"I'm sick of this folly," Lizzie whispered in Jane's ear, then ducked out of the room.

Jane felt it necessary to stay, and do what she could to keep her mother's exuberance in check, lest she attempt to order a new wardrobe for Lydia through the service of Mrs. Hill.

As she listened to her mother crow in excitement, she thought of the fears and worries she'd been facing just two hours ago, and felt all the advantages of what they had gained instead.

ALESADRAN

ACADEMY OF ARTS

WELCOME BOOK

CHAPTER 55

Longbourn House, Heoros, First Moon of Londinium

Mr. Bennet had often wished that, when he and his wife were younger, instead of spending his whole income, he'd saved a portion of his aurum for his family when they'd grown. He wished that more now than ever. The satisfaction of paying off one of the most worthless young men in the system to entice him not to marry his underage daughter might then have rested on his own shoulders, and not his brother-in-law's. He was determined, if possible, to find out the extent of Edward's assistance and discharge the obligation as soon as he could.

In terms of grateful acknowledgment for Edward's kindness, expressed most concisely, he wrote the waive containing his approval of all that was done, and his willingness to fulfill the engagements that'd been made for him. He'd never before supposed that, should Wickham be convinced to break ties, it'd be done with so little inconvenience to himself as the present arrangement.

He'd scarcely be ten aurum a revolution the loser after the hundred to be paid for Lydia's keeping and pocket allowance. That all this could be done with such trifling exertion on his side was another very welcome surprise. His wish at present was to have as little to do with this mess as possible. Once his initial rage, which had produced his activity in seeking her, had subsided, he was ready to return to his leisure.

Though usually slow to act when undertaking business, he was quick to execution in this case. He wished to know further particulars of his debt to his brother-in-law, but was too angry with Lydia to send any message to her. He wasn't sure Mariane had given her access to her comcard again, anyway.

The good news spread quickly through the house, and with proportionate speed through the district. It was a fortnight since his wife had been downstairs, but she now returned to her seat at the head of the table for dinner, and in spirits oppressively high. The success of a daughter, which had been one of her greatest wishes for each of them—though perhaps not in the way she'd expected in this instance—was now her sole focus.

"She may be in the Firefly dorms," said his wife, "if we're willing to advance a bit more. Or she can live in off-campus housing in the Doveworth Sector, though that's quite a distance from the main academy buildings, especially for a first year. I can't bear to think of her missing classes due to the walk."

He allowed her to talk without interruption while the staff remained, but when they'd withdrawn he said, plainly and clearly, "Before you construct a house for her in the center of campus, with a closet the size of our front garden, let us come to an understanding. She'll be given enough money for food per revolution and nothing more. I'm paying enough for the Academy as it is. And as for new clothes, she may tear up her current wardrobe and make a new one to stay in fashion, because I won't advance even an argent for this endeavor."

She stared at him with amazement and horror, but he was certain she had not taken his words to heart, and would be scheming to find a way to convince him otherwise in the coming days.

He was swiftly proven right, but his wife was unprepared for the resentment he carried in regard to this situation, and she was met with unyielding dissent whenever she tried to force his hand. By the time his youngest daughter returned home for one last visit before leaving for Arkulus, his wife had begun to realize he wouldn't budge, and her efforts tapered off.

[LizzieLovesSpace] 31.7-8:31:49.LS

I'm sorry that, in the distress of the moment, I told Darcy so much of my fears for Lydia. Now that she's been separated from Wickham, and is enrolled in the Alesadran Academy, it seems we could've concealed the worst of it from anyone not immediately involved. I don't fear the news spreading through him. There are few people I'd depend on more to keep such a secret (you being one of them). At the same time, there's no one whose knowledge of such an entanglement would mortify me as much as him.

STATUS: RETRACTED

[LizzieLovesSpace] 31.7- 9:08:32.LS

To be honest, I'd hoped . . . well, I thought perhaps I could've won back Darcy's regard. I was feeling rather confident of it on Dyberion. Until news of Lydia struck at the worst time. I don't blame you for this, of course. You were just the messenger. But I can't expect our family's connection to Wickham, even as brief as it was, to not have damaged the gossamer thread of connection we were building.

I'm humbled. Grieved. I want to repent, though I hardly know of what. I feel jealous of his esteem, when I can no longer hope to be benefited by it. I want to hear of him, but there's the least chance of my success in doing so. I'm convinced that I could've been happy with him, now that it's no longer likely we'll ever meet again.

What a triumph for him (if only he knew) that the proposals I'd so proudly spurned a few months ago would now be most gladly and gratefully received.

STATUS: RETRACTED

[LizzieLovesSpace] 31.7-9:45:16.LS

I've come to the realization that Darcy is exactly the man who, in disposition and talents, would most suit me. His understanding and temper, though unlike mine, would be the perfect counterbalance. It would've been an advantageous union for us both. Through my ease and liveliness, his mind could've been softened and his manners improved. And from his judgment, information, and knowledge of the worlds, I would've received the benefit of greater importance. But no such union will exist now. The chance has fled.

STATUS: RETRACTED

[MyMyMissJane] 31.7-9:54:03.LS

Something strange is going on with my comcard. I swear I keep seeing alerts from you, but then I look and there's no message.

[LizzieLovesSpace] 31.7-9:56:38.LS

I'm retracting them. Sorry!
Did you see Uncle Edward's waive?

[MyMyMissJane] 31.7-9:57:49.LS

That makes more sense.
No, Mama has me occupied up here. What does it say?

[LizzieLovesSpace] 31.7-9:59:12.LS

He says Wickham has been removed from the Reserves.

[MyMyMissJane] 31.7-10:00:56.LS

I suppose the aurum wasn't enough to smooth over his defection.

[LizzieLovesSpace] 31.7-10:03:23.LS

I'm not so sure. It's apparently his intention to enter the Star Force proper. He has some former friends who are willing and able to assist him with it. He

■ ■ ■

has the promise of a position in a regiment quartered well beyond the satellites of Londinium. I believe he'll be on Wenhal.

[MyMyMissJane] 31.7-10:05:49.LS
What an advantage to have him stationed so far from this part of the system.

[LizzieLovesSpace] 31.7-10:07:39.LS
My guess is that wasn't entirely his choice, no matter how it's being presented. Wickham's debts are settled in Sollaria, assurances are being made to the creditor here in Heoros and on the Meryton.

[MyMyMissJane] 31.7-10:08:23.LS
When does he leave?

[LizzieLovesSpace] 31.7-10:09:17.LS
Not soon enough.

. . . END COM . . .

CHAPTER
56

Longbourn House, Heoros, First Moon of Londinium

Before her younger sister had come home, Elizabeth was conflicted. She and Jane felt pity for her and the growing pains that would be coming her way. They both also dreaded her arrival, feeling keenly second-hand what they expected Lydia wouldn't: shame and embarrassment for what had led to this situation.

But, while she initially appeared to be the same wild, unabashed, and fearless Lydia they remembered, Elizabeth noticed a change in her.

Her reception had been mixed. There was a lingering resentment for her having put them all through so much, and aside from her mother, who had welcomed her with rapturous exclamations, the responses to her arrival were subdued.

Lydia joined in with perfect and unaffected happiness. Her easy assurance was enough to provoke their father into an expression of austerity, in which he barely spoke.

But when they sat together for dinner that night, Elizabeth began to see something beneath the surface of Lydia's assurance. There was no lack of discussion at the table. Neither Lydia nor her mother could talk fast enough. She seemed to have the happiest memories in all the worlds. But it was as though the talking were a barrier to anything beyond surface level.

"Can you believe it's been three months since I went away?" Lydia asked. "It seems only a fortnight! Yet there's been so much that has happened in that time. Sun and stars! When I went away, I had no idea of being enrolled in my *dream* academy when I came home! Who would have expected!"

Her father stared at the ceiling. Jane looked around in distress. Elizabeth watched Lydia closely, but Lydia's eyes never alighted in any one direction long, and she continued happily. "Do the people around the district know that I'm attending Alesadran? I was afraid they might not know."

Eventually, they finished dinner and made their way to the parlor. Lydia's ease and good spirits continued unceasingly, and Elizabeth started to doubt her initial suspicion.

"I long to see my Aunt Phillips and the Lucases and all the other neighbors so I might share in my good news," her sister said. "I hope all of you have half my good luck in life. If only you had all gone to Sollaria."

"It would've been better that we went together," her mother said. "But my dear Lydia, I hate that you're going so far from me. Must it be so?"

Lydia, with perfect self-satisfaction, said, "Oh, lands! Yes. It'll be a wonderful adventure. And you and Papa and my sisters must come visit me."

Something about the way Lydia said that last bit solidified a suspicion Elizabeth was fostering. She could see it in Lydia's eyes. Elizabeth made a mental note to speak with her sister alone before she left for the academy.

"Perhaps there'll be balls they can come to," Lydia went on. "I'll be sure to find good partners for all my sisters. And I'll design you the most beautiful dress, Mama."

"I'd like that more than anything," her mother gushed.

As Lydia wasn't staying more than a week with them, Mrs. Bennet made the most of the time by having frequent parties at home. It made getting her sister alone rather difficult for Elizabeth. But finally, one morning, as their other sisters were engaged with their mother in some party preparations, Elizabeth and Jane found themselves alone with Lydia in the sitting room. This was as good an opportunity as she was bound to get.

"Have I told you of my schedule?" Lydia was saying to Jane. "Who knew that school could be so amazing? It's not at all—well, it's mostly not—any boring classes. I would say maths are boring, but I do need some of it for measurements and the like. Still, over-all, it's going to be wonderful."

"I'm glad you feel that way," Elizabeth said. "It's a long way from home. It'll help to love the things you'll be doing each day."

"Better distractions," Jane chimed in.

"From the homesickness?" Lydia asked.

Elizabeth nodded.

Lydia scrunched her nose. "Oh, I won't be homesick," she said, though her voice didn't sound so assured as usual. "There'll be too much to do to even think of home."

Elizabeth caught Jane's eye, and saw the same sympathetic smile as her own reflected there.

Lydia eyed them warily. "Stop it, you two. You're projecting things of me that I don't feel."

Elizabeth grew serious. "It's okay to be scared. This is a big step."

Lydia pursed her lips. "No bigger than running away with an officer."

"That wasn't your best decision," Jane said.

Lydia looked at her lap. "I loved him."

"Lyddie, that wasn't love."

"I know, I know. Aunt Mari told me a *million* times. And when she wasn't preaching at me, Mr. Darcy was." Her eyes widened as Lizzie sat back in shock.

"Mr. Darcy?" she repeated, in utter amazement.

Lydia looked uneasy. "Yes. Well. I wasn't supposed to mention his involvement. I promised him so faithfully. But the way you're looking at me, I don't think you're going to let me out of this room without explaining."

"You aren't wrong."

"He was the one who offered me the Alesadran Academy." Guilt washed over her face. "I wasn't supposed to say a word. It was meant to be a secret, but . . . secrets have gotten me in such trouble lately . . ."

It seemed that her sister had learned a lesson or two after all.

"If it was meant to be a secret," Jane said, setting aside her embroidery—the kit Aunt Mari had given her at Winter's Turning—"don't say another word about it, and we'll ask no questions."

"Certainly," said Elizabeth, though she was burning with curiosity. "Not a single question."

"Thank you," said Lydia earnestly. "If you did, I'd likely tell you all."

On such encouragement to ask, Elizabeth was forced to put it out of her mind by making an excuse to leave the room.

But living in ignorance on such a point was impossible. At least, it was impossible not to try for information. Mr. Darcy was exactly in a place, and among people, where he had least to do and least temptation to go.

Reasons for this began rapidly filling her brain, but nothing satisfied her. Those that pleased her most seemed improbable. She couldn't bear the suspense. She snatched her comcard and sneaked into the empty front room.

"My dear aunt," she muttered as she began to type, "if you don't tell me quickly and clearly, I'm not above resorting to schemes to find this out."

[LizzieLovesSpace] 20.8-10:03:26.LS

Are you able to explain why Mr. Darcy—a person so unconnected with any of us—was with you during your search for and separation of Lydia and Wickham? Unless for whatever reason, it's meant to remain the secret Lydia implies it to be. In which case, I'll force myself to be satisfied with ignorance.

[MarianeGardiner] 20.8-10:07:12.LS

I'm surprised at you reaching out for clarification. Your uncle is, too. We didn't expect it to be necessary from you.

[LizzieLovesSpace] 20.8-10:08:37.LS

What makes you think so?

[MarianeGardiner] 20.8-10:10:22.LS

If you're choosing not to understand me, I don't mean to be impertinent. Only the belief that you were of concern in the matter would've allowed your uncle to act as he has. But if you really don't know what I'm implying, I can speak plainer.

[LizzieLovesSpace] 20.8-10:12:39.LS

Please. I have vague suspicions but I can't rely on those.

[MarianeGardiner] 20.8-10:13:59.LS

Prepare yourself for an influx of coms. This may have been better off as a waive.

[LizzieLovesSpace] 20.8-10:14:55.LS

My entire day is at your disposal. I'll be thinking of nothing else.

[MarianeGardiner] 20.8-10:17:03.LS

The day I returned to Londinium, Mr. Darcy was sequestered with your uncle in his office for several hours. He came to tell Edward that he'd found where your sister and Mr. Wickham were, and that he'd seen and spoken to them both. It seems he left Dyberion only a day after we did, and flew to Londinium with the purpose of hunting for them.

[LizzieLovesSpace] 20.8-10:18:41.LS
That alone is beyond my greatest expectations. And yet there's surely so much more to tell!

[MarianeGardiner] 20.8-10:19:01.LS
Indeed. He believed it was his fault that Wickham's true nature wasn't so well known as to impede the interests of any unsuspecting young women.

[LizzieLovesSpace] 20.8-10:20:10.LS
He must share the blame of that between several of the Bennet sisters.

[MarianeGardiner] 20.8-10:27:38.LS
None of you, even Mr. Darcy, can blame yourselves for Wickham's poor character. Meanwhile, Mr. Darcy's character spoke for itself. He attributed his believed failure to his mistaken pride, and confessed that he'd thought it beneath him, originally, to lay his private actions open to the moons. He then called it his duty to step forward and endeavor to remedy the evil he'd brought on himself. I suspect there was another motive, but not one he was perhaps willing to admit to me.

He was in the city for a while before he was able to discover them, but he had more to direct his search than we did. There's a woman named Mrs. Younge, who was once a governess for his sister. She was dismissed for some moral reason he didn't elaborate on, and ended up in lower St. James letting lodgings.

[LizzieLovesSpace] 20.8-10:30:14.LS
I know of her from something he told me on the Kent. She has connections to Wickham. I'd completely forgotten.

■ ■ ■

[MarianeGardiner] 20.8-10:33:05.LS

Yes. He went to her first, and suspected she knew more than she initially let on. It took him a few days to get what he wanted from her. She wouldn't betray Wickham without sufficient bribery, but once she did, he went straight to their hiding place. He met with Wickham first, then insisted on seeing Lydia.

[LizzieLovesSpace] 20.8-10:34:59.LS

What was the initial plan, I wonder. Surely, not Alesadran . . .

[MarianeGardiner] 20.8-10:37:45.LS

He seemed to approach Lydia in the same way he might his own sister. He explained that his first goal was to persuade her that this wasn't a safe or healthy situation she'd put herself in, and offered to return her to her friends as soon as possible. She'd been poisoned to him, however, and wanted nothing to do with him. Her love, she'd told him, was unwavering. Wickham had convinced her they would be married at some point, but it didn't much matter when.

[LizzieLovesSpace] 20.8-10:39:12.LS

Stubborn, naive girl. Of course, no other option could've entered her mind as a possibility.

[MarianeGardiner] 20.8-10:42:49.LS

It was a long time before we were able to break through that hard head of hers. In the meantime, Mr. Darcy shifted his efforts to Wickham. He'd known from his first conversation that Wickham never intended to marry her. Wickham confessed that he was forced to leave the regiment due to some very pressing debts, and didn't hesitate to blame Lydia's flight on her folly alone. He planned to resign his commission immediately. He had neither aurum nor plans.

[LizzieLovesSpace] 20.8-10:43:25.LS

Reckless. And he dragged her with him, only to blame her. I shouldn't be surprised, considering what we know of him. Blame is not something Wickham would lay at his own feet.

[MarianeGardiner] 20.8-10:44:53.LS

Mr. Darcy was thinking the same. He felt that aurum would secure Wickham's agreement to part ways, with the added benefit of showing Lydia what kind of man Wickham actually was. They met many times. Wickham wanted more than he could get, but was eventually reduced to being reasonable.

[LizzieLovesSpace] 20.8-10:46:38.LS

Buying off Wickham again! Brightest Light. Every kind of pride must revolt from such an experience.

[MarianeGardiner] 20.8-10:49:25.LS

If it did, he didn't show it. He also wished not to break your sister's heart completely. I believe he wanted her to feel as though she had made a positive choice for her future to make up for the negative one she had yet to understand. It was at the point that he brought your uncle in. As they were negotiating the particulars of her return, and how best to secure her, the idea of Alesadran Academy was introduced. He believed such an opportunity to be enough to secure her from attempting to run after Wickham again.

[LizzieLovesSpace] 20.8-10:50:55.LS

Alesadran was Darcy's idea?

[MarianeGardiner] 20.8-10:52:47.LS

I believe it was. He has a lot of influential connections, and he had nearly everything settled by Monday. It must have been on some recommendation of yours that he thought to suggest it. Did you show him her sketches on the Kent or in Dyberion?

[LizzieLovesSpace] 20.8-10:54:19.LS
No. I think I mentioned that she'd picked out my dress that day at Pemberley when you met, but that was all.

[MarianeGardiner] 20.8-10:56:08.LS
It seems that was enough to recommend her.

[LizzieLovesSpace] 20.8-10:57:49.LS
People don't gauge the talent of a designer on the appearance of the wearer.

[MarianeGardiner] 20.8-11:00:45.LS
It seems at least one person does. But now that you mention it, I believe we spoke of Alesadran at breakfast that next day, as well. I mentioned Lydia's talent to Miss Georgiana and it sparked a conversation about schooling.

[LizzieLovesSpace] 20.8-11:03:02.LS
But what of tuition? There was a reason it was Lydia's dream school, and not her realistic goal.

[MarianeGardiner] 20.8-11:07:14.LS
Well, Mr. Darcy was very obstinate about the plans. I believe that's his real defect, by the way. He's been accused of many faults, but this is the true one. Nothing was to be done that he didn't do or oversee himself. Though I'm sure your uncle would've settled it all himself (and they battled it out for a long time). Edward was forced to yield. Instead of being allowed to be of use to his niece, Mr. Darcy made sure he would only have the credit for it. This hasn't sat well with him. Your message has lifted a weight on his heart, I know, because you required an explanation that would rob him of his

borrowed feathers and give the praise where it's due. But Lizzie, this mustn't go further than yourself, or Jane, at most.

You know pretty well, I suppose, what all has been done for the two of them. His debts amounted to something over a thousand aurum. Another thousand was given to Alesadran to facilitate Lydia's entrance. He also purchased Wickham's commission in the Star Force.

[LizzieLovesSpace] 20.8-11:07:14.LS

Stars around! He's done all this for a man he despises and a girl whom he barely knows. It pains me to know that we owe someone a debt that we can never return.

[MarianeGardiner] 20.8-11:09:14.LS

His reasons for taking it all upon himself were the same as I mentioned earlier. He believed it was his fault that Wickham's character had been so misunderstood. Perhaps there's truth to it.

But in spite of all this fine talk of his, my dearest Lizzie, you may rest assured that your uncle would never have yielded if we hadn't perceived another interest in the whole affair.

[LizzieLovesSpace] 20.8-11:11:00.LS

You're being vague here. On purpose?

[MarianeGardiner] 20.8-11:14:32.LS

Yes, if you insist on not understanding me.

Anyway, once Lydia was safely returned to us, he went home to his friends, who were still staying at Pemberley. But he insisted on coming back to the city for her interview, should anything arise. There were financial matters to settle once she'd gotten her acceptance. While he was away, we worked on helping Lydia to understand the situation as the rest of us could see it. I tried to be gentle with her in explaining how ill-used she'd been. I know she heard me, but she buried herself in plans for Alesadran and appeared to ignore it all.

[LizzieLovesSpace] 20.8-11:17:08.LS
This seems to be what she's doing at home as well. I'm not sure she has ever felt ashamed or guilty in her life. It's going to take her a while to process it.

[MarianeGardiner] 20.8-11:18:45.LS
I couldn't agree more. So I was patient with her. When Mr. Darcy returned for the interview, he dined with us the next day. I don't believe his presence helped in that regard.

[LizzieLovesSpace] 20.8-11:19:17.LS
She owes the saving of her reputation, her future, to him. I—who am not directly affected, nor who treated him with anything like the distant indifference that Lydia did—am thoroughly humbled by what he has done for her. I can only imagine what she must have been feeling.

[MarianeGardiner] 20.8-11:20:32.LS
It was overwhelming for her, to be sure. But I must take this opportunity to say something I was never bold enough to say before; I really like him. His behavior has, in every respect, been as lovely as when we were on Dyberion. He wants nothing but a little more liveliness, and that—if he marries prudently—his wife may teach him. I thought him very sly. He hardly ever mentioned your name. But avoiding directness seems the fashion.

[LizzieLovesSpace] 20.8-11:21:43.LS
I'm honored that you believe such affection and confidence subsists between us, but I think you may be seeing through the lens of your wishes.

[MarianeGardiner] 20.8-11:22:38.LS

Maybe. I don't mean to be presumptuous. Forgive me! Or, at least, don't punish me so far as to exclude me from Pemberley. I'll never be truly happy until I've seen the entire park.

[LizzieLovesSpace] 20.8-11:24:03.LS

To quote yourself . . . do be serious!

I appreciate what you're insinuating, but I'm not so vain as to put any stock in it. Thank you for all of this. I promise to keep it to myself . . . and Jane.

[MarianeGardiner] 20.8-11:26:13.LS

Happy to be of help, my dear.

. . . END COM . . .

CHAPTER 57

Longbourn House, Heoros, First Moon of Londinium

Mary felt as though she were standing peacefully still while the world moved around her in double-speed. The dust had barely settled from the whirlwind of Lydia's short visit when news of Mr. Bingley returning with the Netherfield kicked the anthill of Heorosian society once again. Her mother could barely sit still, her father was agitated from his wife's constant demands that he go visit Mr. Bingley when he arrived, and all three of her sisters' demeanors were altered.

No real loss had been felt on Mary's side with Lydia's departure to Alesadran—she wasn't as close to her as Kitty—and no gain was anticipated in Mr. Bingley's return—he was never an object of affection for *her*. The only one who should

have been as unaffected as Mary was Lizzie, and yet she seemed somehow the most altered of them all. Mary was curious to know what had
affected her, but she was willing to be patient, and content to observe.

"One advantage of being the quiet one is getting to watch and
listen in on others without them seeming to mind," she told Kitty one
morning, doing her best to keep her sister in higher spirits. While the
rest were in various states of anticipatory agitation, Kitty was struggling with despondency. Mary had been making a concerted effort
to include her in the thoughts she generally kept to herself. "After all,
who minds my overhearing their words when I have no one to tell?"

"You have me," Kitty offered.

"This is very true. And you are quite an astute observer of the
larger social influences, so perhaps I should fill you in on what I've
been seeing and see what you can glean from it all."

This lit Kitty's eyes with intensity, so Mary went on.

"Yesterday, I watched as Lizzie prodded Jane in an attempt to
reveal her true feelings about Bingley. Jane insisted that she wasn't
distressed by the news of his impending return, but rather confused
that Lizzie had even bothered to look to her for a reaction. I, for one,
was also looking to her for a reaction. What would Lizzie and I be
expecting to see there?"

"Some lingering affection, of course," Kitty said. "We all
thought they were a sure thing for a while."

Mary nodded. "But why is it that we thought that? Did Jane
ever whirl about the house the way Lydia might, exclaiming her love
of him? Did she ever say anything at all that might tell us to believe
the rumors?"

Kitty frowned and considered. "Well, no. Not directly. I suppose if you'd been able to overhear her talking with Lizzie about
him, then you'd know more than most."

"I was. But that isn't necessary here, I don't believe. It's in
her manner as much in the moments they're together as it is when
they're apart. Everyone always looks for the way they interact. But

you watch her in the quiet moments and she's different. It's why Lizzie and I both expected her to react to the news."

Kitty considered for a moment. "Yes. I agree. Did either of you ever find out what she was feeling?"

"When Lizzie had all but dropped the conversation, Jane mentioned her consternation that Bingley couldn't leave or arrive to his home without raising speculation. She insisted that we should leave him alone. With that, though, even Mama noticed a change in her. She's not being as serene as she would like us all to think."

"Who could blame her? If I'd been so close to happiness, only to have it ripped from my grasp, I'd be affected by it for . . . ever!"

"You'd heal. She will, too. But fondness doesn't blink out of existence like some distant star." Mary felt regret seep into her. "I wish I could tell her all these things, but she's trying so hard not to seem affected. So I think it's best not to draw attention to her efforts or offer my thoughts on any of it."

"Do you think she'll come around?"

"She did a bit today, I believe. We were sitting together in the back room, looking over the lawn, when Jane told Lizzie that she was beginning to be sorry Bingley was coming to Heoros at all. She's convinced she can see him with 'perfect indifference' but the constant conversation surrounding his arrival—especially from our mother—has gotten under her skin."

"That might be the nearest she's ever come to a complaint about Mama that I've heard from her."

Mary laughed. "You aren't wrong. She softened it immediately by saying she knew Mama meant well. But she was at least honest enough with herself and her emotions to admit she was suffering under the current circumstances."

"I hope she'll find some relief from it all, soon," Kitty said. "Thank you for telling me all this. Maybe I can try distracting Mama when she brings him up the next time."

"I think that's a great idea."

LONDINIUM SAT[SYS

Communications Log—System Storage 30 Days [Planetary]

[Ba_Da_Bing_ley] 26.8-11:00:34.LS

Are you coming with me tomorrow?

[FW.Darcy] 26.8-11:01:49.LS

If you want me there, I'll be there, as promised.

[Ba_Da_Bing_ley] 26.8-11:03:33.LS

Don't be so stiff and formal. You know it's unnecessary.

[FW.Darcy] 26.8-11:04:55.LS

I'm here for you. I owe you this.

[Ba_Da_Bing_ley] 26.8-11:05:48.LS

You do, but don't be so weird about it. It's unsettling.

[FW.Darcy] 26.8-11:07:29.LS

I'm not trying to be. What time do you want to be there?

[Ba_Da_Bing_ley] 26.8-11:08:41.LS

How early is too early?

[FW.Darcy] 26.8-11:10:02.LS

All of this is entirely up to you. I am but an observer.

. . . END COM . . .

CHAPTER
58

Longbourn House, Heoros, First Moon of Londinium

Elizabeth watched with Jane from their bedroom window the night the Netherfield broke atmo. It lit the sky like so many others in the Port District, but there was something mesmerizing about seeing one land so closely, especially at its size. She went to bed that night knowing that the morning would bring a new anxiety to the house.

As expected, that morning, her mother began to mark out the time that must pass before they could send an invitation, with no hope of seeing Bingley before. On the third day following the Netherfield's touchdown, Elizabeth and Jane were coming up the walk on the right side of the house when they spotted two gentlemen disembarking from a Chase-Z16.

It was Mr. Darcy and Mr. Bingley.

Jane gasped and yanked Elizabeth back around the corner where they couldn't be seen.

Elizabeth's astonishment at Mr. Darcy coming to Longbourn was almost equal to what she'd felt on first noticing his altered behavior on Dyberion.

For a fleeting instant, her body suffused itself with the joy of hope—that his affection and wishes might still be unshaken—but her fears returned and the feeling drained away. She'd need to see how he behaved first. It was too early for expectations.

"Stars ignite!" Jane whispered, surprise and concern on her face. "Mr. Darcy's with him."

Elizabeth had never told her of their meeting on Dyberion. Jane, seeing the emotions that must have played on her face, was likely expecting the awkwardness Elizabeth must be feeling in seeing him for the first time since the Kent. Her discomfort was palpable. Her anxiety wasn't misplaced, though the cause was. Elizabeth hadn't found the courage to show her sister Aunt Mariane's waive, or to relate her own change of sentiment toward him. To Jane, he was only a man whose proposals she'd refused, and whose merit she'd undervalued. But to Elizabeth, he was the person to whom the whole family were indebted, and whom she regarded with an interest, if not quite so tender, at least as reasonable and just as what Jane felt for Bingley. Still, Elizabeth was as anxious for Jane as Jane was for herself.

"Do we meet them in the entry, or go around the back?" Jane asked.

Elizabeth peeked back around. They were on the front steps. "The back," she answered. "It would feel odd to follow them in, and they're already at the door."

Jane nodded in agreement, and they rushed quickly around the house to the back door. Once inside, they looked each other over and freshened up as best they could. Jane was paler than usual, but more sedate than Elizabeth expected.

From the front room, their mother's voice drifted to meet them. ". . . so wonderful to have you back in Heoros. It has been quite long since we last had the pleasure of your company."

Elizabeth felt the need for urgency, then, and they both hurried down the hallway, slowing only when they reached the door of the sitting room.

Stepping through, they drew the attention of the two men, who stood near the door. Inside the room, their mother and their younger sisters sat where they'd left them for their walk.

"Oh, there you are, girls," Mrs. Bennet said. "Look who has come to visit!"

Elizabeth greeted them quietly as she walked to the open book and seat she had left before their walk. She ventured only one glance at Darcy as she sat, striving to appear composed and unaffected, hardly daring to meet his eyes.

He looked serious, as usual; and, she thought, more the way he used to look on Heoros. Perhaps it was this moon? More likely he couldn't be what he was with her aunt and uncle when he was around her mother. It was a painful, but more probable, conjecture.

In anxious curiosity, she looked to her sister. Jane's face was flushed, yet she had met them with tolerable ease, her behavior free from any symptom of resentment or unnecessary agreeableness.

Bingley appeared both pleased and embarrassed. Her mother spoke to him with a shameful overeagerness, especially in contrast to her cold and ceremonious addresses to his friend.

Elizabeth, who knew what her mother owed to the latter in preserving the future of her favorite daughter, was painfully distressed by her mother's ill-applied distinction.

Darcy had walked along the edge of the room, catching Elizabeth's attention as he came near. "Are the Gardiners doing well?" he asked.

He would know better than she, having seen them more recently, though he had no idea she knew it. She was too confused by the meaning behind the question to say more than "They are, yes."

He moved past her and sat on the other side of the room, making no other conversation. He hadn't been this way on Dyberion. There, he'd talked to her aunt and uncle when he couldn't talk with her. But now several minutes elapsed without the sound of his voice. Occasionally, unable to resist the impulse of curiosity, she raised her eyes enough to see his face. She found him more often looking at Jane than herself, and frequently nothing but the ground. His expressions held more thoughtfulness and less anxiety to please than when they last met. She was disappointed, and angry with herself for being so.

What was she expecting? Why had he come? She was in no mood for conversation with anyone but him, and to him she hardly had the courage to speak.

"Mr. Darcy, is your sister well?" she finally managed to ask.

He confirmed that she was, but they seemed unable to connect any further.

"I believe, Mr. Bingley, it has been almost a year since we first met," said Mrs. Bennet.

He readily agreed. "Wenhal's moons! It has, indeed."

"I started to worry you'd never come back when you left. People *did* say you meant to leave the place entirely in the winter. I do hope that's untrue. The neighborhood is so much cozier with the Netherfield on its landing." Her mother barely took a breath before shifting subjects. "Speaking of the neighborhood, there were many changes since you went away. Miss Lucas is married and settled. And one of my own daughters has left for the Alesadran Academy on Arkulus. I suppose you've heard of it."

He nodded. "I have. It's quite prestigious. Congratulations to her and to you for such an accomplishment."

Elizabeth dared not glance at Darcy. Instead, she endeavored to change the subject completely. "Mr. Bingley," she said quickly, "are you planning to stay long?"

"A few weeks," he said. "For the hunt."

"When you've secured all your own jewelbirds, Mr. Bingley," her mother interjected, "please come here and collect as many as you please on our lands. I'm sure Mr. Bennet will be vastly happy to oblige, and will save all the best of the swarm for you."

Elizabeth couldn't help but feel the sting of her mother ignoring Darcy. In that instant, she felt that years of happiness couldn't make Jane or herself amends for moments of such painful confusion. The air in the room was a miserable soup of anxious energy. Her only relief was seeing how much her sister's very presence rekindled Bingley's admiration. When she'd first come in, he'd spoken very little to her. But every five minutes he seemed to be giving her more of his attention.

She was as beautiful, as good-natured, and as unaffected as she'd been last year, though not quite so chatty. Elizabeth was sure that Jane didn't recognize the small change in herself, her mind likely too full of thoughts and questions to notice when she was silent.

When the gentlemen rose to leave, her mother seized the opportunity to invite them to dinner in the next couple of days.

Bingley readily accepted.

"You're quite a visit in my debt, you know," her mother added. "Before you went to the planet last winter, you promised to have dinner with us as soon as you returned. I haven't forgotten. I assure you, I was very disappointed that you didn't come back and keep your engagement."

Bingley's face flickered with conflicting emotions, and he said something of his concern at having been prevented by business. Then they went away.

As soon as they were out the door, her mother said, "I'd have invited them this evening, but they deserve better than two courses."

Elizabeth went to the window to watch them leave. Mr. Darcy turned once to look back, and she felt his eyes meet hers. This time, she didn't look away. Neither did he.

His behavior vexed her. She wished that she could, with this one look between them, ask why he'd come, if only to be silent, grave, and indifferent?

Could he not be with her here as he was in Dyberion? If he feared her, why had he come? If he no longer cared for her, why stay silent? Bingley, on the contrary, had been very clearly wishing to reconnect, even if it was only on the level of friendship—though she suspected more. But not his friend.

After watching the place where the Chase had disappeared for a few minutes, she decided she needed to find somewhere secluded to recover—or more accurately, dwell—without interruption. The hangar was the obvious choice. She grabbed the book on the building of a Nebula Dancer, which she'd had open on the table since the morning, and started for her place of comfort. But she'd barely made it off the front porch when Jane called her name. She was sitting in the little swing hanging from the front tree. She had a cheerful look, which showed that she'd been better satisfied by the visit than Elizabeth.

Elizabeth came over to her.

"Now that this first meeting is over," Jane said, "I feel perfectly easy. I know my own strength, and I'll never be embarrassed again by his appearing suddenly. I'm glad he'll dine with us here on Tuesday. It'll show everyone that, on both sides, we meet only as common and indifferent acquaintances."

A laugh burst from Elizabeth before she could stop it. "Stars! Yes, very indifferent," she said, shaking her head. "Oh, Jane, take care."

"Lizzie." Jane set her fists on her hips. "You can't think I'm so weak as to be in danger now."

Elizabeth grinned. "I think you're in very great danger of making him as much in love with you as ever."

CARDS

52 cards split in four suits (Sun, Moon, Star, Comet)
The Knight of Moons, known as the Wolf, always
belongs to the **eclipse** suit and beats ~~...~~
in the pack, in~~...~~

DE

Low ~~...~~
pass ~~...~~
Deal ~~...~~
two, ~~...~~
next ~~...~~

OBJ

To 'rise ~~...~~
wins n~~...~~

BURN

A burn i~~...~~ burn
four of a ~~...~~ st to
card/(s). ~~...~~ y,
winning ~~...~~ her
burn.

BIDDI

Players ch~~...~~ vel.
Optionally ~~...~~ car
being deal ~~...~~
upturn).

PLAY

First upturn~~...~~
the Wolf ma~~...~~
a better card ~~...~~
if they can, o~~...~~
or by the high~~...~~
must lead an ~~...~~

PAY-OFF

Each level rise~~...~~ ~~...~~ pay all
agreed stake to ~~...~~

*eclipse=highest ranking card or suit.   *galaxy=the center space where coins or tokens are pooled

---

Dinner Menu

Spiced Sausage and cauliflower
soup

Emerald Isle Salmon w/lemon
caper crème over wild rice

Petite filet of Torrani beef
accompanied by broiled potatoes dal
Astrea

Smoked half breast and leg of
partridge with a summer salad

Chocolate mousse with Khora berries
and cream

CHAPTER
59

Longbourn House, Heoros, First Moon of Londinium

On Tuesday the large dinner party assembled at Longbourn, and Jane noticed Elizabeth eagerly watching to see where Bingley would sit. Jane did her best not to let that eagerness transfer to herself. But she couldn't help wondering: would he choose, as he had in all their former parties, the seat beside her? Upon entering the room, he seemed to hesitate. But when his gaze fell on her, she couldn't help but smile, and he chose the spot at her side.

Jane felt momentarily triumphant, and then immediately mad at herself for it. That was the easiest choice of seat, regardless of who was sitting around it. As he sat, she saw him turn to Darcy with an expression resembling half-laughing alarm. She couldn't account for it, and she thought best not to try.

"Hello again," Bingley said to her, as kind and cordial as ever. "I hope you've been having a good day."

"I have, thank you," she said. "And you?"

He looked around the room with satisfaction. "Better now that I'm here."

Her heart skipped. Then she remembered that this had been his general way with her from the beginning. This was nothing special to her, and she was a fool to let herself believe that.

She turned her eyes toward Mr. Darcy, and found his trained on Lizzie. They weren't seated near one another, which Jane was sure Lizzie was grateful for. He sat beside her mother. She felt a pang of sympathy. That would not be an easy placement for him. It seemed though, to his benefit, that he wouldn't need to speak much.

It appeared, as she stole glances through the dinner, that when they did speak, both were formal and cold in their manner. Lizzie, when Jane caught her watching any of their interactions, had the most unreadable expression on her face. It was slightly unsettling. She could usually read Lizzie quite well.

Mr. Bingley was perfectly amiable through dinner, and though Jane did her best not to let her former feelings resurface at the slightest provocation, she was not entirely sure she succeeded.

When dinner concluded, they moved to the adjoining room. Tables had been set for gaming, and she resolved to choose a seat before Bingley, so that it would again be his decision whether they sat near one another. Perhaps if she sat somewhere less accessible, she'd have a better idea of what his choice might mean.

Thankfully, her father decided this was the time to invite their guests to scope out the best places for the upcoming jewelbird hunt. "We won't be long," her father had called down the hall, the two men trailing him.

Before sitting down, she and Lizzie went to the drink table to pour themselves something. Lizzie seemed slightly agitated, her responses to Kitty more clipped than usual. Before she could question her, Jane heard the sound of her father's voice in the hall again.

She turned quickly and found a seat at the Twist table. The men came in, and went for the drinks first. Mr. Darcy looked as if he intended to speak to Lizzie, and Jane's heart constricted in anxiety for her. But Bingley and Mary ended up between them. Jane expected her sister to be relieved by this, but instead she appeared more agitated.

To Jane's surprise, Mr. Darcy came over to her.

"Which of the games would you recommend I play, Miss Bennet?"

She was pleasantly surprised by such a question from him. "It depends upon your competitiveness," she told him seriously, eyeing her mother. "Mama will be out for blood. I, on the other hand, am just here for a good time."

He smiled, and it made her think that, had he presented himself this way from the start, Lizzie may not have been able to reject him.

"I'll keep that in mind," he said.

She peered around him at Lizzie, whose face, for once this evening, was easy to read. Her sister very much wished to know what they were speaking of. She was practically glaring in her effort to read Jane's lips.

Mr. Darcy noticed her looking and turned to catch Lizzie's eye.

Her sister's expression instantly morphed into an unbothered curiosity.

Jane almost laughed.

"Excuse me," Mr. Darcy said. "I fear I'm low on drink." He held up his glass, more than halfway full, and gave her a little nod before turning away.

She felt slightly more at ease, her mind not so focused on her own feelings, as she watched him start a conversation with her sister.

They spoke for a minute, but seemed to run out of things to say rather quickly. He didn't, however, move from her side until their mother decided that they were sufficiently primed for game time, and began forcing everyone to sit.

In that moment, Jane realized she'd overlooked an obstacle in her seating plan. Her mother gave Bingley no choice at all. She shooed him straight into the seat beside Jane, with Lizzie on her other side. Claiming the need for one more at the Twist table, Mrs. Bennet gave Mr. Darcy no choice in the matter either, and sat him next to Kitty.

Lizzie looked relatively put out by this, but Jane wasn't sure what to attribute it to. With Bingley beside her, and her favorite game in front of her, though, she didn't concern herself with it for long.

The rest of the evening passed pleasantly, though too quickly, and before they knew it, Bingley's Chase was called to the front.

"I think that went well," her mother said, as they ascended the steps to their rooms in order to change. "The dinner was impeccable. The salmon was cooked perfectly. The soup was fifty times better than what we had at the Lucases' last week. Even Mr. Darcy acknowledged that the Torrani was remarkably well done, and I suppose he has two or three Arkuluan chefs at least. And my dear Jane, envy of the stars, I never saw you look more beautiful." Mrs. Bennet, to say it simply, was in a very good mood.

Jane and Lizzie bid her goodnight at the top of the stairs, and closed themselves into their room as quickly as they could.

"She's right," Jane said, collapsing, not at all gracefully, into her bed. "It did go well. Everyone seemed to really enjoy themselves. I'd be glad to do that again soon."

Her sister sat on her own bed and smiled.

"Lizzie," Jane said warningly. "Don't. You can't suspect me. I assure you, I've learned to enjoy his conversation as a welcome acquaintance, without having a wish beyond it. I'm perfectly satisfied believing, based on his manners to me tonight, that he never wished to be more than we were. He's simply blessed with a greater sweetness of address and a stronger desire of generally pleasing than any other man."

"You're very cruel," Lizzie said, pressing the small button on the side table which spilled a pool of soft, warm light upon her pillow. "You won't let me smile and you're provoking me to it with every word."

"It's so hard sometimes to be believed," Jane said.

"And how impossible in others," Lizzie retorted.

"Why do you insist that I feel more than I do?"

"We all love to instruct, though we can only teach what isn't worth knowing. Forgive me. If you persist in indifference, don't make *me* your confidante."

For the next few days, Jane did just as her sister requested.

She was too uncertain of her own feelings to admit or deny what Lizzie had insinuated.

It had been a week since Bingley had returned to the neighborhood, but he hadn't contacted Jane once via waive. She felt this was further and certain proof that he really was nothing more than a friendly acquaintance.

Then a few days after his visit, Bingley came to the house again, this time alone. His friend had left him that morning for Londinium, to return in ten days' time. He sat with them in the parlor well over an hour, and was in remarkably good spirits. Her mother invited him to dine with them, but with many expressions of concern, he confessed that he was engaged elsewhere.

"Next time you come over," her mother said, "I hope we'll be more lucky."

He eagerly assented. "I'd be more than happy to return without dinner plans," he said. "Name the day."

Jane was in good spirits as well. Boldly, she suggested, "Tomorrow?"

"Yes, absolutely," he said. "I had no plans for tomorrow, but now I do. What time should I come by?"

His alacrity was catching. When had she grown so bold? "My father's hunting jewelbirds at first flight. I'm sure he'd be happy to have you join. Then you could stay for dinner afterward?" she suggested.

He agreed.

That night he sent her a waive confirming that the plans were still set.

It was an innocuous message. Nothing should've been read into it. This was simply part of their new dynamic. Wasn't it?

She went to bed unsettled, doing her best to repeat to her own heart what she'd insisted many times to her sister. She wouldn't get her hopes up this time. She wouldn't.

Bingley was punctual to his appointment. He and Mr. Bennet spent the morning together as planned. Jane knew that her father would find him more agreeable than he expected. There was nothing of presumption or folly in Bingley that could provoke his ridicule, or disgust him into silence. She had faith that he'd not be found wanting. She didn't look deeper into why she was thinking these things, and let herself believe that it was simply a wish for her father to have a nice time.

They returned to the house earlier than expected. None of her sisters were ready except for Kitty, but her mother kept rushing Jane to finish up and entertain Bingley until the rest of them were ready.

Jane looked pointedly at Lizzie. "I'm not going down without you. Mama's . . . scheming." To be alone with him would mean inviting the resurgence of questions and things they'd left unsaid. She wasn't sure of the answers, and the fear kept her from the temptation.

That same anxiety to get them by themselves subsided for the early part of Bingley's visit, but returned again in the evening. After tea, her father retired to the library, as was his custom, and Mary went to her room to study. Two obstacles of the five being thus removed, her mother sat looking and winking at Lizzie and Kitty for a considerable time, without making any impression on them nor realizing that Jane was witness to it all. Lizzie flat out avoided her gaze, and when Kitty did take notice, she very innocently said, "What's the matter, Mama? Why do you keep winking at me? What am I supposed to do?"

"Nothing," her mother said hastily. "Nothing at all. I didn't wink at you."

Her mother's schemes were thwarted.

Dinner passed as pleasantly as the afternoon. Bingley was everything that was charming. His ease and cheerfulness rendered him the most agreeable addition to their evening party, and he bore her mother's every quirk, every embarrassing remark, with a forbearance Jane was particularly grateful for.

She knew she would say nothing more of her indifference, should Lizzie ask tonight. It would please her sister to hear that she might've been correct the other night. But Jane wouldn't give her the satisfaction of hearing it from her lips until she knew for certain she and Bingley could be something more.

After dinner, Kitty, who had been missing their routine since Lydia left, set out the game table for Press. Lizzie bowed out, claiming that she had a waive to write, and left the room with a promise to return shortly.

Lizzie hadn't seemed suspicious. There was a promise of occupation for the whole group. But her mother had become more stealthy in her tactics. And before Jane could catch on to what she was doing, Mrs. Bennet had everyone but Jane and Bingley on a task that required their presence in a different room.

Jane was alone with Bingley again, seated directly beside him at the game table. There was nothing for it now but to talk.

~~Dear~~ Jane

I ~~still love you~~ must speak with you about how ~~we~~ I left things. I've made so many mistakes I don't know where to begin. I should've reached out to you. ~~I thought~~ I don't know what I thought. I'm ~~too damned trusting.~~ I was ~~told~~ ~~persuaded~~ that given the impression that you had no feelings for me, and I was ~~heartbroke~~ hurt that what I'd thought we were was nothing like it. I could've ~~should've~~ sent you a waive. But I ~~was embarrassed~~ was angry at myself. ~~I didn't want you to confirm what I'd been told~~ I didn't see the point of going out of my way to be hurt again. I'd had trouble with my comcard when I first reached Londinium. By the time it was squared away, I was too much of a coward to reach out. I let myself believe that no messages from you was by your choice and not a glitch in the system when the comcard scrapped out.

There were days I wished I could've just run into you somehow and then maybe I'd have the courage to ask you face to face. But you were on Heoros and I was on Londinium. I ~~loved you even then~~ should have paid more heed to ~~my heart~~ my instincts. Nothing but the persuasion that you were indifferent would've prevented my coming back to you on Heoros. ~~They knew the one thing that could keep me from you.~~ The evidence was convincing, at the time. I look back now and I see the truth. I was an ass. There was no excuse for me not to have asked you directly. If you can find it in your heart to forgive me for going dark matter on you, ~~I would very much like the chance to pick up where we left off~~ I'd be forever grateful.

(If she forgives me) I must now be as direct as I should've been before, ~~and tell you that I've loved you since before I left and I love you still.~~ If you never did or no longer do, then I confess that when I left you, I was in love with you. I wish to know if you possibly had the same feelings. Not necessarily the same strength of feeling, but just a confirmation, I hope, that I ~~wasn't completely wrong~~ rather any reciprocation whatsoever?

(If no) Thank you for your honesty. I'm sorry I didn't allow you that opportunity before. It could've saved us from the discomfort of an interrupted friendship. I do hope we can resume that friendship.

(If yes) Is there any hope that, having loved me then, you might still love me now? ~~Because I have never stopped loving you.~~ I still love you. ~~I'd marry you~~ tomorrow if you'd have me.

(too forward)   (Just wing it from here. If I get this far I'll figure it out).

CHAPTER
60

Longbourn House, Heoros, First Moon of Londinium

Elizabeth suspected, as she made her way back to the game table, that her mother had outwitted her. It was far too quiet in the room for Rise to be in progress. She opened the door and carefully peeked in.

Jane was standing with Bingley beside the hearth, apparently in the midst of earnest conversation. Their faces hastily turned to her and they stepped away from each other.

Elizabeth's stomach dropped in surprise, but her heart leapt. *Their* situation was awkward enough, but *hers* as an intruder was worse. None of them spoke, and Elizabeth was on the point of turning away, when Bingley whispered something into Jane's ear, and darted out of the room, flashing her an awkward but endearing half-smile as he passed by.

Widening her eyes in expectant curiosity, Elizabeth came to the couch and her sister all but floated over to join her.

Jane brightened and threw her arms around Elizabeth. "Oh, Lizzie," she said almost breathlessly. "I'm so *very* happy." She pulled back from their embrace, her eyes glistening with joyous tears. "It's too much. I don't deserve such good fortune. All my stars are lucky! Why is everyone not this happy?"

Elizabeth grinned. "So, he *is* in love with you?"

Jane nodded. "More than that. He asked me to marry him."

Her grin turned mischievous. "It's too bad you only see him as a friend."

Jane laughed in surprise. "You were right. I was . . . scared to get my hopes up again."

"Oh, Jane," Elizabeth clasped her sister's hands. "I know. Congratulations. Sincerely. He's a perfect complement to you and I know that you'll be so very happy together."

They sat for a moment just smiling at each other. Then Jane's face shifted and she jumped up. "I have to tell Mama. I wouldn't dare trifle with her patience, or allow her to hear it from anyone but me. He's gone to tell Papa. Stars fall! Lizzie, to know that my news will give pleasure to all our family! How shall I bear such happiness?" She hastened away to find their mother.

Elizabeth, who was left by herself, now smiled at the quickness and ease in which an event was finally settled that had given them so many previous months of suspense and vexation.

This was the end of all Bingley's friends' anxious prudence, and all his sister's falsehoods and scheming; the happiest, best, and most reasonable end.

In a few minutes she was joined by Bingley.

"Where's your sister?" he asked hastily, as he entered.

"With my mother. Upstairs, most likely. She'll be down in a moment, I'm sure."

He then closed the door behind him and came up to her.

"Congratulations, by the way," Elizabeth said. "I have no doubts that your future together will be filled with happiness."

It was an evening of uncommon delight to them all. Jane had a glow of such sweet admiration to her face that she looked somehow more beautiful than ever. Kitty giggled and smiled. Mrs. Bennet couldn't give her consent or speak her approval in terms warm enough to satisfy her feelings, though she talked to Bingley of nothing else for half an hour. When Mr. Bennet joined them, his voice and manner plainly showed how really happy he was. Not a word, however, passed his lips in allusion to it, until their visitor took his leave for the night.

As soon as Bingley was gone, he turned to Jane and said, "Congratulations, my sweet Jane. You'll be very happy, and I have no doubt you'll do very well together. Each of you are so complying, that nothing'll ever be resolved on; so easy that every servant will cheat you; and so generous, that you'll always exceed your income."

"Exceed their income! My stars!" cried his wife. "What are you talking about?" She turned to Jane. "I knew how it would be. I always said it must be so in the end. I was sure you couldn't be so beautiful for nothing! He's certainly the handsomest young man in the system!"

It didn't take long before her younger sisters began to make requests for the future.

"Would I be able to use the Netherfield library for my studies?" Mary asked.

"Someone should use the books," Jane said fondly, glancing at Elizabeth, who quickly recalled Bingley's admission of neglecting his library himself.

"Can I help plan the next Netherfield ball?" Kitty inquired.

"I'm sure you'd be more than welcome."

"Since we're making requests," Elizabeth said slyly, "can I borrow the moon-hopper for flight practice?"

Jane's laugh sparkled like sunlight on water.

That night, when they were finally alone again in their room, Jane, tucked snugly in her bed, turned to face Elizabeth. "He's made me so happy," she said, "by telling me that he was totally ignorant of my being on Londinium last spring. I didn't think it was possible."

"I suspected as much," said Elizabeth, mirroring her sister in her own bed. "But how did he account for it?"

"It must've been his sister's doing. They certainly were not supporters of his attachment to me. I can't be surprised, since he might've chosen someone more to his advantage in many respects. But when they see, as I trust they will, that their brother is happy with me, they'll learn to be content and we'll be on good terms again. Though we can never be what we once were to each other."

"That's the most unforgiving speech I've ever heard you utter," Elizabeth said. "Good for you. It'd vex me, to say the least, to see you again the victim of Caroline Bingley's pretended regard."

"Can you believe this, Lizzie?" Jane went on. "When he left for Londinium last November, he really loved me, and nothing but the persuasion of *my* being indifferent could've prevented his coming back again."

"He made a mistake, to be sure. But it's to the credit of his modesty."

This naturally introduced a shower of praise from Jane on his modesty, and the little value he put on his own good qualities. Elizabeth was pleased to find that he hadn't betrayed the interference of his friend. Jane had the most generous and forgiving heart in the system, but Elizabeth knew it was a circumstance that could still prejudice her against him.

"I'm the luckiest creature that ever existed," cried Jane. "Lizzie, why am I singled out this way from my family and blessed above them all? If I could see you as happy—if there was but another man for you!"

"If you were to give me forty such men, I'd never be as happy as you. Until I have your disposition and your goodness, I can never have your happiness. No, no, let me sort through the men for myself. Perhaps, if my stars are very lucky, I may meet with another Mr. Collins in time."

Longbourn

CHAPTER
61

Longbourn House, Heoros, First Moon of Londinium

One morning, about a week after Bingley and Jane's engagement, as they sat around together in the dining room, their attention was collectively drawn to the window by the sight and sounds of an unfamiliar ship landing on the Bennets' launchpad.

It was too early in the morning for visitors, and Elizabeth knew no one who had access to a Shrike series transport. As it was certain, however, that someone was coming, Bingley, who had been spending nearly every day with them since the engagement, requested that Jane accompany him to the front garden and avoid the confinement of an intrusion. Jane instantly agreed, and they set off, leaving Elizabeth and the rest of her family to wonder at who might be coming. Soon the housekeeper opened the door and the visitor entered.

It was Lady Catherine de Bourgh.

They were all prepared to be surprised, but their astonishment was beyond expectation. Kitty and her mother seemed in particular shock, though neither had ever met the woman.

"Lady Catherine," Elizabeth said, almost as an exclamation. "What a surprise. Please, come in."

Her ladyship entered the room with a more than usually ungracious air, made no other reply to Elizabeth's greeting than a slight inclination of the head, and sat down without saying a word. No request of introduction was made, and her family were left to watch her in silence.

Mrs. Bennet was so in awe of such a guest that she received her with the utmost politeness.

Lady Catherine didn't respond. She sat for a moment in silence, then said very stiffly to Elizabeth, "I trust you're well, Miss Bennet. That lady, I suppose, is your mother."

Elizabeth replied very concisely that she was.

"And *that* I suppose is one of your sisters."

"Yes, madam," said her mother, delighted to speak to Lady Catherine. "She's my youngest still currently at home. My youngest of all is lately enrolled in Alesadran Academy, and my eldest is somewhere on the grounds, walking with a young man who will soon become part of the family."

"You have a very small park here," returned Lady Catherine after a short silence.

"It's nothing compared to Rosings, my lady, I'm certain. But I assure you it's much larger than Sir William Lucas'."

"This must be a most inconvenient sitting room, in summer. The windows are full west."

"We never sit in here during the setting days," Mrs. Bennet assured her. "May I take the liberty of asking your ladyship whether you left Mr. and Mrs. Collins well?"

"Yes, very well. I saw them the night before last."

Elizabeth now expected that her ladyship would produce a package for her from Charlotte, as it seemed the most probable motive—though still rather improbable—for coming all this way. But nothing appeared, and she was completely puzzled.

Her mother, with great civility, offered some refreshment to their guest. But Lady Catherine very resolutely, and not very politely, declined. She stood and said to Elizabeth, "Miss Bennet, there seemed to be a prettyish kind of little wilderness on one side of your lawn. I'd be glad to take a walk in it, if you'd favor me with your company."

"Go, my dear," her mother quietly insisted. "Show her ladyship the different walks. I think she'll be pleased with the viewing house by the pond."

Elizabeth obliged. As they passed through the hall, Lady Catherine opened the doors to the dining parlor and drawing room, and pronounced them, after a short survey, to be decent enough rooms.

A custom-designed land transport was parked in the drive. Elizabeth saw that a pilot was waiting in it.

They proceeded in silence along the gravel walk that led to the copse; Elizabeth was determined to make no effort for conversation with a woman who was more than usually insolent and disagreeable.

She couldn't help but wonder at how she ever thought Darcy was like the woman.

As they entered the copse, Lady Catherine began speaking. "You can be at no loss, Miss Bennet, to understand the reason for my journey here."

Elizabeth looked at her with unaffected astonishment. "You're mistaken, madam. I haven't been able to account for the honor at all."

"Miss Bennet," her ladyship retorted, her tone angry. "I'm not to be trifled with. However insincere *you* may choose to be, you'll not find *me* so. I am celebrated for my sincerity and frankness. In such a moment as this, I'll certainly not divert from that. A report of a most alarming nature reached me two days ago. I was told that not only was your sister on the point of being most advantageously married, but that you, Miss Elizabeth Bennet, would soon afterward be united to my great-nephew. Though I *know* it to be a scandalous falsehood, I wouldn't insult him by supposing it possible. I instantly resolved on setting off for this place so that I might make my sentiments known to you."

"If you believed it to be impossible," said Elizabeth, coloring with astonishment and disdain, "I wonder why you took the trouble of traveling so far. What could you mean to do?"

"Insist at once upon having such a report universally contradicted."

"Your coming to Longbourn," Elizabeth replied coolly, "would rather be a confirmation of it, if indeed such a report exists."

"*If*? Do you pretend to be ignorant of it? Has it not been industriously circulated by yourself? Do you not know that such a report has been spread abroad?"

"I never heard that it was."

"And can you declare that there's no *foundation* for it?"

Elizabeth took a steadying breath. "I don't pretend to possess equal frankness with your ladyship. *You* may ask questions which *I* shall choose not to answer."

"Stars alight! This is not to be borne. Miss Bennet, I insist on being satisfied. Has Mr. Darcy made you an offer of marriage?"

"Your ladyship has declared it to be impossible," she retorted, her voice cold.

"It ought to be so. It *must* be so while he retains the use of his reason. But *your* arts and allurements may, in a moment of infatuation, have made him forget what he owes himself and his family. You may have drawn him in."

"If I did, I'd be the last person to confess it."

"Miss Bennet. Do you know who I am? I haven't been accustomed to such language as this. I'm almost the nearest relation he has in the worlds, and am entitled to know all his concerns."

"But you aren't entitled to know *mine*. Nor will your behavior ever induce me to be explicit." Why had it fallen to Elizabeth to be so often scolding wealthy elites into being polite?

"This match can never take place. Never. Mr. Darcy is engaged to *my daughter*. Now what do you have to say?"

"If he is, then you have no reason to suppose he'd make an offer to me."

Lady Catherine hesitated for a moment and then replied. "The engagement between them is a peculiar kind. They've been intended for each other since infancy. It was *his* mother's wish as well as mine. While in their cradles, we planned their union. Now, at the moment when the wishes of both women would be accomplished, to be prevented by a young woman of inferior birth—of no importance on any world—so wholly unconnected with the family! Do you have no regard for the wishes of his friends? Are you lost to propriety and delicacy? Have you not heard me say that he was destined to my daughter?"

"Yes, I'd heard it before. But what's that to me? If there's no other objection to my marrying Mr. Darcy, I certainly won't be kept from it by knowing that his family wanted him to marry elsewhere. You both did as much as you could to plan the marriage. Its completion depended on others. If Mr. Darcy isn't bound by honor or inclination for her, why can't he make another choice? And if I'm that choice, why shouldn't I accept him?"

"Because honor, decorum, prudence—no, interest—forbid it. Yes, Miss Bennet, interest. Don't expect to be noticed by his family or friends, if you willfully act against the inclination of them all.

You'll be censured, slighted, and despised by everyone connected with him. Your alliance will be a disgrace. Your name will never be mentioned by any of us."

"These are great misfortunes," Elizabeth replied. "But the wife of Mr. Darcy must have such extraordinary sources of happiness attached to her situation that she could, on the whole, have little cause to regret."

"Obstinate, headstrong girl! Galaxy's end! I'm ashamed of you. Is this your gratitude for my attentions to you last spring? Is nothing due to me on that score? You must understand, Miss Bennet, that I came here with the determined resolution of carrying my purpose, nor will I be dissuaded from it. I don't submit to any person's whims. I've not been in the habit of brooking disappointment."

"*That* will make your ladyship's current situation more pitiable, but it won't have any effect on *me*."

"I won't be interrupted. Hear me in silence."

Elizabeth bristled.

"My daughter and Mr. Darcy are formed for each other. They're descended from royals and from respectable, honorable, and ancient landed families. Their fortune on both sides is splendid. They are destined for each other by the voice of every member of their respective houses. And what is to divide them? The upstart pretensions of a young woman without history, connections, or fortune. Is this to be endured? It mustn't, and won't. If you were sensible of your own good, you wouldn't wish to quit the sphere in which you've been brought up."

"Marrying Mr. Darcy doesn't change my sphere. He's a gentleman. I'm a gentleman's daughter. So far, we're equal."

"True. You *are* a gentleman's daughter. But who is your mother? Your uncles and aunts? Don't imagine me ignorant of their condition."

"Whatever my connections may be," said Elizabeth, her blood rocketing through her veins as she clung desperately to composure, "if Mr. Darcy doesn't object to them, they can't be anything to *you*."

"Tell me once and for all, are you engaged to him?"

Though Elizabeth wouldn't, for the mere purpose of obliging Lady Catherine, have answered this question, there was nothing else to say after a moment's deliberation but "I'm not."

Lady Catherine seemed pleased.

"And will you promise me never to enter into such an engagement?"

"I'll make no such promise."

"Miss Bennet, I'm shocked and astonished. I expected to find a more reasonable young woman. I won't go away till you've given me the assurance I require."

"I hope you're comfortable. Because I'll *never* give it. I'm not going to be intimidated into anything so unreasonable. Your lady-ship wants Mr. Darcy to marry your daughter. But would giving you the wished-for promise make *their* marriage at all more probable? Supposing him to be attached to me, would *my* refusing to accept him make him wish to offer his love to *her*? Allow me to say, Lady Catherine, that the arguments with which you've supported this extraordinary petition have been as frivolous as the action was ill-judged. You've grossly mistaken my character if you think I can be worked on by such persuasions as these. How far Mr. Darcy might approve of your interference in *his* affairs, I cannot tell. But you certainly have no right to concern yourself in *mine*. I must beg, therefore, to be harassed no more on the subject."

"Oh, I'm not done. To all the objections I've already urged, I have still another to add. I'm no stranger to the particulars of your youngest sister's infamous flight. I know it all. That the acceptance into the Alesadran Academy was a patched-up business at the expense of your father and uncles. And is *such* a girl to be Mr. Darcy's sister? Stars that fall! Are the shades of Pemberley to be thus polluted?"

"You can *now* have nothing further to say," Elizabeth answered resentfully. "You've insulted me in every possible way and I must beg to return." She turned and started back to the house.

Lady Catherine followed, highly incensed. "You have no regard, then, for Mr. Darcy's honor and credit? Unfeeling, selfish girl! Don't you consider that a connection with you must disgrace him in the eyes of everybody?"

"Lady Catherine," she replied over her shoulder, "I have nothing further to say. You know my sentiments."

"You're resolved to have him?"

"I've said no such thing. I'm only resolved to act in the manner which will, in my own opinion, constitute my happiness, without reference to *you*, or to any person so entirely unconnected with me."

"You refuse, then, to oblige me. You refuse to obey the claims of duty, honor, and gratitude. You're determined to ruin him in the opinion of all his friends, and make him the contempt of the worlds."

"Neither duty, nor honor, nor gratitude," replied Elizabeth, stopping to turn to her ladyship, "have any possible claim on me in the present instance. None of these would be violated by my marriage with Mr. Darcy. With regard to the resentment of his family— or the indignation of all the worlds—if the former, it wouldn't give me one moment's concern, and the latter would have too much sense to join in the scorn." She turned on her heel and walked on.

"And this is your real opinion—your final resolve! Very well. I'll know how to act now. Don't imagine, Miss Bennet, that your ambition will ever be gratified. I came to try you. I hoped to find you reasonable, but, depend upon it, I'll carry my point."

Like an angry goose, Lady Catherine talked on, chasing her heels, till they stopped at the door of the custom transport and, turning hastily around on the step as she entered, added, "I take no leave of you, Miss Bennet. I send no compliments to your mother. You deserve no such attention. I'm most seriously displeased."

Elizabeth raised her eyebrows and said nothing. Without attempting to persuade her ladyship to return to the house, she walked quietly into it herself. She heard the vehicle glide away as she proceeded upstairs. Her mother impatiently met her at the landing to ask why Lady Catherine wouldn't come in again and take refreshment.

"She chose not to," said Elizabeth. "She had to go."

"She's a fine-looking woman. And her coming here was so prodigiously civil, for she came, I suppose, to tell us the Collinses were well. I suppose she had nothing particular to say to you, Lizzie?"

Acknowledging the substance of their conversation was impossible. "I'm feeling unwell, Mama. I'm going to lie down." Then she swept past and into her room, trapping herself safely behind her door.

To: Mr. Bennet, Longbourn Estate, Landings District, Heoros

From: William Collins, Hunsford Parsonage, Kent Orbital Station

Subject: Congratulations and Concern

Dear Sir,

Such news has reached me, through the family of my beloved wife, that warranted a waive to you.

I must first congratulate you most sincerely on the upcoming nuptials of your eldest daughter. I know this to be a time of great happiness for your entire family, having so recently been married myself. The Light has truly shone upon us all and I will keep them in my daily devotions so they may never stray into darkness.

On that score, however, I must caution you on the decisions of two of your other daughters, which we've learned of by the same authority.

Your daughter Elizabeth, it is presumed, will soon be engaged as well. Mr. Darcy may be reasonably looked up to as one of the most illustrious persons in the Londinium system. He is blessed with splendid property, noble relations, and extensive patronage. Yet in spite of all these temptations, let me warn you both of the follies of accepting this gentleman's proposals.

His distant relation, the esteemed Lady Catherine de Bourgh, does not favor the match. After mentioning the likelihood of this marriage to her ladyship the other night, she immediately expressed what she felt on the occasion. I knew she would never give her consent to what she deemed so disgraceful a match. I thought it my duty to give the speediest intelligence of this to your daughter, so that she and her noble admirer may be aware of what they risk and not run hastily into a marriage which isn't properly sanctioned.

Finally, I am truly rejoiced that your daughter Lydia's poor choices have been so well hushed up. I mustn't neglect the duties of my station, or refrain from declaring my amazement at hearing that you've rewarded her with such a placement. It was an encouragement of vice, and had I been the head of Longbourn, I'd absolutely have opposed it. You may certainly forgive her, but never then treat her better than your other, more obedient, daughters.

Congratulations again to your daughter Jane.

With all this talk of children I should like to add that congratulations are in order for myself and my wife as well. We are expecting a young Collins of our own next year. But I will save the particulars for another waive, so that my own joy for my future child does not dilute my words of warning to your present ones.

By the Light,
William Collins

CHAPTER 62

Longbourn House, Heoros, First Moon of Londinium

The discomposure Elizabeth experienced after Lady Catherine's extraordinary visit wasn't easily overcome. It took many hours before she could think of it less than incessantly. It appeared that the woman had actually taken the trouble of traveling across the system for the sole purpose of breaking off Elizabeth's possible engagement with Mr. Darcy. Was it rational? Where could she have heard such a report? Perhaps *his* being the close friend of Bingley, and *her* being Jane's sister, was enough to supply the idea. She hadn't forgotten to consider that her sister's marriage must surely bring them more frequently together.

She couldn't help feeling some uneasiness thinking of the possible consequences of Lady Catherine persisting in her interference. From what she'd said, it occurred to Elizabeth that she'd likely approach Mr. Darcy as well. She didn't know the exact degree of his affection for his great-aunt, or his dependence on her judgment, but it was natural to suppose that he thought much higher of Lady Catherine than *she* could. It was all but certain that, in enumerating the miseries of a marriage with Elizabeth, Lady Catherine would address him on his weakest side. With his notions of dignity, he'd probably feel that the arguments which Elizabeth had considered weak and ridiculous contained much good sense and solid reasoning.

If he'd been shifting off course from her before, which seemed likely, the advice and entreaty of Lady Catherine might settle every doubt. In that case, he wouldn't return again.

Elizabeth determined that if, in a few days, Mr. Darcy should send an excuse to Bingley for not keeping his promise, she'd under-stand it to be because of her ladyship. She'd then give up every wish and expectation of him. If he was satisfied in only regretting her, when he might've obtained her affections and her hand, then she'd soon cease to regret him at all.

The next morning, as she was going downstairs, her father came out of the library.

"Lizzie," he said. "I was off to look for you. Come here."

She followed him back into the library. Curiosity to know what he had to tell her heightened her suspicion of it being somehow connected to the comcard in his hand. It suddenly struck her that it might be a waive from Lady Catherine, and she anticipated with dismay all the consequent explanations.

She followed her father to the fireplace, and they both sat down.

"I received a waive this morning that has astonished me exceedingly," he said. "As it mainly concerns you, I thought you'd want to know its contents. I didn't know that I had *two* daughters on the brink of matrimony. Let me congratulate you on a very important conquest."

Heat bloomed in Elizabeth's cheeks at the instant conviction of it being a waive from Mr. Darcy, rather than Lady Catherine. She had no idea whether to be pleased that he explained himself at all, or offended that his waive wasn't addressed to her.

"You look conscious of this. Your mind is sharp in many regards, but I think I might defy even *your* discernment, to discover the name of your admirer. This waive is from Mr. Collins."

"Mr. Collins! Great eclipse! What can *he* have to say?"

"Something very succinct and to the point, of course." He handed her the comcard and she read the waive quickly, her emotions swirling like leaves in wind, nothing settled.

When she returned the comcard to his hand, he said, "Could he have selected any man whose name would give less credibility to this rumor? Mr. Darcy, who never looks at any woman but to see a blemish, and who probably never looked at *you* in his life! It's admirable."

Elizabeth tried to laugh along with her father, but only forced a reluctant smile. Never had his wit been directed in a manner so disagreeable to her.

"Lizzie, you look as though you didn't enjoy this. You're not going to be demure, I hope, and pretend to be affronted at such a report. For what do we live, but to make sport for our neighbors, and laugh at them in our turn?"

"Oh," cried Elizabeth, distracted, but trying not to seem so. "I'm excessively entertained. But it's so strange."

"Yes. *That* is what makes it amusing. Had they fixed on any other man, it would've been nothing. But *his* perfect indifference, and *your* pointed dislike, make it so delightfully absurd! As much as I despise typing out waives, I wouldn't give up Mr. Collins's correspondence for anything. No, when I read a waive of his, I can't help giving him the preference. What did Lady Catherine say about this report yesterday? Did she come here to refuse her consent?"

Elizabeth could only laugh at this question. It'd been asked without the least suspicion, and she wasn't distressed by his repeating it. She had never been more at a loss to make her feelings appear what they weren't. It was necessary to laugh, when she'd rather have cried. Her father had mortified her with what he said of Mr. Darcy's indifference. She could do nothing but wonder at such a lack of discernment, or fear that perhaps, instead of his seeing too *little*, she might have fancied too *much*.

LONDINIUM SAT[SYS
Communications Log—System Storage 30 Days [Planetary]

[Ba_Da_Bing_ley] 12.9-15:25:10.LS

I've found the perfect way to celebrate the engagement. The timing is incredible, but tight. We can't pass it up.

[MyMyMissJane] 12.9-15:26:01.LS

If you're excited for it, so am I. Where are we going?

[Ba_Da_Bing_ley] 12.9-15:27:38.LS

There's a ship passing orbit tomorrow. The Parallax. It has a spacewalk arena.

[LizzieLovesSpace] 12.9-15:28:55.LS

Yes! I know exactly the one you're talking about.

[Ba_Da_Bing_ley] 12.9-15:29:38.LS

Be careful, Elizabeth, you may become my favorite sister.

[LizzieLovesSpace] 12.9-15:30:49.LS

It's an honor, favorite soon-to-be-brother! When do we leave?

[Ba_Da_Bing_ley] 12.9-15:32:09.LS

Early. The ship's a flyby. If either of your younger sisters are interested, the age restriction won't be a problem, and there's plenty of room in the transport for them both.

[LizzieLovesSpace] 12.9-15:34:14.LS

Mary says she'd rather visit your library while you're away, if you'd allow it?

[Ba_Da_Bing_ley] 12.9-15:35:27.LS

Definitely. Someone should be reading those books!

[MyMyMissJane] 12.9-15:35:50.LS

Kitty would like to come along. It'd be good for her, I think, to get out of the house and do something fun.

[Ba_Da_Bing_ley] 12.9-15:36:59.LS

Wonderful. Darcy, will you be back in Heoros tonight, or would you need to meet us on the Parallax?

[FW.Darcy] 12.9-15:40:14.LS

I'll be back tonight and ride with you in the morning.

[Ba_Da_Bing_ley] 12.9-15:41:28.LS

The plan is set! Liftoff from Netherfield Landing at, say, 7. See you all then!

[FW.Darcy] *LIKES MESSAGE*

[MyMyMissJane] *LIKES MESSAGE*

[LizzieLovesSpace] *LIKES MESSAGE*

. . . END COM . . .

CHAPTER 63

Parallax StarSeeker, Independent Orbit, Londinium Lunar System

Darcy was looking forward to the experience of the space walk. He was also looking forward to the company, though both gave him some anxiety.

When they filed into the Netherfield's transport, which Bingley had dubbed the Hopper, he was glad to get in first and claim his seat, so that his proximity to Elizabeth wouldn't be up to him. But the consequence of their entry order meant he couldn't be sure whether her choice was intentional. Bingley and Jane took their places next to him on the starboard bench, which left Elizabeth to sit across from him and Kitty beside her.

The Hopper ascended. Darcy stole glances at Elizabeth, who seemed almost determined not to meet his eye, the warm gold of the sky glowing against her skin as they broke through the atmosphere. Bingley whispered excitedly to Jane beside him. Kitty was turned, her eyes watching the moon fall away.

Darcy finally caught Elizabeth's gaze. "Have you ever done something like this before?" he asked, to keep the silence between them from growing into awkwardness.

Her eyes brightened. "No, but I've heard it's an incredible experience."

"I wonder if it'll live up to the flight you took last year," he offered.

She looked up through the ceiling's windows and was silent for a moment, a small smile on her lips. "I guess we'll find out soon enough."

Kitty turned back around in her seat, catching something of Bingley and Jane's conversation. "So there won't be anyone else in the arena? Really?"

"We'll be the first in," Bingley said. "It doesn't open to the ship's occupants until ten. We have the place to ourselves for two hours."

"Moons align! I can hardly wait," Kitty said. She spent the remainder of the flight involving them all in conversation about what was ahead of them. She seemed to favor Jane and Bingley, a nervous edge to her voice any time she tried to include Darcy. The strange mix of eagerness and shyness reminded him of Georgiana. He felt a pang of disappointment that he couldn't bring his sister along with them. He resolved to look into the ship's circuit and take her when he next had an opportunity.

The Parallax loomed as they moved toward it, a white orb in the dark sea of the void. They docked without issue, and disembarked. Where the hull was bright white, the walls of the corridors were a stately slate and steel. Jane and Bingley walked in front with the host, who'd met them in the docking bay, and who was now guiding them to the arena. Kitty walked between Elizabeth and Darcy, anticipation practically radiating off of her. Elizabeth occasionally pointed out a poster set in the walls featuring visuals of the ship and light schematics of its various levels. From what they could tell, using these in combination with their view as they'd approached in the Hopper, the arena was set off from the main circle of the StarSeeker. This, he supposed, was how the arena was able to maintain a separate gravity field.

They were led to a small lobby with a large desk in the center, a bank of windows on the left where the arena seemed to float beside it, and a wall with three doors on the right. Behind the desk was an airlock.

Their host introduced them to the two employees behind the desk, and the five of them were quickly swept into the process of being fitted for the necessary accessories. They were brought into the room behind the first of the three doors, where there was a wide bench on one side and a few compressed racks of clothing.

The man who'd led them into the room began a speech he'd clearly given many times. He was kind and to the point, and expanded each rack timed with the speech in an almost theatrical flourish. "The outer walls of the spacewalk won't be visible when you're inside the dome. You won't be tethered. It can be unsettling, but I assure you the walls are indeed there. There's also a debris field. The rocks are fake, they will not hurt if you slam into them. They're meant as stopping points, handholds, launchpads . . . whatever you can think of. Now, for your peace of mind, and as a safety failsafe, you'll be fitted for heat redundancy in pants, vests, jackets, and the like that can be worn with your current clothing. You will also be given this halo helm, which will expand in the event of a breach in the walls." The man showed them how the thin metal headpiece fit around the crown of Kitty's head, and demonstrated how it worked as he spoke. "This piece will transform to allow a pocket of breathable air, recycled through this hose connected to the halo here," he tapped the back of her head, "and down into this small canister backpack. The straps here are adjustable. Finally, we'll be fitting you for thrust boots. If you find yourselves in a position in the arena where you can't course-correct, switch the thrust boots on, point your feet away from where you're trying to go, and the boots will assist you."

When they'd been properly fitted, they were led to the changing rooms, which were behind the other two doors.

Elizabeth was the first one dressed. Darcy, the second. She'd kept her yellow dress on, her white warming-pants replacing the yellow ones that had poked through the slit. Her white warming-vest fit her form as though it were tailored for her. He was so consumed with taking in her details, he was startled to find her eyes doing the same to him until their gazes met. In that moment, she looked almost as if she wished to say something to him. Then Bingley emerged from the dressing room, and she quickly looked away.

Once everyone was ready, the airlock was opened, and the party entered. Doors hissed shut, buttons pressed, more doors, and then they lifted off their feet, gravity releasing them all.

"Through the tunnel," said a voice over the com.

What Darcy had expected to be a tube elevator was instead a tube of ladders, which they were clearly meant to use to help pull themselves through to the arena.

Elizabeth caught on first. She tipped sideways, grabbed a rung, and pulled herself along. Darcy copied and followed her at once, reorienting his mind to the loss of gravity—and the concept of a floor. With one pull, he sailed forward, feeling momentarily like a ship cutting through atmo.

Emerging into the arena didn't feel like it. Instead, it felt as though he'd been ejected into the void. Along the wall with the tube was a decently sized platform which appeared as a rocky flatland with various sitting areas molded to look like stones. He let his mind call this the ground, and shifted to stand on it.

As he looked around on what felt like a half-exploded comet—rocks floating in the void at various distances from the platform—Bingley, in his bright blue, sailed past.

"Come, Darcy!" he called with a laugh. "You can't possibly stay on the wall for *this*!"

Elizabeth laughed, too, and Darcy turned around to see her floating a little way above him. Glowing in white and yellow, with the gold metal halo helm ringing her dark hair, she looked like a goddess of Everlasting Light. He half expected her to drop aurum coins down to him, her supplicant.

Jane more cautiously emerged from the tube, and followed Darcy's path. When she'd oriented herself to stand beside him, she smiled a Bingley-like smile and said, "Now's the time to enjoy ourselves." Then she crouched, and launched herself toward her husband-to-be.

"Kitty," Elizabeth called. "Are you—" Before she could finish the question, her sister shot through the tube as though she'd been launched, a blur of gray and lavender. She practically screamed with excitement, bounced off the nearest floating stone-like debris, and careened out of sight.

He shook his head, and pushed off, joining the others at a large fake boulder close to the entrance.

"I wonder how far away the edges are," Jane said.

"It feels dangerous to try for them," Elizabeth admitted. "And yet I'm tempted."

"If anyone can find the wall, it's Darcy," Bingley teased.

Darcy's mouth turned up at the corner but he didn't dignify Bingley's jest with a full smile. "You aren't wrong," he said, and pulled himself to the other side of the boulder. Feeling emboldened, he said, "Anyone coming with me?"

He noticed a glint in Elizabeth's eye as she turned to her sister. They pushed off each other and headed in different directions.

Bingley exclaimed in surprise, then scrambled to chase after Jane.

Darcy chose a direction similar to Elizabeth, but slightly more outward.

He went this way a while, until out of nowhere, Elizabeth rounded one of the floating rocks, and with no way to stop herself, slammed into him head on.

He grabbed onto her arms before she could swing away in a different direction, and they whirled uncomfortably until his back slammed into another floating rock. He was thankful that unlike normal rocks, these were engineered for this space, and gave a bit in the impact. Elizabeth was able to catch a handhold and between the two of them they managed to slow to a stop.

Both sucking in air and wheezing, they found a seat on the faux rock, hooking their legs and feet into the strategically placed insets to check themselves for damage.

"Are you all right?" he asked her, looking her over.

She had her elbows on her knees and her head in her hands. After a couple of deep breaths she lifted her head and nodded. "I think so. I'm so sorry. I—"

"No, don't be," he said, cutting off her excuse. "It's the nature of the activity, I dare say."

She studied his face for a moment. He didn't know what to say, but something in his gut told him that he shouldn't speak.

"Stars! You're bleeding," she said, and reached a hand to his face. With a swipe of her thumb above his right eye, she pulled her hand away with a red streak along it. She cocked her head and looked at the cut with a faint, almost absent smile. "The blood isn't dripping. It's pooling." Her eyes drifted down to meet his, and with an unexpected and rapidly growing intensity, she held his gaze.

When the galaxy of thoughts this caused expanded beyond his comfort, he looked away. "Is it bad?" he asked, pulling a fabric square from one of his pockets and dabbing his forehead. He lowered the square to check. "No," he answered himself.

Elizabeth had gone quiet. He looked over to see her frowning at her hands.

He was on the verge of asking whether a finger had been injured when she looked up at him.

Her words came out in a rush, steadying as she went on. "Mr. Darcy, I have to be selfish for a moment. I've been so uneasy and I can't stand it any longer. I can't continue to pretend that I don't know what you've done for my sister—the unparalleled kindness of it. Ever since I've known about it, I've been so anxious to tell you how grateful I am. If the rest of my family knew . . ."

Whatever blood remained in his face drained from it instantly. "I'm sorry—*so* sorry," he replied earnestly, "that you were ever informed of what may, in some mistaken light, have given you uneasiness. I didn't think Mrs. Gardiner was so untrustworthy."

"Don't blame my aunt. Lydia accidentally betrayed your involvement. And then, I couldn't rest until I knew the details. I will thank you a thousand times, in the name of all my family, for your generous compassion. You took on so much trouble for the sake of discovering them."

"If you *do* thank me," he replied, "let it be for yourself alone. I won't deny that my wish of bringing you happiness was a great inducement. But your *family* owe me nothing. As much as I respect them, I thought only of *you*."

Elizabeth was quiet again. She stared intently toward a portion of the arena that, when he glanced in that direction, revealed Jane and Bingley in some sort of weightless, directionless dance.

Seeing that joy between them, coupled with this confession of Elizabeth's, shot adrenaline through him, and with it, the bravery to say, "You're too generous to trifle with me." He turned to her again. "If your feelings are still what they were last April, tell me so at once. *My* affections and wishes are unchanged. But one word from you will silence me on this subject forever."

In the seconds between his question and her answer, the silence was so profound that he feared the outer walls had been breached, and was anticipating the activation of the halo helm. But then she spoke, and he breathed in again.

"The way I felt last April is . . . so entirely different that I can hardly believe I'm the same person," she said quietly. "I can only express this change in sentiment by saying that . . ." Her gaze held his. "Had the woman you sit with here in this moment been approached by you in that house on the Kent, she would've accepted you with pleasure and gratitude."

The happiness which this reply produced was so intense that he could hardly form the words to respond. "Elizabeth," he breathed, and she dropped her gaze. "What I felt for you then has only grown stronger. Being with you at my home, seeing you interact with your family, my friends . . . I love—" His throat tightened with such a bold admission, knowing the risk he was taking, again. "I love you. And it's the greatest wish of my heart to never be parted from you from this moment on."

She looked at him again with that same fervent intensity as before. "Then it's *my* greatest wish to grant *yours*."

They sat on the rock, lost to time. From this vantage point, they might as well have been lost to the universe as well. There was too much to be thought and felt and said for attention to anything else.

After a while, he broke the silence. "You know," he said, taking her hand in his, "we have Lady Catherine to thank for this moment."

"Oh?"

"She found me on Londinium. Told me of her journey to Longbourn, its motive, and the substance of her conversation with you. She dwelled emphatically on your every affronting or unsettling word, believing such news would assist in her efforts to obtain the promise from me that she couldn't get from you."

"Unlucky for her, it had the opposite effect?" Elizabeth ventured to finish, twining her fingers in his and sending a current through every cell in his body.

"It taught me to hope," he said, "as I'd scarcely allowed myself to hope before. I knew enough of your disposition to be certain that, had you been absolutely, irrevocably decided against me, you'd have told Lady Catherine frankly and openly."

Elizabeth blushed and laughed as she replied. "Yes, you know enough of my *frankness* to believe me capable of *that*. After abusing you so abominably to your face, what scruples could I have in abusing you to all your relations?"

He grimaced. "What did you say of me that I didn't deserve? Though your accusations were ill-founded—formed on mistaken premises—my behavior to you at the time merited the severest disapproval. It was unpardonable. I can't think of it without abhorrence."

"We won't compete for the greater share of the blame of that evening," said Elizabeth, the loose strands of her hair drifting around her as if in a breeze. "Neither of our conduct, if examined closely, would be faultless. Since then, I hope, we've both improved in civility."

"I can't forgive myself so easily. The recollection of what I said then—of my conduct, my manners, my expressions during the whole thing—is now, and has been for many months, inexpressibly painful to me. Your reproof was so well applied, I'll never forget it." He looked away from her—into the dark beyond the arena's floating rocks, that moment playing in his mind's eye. "'Had you behaved in a more gentlemanlike manner.' Those were your words. You can't know how they've tortured me; though it was some time, I must admit, before I was reasonable enough to allow their justice."

"I was certainly very far from expecting them to make so strong an impression. I had no idea that you might feel them in such a way."

He turned back to her. "I can easily believe it. You thought I was devoid of every proper feeling. The shift in your face—I'll never forget it—as you said that there was no way that I could've induced you to accept me."

"Don't repeat what I said then. These memories won't do. I assure you that I've long been most heartily ashamed of it." The effects of zero-gravity had them both, though tethered by hand- and footholds, lifting, balloon-like, in their seats. He couldn't help feeling it reflected his internal emotions.

"What of the letter? Did it eventually make you think better of me? When you first read it, could you give any credit to its contents?"

"Not at first. But gradually. After a hundred or so readings of it, all my former prejudices disappeared."

He chuckled a bit at this. "I knew what I wrote would give you pain, but it was necessary. I hope you've destroyed the letter. There was one part especially—the opening of it—which I'd dread you having the means of reading again. I can remember some lines which might, justly, make you hate me."

"The letter shall certainly be burnt," she proclaimed, "if you believe it essential to the preservation of my regard. But while we both have reason to think my opinions not entirely unalterable, they aren't, I hope, quite so easily changed as that implies."

"When I wrote that letter, I believed I was perfectly calm and cool. I'm convinced now that it was written in a dreadful bitterness of spirit."

"Perhaps it began in bitterness, but it didn't end that way," she said. "Let's think no more of the letter. The people who wrote and read it are entirely different from us. All the negativity we connect to it should be forgotten. What is that old saying? 'Think only of the past as its remembrance gives you pleasure.'" Her smile was suffused with warmth.

"*Your* retrospections are completely devoid of reproach. The contentment arising from them is innocence." He squeezed her hand a little tighter, and looked down at her soft fingers entwined in his. "With *me*, that's not the case. Painful recollections will intrude and I won't repel them. I've been a selfish being all my life, in practice, though not in principle. As a child I was taught what was *right*, but I wasn't taught to correct my temper. I was given good principles, but left to follow them in pride and conceit. Unfortunately, as an only son—and for many years an only child—I was spoiled by my parents. Though they were good themselves, they weren't incapable of some failures. I was allowed to think meanly of the rest of the worlds' sense of worth compared with my own. I was this way from eight to twenty-eight. I still might be—" he looked into her eyes and moved his hand to caress her cheek—"had it not been for you, dearest, loveliest Elizabeth. What don't I owe you? You taught me a lesson—hard at first, but most advantageous. By you, I was properly humbled." He grabbed the handhold again to keep from floating away. "I came to you without a doubt of my reception. You showed me how insufficient all my pretensions were of pleasing a woman worthy of being pleased."

She sucked her bottom lip in her teeth, then she asked, "Had you persuaded yourself that I'd accept you?"

"I had. What vanity. I believed you'd be wishing for and expecting my proposal."

She frowned slightly. "My manners must've been at fault, though not intentionally, I promise. I never meant to deceive you. How you must've hated me after *that* evening."

"Hate you! No. I was angry, perhaps, at first. But my anger soon began to take the proper direction."

She shifted to face him. "I'm almost afraid of asking what you thought of me, when we met at Pemberley. You blamed me for coming?"

"No. I felt nothing but surprise."

"Your surprise couldn't have been greater than *mine* in being noticed by you. My conscience told me that I deserved no extraordinary politeness. I admit, I didn't expect to receive *more* than a common civility."

"My goal *then*," he said, "was to show you, by every civility in my power, that I wasn't so mean as to resent the past; and I hoped to garner your forgiveness, lessen your ill opinion of me, by letting you see that your words had been heeded. How soon any other wishes introduced themselves, I can hardly tell. I believe it was about half an hour after I'd seen you."

She grinned.

"Georgiana was delighted to meet you," he told her. "She was disappointed by the sudden interruption."

"Moons collide! If only Lydia had stayed in Sollaria," Elizabeth sighed ruefully.

"I disappointed her further by changing my plans with her and following you from Dyberion. My quest after your sister was formed before I'd left the inn."

"Was that why you were so grave and thoughtful in the suite?"

He nodded. "I had much to plan and very little time to execute it."

"Thank you again for all that you've done in that regard."

"Please, think no more of it," he said softly.

They sat for some time in companionable silence. Jane floated by, laughing as Bingley chased her. A little while later, Kitty shot by, waving, before reaching a new rock, absorbing the impact with her feet, and then flipping herself head over heels as she launched, spiraling away into another area of the arena.

"We really ought to be enjoying space more on this spacewalk," Elizabeth noted absently.

Darcy thought for a moment, then stood, pulling her up with him. He offered her his other hand. She took it. "Lift off," he said, and gently jumped.

They floated free and slowly, keeping tethered to one another with their hands.

Elizabeth laughed as they rotated lazily toward another faux rock. She looked around. "I wonder what became of Jane and Bingley."

"Off doing similar, I imagine," he said. "They have much to discuss, what with their impending marriage."

She looked a little wistful as she said, "I'm glad they found their way back to one another."

He very seriously replied, "I am, too. He sent me word within minutes of her acceptance."

"And were you surprised?"

"Not at all. When I left, I felt sure it'd happen soon."

"That is to say, you'd given your permission—"

"I wouldn't say—" he objected half-heartedly.

"I guessed as much," she finished.

He capitulated with a shrug. "When we returned to Heoros—before we came to see you," he said, "I made a confession to him, which I believe I ought to have made long ago. I told him everything that had occurred to render my interference in his affairs absurd and impertinent. He was greatly surprised. He'd never had the slightest suspicion. I told him also that I had reason to suspect my interpretation of your sister's feelings was incorrect. I also confessed to one thing that, for a time—and not unjustly—offended him. I couldn't allow myself to conceal that your sister had been in the city for three months last winter, that I'd known of it, and had purposely kept it from him. He was angry. But his anger, I'm persuaded, lasted no longer than his doubt remained uncertain in regard to your sister's affection. We came to discover the truth, and, I hoped, to salvage his good opinion of me."

"So that's why you were so serious and quiet?"

He felt a stab of shame at this. "Yes. The night before I left for Londinium, I told him that everyone could see that his attachment to her was as strong as ever, and that I felt no doubt of their happiness together. I'd closely observed her during those visits, and I was convinced then of her affection."

"And your assurance of it, I suppose, carried immediate conviction to him."

"It did. Bingley is unaffectedly modest. It prevented him from depending on his own judgment in so anxious a case, but his reliance on mine made everything easy. He'd been halfway to forgiveness before I gave him the final verdict. He's heartily forgiven me now. With the caveat that I could only respond with an enthusiastic yes to anything he might ask of me in the next year."

Her laugh sparkled in the relative quiet of the arena. "Thus your willingness to come here today?"

"What a fortunate turn of events," he said, thinking of how, in helping his friend secure happiness, it had led to securing his own— even greater—joy. What fortune, indeed.

BEGINNER'S GUIDE
POINTS OF INTEREST
GAMES TO PLAY

THE PARALLAX*spacewalk*
ACTIVITY GUIDE

CHAPTER 64

Parallax StarSeeker, Independent Orbit, Londinium Lunar System

Elizabeth had been so wrapped up in her conversation with Darcy that it wasn't until Jane came flying toward them, saying, "Where have you two been?" that they realized how long they'd been apart from the others.

"We've been searching for you for a while," Jane continued. "Kitty's waiting at the entrance. This place is bigger than it appears from the outside."

Bingley bounded from rock to rock, exclaiming, "There you are!" as he caught up to them. He'd taken extremely well to the lack of gravity.

"We've both been wandering the outer limits," Elizabeth replied.

"Then we ran into each other," Darcy added.

She turned to look at him. Had he just made a joke? "We ended up talking and . . . lost track of the hour," she said, her face warming.

This seemed not to incur any suspicion of truth on Jane or Bingley's part.

The return to their ship, then to Heoros, passed easily, talk of the arena experience dominating the conversation. They spent the afternoon at Longbourn, playing games and describing their experience on the Parallax in detail for the members of her family who missed it. The acknowledged lovers talked and laughed, the unacknowledged were silent. Darcy seemed the type whose disposition meant happiness wouldn't overflow in mirth. Elizabeth, agitated and confused, rather *knew* that she was happy than *felt* herself to be.

Besides the immediate embarrassment, there were other worries before her. She anticipated what her family would feel when her situation became known. Aware that no one aside from Jane liked him, she feared that the others' dislike was too severe even for his fortune and consequence to overcome.

When the gentlemen had left, and the day had given way to night, Elizabeth, alone in her room with Jane, finally opened her heart to her sister. She told her what had really happened during their spacewalk, and Jane, who was standing just inside the doorway to their closet, exclaimed in a whisper, "You're joking," and grabbed the doorframe in her shock. Her hand slipped, depressing the button which triggered the closet door. It whooshed shut behind her, and she gasped, startled.

Elizabeth would've chuckled, but the pure disbelief in her sister's eyes tempered her.

Jane shook her head, eyeing the closet door, then crossed the room to her bed. "Lizzie. This can't be true. Engaged to Mr. Darcy? No, you won't deceive me. I know it's impossible."

Elizabeth, cross-legged on her bed, lifted her hands in exasperation. "This is a wretched beginning. You were the single person I could depend on. No one else will believe me if *you* don't." She waited for Jane to settle herself across from her. "I'm being earnest. I'm telling you nothing but the truth. He still loves me, and we're engaged."

Jane's look of doubt had barely faded. "Oh, Lizzie, it can't be. I know how much you dislike him."

Elizabeth bore this with patience. "You know no such thing. *That* should all be forgotten. Maybe I didn't love him as well as I do now, but in such cases as these, a good memory is unpardonable. This is the last time I'll remember it myself."

Jane still looked amazed and uncertain.

"Jane. With all sincerity, I love him. I mean every word. I wouldn't lie to you about this."

"Stars in the sky! If it's the truth, then I have to believe you," Jane cried. "My dear Lizzie, I—congratulations! But, are you certain? Forgive me, I'm trying to understand. Are you certain that you can be happy with him?"

"Without a doubt. It's settled between us already. We'll be the happiest couple in the galaxy." She smiled, but it faltered slightly. "But . . . are you pleased, Jane? Would you like to have such a brother?"

Jane smiled back. "Very. Very much. Nothing would give me—or Bingley—more delight. But we considered it. We hoped for the possibility of it. Do you really love him well enough? Are you certain that you feel what you ought to?"

"Yes! You'll only think I feel *more* than I ought to when I tell you everything."

"What do you mean?"

She took a steadying breath, then said, "I love him better than I do Bingley. I'm afraid you'll be angry."

"Lizzie," Jane scolded, her face scrunched in consternation. "*Be* serious. I want to talk very seriously. Let me know everything, starting with how long you've loved him."

"It's been coming on so gradually that I hardly know when it began." Then she smirked, unable to resist. "But I believe it was from the first moment I saw his beautiful grounds at Pemberley."

Jane's face deadpanned. Elizabeth held hers steady. They locked their gaze, Jane's eyes revealing a world-wearied older sister, annoyed by the antics of her younger. Elizabeth fought and lost to the grin spreading on her lips.

"I'm sorry. I'll be serious. I promise," Elizabeth entreated, and the daggers abated from Jane's eyes. With great solemnity, she added, "It *was* in Dyberion, but because of *him*, not his belongings."

"Then I'm happy," Jane said. "As happy for you as I am for myself. I always saw the value in him. His love for you aside, I would've held him in esteem. But now, as Bingley's friend and your husband, there can only be Bingley and yourself more dear to me." She launched herself off the bed and threw her arms around Elizabeth. She squeezed her uncomfortably tight, then pulled back quickly. "But you've been very sly," she scolded warmly. "You told me so little of what passed at Pemberley and North Tōmbal. I owe what little knowledge I have of that to someone else."

"Bingley?" Elizabeth guessed. With Jane's affirmation, she told her the motives of her secrecy. She'd been unwilling to mention Bingley; and the unsettled state of her own feelings had made her equally avoid the name of his friend. But now she could reveal to her sister Darcy's share in Lydia's recovery. All was acknowledged, and half the night spent in conversation.

LONDINIUM SAT[SYS
Communications Log—System Storage 30 Days [Planetary]

[LotteLu] 13.9-18:32:29.LS

Lizzie! I'm so sorry for my husband and Lady Catherine. I just learned what he said. I'm certain that her coming such a distance just to say the same was no kinder experience. That was absolutely uncalled for.

[LizzieLovesSpace] 13.9-18:35:33.LS

It wasn't ideal, but I'm fine. With the bad comes good. If it weren't for your husband's waive, I wouldn't have heard the news. Congratulations are in order, I believe.

[LotteLu] 13.9-18:37:12.LS

I wish I could've told you first, but yes! I'm due in autumn.

[LizzieLovesSpace] 13.9-18:39:43.LS

How are you feeling about it? Are you being well cared for?

[LotteLu] 13.9-18:44:56.LS

More nervous than I was to marry and move to a house floating in the void, that's for certain. But one thing I can count on from Lady Catherine is an abundance of attention to all of my needs. I'm happy, though. Looking forward to what my days will be when there's another Collins vying for my attention. Though I already dread the day when the baby is old enough to talk. I imagine I may need to escape them both for any chance at a quiet moment!

[LizzieLovesSpace] 13.9-18:47:29.LS

Well, you have a standing invitation to Pemberley any time quiet is desired. I'll offer you lemon-moss tea, a good book, and a room to yourself.

[LotteLu] 13.9-18:48:43.LS

Pemberley??!

[LizzieLovesSpace] 13.9-18:50:38.LS

Oh, yes, I have good news of my own. You're only the second person who knows, so keep this to yourself for now, please.

[LotteLu] 13.9-18:52:45.LS

Elizabeth. Bennet. Are you telling me that—what are you telling me? Are you engaged to Mr. Darcy? I knew I saw something between you when you were both here!

[LizzieLovesSpace] 13.9-18:55:01.LS

You're very perceptive, my friend. There's so much to tell you, but it'll have to wait a bit longer. I promise to send you a very long waive explaining it all. But first I need to tell my parents!

[LotteLu] 13.9-18:57:12.LS

Good luck!

. . . END COM . . .

CHAPTER
65

Longbourn House, Heoros, First Moon of Londinium

Elizabeth and Jane dragged themselves from bed on the later side of the next morning, and were so slow to get ready that they missed breakfast entirely. They'd barely pilfered the remnants of their missed meal from the kitchen when their mother cried out, "Stars around us! If that disagreeable Mr. Darcy isn't coming here again with our dear Bingley! Why is he always visiting here? I thought he'd be hunting jewelbirds or something, not disturbing us with his company." She spotted them, then, as they tried, and failed, to sneak back upstairs with their food. "Lizzie. Take him on a tour of the countryside today. Get him out of Bingley's way."

Elizabeth could hardly help laughing at such a convenient proposal. It was vexing, though, that her mother was always saying such harsh things about him.

As soon as they entered, Bingley looked at Elizabeth so expressively, and clasped her hands with such warmth, that it left her in no doubt that he'd become privy to the good news. Soon after they arrived, he leaned in to her ear to say, "I'm sorry I don't have another spacewalk for you to get lost in again today."

"Luckily for you, my mother had the same idea," she whispered back.

And indeed, within minutes, her mother pulled her aside. "I'm sorry to force you into having that disagreeable man all to yourself, Lizzie," she said. "But I hope you won't mind entertaining him. It's all for Jane's sake, you know. And there's no need to talk to him much. Just every now and then. So, don't inconvenience yourself any more than is necessary."

Elizabeth solemnly agreed.

Under the guise of convincing him to join her in the gardens, she and Darcy quietly decided that it was best to tell her father sooner rather than later. He offered to give the news himself. She agreed under the condition that she be the one to tell her mother, and to tell her alone. Whether Mrs. Bennet were violently set against the match, or violently delighted with it, it was certain that her manner would do no credit to her sense. Elizabeth couldn't bear that Darcy would be witness to any first reaction of her mother's.

Before they set out for the gardens, while her father was in his library, Darcy stepped in to speak with him. Her agitation on seeing this was extreme. She didn't fear her father's opposition, but she knew that he'd be unhappy. The idea that *she*—his favorite child—should be distressing him by her choice, filling him with fears and regrets, was a wretched thought. She stood in the hallway in misery until Darcy appeared again in the doorway, and was a little relieved by his smile. "Your father wants you," he said softly, setting his hands on both her shoulders. "I'll wait right here."

When she entered, her father was pacing the room, looking grave and anxious.

"Lizzie," he said. "What are you doing? Are you out of your senses, accepting this man? Haven't you always hated him?"

Stars, how she wished that her former opinions had been more reasonable, the words she'd spoken about him more moderate. It would've spared her from explanations and professions that were exceedingly awkward to give. But they were now necessary, and she assured him, with some confusion on his part, of her attachment to Darcy.

"In other words, you're determined to have him," her father said, no longer pacing. "He's rich, to be sure. And you'd have more fine clothes and ships and transports than Jane. But will they make you happy?"

"Do you have any other objection to this than your belief in my indifference?"

"None at all. We all know him to be a proud, unpleasant sort of man. But this'd be nothing if you really like him."

"I do. I do like him," she replied, tears springing to her eyes. "I love him. Truly, he has no improper pride. He's perfectly amiable. You don't know what he really is. Please, don't pain me by speaking so severely of him."

Her father sat in his reading chair, elbows on the arms, steepling his fingers under his chin. "Lizzie, I've given him my blessing. He's the kind of man whom I'd never dare refuse any-thing which he condescended to ask. I now give it to *you* to decide, if you're resolved on having him. But let me advise you to think better of it. I know your disposition, Lizzie. I know that you could be neither happy nor respectable, unless you truly esteemed your husband—unless you looked up to him and felt he was your equal. Your lively talents would place you in the greatest danger in an unequal marriage. You'd scarcely escape discredit and misery. My dear, don't let me have the grief of seeing *you* unable to respect your partner in life."

Elizabeth, with as much solemnity and sincerity as she could muster, assured him that Darcy really was the object of her desire. She explained the gradual change which her estimation of him had undergone, relating her absolute certainty that his affection wasn't the work of a day, but had stood the test of many months' suspense. She enumerated with energy all his good qualities. And finally, she conquered her father's incredulity.

"Well, my Lizzie," he said. "I have no more to say. If this is the case, he deserves you. I couldn't part with you to anyone less worthy."

To complete the favorable impression, she then confessed what Darcy had voluntarily done for Lydia.

He heard her with astonishment. "Land's sake! This is an evening of wonders! So Darcy did everything—set the interview, gave the money, paid the fellow's debts, and got him the commission? This is even better. It'll save me a moon of trouble and economy. Had it been your uncle's doing, I would've paid him. But these passionate young lovers carry everything their own way. I'll offer to pay him tonight, he'll rant and storm about his love for you, and that'll be the end of the matter."

He chuckled at this. Then he focused on some point in the distance for a moment. "Ah! So this accounts for your embarrassment the other day when I was reading Mr. Collins's waive." He laughed again. "Well, then. Go on back to your lover."

"I will, if you promise to wait and let me tell Mama in my own time."

"Of course, my dear. Now, go. And if anyone comes to confess their love for Mary or Kitty, send them in. I'm quite at my leisure!"

Elizabeth's mind was now relieved from the weight of a moon. She returned to Darcy, suffused with tranquility. Everything was still too recent for gaiety, but there was no longer anything material to be dreaded, and the comfort of ease and familiarity would come with time. "Let's take my mother's advice and lose ourselves outside."

They walked in quiet contentment for a while, Elizabeth absently leading him to one of her favorite spots. Soon they found themselves on a tree-swing bench, overlooking a pond hidden in the nearby wooded glen, words flowing easily between them.

His presence beside her was quickly becoming a comfort. "How could you have fallen in love with me?" she asked him playfully. "I can understand going along easily enough, once you'd made a beginning. But what could've set you off in the first place?"

"I can't pinpoint the hour, or the spot, or the look, or the words, which laid the foundation. It was too long ago. I was in the middle before I knew I'd begun."

"My beauty you had withstood, early on," she teased. "As for my manners, my behavior to *you* was at least always bordering on uncivil, and I never spoke to you without wishing to give you some pain. Be honest. Did you admire me for my impertinence?"

He smiled. "For the liveliness of your mind, I did."

"You might as well call it impertinence. It was very little less. The fact is, you were sick of civility, of deference and officious attention. You were disgusted with the women who were always speaking, and looking, and thinking for *your* approval alone." She thought of Caroline. "I roused and interested you because I was so unlike *them*. You might've hated me for it. But in spite of the pains you took to disguise yourself, your feelings were always noble and just—and in your heart, you thoroughly despised the people who so assiduously courted you." She traced the lines of his palm, which lay face up in her other hand. "There. I've saved you the trouble of accounting for it. All things considered, I think it was perfectly reasonable. You certainly knew no actual good of me. But nobody thinks of *that* when they fall in love."

"Wasn't there good in your affectionate behavior for Jane while she was ill on the Netherfield?" he countered.

"Dear Jane. Who could've done less for her?" She slid her hand into his, savoring the shivers of pleasure that chased across her skin with his touch. "But make a virtue of it, by all means. My good qualities are under your protection, and you're in charge of exaggerating them as much as possible. In return, I will find occasions for teasing and quarreling with you as often as needed." She pulled her hand away to emphasize her seriousness. "I'll begin directly, by asking you what made you so unwilling to come to the point at last. What made you so shy of me when you and Bingley first came back to Heoros and dined here? I know that you were observing Jane, but why did you look as though you didn't care for me?"

He held her gaze. "You were just as silent as I was. You gave me no encouragement."

"I was embarrassed."

"So was I."

"You might've talked to me more when you came to dinner," she said, unable to stop her slight pout.

He cupped her cheek in his hand. "A man who felt less, might."

She couldn't help but lean into his palm. "Count my stars lucky that you have such a reasonable answer. But I wonder," she said, bringing her hand up to his, "how long would you have gone, if left to yourself. When *would* you have spoken, if I hadn't asked you? My resolution of thanking you for your kindness to Lydia had quite the effect, I'm afraid. What becomes of my morals, if our comfort springs from a breach of promise?"

He turned his hand and closed his fingers around hers. "No need to distress yourself. Morality still resides. I'm not indebted for my present happiness to your eager desire of expressing gratitude. After Lady Catherine's meddling, I was determined to know everything as soon as I was able."

"Lady Catherine has been of infinite use," Elizabeth noted. "That ought to make her happy. She loves to be of use. Now tell me: Did you come down to Netherfield Landing only to study Jane? Or did you intend on something more serious?"

He looked out over the little pond, lost for a moment in thought. He turned back to her. "Outside of what I owed Bingley, my purpose was to see *you* and to judge, if I could, whether I might ever hope to earn your love."

"Will you ever have the courage to break the news to Lady Catherine?"

"I'm more likely to want for time than courage," he said. "But it ought to be done. If you give me a bit to compose my thoughts, I can grab my comcard and write the waive right away."

"I should probably take this opportunity to tell my mother, too."

He nodded. "Shall I meet you inside in half an hour?"

"Yes. Perfect." And before she could think herself out of it, she leaned in and kissed him. The warmth and softness of his lips sent a shockwave through her and she pulled back. "For courage," she whispered, and darted out of the glen.

Entire body still buzzing from what she'd just done, she sought her mother out. Mrs. Bennet was in her room. Fearful of losing the courage she'd bought herself, Elizabeth made the announcement without preamble.

The effect of her words was extraordinary. On first hearing it, Mrs. Bennet sat quite still, unable to utter a syllable. For several minutes, she seemed not to comprehend what she heard. Elizabeth was on the verge of running to her room to try again a different day, when her mother finally recovered enough to fidget in her chair, get up, sit down, wonder, and bless herself.

"Land's sake! Stars align! Mr. Darcy! Who would've thought! And is it really true? Oh, my sweet Lizzie! How rich and great you'll be! What jewels, and trips, and transports you'll have! And books, too—I know you love those. Jane's possessions will be nothing in comparison to it all. I'm so pleased. So happy. Such a charming man—so handsome and tall! Stars!—my dear Lizzie. Please apologize for my disliking him so much before. I hope he'll overlook it. Dear Lizzie. A house in Cloudtop! The Pemberley Estate!" She practically gasped as she said this. "Three daughters attaining such successes. Two married! Ten thousand per revolution!"

This was enough to prove that Elizabeth's choice to do this privately was the wise one. Rejoicing that such an effusion was heard only by herself, she slipped away.

She had only a few minutes of freedom in her own room before her mother followed her in. "My dear, I can't think of anything else! Ten thousand aurum, and very likely more! Oh, you must be married somewhere majestic. My dear, tell me, what dish is Mr. Darcy particularly fond of? I'll order it prepared for tomorrow."

This was a sad omen of what her mother's behavior to the gentleman himself might be. Elizabeth found that, though in the certain possession of his warmest affection, and secure in her relations' approval, there was still something she could wish for. But the evening passed off much better than she expected. Her mother stood in such awe of her intended son-in-law that she ventured not to speak to him unless she could offer him attention or mark her favorable regard to his opinion.

Elizabeth had the satisfaction of seeing her father taking pains to get acquainted with him, and Mr. Bennet soon assured her that Darcy was rising every hour in his esteem. "I admire my sons-in-law highly," he said. "Collins would've been my favorite. But I think I'll like your husband well enough as an alternative."

LONDINIUM SAT[SYS
Communications Log—System Storage 30 Days [Planetary]

[LizzieLovesSpace] 15.9-9:30:24.LS

I should've thanked you properly, and sooner, for the information you gave me the other day.

[MarianeGardiner] 15.9-9:32:15.LS

No thanks necessary, my dear.

[LizzieLovesSpace] 15.9-9:34:01.LS

To be honest, I was mad that you supposed more between me and Darcy than really existed. But now suppose as much as you'd like. Give rein to your fancy and indulge your imagination. Unless you believe me to be actually married, you won't be too far off.

[MarianeGardiner] 15.9-9:38:23.LS

If you are teasing me, Lizzie, I will never visit you again.

[LizzieLovesSpace] 15.9-9:40:12.LS

But then how will you see all of Pemberley's grounds?

[MarianeGardiner] 15.9-9:42:10.LS

Oh, Lizzie, I'm so happy to hear this! Congratulations!

[LizzieLovesSpace] 15.9-9:44:03.LS

Thank you to Wenhal and back for not going to Kaels! I'm the happiest creature in the universe. Others might have claimed to be, but it's me. I'm happier even than Jane. She only smiles. I laugh!

[MarianeGardiner] 15.9-9:48:39.LS

I just told your uncle. We are laughing with you!

[LizzieLovesSpace] 15.9-9:50:01.LS

Thank him a million times for me for all the help and good will he gave my future husband. Darcy sends you all the love in the worlds that he can spare from me.

■ ■ ■

[MarianeGardiner] 15.9-9:51:45.LS

Pemberley next winter?

[LizzieLovesSpace] 15.9-9:53:05.LS

It wouldn't be a proper holiday without you!

. . . END COM . . .

CHAPTER
66

Netherfield Landing, Heoros,
First Moon of Londinium

Jane sat beside Lizzie at the long banquet table, tucking the train of her wedding dress carefully under her as she did. "The evening has turned out more perfect that I could've hoped."

Lizzie, who was seated beside Georgiana Darcy, looked so beautiful in her midnight blue gown, her dark hair falling in waves along one shoulder. She smiled over the rim of her glass of Gleam. "We were just talking about that. You couldn't have asked for better weather."

"And the swarm of jewelbirds that flew behind you as you said your vows?" Georgiana added. "Absolutely magical! I had no idea they shimmered like that when they flew."

"Aunt Phillips insists Bingley paid for that to happen," Lizzie added with a roll of her eyes.

Jane knew that Lizzie had been struggling to tolerate Aunt Phillips since her engagement was made public. Though the woman stood in too much awe of Darcy to speak to him with the same familiarity that Jane's new husband's good humor encouraged, whenever she *did* speak, it caused Lizzie to cringe. Her sister did what she could to keep Darcy shielded from the notice of her aunt and her mother, both of whom put her on edge when they spoke to him. But it couldn't always be avoided. Jane felt Darcy had borne the interactions well, however.

Georgiana whispered something to Lizzie, and Jane watched them with satisfaction.

Darcy's sister had been so overjoyed by the news of her brother's success in claiming Lizzie's heart that she had practically shorted out his comcard expressing her delight. He very quickly diverted her directly to Lizzie's coms, and it took them no time at all to become fast friends. Georgiana's earnest joy to be gaining a sister had made Lizzie feel as welcome and loved as Jane knew her sister had always deserved.

She looked out across the ballroom floor, placed in the middle of the beautiful grove where she'd been married just hours before, and caught sight of her own new sister.

Caroline's congratulations to Jane and her brother had been all affection and sincerity. She even wrote to Jane on the occasion, to express her delight and repeat all her former professions of regard. But even without the comparison of Georgiana to draw from, Jane was not deceived. She was, at least, affected. Perhaps she could never rely on Caroline in a sisterly way, as Lizzie and Georgiana would, but she resolved always to be kinder than Caroline deserved. Especially since her new sister had finally dropped her resentment toward Lizzie. She was still nearly as attentive to Darcy as before, but she gave Lizzie the proper deference as his soon-to-be wife.

Whatever Caroline's motives for the change, Jane was glad for it all the same.

"Oh, *there's* Charlotte," Lizzie said, pulling Jane's attention back to the present. She turned to see their friend making her way carefully back from the house, one hand cradling her baby bump, the other keeping her silver dress from trailing in the grass.

"My only complaint for the entire evening," Charlotte said as she reached them, "is that your restrooms aren't closer."

Lizzie chuckled and gestured for her to join them at the table. Charlotte gratefully obliged.

"If I were consulted on such matters, as I ought to have been," Lizzie said with mock austerity, "*I* would have had far more accommodations."

Georgiana laughed. "You sound exactly like Lady Catherine."

"I *was* enjoying my time away from her, Eliza," Charlotte scolded with a smile. "Now that you've brought her to mind again, I shall sleep terribly."

Charlotte and her husband had come to stay with her parents quite soon after the announcement of Darcy and Lizzie's engagement. Lizzie said that the great lady had been rendered so exceedingly angry by the contents of Darcy's waive that Charlotte—who had rejoiced in the match as much as Jane had—was anxious to get away until the storm receded.

"Did you think you bought peace for nothing?" Lizzie said. "My poor fiancé has been weathering your husband's excessive attention for the better part of your visit."

"Look, he's doing it right now," Georgiana noted.

Lizzie laughed. "So he is!" A look of pity crossed her face, and she stood. "Excuse me. I must rescue him."

The three of them watched her cross the dance floor and slide her hand into his. She made some sort of apology to Mr. Collins and then pulled Darcy with her among the dancers. The two of them, in their matching dark blue, stood in the center, orbited by a constellation of colors, looking at one another with a gravity all their own.

He ran a hand through her hair, his face the very picture of adoration. Lizzie looked as if she could see nothing but him, and the amber glow of sunset seemed to be radiating from inside her. In that moment, Jane believed she could not be any happier.

But then her husband's voice was in her ear and she knew that wasn't true. "Hello, my love," he whispered, leaning close enough that his breath tickled the side of her neck. She shivered. "Would you please honor me with a dance?"

She turned to look him in the eye, their breath mingling, her lips yearning to touch his. "It would be my pleasure."

NOTES

My wife's maternal happiness has reached its peak. She has now officially gotten rid of her two most deserving daughters. One might wonder whether this accomplishment produced so happy an effect as to make her a more sensible, likable, well-informed woman. Luckily for me, she's remained her occasionally nervous and invariably silly self. I wouldn't relish such unusual domestic felicity as a stable wife.

I miss my dear Lizzie exceedingly. My affection for her draws me more often from home than anything else could do. And I adore going to Pemberley. Especially when I'm least expected.

I miss my lovely Jane and her husband as well. They remained at Netherfield Landing only a year before certain of her relations wore down even his easy temper and her affectionate heart. He bought an estate on Dyberion. Jane and Elizabeth are now within thirty miles of each other. A convenient distance on my occasional drop-ins.

Kitty has had the distinct advantage of spending a great deal of time with her two older sisters, as she's been taken under the wing of her newest sister at Pemberley. In such superior society, she's improved greatly. Miss Georgiana is a sweet girl, and a much more sensible companion than Kitty was used to in Lydia. She was never so ungovernable in temper as Lydia. But removed from her younger sister's influence and example, she's become less irritable, ignorant, and insipid.

Lydia invites her frequently to come stay at the Academy campus, promising fun. I'd like to keep her influence at a minimum for now. She's thriving on Kaels. While humbled by the experience that led her there, she's still as exuberant and self-involved as ever. But the ability to nurture her love of fashion and her talent for design has been invaluable. I'm sure the schedules and strict policies are the main foundation for her newly formed sense of responsibility and dedication, however. So we will wait and see what becomes of her after the Academy.

I'm left with Mary, the only daughter who remains consistently at home. With the others gone, she's drawn by necessity away from her academic pursuits, in order to keep her mother company. She's obliged to mix more with the worlds, and without her sisters to compare her to, she seems to be thriving. She's a good girl. More studious than my Lizzie, but with a better temper and mind than her younger sisters. Given time, she may understand my humor enough to converse the way Lizzie and I did. I'll keep working with her on it.

CHAPTER
67

Pemberley District, Dyberion, Fourth Moon of Londinium

Darcy cleared his throat in warning as Elizabeth maneuvered their transport through the thin gap in the Moon's Teeth.

"Do. Not. Say. A. Word," she said. She was glaring through the viewport in concentration; strands of her hair had fallen loose from their tie to frame her face. The muscles in her arms were taut as she guided the steering. She was as tense as a spring. He loved her like this, full of kinetic energy that would come off of her in waves later. He smiled to himself. Perhaps it was the Gardiners' presence in the rear of the ship, or what he had waiting for her when they returned home, but he suddenly recalled the conversation they'd had that fated day she'd first come to Pemberley.

"And you were worried you'd never be able to fly this low without being distracted," he muttered.

This made her chuckle, but she didn't look at him. "I believe that was *you*."

"No, I distinctly recall telling you I prefer the views to flying."

"What views? You've had your eyes on me this whole flight."

"Can you blame me?"

Her response was half laugh, half exhalation from the effort of curving the ship around the last of the Teeth. Then she turned her eyes to meet his and he was lost in the dark pools of them at once.

She arched a brow. "Yes. That was some of my best flying, and you missed it entirely."

"I didn't miss an inch of it," he said, looking her up and down.

Now it was Georgiana's turn to clear her throat. "There *are* other people in this craft, dear brother," she said loudly from her seat. "Though I'm not certain which is more fun to watch. The flying, or the flirting."

"It was the flirting," Mariane chimed in.

He almost laughed in his surprise. Georgiana, who held Elizabeth in the highest esteem, had generally been in awe of his wife's lively, sportive manner of talking to him. It seemed she had reached the point where she felt brave enough to try it herself.

"Elizabeth, you're a bad influence," he said. He crossed his arms and took on as fatherly a stance as he could. "What happened to the sister whose respect of her older brother so often outweighed her affection?"

"We younger sisters *grow up*," Georgiana said confidently, putting her feet on his empty seat and leaning back in her own.

"She's not wrong," Edward said, turning from the window to throw a wink in Darcy's direction.

"Indeed," Mariane added. "Look at how Lydia has flourished. It's a wonder Georgiana took as long as she did to discover you can be teased by a sister as readily as by a wife."

"Oh! Speaking of Lydia," Georgiana said, "Did you see the floor plans for her fashion house on Itavia?"

"I did. Jane was showing me just yesterday. With her and Charles's investment, they have to sign off on everything."

Georgiana sighed wistfully. "I can't wait to see it in person. Even Lady Catherine said she'd buy one of her dresses for Anne."

His great-aunt had come a long way from her initial reply to his informing her of his engagement. At the time, she'd been so very abusive, especially of Elizabeth, that he cut all contact with her. It was only through the grace of his wife that he was persuaded to overlook the offense and seek reconciliation. Elizabeth had cited as her reasoning that Lady Catherine was the only family that remained to him. But he looked around the transport and disagreed. What family he would've lost in Lady Catherine, he'd gained twice over in the Gardiners.

He loved them as though they were his own, and he would never be without gratitude for the two people who, by bringing Elizabeth to Dyberion, had been the means of uniting them.

As though sensing herself on his mind Elizabeth's hand snaked around his wrist and gently pulled him toward her. "You're lost in thought," she said gently.

He glanced out the viewport. Elizabeth had turned them toward home. He was anxious for what awaited her there, yet as content as he ever was in her presence. He leaned down and kissed her on the top of the head. "Just glad to have survived the teeth," he teased.

She gasped in playful incredulity as he walked back to his seat. "We aren't home yet," she warned.

Despite her veiled threat, she landed them safely back at Pemberley just as the sun set, and the group started up the hill road to the main house in the gloaming dark.

The entire party were accessories to his scheme. The Gardiners dutifully plied Elizabeth with conversation, keeping her occupied with questions about and praise for her flying. Meanwhile, Georgiana ran ahead to check the progress with Mrs. Reynolds.

Halfway up the hill, he spotted Georgiana from the light of an upper window in the house. She gave him the all clear, and he very stealthily signaled the same to Edward and Mariane.

The two eased off, allowing Darcy to take Elizabeth's hand and walk beside her.

She was brimming with energy from the flight. Meanwhile, his heart was climbing into his throat. He knew that she'd appreciate what he'd done, but his expectations were high, and he was eager to please her.

As they rounded the corner of the house, Elizabeth stopped. "What?" she gasped.

The lawn had been transformed. A veritable sea of phospho-drops had been placed among the mallow-moss, turning the usually viridian yard a brilliant blue. At its center, where her presence had once shocked him into stillness, there was now a pallet of lush cushions beneath a sheer tent. Beside the pallet was a low table filled with all her favorite foods, a bottle of Arkuluan Red, and two glasses.

"Happy anniversary," he said.

She looked at him. "But it's not—" Her gaze shifted to the Gardiners and recognition washed over her face—"oh."

"Braving that tour of Pemberley doesn't look so bad in retrospect, does it?" her aunt said, grabbing her hand.

Elizabeth was wide-eyed with wonder. "You were in on this?"

Her uncle patted her cheek. "Of course."

Her aunt blew her a kiss as the two of them headed inside, where they, and their children, would entertain Georgiana for the night.

Elizabeth turned to Darcy then, bemused.

"Do you like it?" he asked. "Three years ago, today, you reappeared in my life, and you gave me hope. I thought we could spend the evening right here under the stars, where I first saw you in our home, and where some part of me knew you belonged."

She said nothing for a moment. Then she threw her arms around his neck and kissed him deeply. He pulled her body tight against his own, the heat of her radiating through him, tangling with the blaze alight in his heart. The feeling threatened to consume him, and the kiss turned urgent in the wanting. He needed her like air in the void. Three years, twenty, a hundred and five . . . it didn't matter. His love for her would outlast the very stars. When it did, they'd still be shining in the dark.

ACKNOWLEDGMENTS

I HAVE WORDS FOR DAYS WHEN I WRITE MY STORIES, but somehow so few of them seem worthy enough to thank everyone who helped me turn this one into the book in your hands (or your ears, if you're listening to it). This will be the most concise I have ever been in my life. Nearly everyone mentioned on these pages can attest to that.

The first thank-you goes to my husband and my daughters for putting up with all my stressful days and sleepless nights.

Josh, your utter faith in me is unparalleled. I wouldn't be where I am or who I am today without you.

My sweet Maren, thank you for painting me the prettiest lines on my hardest day.

Madeline, my shining star, thank you for being my light so many times when I was lost in the dark.

Of everything I create in this life, dearest darling baby girls, I will always be proudest of you.

Andrea Twaddle, I can't properly express how grateful I am that you've been a part of this book's journey. The love my Bennet sisters have for one another is absolutely entwined in my experience with you. You're my favorite.

Michelle Ladner, there is no way to do the depth of our friendship justice without a novel of its own. Thank you for being the Sam to my Frodo in both life and writing since the day we met. I wouldn't have had the courage and confidence to lean into my own voice without you.

Mom and Dad, I was blessed to have been given parents who encouraged and nurtured my creativity in a thousand little ways throughout my life. Doubtless, my brazen optimism can be attributed to your love and support.

Bebe & Pops, thank you for always being there for us and the girls. You are the best village anyone could ask for. I will be forever grateful to have lucked into in-laws like you.

Mika Kasuga, you've been the champion of this story from our very first conversation. I couldn't have dreamed up a better person to entrust it to. You've been so much more than an editor and have made me feel like part of the team.

Erik Jacobsen, I can't thank you enough for sculpting the colorful clay of my ideas into a polished book, and allowing me to collaborate on so much of what usually gets to be just you. You worked yourself as hard as I did to make this happen, and I'll never forget it.

Mahalaleel M. Clinton and Alison Skrabek, thank you for your endless patience as I navigated through the process of turning the rough edged manuscript into a polished book. Your help was invaluable, and I'm so thankful to you and everyone at Union Square who cheered on, lifted up, and helped bring to life this book. Thank you all for putting your faith in me and contributing in all your many ways!

My unending gratitude goes to the Unhurried Scribblers Society—Katie, Naomi, Kelsie, Marylyn, Jeannie, (and Andi and Michelle again). Thank you for all your critiques and camaraderie. I'm so glad to have such a great group of writers to spend time and grow stories together with.

Nathanna Érica, I'm incredibly honored to include your art in my story. Your work brings me so much joy, and I thank you a thousand times over for being willing to contribute to mine.

Spencer Twaddle, thanks for being you. You embody Mr. Bingley right down to the handwriting, and I'm so very glad to call you family!

Briana Crotinger and Joel Daniel Phillips, I am so lucky to have such talented artist friends. Thank you for pausing your busy lives for a brief moment to troubleshoot my work when I panicked.

Special thanks to the cast of Critical Role for entertaining me throughout the months of work I spent drawing for this book. The fact that I'm now designing for you in the midst of final edits for the same book is possibly the most serendipitous thing that has ever happened to me.

Special thanks also to the composers of the Bridgerton soundtrack for being the background music in the months of my writing for this book. It is not lost on me that this, too, was connected even further to my story by the fact that the creator of the Bridgerton books was the first person I sent an early copy to.

Julia Quinn, I am profoundly grateful to you for your kindness in not only simply responding to that first email of mine, but for taking the time out of your incredibly busy schedule to read my work. You are amazing and I'm so glad to know you.

And finally, to you, the person reading (or listening) to this right now—all of you who took a chance on this book—thank you for trusting me with your time and attention (and suspension of disbelief). That you were drawn in enough to read it, either by my art or the premise, or maybe both, makes me so happy. I'm forever grateful for each and every one of you.